BETWEEN MOUNTAINS

Maggie Helwig

Between Mountains

Chatto & Windus
LONDON

Published by Chatto & Windus 2004
First published in Canada in 2004 by Knopf Canada

2 4 6 8 10 9 7 5 3 1

First published in Great Britain in 2004 by
Chatto & Windus
Random House, 20 Vauxhall Bridge Road,
London SW1V 2SA

Random House Australia (Pty) Limited
20 Alfred Street, Milsons Point, Sydney,
New South Wales 2061, Australia

Random House New Zealand Limited
18 Poland Road, Glenfield,
Auckland 10, New Zealand

Random House (Pty) Limited
Endulini, 5A Jubilee Road, Parktown 2193, South Africa

The Random House Group Limited Reg. No. 954009
www.randomhouse.co.uk

A CIP catalogue record for this book
is available from the British Library

ISBN 0 7011 7691 1

Papers used by Random House are natural, recyclable products made from wood grown in sustainable forests; the manufacturing processes conform to the environmental regulations of the country of origin

Typeset in Janson by Palimpsest Book Production Limited,
Polmont, Stirlingshire

Printed and bound in Great Britain by
Mackays of Chatham plc, Chatham, Kent

Part One

HISTORY

I

The Zone of Separation

13 July 1999

It was just before dawn when the trucks began to move. Behind the city the hills were barely visible, black masses in an indigo sky.

A stray dog darted for cover as headlights broke the darkness. Some distance away, a helicopter rose, hovered.

The trucks turned to create roadblocks at key intersections. Men climbed down with machine-guns in their arms. At several points across the city this occurred.

A small brown-haired man was sitting at the window of his hotel room, a laptop balanced on his knees. He was drinking instant coffee from a plastic cup, awkwardly, holding it by the rim so that he wouldn't burn his fingers. It was exceptionally bad coffee. When he heard the engines, he put the cup on the floor, pushed aside the sheer white curtain and saw two of the trucks, passing in front of the apartment block across the street. He watched until they turned a corner and were gone. Setting the laptop down beneath his chair, he picked up a digital camera and a laminated card on a metal chain and hung them around his neck.

In the deserted silence of the early morning, he could hear his own footsteps on the hotel's worn green carpet. The plaster walls were cracked and swollen with damp. At the front desk the night clerk, a thin teenager, was reading a movie magazine with furious concentration, twirling a bit of dark hair around her finger. Her eyes flicked briefly towards him as he passed, but she didn't raise her head. Outside, the streets were empty; then he heard the rumble of another truck, and stood against the wall as it passed. When it turned west at the corner, he followed.

At the edge of the park, he saw the light of a single taxi, as the driver started the engine and turned the car away, avoiding what might be trouble. Walking under a canopy of oak trees, the reporter listened for the sound of the heavier motors, and turning the next corner he found them, one truck parked sideways across the intersection, a very young, very tall soldier standing beside it. The young man gestured sharply towards him. The reporter raised the card and pointed to it, mouthing 'Press' without making a sound.

'Go home,' said the young man, in accented English. Was he German? Dutch? His accent was soft, and in the dark it was hard to make out the flag on his shoulder. The reporter peered around the broad khaki chest, and saw, about halfway up the street, a knot of soldiers gathering in front of a small block of flats. With a single sharp movement, one man kicked the door in, and the others poured through the gap. A light flickered on in a neighbouring building, and quickly went out again.

'Who are you after?' asked the reporter.

'I told you, go home. Nothing for you to do here.'

'Always something for me to do.' He smiled. But this soldier was too young, he took himself seriously. He was impressed with the gravity of his mission, and instinctively certain that the press must be unwelcome.

'How many times I have to tell you to go home? You only put yourself in danger.'

'Is he dangerous, then, the man you want?'

'They all are dangerous. What do you suppose?'

Other motors were idling, a street or two away.

'Is it more than one tonight? Sounds like more than one.'

'You can think of any reason I should tell you?'

From inside the building there was a muffled shout, but only one. No gunshots. Then the soldiers were out the door again, a heavy grey-haired man walking stiffly between them. A soldier pushed him down onto his knees, another yanked his arms behind his back, twisted plastic handcuffs around his wrists.

The reporter whistled. 'Wow,' he said softly. 'You finally came for him.' He lifted the camera and shot around the Dutch – probably Dutch – soldier's body. The young man scowled but made no move to stop him. 'That was stupid,' he said.

They were pushing the man into one of the trucks. The sound of the helicopter was louder, rising over the rooftops. The young soldier turned away, looking back with a quick warning shake of his head, and the trucks were gunning their engines, moving fast, not worried about noise now, up the street and out of sight.

The reporter stood at the corner and waited. A few lights came on, curtains twitched. One head appeared at a third-floor window, then vanished again. The lights, one by one, went out. He was thinking of going back to the hotel when he heard gunfire, down beyond the park. A pistol first. Then machine-guns responding.

His body reacted, tossing him into a doorway, his face pressed into the stone surround. He still dropped to the ground, sometimes, when he simply heard a door slam; real gunfire was an instant return to the years of the siege. The noise only lasted a few seconds but he stood longer, his arms flexed, sweat trickling down his neck. But this was nothing too new or strange. Nothing you couldn't get used to.

There were distant voices, agitated. He moved forward carefully, his body still close against the walls. The sky was paler now, a bruised wet blue, the shapes of the city emerging from darkness. He ducked across the street towards the park, heard cars driving away. At the intersection of the main street he stopped.

No one was there any more, but even in the half-light of dawn the pools of blood were unmistakable. He looked around the empty pavements, raised the little camera again.

A man appeared round the opposite corner and crossed over. He too saw the blood, and quickly turned away, pushing his hands deeper into his pockets.

'Excuse me,' said the reporter, speaking in Bosnian. 'Do you know what happened?'

The man looked at him. 'Something bad,' he replied in English. 'Something bad happened here.'

The helicopters rose, turned. They moved swiftly over the hills and rivers of the small country. They carried soldiers and equipment. They carried a prisoner, a dead man and a dying man. The hills were green; rough and pretty in the early morning. The dying man flailed with one arm, not knowing what he meant to say, pink foam on his lips. There were medical supplies on the helicopter, they were flying towards a hospital, but they would not be able to save him. The dead man lay unattended, covered by a tarpaulin.

Between the hills of this country, men and women were digging. They pushed through the heavy earth, wearing boots and overalls and wide-brimmed hats. You wouldn't have thought, if you saw them there by the pine trees, that they were police officers. They might have been digging up orange and sky-blue frescoes, the bull dance at the palace of Knossos. Bowls of hardened grains, parched and desiccated meats and fruits. Ivory-handled knives, small bells, leather belts. They might have been digging up little models of horses for children to play with, or goddess figurines holding handfuls of snakes, or hammers and awls.

The dying man closed his eyes, the morphine entering his bloodstream. A great peace. All his fears and burdens lifted away and he moved gently towards sleep. He felt such relief. Surely, now, everything was all right.

A few moments later his heart stopped.

In the trenches they were digging up bodies, partly rotted, the flesh beginning to melt together. The photographs, later, would have a strange beauty, the tangled arms and legs, clothing and hair and bones, emerging from mud as if it was clay and they were art, something sculptural. But the women and men digging up the bodies were only aware of the smell. They would shower two, three, four times a day, but their own skin and hair would still smell sweet and corrupt like decaying flesh, and when they went into town people would move away from them in the shops and cafés.

They would separate the bodies carefully, drawing them out one by one, trying to ensure that limbs and pieces of flesh did not fall loose. Whole bodies when they could, then parts of bodies. The backpacks, leather jackets, running shoes. Wallets and small change, photographs eaten away by water. A cat's-eye marble. The blindfolds. The bits of rope that had tied the wrists.

Out of the dark earth we draw the forms of our desire. And here as well. This too was human desire, the sight of those bodies in the trench. The bearded men who lined other men up at the edge would have said, as they opened fire, that they wanted only the things that everyone wants.

A man pinned under his son's dead body in the mud.

The helicopter rises, passing above the graves on the hillsides.

Something bad happened here.

* * *

The first thing that Daniel did when he came back into his hotel room was to trip on his cup of coffee, spilling it out over the hotel carpet. He made a quick grab for his laptop and then stood there, stupidly, watching the brown liquid spread across the floor, remembering that he hadn't shut the computer down and that there was something wrong with the battery, wondering whether to unplug it right away and put it on the bed, or try to shut it down where he was. Awkwardly he cradled it in one arm, saving his files and shutting down with the other hand while cold coffee seeped through his thin canvas shoes, feeling sure there must be a better way to manage this, aside from buying a laptop that would actually run on its battery like it was supposed to. Besides which, he thought, the hotel could potentially charge him for the damage to their carpet.

As he wiped at the stain with a towel, he had the distinct feeling that the situation was out of his control. He wanted an aspirin, and he was unhappy with the image he was presenting. He was fairly certain that nobody, if asked to picture a war correspondent, would think of a little man with thinning hair and thick glasses, mopping up coffee on his hands and knees from a hotel floor.

When he eventually felt he had blended the stain with the other stains well enough to avoid legal liability, he plugged the laptop in again, arranged it on his knees, and downloaded the photographs. It was early daylight now, the city's crowded life resuming, the makeshift stalls selling hair ribbons and chewing gum and pornographic magazines opening up for the morning, a thin wash of pink in the sky. Some people were grouped at corners, talking, others walking quickly along the narrow pavement.

The arrest photograph was more or less usable, once it was blown up and cropped; fuzzy, but acceptable. He opened another file on the computer, then punched a number on his mobile phone, and fitted it onto his shoulder as he typed.

13 July 1999, Banja Luka, Bosnia-Herzegovina

NATO troops in the Serb-controlled sector of Bosnia have carried out a successful arrest of former Bosnian Serb official Nikola Marković.

Marković, accused of involvement in the 'ethnic cleansing' of northern Bosnia during the 1992-95 war, was apprehended at his home in the city of Banja Luka early this morning, and went peacefully with the arresting soldiers. However, a second raid . . .

'Well, you know, you may as well confirm Marković right now because I saw him, so a no comment's just going to make you look . . . Because I cover this town. I know when something's going to go down, right? Sure, you go and ask then, I'll hold.'

While he waited, he put the laptop down on his chair, carried the phone to the wardrobe and began to go through his jacket pockets. No aspirin. He collected a used-up ballpoint pen, some receipts and a couple of beer bottle tops, and threw them into the bin. There was a click at the other end of his phone.

'So you will confirm his arrest? Excellent. And he's on his way . . . Yep. Now, there was something else that happened. Are you prepared to go on record . . . Okay, you understand I'm doing this in a spirit of sharing? I heard shots, I saw blood. Lots of blood. And I will have to report this, but if you talk to me now you get to put a shape on it before . . . Mmm-hmm, you go check it out then . . .'

On the next hook was his flak jacket, unused for several years now. He began going through those pockets as well.

It was heavy even to shift on the hook, the fabric covering a structure of ceramic plates and layers of Kevlar. He felt a weird twist of something almost like nostalgia, remembering the weight on his shoulders, the smell of snow and death.

There were tiny scraps of paper in the pockets, which he piled on the desk; and, wonder of wonders, a nearly empty aspirin bottle, stamped EXP JL 97. He shrugged – never heard of anyone dying from stale aspirin – and chewed down two tablets without water.

'Hello? Ah, brilliant.' He moved quickly back to his chair and picked up the laptop, scrolled upwards and began to retype his lead sentence. 'Just give me as much as you can, right?'

A NATO soldier was injured, and a suspected war criminal killed, in a botched arrest raid in Banja Luka this morning. A second action met with more success, as another indicted suspect was apprehended peacefully.

According to NATO sources, Dušan Jovanović opened fire on arresting troops, seriously wounding the soldier, whose name and nationality were not disclosed . . .

He finished typing the story, and emailed it out with the photo. Closing the laptop, he picked up a black pen, walked over to a Wanted poster taped to the bathroom door, a series of grainy photos and captions, and crossed out two faces.

In an old city by the North Sea a woman was walking to work, a cigarette in one hand and a briefcase in the other. From her slightly run-down residential street, she turned north onto a broad cobbled avenue, the trees shielding red-brick mansions, now mostly converted into embassies. The road curved, led her along the side of a wooded park where two grey herons stalked in the shallows of a small canal, then opened onto a street noisy with four lanes of traffic, and lined with tall glass-walled hotels. She crossed at the intersection, and walked past a metal barricade towards a yellow stone building that had once been an insurance company office.

Entering the security booth, passing through the metal detectors, she divested herself of particulars. That she was:

age forty, sex female, citizenship French. Hair blonde turning grey, build slight, height average, chronic medical conditions none. Opinions about the bread-queue massacre, her father, Josef Stalin, the Inter-Entity Line, modern poetry, Josip Broz Tito, the Field of Black Birds, where to buy cheese on the rue St-Jacques, all these she had to remove.

What remained – mother tongue Serbo-Croat, perfect command of French, fluent command of English and German, some knowledge of Albanian and Italian. Professionally licensed to interpret in simultaneous and consecutive modes.

This was her part in the drama.

Serbo-Croat, of course, presented some difficulties because it no longer technically existed.

Interpreters shall not exercise any form of influence or power over their listeners.

Interpreters shall convey with the greatest accuracy and fidelity, and with full neutrality, the meaning of the speech which they interpret.

Interpreters shall convey the whole message, including the inflections and intonations of the speaker. An interpreter should provide the most accurate form of a word in spite of any vulgar or derogatory meaning.

Interpreters shall not correct an erroneous fact or statement, even if it is a patent mistake or untruth.

Interpreters shall maintain professional detachment at all times.

Lili felt something in the air as soon as she left the security booth, a soft murmur of excited sound. There was an unexpected cluster of journalists in the small lobby, talking on mobile phones and looking for press officers. One of them moved towards her.

'I'm sorry,' she said in English, walking quickly past. 'I can't speak to the media.' Holding her staff pass up to the automatic sensor, she went through a set of revolving doors at the side of the lobby and entered the restricted area. As she walked up the stairway to the courtrooms, she passed one of the English interpreters and raised an eyebrow interrogatively. He shrugged, palms out.

She went through a series of narrow corridors, cramped offices hastily constructed from plaster and plywood, and into the cluttered slice of a room that served as an office area for herself and several others. Vanja was sitting at the desk, studying a legal dictionary and drinking coffee.

'There's journalists all over the lobby,' said Lili. 'Any idea what's up?'

'Not a clue,' said Vanja. 'I don't think even the press officers know, they were on the phones trying to get briefed when I came in. Maybe the prosecutor's issuing a big indictment.' She flipped a page of the dictionary. 'So how are you handling this massacre versus mutilation issue?'

'Large numbers killed usually works for me. It does depend, though, doesn't it?'

'I think sometimes we could just go with killing *per se*.'

A security guard arrived to open the doors, and they walked up a few steps into a small soundproof booth at the side of Courtroom Three. From her briefcase, Lili took a bottle of water and a binder full of papers, and arranged them on the desk in front of her. She fitted the earphones over her head, adjusted the mike, and waited.

Her booth was built high up, above the heads of the people who were gradually filling the little courtroom. From where she sat, she looked directly over the prosecution team, who were sorting through documents at their table while clerks wheeled in carts full of huge ringbinders. Against the wall to her right was the taller desk where the three judges would sit in their black and red robes, and directly facing her the defendant, a square-shouldered man with a walrus moustache. An armed security guard sat beside him, his team of lawyers at another row of tables.

A robed court official stood at a microphone and recited, 'All rise, *veuillez-vous lever*,' the French badly mispronounced. The judges entered, the courtroom sat, and Lili turned on her microphone and began to speak.

'. . . prosecution's motion to amend the first amended indictment will be decided in due time, but for the moment the court will turn to consideration of the defence motion . . .' She received the proceedings in English through her earphones, and relayed them, seconds later, in the language which currently had no fixed name, but in consideration of the defendant might be called Serbian.

After thirty minutes she handed over to Vanja, who sat in a chair beside her. She closed her eyes for a moment and took a sip of water. She would listen for thirty minutes as Vanja interpreted, and then resume; and they would continue like this, handing off at measured intervals, for several hours. They could work for a total of six hours in a day, no more. It was essential that they did not become too tired, that they did not wander or daydream or lose the thread of words. An exhausted interpreter could fall behind, mistake an idiom, she could compromise the integrity of the trial in ways that could never be recovered. It was a matter of perfect attention. The ideal was transparency, a self-effacement thorough enough that no one in the room would remember they were there.

As a child, Lili was brought up to believe in the Party, the good old hard-line Party that Tito had betrayed, causing her parents to leave Belgrade in a fit of political pique. And for a while she did believe, with a vague and fervent passion, in many things of which she had scarcely any detailed concept. She believed in discipline and authority, in sacrifice. She believed in austerity and historical inevitability, in progress and justice. She believed in the future, in some magnificent unavoidable future without borders or wars, a time of solemn and perfect equality, of happiness in the far distance.

She believed, in a highly abstract sense, that it might be necessary to kill for this future, but she preferred to imagine herself dying for it, on some elusive barricade.

The extreme sweetness of nostalgia, for Lili, would be most tied up with the Fête de l'Humanité, which seemed then far away and the size of the world itself. The music, the sweet autumn air; *crêpes sucrées*, garlic sausages and almond cakes from the Basque country, and all the people, for miles and miles she thought, the bright colours of their clothes. Driving home late at night, leaning half-asleep against her mother, the sound of fireworks still in her ears.

A thin girl in a navy-blue skirt, she would walk for hours up and down the streets of Paris in the rain, delivering packages of leaflets and *L'Humanité Dimanche*, convinced that in some way she was doing this for the proletariat. At the age of nine – eventually she would find this funny – she fiercely proclaimed the May '68 uprising to be undisciplined and childish. Students fought with the police almost under her window, she walked in the street past graffiti that would become famous around the world – *Under the city, the beach; Be realistic, demand the impossible*. But she resisted the taste of astonishment in the air, she continued to believe in that clearly organized future made up of some combination of auto workers and architecture. She had pictures of Marx and Lenin and Maurice Thorez in her bedroom.

So she did know something about them, the men who had brought the Balkan wars about. Though their vision was not the same as hers, though it was all about nations and borders and blood and soil, she did remember what it was like to believe in history. To believe that history would explain it all, would make you right, would justify any amount of death. That it would converge on a single explosive point. And you yourself would be there.

Of course, for most of the men who came into the court it was not so complex. Some of them plainly, straightforwardly enjoyed degrading and hurting other people. A lot of them just did what they were told, because they couldn't think of anything else to do. Sometimes it was greed, or fear that if they didn't kill first it would be done to them; if they believed in anything, it was no more than a collection of weird fairy tales about their neighbours that they had recently heard on the television. Most of them were confused about what they had really felt. Almost all of them claimed to have very little memory of what they had or had not done.

Daniel looked through the bits of paper he had found in the pockets of his flak jacket, wondering why he hadn't cleared them out before now. They were a strange assortment – some café receipts, a ticket to Sarajevo's international film festival – and he remembered the mad dashes across Sniper Alley to get to the films and the concerts, to the theatre, remembered that people had made these crazy expeditions partly to drive home a point – *we are Europe too, you must care about us* – but also because they really did want to see the films. Everything from *Aladdin* to *I Burned Their Legs*.

The rest of the papers were notes to himself, almost all of them so cryptic that even he couldn't understand them any more, scribbled in cars veering along back roads at night perhaps. *pale nr checkpoint that guy, cut yer head off, ha ha*, he deciphered from one scrap. *selima k, x-files, has theory*, said another. He was sorry that he couldn't recall what Selima K's theory about the *X-Files* had been. Indeed, he couldn't figure out how Selima K, in a city under siege since 1992, would have heard about the *X-Files* at all. Was a friend in Berlin or London sending envelopes full of plot summaries through one of the aid agencies?

A bit regretfully, he threw all the papers into the bin, checked his watch, and decided to buy some groceries. He felt weightless and sore-eyed from exhaustion but knew that he wouldn't be able to sleep, with the bright sunlight pouring in the window, and the nervous energy of coffee and an exclusive story just filed buzzing in his head, his heart beating slightly too fast. There was nothing for it but to walk around Banja Luka, look for street reaction maybe. Get on the phone later and see if any levels of government had a comment.

He went into the market first, weaving through the crowds between stalls made of sticks and plastic, piled with cheap jeans and cosmetics, fruits and vegetables. A woman smiled at him as she sold him a bag of apples, but when he asked her about the arrests her face went blank and she turned away. Inside the old grey hall, among the smells of cheese and coffee and votive candles, it was much the same, his questions sending a chill through the room, the open pleasant expressions of the stallholders pinching in sudden hostility. He bought a jar of honey; then he left the market and walked towards the river, passing groups of hard-muscled young men, some of them in the uniform of the army of Republika Srpska. A white UN minivan drove by, slowly, on no special mission.

Across the bridge, where the Vrbas river glittered teal green in the morning sunlight, he walked further into the residential streets, along the crumbling pavements, past white and pale yellow houses sheltered by apple trees and climbing ivy. When he had first come here, these streets looked like any neighbourhood, small, plain. Then painted slogans started to appear on the walls – *Muslim*, *Croat*, *Serb* – and the homes that were not labelled *Serb* began to be smashed, burned, peppered with bullets. Then the shelling. Murders in the night. The soldiers' trucks racing down the centre of the street, loaded with televisions and VCRs, the women driven weeping into railway cars heading for Zenica; the men to the camps, the barbed wire, the things that happened there. Now the slogans were gone, the houses under repair in a haphazard way, the population almost exclusively Serb. A cleansed city.

One spring night while he was in Sarajevo, Banja Luka's beautiful Ferhadija mosque had been dynamited. The burned patch of waste ground stood outside his hotel, a part of the landscape he walked by daily.

He wondered what it meant that in some way he did love this city, when he had seen only the final moments of its real life, and knew that it was now an angry remnant, a kind of reanimated corpse. He wondered what it meant to say that he loved this poor lovely country, its green mountains and fast rivers, its old streets and its rock-and-roll kids, when he had never really seen it at peace; if the only thing he really loved was the war, the drama, the terrible poignancy of this wound at the heart of Europe.

Turning onto a street of small shops, their signs a mixture of Roman and Cyrillic letters, he was brought up short for a moment outside a window filled with rubber masks. The faces of Radovan Karadžić and Ratko Mladić stared out at him, blank, multiple, surrounded by flags. I could make this a metaphor of Republika Srpska, he thought, but that wouldn't be quite true either, not exactly. He thought of the Serbian refugees from the Krajina, who had not particularly wanted this war, most of them; who had just been shuffled from place to place until they ended up staying somewhere, maybe here. Not all of them wanted to put on these plastic masks. Still, he took out the digital camera and shot off a few quick pictures.

When he crossed the river again, the sun was high and hot. He walked along the street below the sixteenth-century fort, where elderly women stood above piles of worn blue jeans and lace doilies, part of Banja Luka's small frenzy of commercial activity, a feverish weak economy in a permanent grey zone. He checked his watch and stopped at a small café, where he ordered burek and coffee and took out his mobile, punching numbers in quickly.

By the time the morning session in Courtroom Three wrapped up, Lili was aware of the strain around her temples. She massaged them quickly with her thumbs, then shuffled her papers back into their binders. The security guard locked the door of the booth as they left.

Vanja sat at her desk and pulled a sandwich out of her bag. 'Want a bite?' she asked, holding half of it towards Lili. 'It's smoked eel, it's not bad.'

'Thanks anyway, but I'm going for a cigarette. See you in a bit.'

She went across the hallway to the rather uninteresting cafeteria, picked up a bowl of pea soup with sausage and carried it to a table in the smoking section. She was just sitting down when she heard her phone ringing inside her briefcase.

'*Zut*,' she muttered, realizing that both she and the security guard had overlooked it, and that it might have rung while she was working. She unfastened the briefcase and pulled it out. '*Allô?*'

'Lili? It's me, Daniel.'

'Oh,' she said. 'Oh. Daniel.' She found herself glancing around the room, checking to see if anyone was sitting near her, then thought that she was being silly, there was no need for that.

'You're at lunch, right? I mean, your phone's on, so it's okay to call?'

'Sure, I guess so.' It was good to hear his voice, after all.

'It's not ideal, but . . . how are you?'

'I'm good, I'm cool, I'm just bouncing around here and I have to talk to somebody. You remember my old pal Nikola Marković?'

'Oh yes, the nutter. The one with the singing and the emotional problems.'

'The very one. Well, I guess you guys had a sealed indictment on him after all, because NATO picked him up a few hours ago, and on top of that—'

'Wait, wait.' She held up her hand as if he could see her. 'Think about what you're telling me,' she said softly.

'That they . . . oh.'

'Exactly. He's under the jurisdiction of the tribunal now. I don't say one word about him, and you don't tell me. And anything I said before in this conversation, I didn't say it, all right? It's gone from your records.'

'Lili, I wasn't calling you for a quote.'

'Nobody trusts a journalist, my friend. You must learn to live with that.'

'Well, goddamn, this is my best story for ages. An adventure on the streets of Banja Luka. Exclusive photos. Wild times in the not very big city.'

'Are you drunk or something?'

'It's barely lunchtime. What do you think I am?' She reached for a cigarette, turning slightly in her chair to face away from the neighbouring tables. 'What I am,' Daniel went on in his slightly giddy voice, 'what I am is definitely sleep-deprived, because I got this tip that something was going down tonight, last night, whatever, so I spent the whole night sort of spooking around the streets waiting to see what was going to happen, and it wasn't till I finally went back to the hotel to get some coffee around dawn that . . . well . . . the things happened that happened, you know.'

'I do feel this is a conversation I shouldn't be having. Could we possibly change the subject?'

'Sorry. I'm kind of preoccupied.' She could hear him chewing something. She lit her cigarette and breathed in. 'Well, I can tell you the reason this is important to me is that AFP is giving me trouble again. They're not exactly threatening my *per diem*, but there's been an awful lot of muttering about how much time I spend in Bosnia. Kosovo, they say, why didn't you stay in Kosovo? I filed a dozen stories from Kosovo last month, but this isn't good enough for them. Apparently. Anyway, this time I got them some bloodshed, so they have to be happy.'

She wanted badly to ask him what he meant about bloodshed, she was genuinely curious, and she wanted to make sure that he hadn't been in too much danger. She was bound to hear the whole story within a few hours, this was a purely symbolic withholding, something of no legal or ethical weight. But she didn't ask.

'Talk to me, Lili.'

'I'm just sitting here in the cafeteria, thinking that my soup looks quite unpleasant. I'm not adjusting easily to the Dutch cuisine.'

'I'm sorry.' Daniel hesitated at the other end of the line. 'I should phone you tonight, shouldn't I?'

'I think that would be a better idea.'

'Okay. I'm sorry. I didn't really expect to reach you.'

'It's all right, it's all right, Daniel. I'll talk to you later.'

She hung up, turned the phone off, and studied her soup, which was now lukewarm. She pushed the bowl away and went back to the counter for a cheese sandwich.

Normally Lili worked in the French booth of Courtroom One, but with some kind of epidemic of summer colds laying the language staff low, she was assigned that day to the Bosnian/Croatian/Serbian booth of Courtroom Three, where at the moment the judges were hearing pre-trial and sentencing proceedings.

The defendant sat in the witness chair with his earphones on – Vanja and Lili would be transmitting the words of the lawyers to him, in the language which might in this instance be called Croatian. He was not someone of great importance; one of the local thugs who ended up in the court sometimes, a step up the chain of command towards someone bigger. Convicted last month of a series of crimes in a particular corner of Bosnia, and sensing that his options were running out, he had recently decided to argue diminished responsibility on the grounds of mental instability. Currently he was engaged in an attempt to convince the court that he had believed himself to be taking orders from a particular, and evidently criminal, ram who lived on a nearby farm.

'Because you know, sheep have always been pretty bad characters for me. They're just trouble, however you look at it. Now, cows are different. I never had a problem with a cow, I would say they're fine animals.' He paused and took stock. 'Of course, I understand now that the sheep themselves weren't really talking to me. This was an aspect of my mental condition at the time.'

'But you're answering my questions coherently now. You're talking about these things in a very objective way. To what do you attribute your remarkable improvement?'

The defendant chewed his thumbnail. 'I have a healthy lifestyle in the prison,' he offered at last.

A corner of the lawyer's mouth twitched. 'I see. Could you expand on this healthy lifestyle for us?'

'Well, hmm.' The defendant frowned thoughtfully and looked around the room. 'I watch a lot of educational television,' he said in an optimistic tone. 'And they won't let me drink alcohol.' One of the young court officers put her hands over her mouth and looked quickly down at the table.

She walked home, when the court had closed, in the lengthening shadows of the early evening. When she reached her own neighbourhood, she detoured south, onto narrow streets lined with identical tall brick houses, little shops, people speeding past on bikes and mopeds. She went into the grocery store to buy olives and fruit and Turkish flatbread, and while she waited at the till she heard the story on the radio, as she had expected. 'A British special forces soldier and a Bosnian war crimes suspect were killed this morning in the Serb-controlled area of Bosnia,' the Dutch announcer read, 'while a second suspect was arrested without incident. Dutch troops were reportedly involved in both arrests. The soldier, whose name has not yet been released . . .'

She was living in a furnished flat on the second floor of a house on Laan van Meerdervoort, above a friendly small bar, and directly next door to the former home of a nineteenth-century banker who had made a local reputation by painting impeccably bourgeois pictures of sand dunes. His home had now been turned into a museum dedicated to his works, a fact Lili tried to avoid remembering.

It was a nice enough flat – the bedroom had a little balcony overlooking the back yard, and a pretty blue quilt on the bed, and the living room with its kitchenette had wood floors in decent condition. She was not unaccustomed to living among the furniture of strangers, but she found herself doing odd things, uncharacteristic things, to make it her own. She had acquired the Dutch habit of bringing flowers home, something she never did in Paris; there were white roses in a vase on the table, a day old and just starting to wilt at the edges, their sweet, acrid scent drifting gently through the room.

Daniel didn't phone until nearly midnight. She was lying on the couch with a blanket around her legs, reading a copy of *Vreme* which she subscribed to from Belgrade at considerable expense, and wondering if she should go to bed.

'Sorry,' he said, his voice a bit fuzzy. 'I fell asleep sometime in the afternoon.'

'That was probably for the best.'

'So how was your day?'

'Fine.' She folded up the paper. 'I gave up about the soup and ate a sandwich. Honestly, Daniel, I don't know why you even ask me about my day.'

'I'm sure there are things you could tell me. I don't know, gossip about the other interpreters, who's sleeping with who.'

'Of course, because if I knew that, I would certainly divulge it to a reporter.' She stretched one arm behind her head. 'So I heard on the radio that two people were killed. Jovanović and a soldier.'

'Yeah. Initially the word from NATO was that the soldier was only wounded, but I hear he was gone before they reached Tuzla. Does this mean you can talk about Jovanović?'

'I suppose so. He's out of our jurisdiction now.'

'Out of every jurisdiction but God's, isn't he? Rescued from justice by death.'

'Whatever made him think he could shoot his way out? Were you there?'

'No, I got there just after. I was watching them arrest Nikola – which was kind of strange, in the end. I don't think he saw me. I guess Jovanović was a fair marksman though, I mean, taking down a guy from the special forces is no small task.'

'It's still not how I would choose to die.'

'Well. No.' Daniel paused. 'So there's another thing I need to talk to you about.'

'Oh yes?' Lili sat up, wondering about the edge of apprehension in his voice.

'See, after I phoned you before, I was talking to the *Sunday Times* woman in Holland. She's putting together a fairly major feature on Marković, and because I had this, as it were, relationship with him, she wanted me to drive up there for a bit to work with her on background.'

'Uh-huh.'

'Well, obviously I'm going to do it, in fact I'm coming in tomorrow.' He cleared his throat. 'What I need to know,' he said sharply, 'what I need to know is whether I know you. While I'm in town.'

Lili rubbed her forehead. 'I hate these conversations, Daniel.'

'Look, okay, but I just need to know.'

'I'm not sure.' She exhaled softly. 'I mean, there would have to be a lot of limitations.'

'Right, and the limitations would be . . . what, then?'

'I do want to see you, Daniel. Really I do. You must know that.'

'I don't . . . Listen, I'm just saying I'm going to be there by tomorrow night, and I need you to tell me what the rules are.'

'Let me think.' She pulled her knees up to her chin and folded her free arm around them, feeling miserable. 'Let me think a minute. I just can't guarantee that this is not a problem.'

The prisoner arrived at the Scheveningen Detention Centre late at night. A few kilometres east of Lili's flat, they took him from a van under armed guard and led him inside. They had earlier changed the plastic handcuffs for metal; now they uncuffed him, took his fingerprints and photograph, and searched him thoroughly. They removed the change in his pockets and a small penknife, writing down these items on an inventory sheet. He was advised of his right to contact his family, and the diplomatic mission of Bosnia-Herzegovina, and also advised that he could defer these calls until morning should he prefer. He could immediately, or in the morning, contact legal counsel. In the event that he could not afford legal counsel, the court would provide counsel for him. They advised him that he would be examined by the medical officer the next day, and that he would appear before the court in the near future to be formally charged. He was given a pamphlet explaining his rights as a prisoner, the disciplinary requirements of the prison, and the process by which he could file complaints.

He was taken to his cell and provided with bedding and a pair of pyjamas. The cell contained a small bed, a desk, a coffee-maker, a barred window with curtains, an alcove with a toilet and shower. It was explained to him that he could have a cable television installed if he wished, but that this would have to be done at his own expense.

It was strange, discomforting, how carefully they treated him; without warmth or courtesy, but not cruelly; precise and measured. Perhaps it would have made him happier if they were brutal, if they had smashed his teeth and put him in a tiny concrete chamber – he could have courage, then, and honour, he could more easily believe that he was persecuted by mad irrational enemies, that he was a soldier in a long battle. The men who had arrested him had been fighters like himself, he believed. They had hit him a few times in the helicopter. He hadn't minded that; he understood war. But not these jailers here.

Perhaps that was why they were so meticulously proper. With cold civility, they would set out to strip him of his last beloved dreams of persecution.

II

Like a Two-edged Sword

14–31 December 1995

Daniel had met Lili for the first time in Paris, at what you might call the end of the wars, or at least some of the wars.

Late in 1995, he flew out of Sarajevo, went to the Elysée Palace and watched them sign the treaty, a collection of men in suits, smiling, scowling, rambling weirdly on about history and the future and their own extreme good intentions.

The president of Bosnia, looking grey and emotionless, signed an agreement to slice his country into two things called entities, with something between them that was and was not a border, two bitter enclaves, and the multi-ethnic Bosnia that people had once believed in, had endured a four-year siege to protect, was finally finished. Cleansed.

Suddenly Daniel couldn't feel his hands, and had to stare down at them for a long time to make sure they were there.

There was a transit strike in Paris that day. He ran to his hotel in a cutting wind, pulling his leather jacket tight, thin rain whipping against his face; dodging at intersections, anticipating sniper fire. He lay down on the bed with his wet shoes still on and covered his face.

It got dark outside.

At some point in the night he turned on the light, found a bottle of duty-free Scotch and a toothbrush glass, and drank until dawn. Then he lay down again and slept. In his dream, he was lying on the floor of a hotel room in Sarajevo, the blinds drawn, earth and rocks piled on top of him.

He couldn't seem to get enough sleep. He would wake up, and his arms and legs would be so leaden with exhaustion that he could barely reach for his watch on the bedside table. He lay in bed, as far as he could later work out, for about two days, never waking quite fully enough to separate his dreams from the passage of actual time. He would make his way down the hall to the toilet and back, only half-aware he was moving, then fall into the bed again.

Finally he sat up and looked around the room. It was not like the Holiday Inn, this room. That was important. It was full of odd bits of old furniture, chairs and a table and an oversized armoire, cracked and wobbly. The sheets and pillows were clean but didn't match; there were no pictures, but wallpaper with a faded floral design. An old plaster rosette on the ceiling, a frayed pink rug.

He got up, showered and shaved, put on clean clothes. He looked at his watch. It was three in the afternoon. The bottle of Scotch on the table was not quite empty; he poured out the remainder and drank, then went downstairs to find something to eat. He was feeling better. Unquestionably, he was feeling better. These things happened now and then, they were bound to happen, but it was something you got through.

He paused in the doorway of the hotel, automatically charting the safest route. There was a little café across the street that would probably make him an omelette in mid-afternoon, and he found himself calculating that there was not much exposed ground to cross, then forcing himself to remember that this was Paris, that there were no snipers in the neighbouring buildings, not for now at any rate.

He walked to the café with deliberate slowness, though it

seemed wrong, unnatural, almost a betrayal. It was warm and smoky inside. Two teenage boys were playing a video game in the corner. He sat down at a table and found himself nearly weeping with relief.

He ate a cheese omelette, bread and butter, apple tart, drank three cups of *café crème* with sugar. The food was wonderful. Both his guilt and his well-being were somehow complete, each having a full existence alongside the other.

As he sipped his coffee, holding the cup close to his face to feel the warmth, he watched the people passing in the street. A woman walked by who troubled him faintly, as if he knew her. As if she had something to do with the wars. A thin woman, with washed-out blonde hair, carrying a paper bag and a briefcase. He watched her as she stopped at a heavy wooden door down the street from the hotel, took a key out of her pocket and let herself in.

This worried him for a moment, but not for too long. He was all right now. He would go back to the hotel and phone the AFP office, tell them he'd come down with food poisoning or the flu. He doubted that they would want a story on the signing ceremony from him at this point, but perhaps there was some colour that would be useful. He would check his bank account and see if he could take a bit of time off, stay here for a week or two. There was still a feature he was working up for the *Independent*, he could finish that one here.

In the morning he walked through the slanting streets of the Fifth, past the great masses of the *grandes écoles*. There were bright little Christmas displays in the shop windows, glittering white and silver. Wandering with no particular destination in mind, he found himself in a scruffy terraced park, built up around the ruins of an ancient amphitheatre. A few men were playing boules in the sandy arena. In a playground under bare trees, a small child rocked on a plastic horse.

He sat on a bench and clenched his teeth, resisting the image of a mortar smashing down onto this park, this pearl-grey morning. He told himself that this was the normal world, the sane world. He thought, for reasons he could not begin to fathom, of Hitler's bunker in Berlin.

At the corner of the park was a sign directing tourists to the mosque. He thought that it would be a good thing to go there. He'd known quite a few Bosnians who were called Muslims – had Muslim names or something – and only a handful of them, mostly old people, went to a mosque at all; but still it seemed like a thing to do that day.

He must have gone inside through the wrong entrance somehow, because he found himself wandering through a long and confusing network of yellow hallways with low ceilings. A group of schoolgirls, some of them wearing headscarves, ran past him shrieking and giggling. He could feel the damp heat in the air from the steambaths, somewhere near by in the building.

He came out of the corridors to a courtyard garden, partly neglected this time of year, small puddles of green water in the broad ceramic pools, the more fragile plants and flowers bitten brown by frost, others growing half-wild along the bright tiled walkways. Through a filigreed archway into a second courtyard, inlaid with delicate mosaic, blue and white and green, and behind a doorway, veiled by screens, the singing murmur of prayer. He looked up towards a pale sky feathered with clouds. *Peace*, he thought. *This is peace. Some kind of peace.*

He noticed her a second time while he was buying lunch, tomatoes and a tin of sardines, in one of the little groceries near the hotel. It had started to rain a bit, and she was at the corner trying to flag down a taxi, wearing a dark jacket and a translucent blue-green scarf, smoking a cigarette. And he had that sense again of familiarity and tension, that he had seen her before, that she was somehow tied up with things, with something. He felt a slight chill, a small clench in his stomach, and he wondered if this was part of what you went through, seeing people you thought had been there. Revenants. Maybe they would be everywhere in Paris. He would walk down St-Germain and see someone who had died outside his window, or someone who had fired shells down at the city from the hills.

He went past the entrance of his hotel, towards the door he had seen her opening. On the stone arch there was a row of doorbells for different apartments, and against one he saw a name that stood out, L. Stambolović. A Serbian name.

Maybe she was related to someone, maybe that was it, a certain shape of the face he had recognized. He wondered if he would see her again.

Crossing the bridges, he found, was very difficult. The Pont St-Michel seemed particularly bad, a target for snipers from several directions, nowhere to take cover. He went over only once, in a hasty scuttle. The Metro was still half-paralysed by the strike, the streets a tangle of irritable traffic. He decided that he would stay on the Left Bank for the time being.

He sat in his hotel room, working on his feature about the Dayton agreement, cutting bread and cheese with a penknife.

'I don't know where I live now,' says Srdjan. A Bosnian Serb, engaged to a Muslim girl, he fled to Belgrade when the war came to his town. Last year, he was kidnapped from a Belgrade restaurant and driven to the front lines. 'I killed some people,' he says in a monotone. 'I tried not to, but if I didn't they would have killed me.' I ask him who 'they' are, and he explains that he means his commanding officers.

He is glad that the fighting is over, but he does not expect to see his girlfriend again. Perhaps she is dead; if she is alive, he expects that she will not speak to him. 'I don't have any country now. I don't know where I can go. Do you think I could go to Australia?'

He was sitting in the Luxembourg Gardens. He had never really understood French parks, dry and barren with their sculptured trees and broad sandy *allées*. White marble statues in histrionic poses and clusters of green metal chairs around a huge fountain. There were fenced-off areas where children were playing, a sandpit and a climbing frame, an expensive merry-go-round, and the park was a bit less formal around these, so he was sitting on a bench reading the *Guardian*, the late afternoon cool but not really cold. The ground was muddy from an earlier rainstorm.

According to the paper, there were demonstrations going on daily in Paris, strikes across the country – wages, social service cutbacks, all the usual issues. Somehow he was not surprised that it had taken him this long to find out, and from a foreign newspaper yet. He no longer expected to understand what went on in the world beyond Bosnia. Still, it wasn't very professional, to miss all that.

A little boy screamed.

Daniel jumped up, his newspaper falling to the ground.

Under the climbing frame, the boy pulled himself to his feet. There was some blood on his face. Blood running down his face.

Oh my God.

Daniel felt his knees giving way underneath him, cold sweat soaking his back.

Oh my God. The little dead bodies on the ground.

The little dead bloody bodies.

He grabbed for the back of the bench.

A little baby in a pool of blood. The baby's arm. Across the street.

The boy's mother was picking him up, cleaning his face with her handkerchief. He sniffled a bit, wriggled down from her arms.

The little mutilated bodies, the blood.

Daniel held on to the bench, and then his throat convulsed, and suddenly he was vomiting, his stomach contents heaving out onto the gravel, burning his throat. When there was nothing left, he spat up strands of bile; then finally, his body went limp and he groped his way back onto the bench, sat down shaking. The mothers were staring at him, a drunk in the park, a disturbance. He wiped his mouth with the sleeve of his jacket. The sky was thick and violet, the sun setting in streaks of light over Luxembourg Palace.

A few evenings later he was in the grocery again, as a chilly rain splattered down outside, trying in his very poor French to chat politely with the man behind the counter, something about the *mauvais temps*. As he turned towards the door he saw the blonde woman, standing by a shelf of canned vegetables, watching him with an amused half-smile.

'Here's a piece of advice,' she said in a low voice, her English only lightly accented. 'It's silly to buy your cheese here, you want to go to the *fromagerie* down the road. This is just, you know, plastic cheese they have here.'

Daniel coughed and nodded, not sure how to respond to this.

'I saw you at the Elysée,' she continued, and right away it came together in his mind, yes, he had a clear memory of her, slight and pale, standing towards the back of the room as he fell apart in his chair. 'You're a journalist?'

'I am, yeah. Mostly stringing for AFP, but I write for some

of the British papers too. I like to freelance, I like the flexibility.'

'Are you based here?'

'No. No, I just came over for the signing.' She had hazel eyes; he noticed that because it was something you rarely saw, proper hazel eyes. 'I'm in Bosnia most of the time. That's my beat, the Balkans.' He watched carefully for her reaction, and he thought he felt an apprehension, something, but he couldn't be sure. People reacted to the word Bosnia anyway. 'What about you? Were you with one of the delegations?'

'Oh no,' she laughed. 'No, I'm not a politician. I'm an interpreter. I was just there as part of the background, but you know they didn't need me. It's not as if anyone was listening to each other.'

They walked towards the door together. 'My name is Daniel, by the way, Daniel Bryant.'

'Pleased to meet you, Daniel. I'm Lili.'

'You live down that way?' She nodded. 'Because I was just walking past and I noticed a name on the door, Stambolović . . .'

Her shoulders tensed slightly. 'Yes. That is me,' she said slowly.

'And I did recognize that it was a Serbian name, so . . .'

'So you want to know if I'm one of those people who likes to sit up in the hills lobbing mortars onto primary schools?' Her face had shut down, her eyes flat and guarded. They were standing in the rain, beside the trays of ice where the grocery store displayed its fish. Daniel could smell the slabs of cod, feel the crushed ice under his running shoes. Christmas lights were shimmering on Gay-Lussac, winter fireflies.

'Oh God, I didn't mean any offence.'

'Yeah, it's okay. It's not your fault. Maybe I'll see you around.' She turned and began to walk away.

'Listen.' He reached out quickly, his hand brushing her sleeve. 'Would you have a drink with me? Let's talk, okay?'

Lili paused, shrugged, looking at the pavement. 'Sure. Why not?'

Inside the little café, they ordered coffee and cognac, and Lili lit a cigarette. 'So okay,' she said briskly. 'The mandatory ethnic background. My father was Serbian from Belgrade. My mother's Albanian from Priština. I was born in Belgrade, but we moved to Paris when I was three years old, and if you want to ask me what I am – because this is the first thing people ask me these days, 'what are you?' – well, I suppose I'm French.'

Daniel sipped his cognac. 'I was in Belgrade a little while ago,' he said. 'I was writing a feature about the Women in Black.'

Lili's face seemed to soften a bit. 'Oh yeah? That's good.' She took a drag on her cigarette, pushed a wet strand of hair off her forehead. 'That's good, they don't get enough coverage.' They were both quite aware of what they were doing, the subtle exchange of code words, the careful testing of political positions.

'So how did your family end up coming to Paris?'

'Oh, my father didn't get along with Tito.' She exhaled smoke. 'Who you must admit looks pretty bad in comparison with all the freedom they've got there now.'

'He was a dissident, was he?'

She smiled sardonically. 'Not the kind you're thinking of. He was a Stalinist, my father. He loved the French Communist Party, they were more Stalinoid than the Soviet Union nearly. I grew up in this little self-contained communist world, we had a communist doctor, communist dentist, communist plumber. I had this subscription to a communist magazine for children, *Pif le chien*. Pretty weird education, overall.'

'Is he still . . . ?'

'He died a long time ago.' She looked out of the window, her expression veiled again. 'When I was a teenager. He was a lot older than my mother.' She was silent for a moment, then turned back to him. 'What about you, then? What's your story?'

Daniel shrugged. Lili tipped her head to one side questioningly, and he noticed that she was wearing small gold and green earrings. He was still interested in her eyes. 'I'm from Canada originally. Haven't been back there for ages. My permanent address is said to be in London, but it's rented out right now. For the last few years I've pretty much lived in the Sarajevo Holiday Inn. Writing war pornography for the masses,' he added bitterly.

Lili nodded and said nothing. 'You know,' he went on, 'you start off with this idea that you're going to tell people the truth about what's happening, that it'll make an actual difference? I mean, what a bunch of crap. Whatever you write, people just read it like some kind of thriller about Balkan serial killers. And body parts, they like those body parts. So that's what the fuck I do.'

Lili tapped ash off the end of her cigarette. 'You stayed, though,' she said quietly.

'I had to.' Daniel signalled the waiter for another drink. 'I had to, I know all these people now, I had to see it through. I'll be going back soon.' He drummed his fingers on the table, tense; he almost wished he was a smoker, he could ask her for a cigarette, it would give him something to do with his hands. 'Go back and watch the fuckers get away with it. Just carve up the whole place and get away with it. My good buddy Radovan and his gang of merry pranksters.'

'There is the tribunal,' said Lili in her soft voice.

'Yeah, it's a nice idea. The UN has lots of nice ideas.'

He felt the same wild impulse he always felt, when he was talking to someone from the outside – a hunger to tell her about everything, every awful detail, the concentration camps and the mass graves, the sheer dirty exhaustion and psychosis of the city under siege, about the UN shining their spotlights onto people escaping over the airport tarmac and giving the snipers a clear shot, about what happened at Srebrenica. He had a vision of himself as a crabbed old man, wandering darkened streets and seizing passers-by. *I only am escaped alone to tell thee.*

He told her a story about the prisoners at Keraterm, and she listened seriously, impassively. He appreciated that; no exclamations of horror, no attempts at reassurance, just a grave calm, like a doctor noting the symptoms of a terminal disease.

'Okay, you know what, that's enough,' he said. 'I don't want to . . . let's talk about something else.'

So as Lili worked her way through her pack of cigarettes they talked about books, about Balkan literature, of which she seemed to have an encyclopaedic knowledge. 'I don't know, there are quite a lot of them,' she shrugged. 'Every second person seems to be a writer, I mean a serious writer. It's like a hegemonic career choice, well, that or a psychiatrist. Good old Radovan has it on both counts, of course. You have to question the function of literature, when you think about that.' She ground out one cigarette and reached for another. 'You know everyone's always quoting Auden, about poetry making nothing happen?'

Daniel nodded.

'Well, this is not true at all. It's just that the only things that it makes happen are evil. This whole war was invented by writers. They wrote it all out beforehand, the nationalist ideologues, the novelists, the poets, and then the second-raters like Karadžić filled in the details. Of course,' she gestured dismissively, 'it had to get down to the TV and the folk music in the end to, you know, generalize it across the population.'

She sighed and looked out the window of the café again. 'But the paradox,' she said, 'is that the others, the writers without the big ideologies, the great writers, the human ones – these are the ones who could make nothing happen at all. Certain writers could start a war that might last for ever, but the others couldn't stop it for a single day.' She shrugged and looked back towards him. 'I'm not really such a defeatist, honestly not. But it does make me sad sometimes.'

She checked her watch. He found himself staring at her wrist, fascinated by its delicacy, and it occurred to him that he'd probably had too much to drink.

'You know what, Daniel, I really have to go. But listen, if you're still here on Saturday evening, why don't you come to my flat? Since you seem to know where it is already,' she added drily.

'I'd like that,' said Daniel.

'I could lend you some books. Anyway it's good for me to have a chance to talk to an English-speaker. I need to keep in practice.'

They left the bar together. 'Your English sounds pretty well perfect to me.'

'Oh, not at all. No, it's my third language, you can never master a third language really. I make mistakes if I'm under pressure, and also I'm not very colloquial. This is part of what makes you interesting to talk to, you've got this salad of British and American slang. It's very educational.' She nodded to him at his hotel door. 'I'll see you on Saturday.'

He watched her moving around her small kitchen, making coffee, slicing fruit, putting pastries on a tray, and felt like he might as well be back in the Balkans, the helpless recipient of determined hospitality – that family in Goražde cutting up their last wrinkled cucumber and insisting that he eat it. Possibly Lili was not so completely French as she claimed.

With a journalist's unconscious reflexes, he scanned the flat, looking for the personal detail, the first paragraph hook. It was bright and very neat, and not without character, but it seemed rather lightly inhabited, as if she was not there very often. Lots of books – he counted six languages in two different alphabets; bright-coloured cushions and a copy of *Le Monde Diplo* on the couch. No photographs. Several oddly shaped white ceramic bowls on the shelves, decorative rather than utilitarian. A couple of framed prints he didn't recognize; one of them simply the words *et après ça?* in big white looping script, on a black background.

'Have you ever been back there?'

'Oh,' she said carefully, 'not for a while. A long time before the wars. When I was little we used to go in the summer to visit my aunt and uncle in Istria, on the coast. Though my father always had this plan that we should go to Albania instead, and he could explain to them why the Chinese were historically deviationist. My mother never liked that idea much. Would you rather have coffee or a glass of wine?'

'You've already made the coffee.'

'Well, yes, but you don't have to feel committed to drinking it. These pastries are very good, by the way. They're from the *patisserie* just up the street, you should go there before you leave.'

He wanted to know if she had a lover. It seemed certain that she must.

'Coffee's fine. Really.'

'*D'accord.* No problem.'

She was wearing black – trousers and a soft top – and the same earrings as before. He wanted to stand up and touch her,

her pale hair, her narrow shoulders. It was possible that there was an implicit invitation here to spend the night with her. But he had no idea how to navigate the maze of French and Balkan and British and Canadian social codes, no sense at all of what was really happening, so he stayed where he was.

Lili was standing by her bookshelves with her coffee now, scanning the books. 'You know what irritates me?' she said. 'These people who keep insisting they speak three different languages. I mean, I'm qualified to interpret into this language, okay? I know something about it. It's hardly even three proper dialects. And I know all about how languages develop and change, it's part of my field, but these new words they're making up, the Croats especially, they're just painful. Though it's greatly inflated my official language competence, I can tell you that.'

'I saw somebody killed one time for using the wrong words,' said Daniel. 'Sliced right open.' He didn't mean to say that at all. He felt idiotic, ridiculous, but the words kept coming out in a jerky convulsive rush. 'Other guy just cut right through him, like that, under his ribs. My God. And he died slow. He didn't die quickly. It was very bloody. Horrible.' He was shaking as he tried to stop himself from talking any more. 'I had this line running through my mind the whole time. *The word of God is like a two-edged sword.* Didn't make any sense at all in the situation. I don't even know where it's from. It just kept going through my head.'

'It's from the Bible,' said Lili.

'Yeah, well, I kind of figured that.' He looked at her, leaning against the bookshelf with that serious calm, those steady hazel eyes. She seemed completely unshockable, and for the first time he wondered exactly what her work involved. 'What do you do?' he asked, and it came out abrupt, harsh, as if he were asking *which side are you on?*

Lili sat down slowly on the couch and reached for her cigarettes. 'Okay,' she said. 'The first thing you have to understand is that, in everything I do, I'm bound by complete confidentiality. I can never tell you one specific detail of what I work on. This is a standard part of all interpretation work. But in general terms – I do some academic conferences here in Paris, some trade delegations, that kind of thing; sometimes I lecture at the university, in the school of interpretation. I also work out of the country quite often; my concierge sublets the flat if I'm away for a month or more. I do a lot of work for the European Community in Brussels. Also I work at NATO meetings. And sometimes I go to Geneva on contracts with various UN agencies. So what I'm trying to say is, I'm not unfamiliar with these stories, with . . . this kind of material. I have been sometimes quite intimate with some of this information.' She blew out smoke, gently. 'What I do is, I speak for people in the languages they need. Because I believe . . . well, that people can talk to each other. That they should. That what happened back there – let me get it right, what Milošević and those people made to happen – it wasn't necessary. It just wasn't necessary for them to do that.'

Obscurely, Daniel felt the nausea gathering in the pit of his stomach again, a hot tangle of emotion rising through his chest. He looked down.

'Okay, don't even say it,' snapped Lili. 'I know how stupid that sounds.' She jumped up, walking restlessly around the room. 'You were in Sarajevo. And all the time the UN was saying, talk to each other, talk talk, and the men up in the hills are just shooting you for entertainment. I know, I know.'

Daniel nodded mutely, wondering if he would ever be able to have a normal conversation again.

'I was at the meetings.' Her face was pinched with a mixture of feelings he couldn't quite identify, anger, guilt. 'All those meetings, all the internationals. People saying, you know those Balkan types, they're just deranged with hatred, it's their nature. People saying the Muslims are really shelling themselves, because, I don't know, they're so Balkan, they're so insane. Nothing for us to do. Let's just have a chat.' She stopped at the window, looking away from him, her arms folded. 'As an interpreter, I don't have opinions, I don't have beliefs. I convey every person's words with all the accuracy I can. I hope for the best. Maybe sometimes it is better than nothing.'

'And as a person, Lili?' He stretched out a hand in her direction, palm raised like a question.

'As a person? I do what I can. Not much, I suppose. I sign open letters in the newspapers. Once in a while I can talk to people with some influence. I interpret for certain groups without charge. Outside of my job, what am I? A traitor to Serbia, according to some people. Or sometimes *šiptar*, you know, dirty Albanian. Slave to Muslims is another one I've heard.' She shrugged. 'This is no big problem to me. I'm just trying to say, I do what I can.'

'Okay,' said Daniel, just able to summon words again. 'I mean, I think I understand that.' He let out a breath. 'I will have a glass of wine, if you don't mind.'

She moved towards the kitchen, and he thought her hands were shaking as she poured the wine, and he tried to direct the conversation away from the war again, to talk about her apartment, the strikes – Lili had marched with the language teachers a few days ago – about anything that didn't make him sound like a lunatic, like the man he used to see in a park in London lecturing people about salvation through UFOs.

Later, she insisted that he take away English translations of Ismail Kadare and Danilo Kiš. She didn't need them, she said, she had the original versions, she was only reading the translations for practice. 'Anyway you can post them back to me sometime. I suppose they'll have mail in Bosnia again eventually. I wish I could give you something by Sidran, but I have nothing in English.' She tucked her card into one of the books. 'If you're back in Paris any time, you could call and see if I'm here.'

At the doorway she kissed him on both cheeks, a polite meaningless gesture, and he hugged her lightly, smelling her perfume. He rode down in the tiny rickety lift, a dark-haired girl who looked like a student almost pacing him down the curving stairway.

The next day he got on a flight to Zagreb, and started looking for UN planes going back into Sarajevo.

He didn't really expect to talk to her again. He was used to these intense and transient connections, they were starting to seem like a normal way of life. Then on New Year's Eve, still waiting for a spot on a UN plane, he found himself in a particularly dreary hotel in a backwater of southern Serbia, listening to a cluster of depressed and paranoid youngsters trying to work up some kind of entertainment for themselves under his window, and in a moment of self-pity he called Lili's number. To his complete astonishment, she answered.

'Oh, I had some invitations,' she said. 'I just didn't feel like going out. Too many people asking what are you and all that.' He could hear the flick of her lighter, an exhalation of breath. 'It's good to hear from you, Daniel. Are you well?'

'Me? Sure. I'm just hangin' with the small-town juvenile delinquents.' He lay back on the bed, feeling suddenly cheerful. 'Vlad swore up and down I'd find dissidents here, but it's perfectly clear now that he made it all up. If I was at least in Belgrade I could be listening to *Radio Bat*.'

'Oh my God, do you know Fleka? People send me tapes

of that man, he's certifiably insane, I'm going to ask him to marry me. Have you ever met him?'

'I don't believe it,' laughed Daniel. 'You're a fan-girl! All this intellectual talk is just a cover for a DJ fan-girl.'

'Yes, I made up the whole thing about teaching at the Sorbonne, you know. I actually work at the comic book store on rue St-Jacques.'

'Well, *sretna nova godina* to you anyway.'

'And *bonne année* to you too. Now tell me what's happening in Sarajevo.'

'There are ten places in the world that are worse,' said Daniel.

'Excuse me?'

'Never mind. It's my New Year's Eve joke. I'll explain it to you sometime.'

This was maybe the beginning of their friendship as he recognized it, an irregular succession of phone calls and emails that made her a constant and somewhat disembodied part of his life. And while his stories continued to go out on the international wires to people who could only vaguely locate Bosnia on a map, the reader in his head was increasingly a blonde woman with a Serbian name who knew poetry and spoke half a dozen languages.

It would be more than three years before he saw her again.

III

As I Walked Out One Evening

September 1997

The preliminaries were not on tape, of course – Daniel's approach to Marković in the bar one night in the autumn of 1997, pleasant, apparently guileless, making the fullest use of his unthreatening and profoundly unmilitary appearance, his lack of height, his softness, his poor eyesight. Let the man think that Daniel admired him, unwillingly perhaps, maybe even envied him; anything to get him talking.

Though he had some idea, in advance, that Marković wanted to talk. He had been around the city, heard rumours of odd emotional outbursts, he thought he could recognize someone on the verge of snapping. That look in the eyes. The need for some kind of priest; and in the world as it stood, it would more often than not be a journalist who would step into that role.

There were the negotiations over the tape recorder itself, over the conditions and necessities that would surround this interview, all of these going obviously unrecorded. The tape picked up as Daniel was in mid-sentence, clearing up another detail.

'. . . *Srpski ili Engleski?*'

'English will be fine. I was associate professor of literature at University of Ohio, you know. We Serbs are not all savages.' Marković laughed, not a particularly friendly laugh.

There was a clinking sound as the waiter set two glasses on the table.

'When were you there? In Ohio?'

'From 1980 to 1988. I returned because it was time of great change in my country and I felt that I was needed. Also because irrational academic politics of United States were preventing my promotion to full professor. This policy of affirmative action of women and blacks, really, how can people live together in such a manner? These policies only spread ethnic hostility.'

'So you came back here with some better ideas about avoiding ethnic hostility?'

'Hmm. I suppose that you could say so.'

'I guess they didn't work very well, then.'

That humourless laugh again. 'What could I do? The Slovenes, the Croats, the Muslims, they all had this compulsive need for separation. It almost was like some kind of mental illness. We say, let us keep it all together, but in the end, what could we do?'

Daniel's pen was scratching in his notebook, but for the moment he made only a soft non-committal noise. It was a fine balance, how hard he could push at any given moment; and they were not far into the interview yet. Soon the momentum would start to take over; after that, he could rely on the fact that the desire of almost everyone in the world to talk about themselves was huge, insatiable, and if you let them go on talking about themselves for long enough they would tolerate, even welcome, almost any questions you might ask.

'Let's go back a bit, shall we? Could you tell me about your history?'

'Surely. I was born in 1944. At the approximate same time, my father was killed in Jasenovac concentration camp by Croat Ustashe fascists. In 1950 my mother died of cancer brought on by stress of widowhood. Any more questions?'

'It must have been difficult for you.'

'It is not a question of my difficult childhood. It is a question of the history of the Serbian people. Always we are persecuted, always we are defeated, but never are we finished. You are familiar with Serbian literature?'

'Just a bit.'

'This is important. You must understand our literature to understand our soul.'

'I've read Ivo Andrić.'

'Yes, a good start. Also you must read our epic poems. Petar Njegoš and so. You will understand that the Serbs choose a heavenly kingdom over a kingdom on earth.'

'I don't quite get it.'

'No, I suppose that you would not. But you see, through all our terrible history we are thinking only of freedom, of liberation, never of our lives. And if you imagine it, so many wars, so many victims, the Serbian mothers and children, our men killed and horribly tortured by the Turks and the Ustashe fascists, it is the biggest state in heaven, for sure.'

'So this is the heavenly kingdom?'

'After a fashion. This is the soul of the Serbian people.'

'Okay, but hang on, let's keep one eye on reality here. You were fighting in a war just now. And this was for territory on earth. You weren't just renouncing, you know, just saying, well, let it go, we have our heavenly kingdom. You were fighting.'

'We were *hit*. Of course when a man is hit, he hits back. They were striking at the bones of our fathers. We are supposed to give up the lands where our millions and millions of victims are lying buried? Only an animal could do that. No, not even an animal.'

'Okay, you know what I'm hearing right now? It's the same kind of rhetoric I'm hearing every day.' One of them must have signalled for another round of drinks; the tape recorded the clink of glasses on the table again. 'You're an intelligent person. Can we get past the mysticism and deal with what actually happened?'

'You are very typical North American. You have lost all sense of the presence of history.'

'Well, humour me, okay? You're telling me your position is, the Serbs never started the fighting, you only responded? Is that right?'

'Of course. If one is provoked, one retaliates. And of course one must retaliate strongly. Maybe we were too weak in World War Two, we let our fathers be killed you could say, maybe we needed to make up for that now.'

'And if I said that the evidence doesn't exactly support your position . . .'

'Evidence,' snorted Marković. 'What is this evidence? You people in the media, you tell to each other stories, and then you tell them a few more times, and you start to think they are true.'

'What about the attacks at the Plitvice Lakes, for instance? What about the shelling of Dubrovnik? What about Vukovar?'

'Well, I was not in Croatia, of course, so I cannot tell you first-hand thinking of people there. Certainly I know many atrocities are said to be committed against Serbs as well.'

'Then let's talk about Bosnia. Because we know who fired the first shot there. Why did Serbian paramilitaries fire on an unarmed crowd on the Vrbanja Bridge? Why were there JNA gunners up in the hills that day?' Daniel spoke quietly, hoping that this would somehow offset his words – this was the moment when Marković might stand up and walk away.

The metal table rattled. 'They were trying to take away our country! Do you even understand what would have happened? That they would have made Bosnia a Muslim country, that they would have driven out all Serbs, killed us all, destroyed us?'

'Do you believe that's what would have happened? Even though there were Serbs in the Bosnian government?'

'Those were not real Serbs. Not in their hearts. I *know* that is what would have happened.'

'Why do you believe that?'

'Because I know, because I know in my heart.'

'Maybe,' said Daniel, his voice very low, 'you think that's what they would have done, because that's what you did to them. Not in theory. For real. I saw Omarska. You know that.'

There was a long silence. 'You do not understand the nature of war,' said Marković. 'You expect in a war, we should be polite. We should be rational. Making always very moderate decisions. But it was like a kind of chaos. Everything was on fire. Everyone went too far.'

'Some further than others.'

There was another silence. Marković called to the waiter.

'No more for me, I think,' said Daniel.

'You cannot keep up?' snapped Marković. 'Again a very typical North American.' The sound of a single glass being set down on the table. 'A lot of these things were very much created by media,' Marković went on. 'I do not know how deep is your education. You are familiar with Baudrillard and so? The manner in which the semiosphere becomes self-sustaining?'

'We'll pretend I don't know Baudrillard, okay?'

'Let me put it in concrete terms. These public relations agencies made up some stories which were very attractive to people, due to their desire for sensational and terrible events.'

'Hang on. I was *there*. I *saw* these things. I saw the cleansing, right here in this city. I saw the camps. Are you telling me this was actually just the semiosphere rotating around or something?'

'Listen. War is terrible. Terrible thing. People go out of

control. This is the nature of war, everyone is affected in that way.'

'So people went out of control.'

'Some people, many people. You think you can explain it all? This is not how war happens.'

'Okay. Tell me how it happens.'

'I know what you think about Serbs. But we only wanted to do good, can you see this? You start with ideas, the ideas that you start with are good ones. But it becomes . . . it becomes as if things move very fast. Mistakes are made, and then people, well, people do certain things, and soon, you see, it is all too late to stop. You think you can make sense of this, but there is no sense. You try to make a story out of it, but it is not a story in that way.'

'I never thought it was a story,' said Daniel softly. 'I always thought it was real.'

'So. It was real. It was complicated. Mr Bryant, I cannot say that I am proud of certain things that happened. They happened. It was somehow not what we intended.'

'Things just "happened"? Nobody did them?'

'Well, of course people did them. And I told you, I am not so proud of everything. Okay, we were not in control of ourselves. It was just like, it was like some strange time, like an insanity. I do not like to look back . . . I do not like to think about some of these things. It is not something I enjoy to talk about.' Marković summoned the waiter again, his voice beginning to slur. 'Certain things perhaps we should admit.'

'You keep saying that phrase. Certain things.'

'You know what things I mean.'

'I'm not sure. Tell me what you mean.'

'You know . . . in Omarska and so on . . . in those camps . . . you know, things did happen there that – I mean, it was not exactly like in Germany, not exactly. But I do not enjoy to think . . . Probably we should admit this, that it was pretty well something bad that happened there. And some other places. Probably is better for us to admit this. But not helpful to talk about too much.'

Daniel was silent. The waiter put another glass on the table.

'Perhaps we are a backwards people in a certain manner,' said Marković. 'Perhaps it was too much to expect for us to live together. If we look at the facts, we can see that Bosnia was destroyed. Therefore we can assert that it was necessary that Bosnia be destroyed. History cannot happen differently from how it happens.'

'I don't believe that. I don't believe that history exists like that. What about all the people who did live together? What would you do with my friend who's got a Serbian father and an Albanian mother? Cut her in half?'

'It is a difficult problem.' Marković was subdued, as if he had purged himself. Daniel wondered what he was expected to do now – deliver a penance and mutter *absolvo te*, or the equivalent in Church Slavonic? But he did not, at the moment, feel that way inclined.

'Have you been following the Hague Tribunal?'

'Not very closely.'

'I notice there's no public indictment against you. Any theories why that is?'

'No.'

'Do you suppose there's a sealed indictment? Do you consider yourself a criminal?'

'Oh, what is a criminal anyway? Was I mentally responsible? I hardly can remember the processes of my mind any more. If I am a criminal I am not getting much profit from it, just look around this city. Who would even want to live here?'

'So why do you stay?'

'You *know* that, Mr Bryant. You said yourself, *sealed indictment*. Where would you suggest else that I could go? The lovely attractive country of Belarus?'

'Do you ever wish you'd stayed in the United States?'

'Well, that is another difficult question.' The waiter muttered something, Daniel muttered something back. 'Perhaps I would feel more honourable about myself now if I had done. But it is a pretty silly country, you know.'

'Yeah, well, no argument there.'

'As I earlier said, they have no sense of history. It is like a country of little children. In fact I am very charmed by American songs. They are like little songs of elementary school.' He cleared his throat and, quite to Daniel's amazement, began to sing. '*A song of love is a sad song, hi-lili, hi-lili, hi-lo/A song of love is a song of woe, don't ask me how I know* . . . Do you know the origin of this song, Mr Bryant?'

'It's from a movie, isn't it?'

'It is from a movie about a young woman who falls in love with a hand puppet. The girl and the puppet sing this song together. That is tragedy to an American, to fall into love with a hand puppet.' The sound of Marković lighting a cigarette. 'I would watch these musical movies on the television. At late night they have many musicals, you know? I have to say that it was a good time in a way. But you must understand, in the end I had responsibility to my own country.'

'What did you teach when you were there?'

'Primarily the literature of Yugoslavia. But I also have some expertise in English literature. The nineteenth-century novel. I am a great admirer of Jane Austen.'

'Really? I would have thought, I don't know, if your taste runs to epic and history . . . maybe Shakespeare, maybe Kipling?'

'You see? You too think that people can be reduced to a

simple thing. Do not think that you would not have done the same thing as me, Mr Bryant. I suppose that you would have.'

Daniel was quiet for a moment. 'Maybe. Maybe me, personally – I would have done. Could be.' His pen tapped on the table softly. 'But here's the thing. I know people who wouldn't. Actually, I know people who *didn't*. I know people who were there, and they didn't do what you did. Say what you want about history, there are people who didn't go along.'

'They were few. And weak.' A strange tone came into Marković's voice, something that carried a drift of memory, and if this had been someone else, Daniel might have called it wistful. 'I do at times think of . . . well, maybe it would have been better for us all if they were stronger. But that is not the way that history came about.'

After the last tape ended, Daniel left the bar and walked down Kralja Petra, the wide street dark with rain. He passed the wall of a building where someone had scrawled in huge letters, *THIS IS SERBIA!* Beneath it someone else had written, in a smaller and neater hand, *This is a post office, idiot.*

IV

The Human Fish

13–14 July 1999

It took time to book in a new inmate at Scheveningen. When they were finished with Marković, it was late at night.

In the hallway outside the cells, he telephoned his wife, spoke briefly on the same phone to a court-appointed lawyer. He paced his cell, looked out the small window. The guards patrolled the halls, looking in on him often, apparently expecting him to knot his bedsheets into a noose or smash his head open against the toilet.

He lit a cigarette; an unfamiliar brand, tasteless and weak. He sat on the bed, awake, wondering when it would be dawn.

As well as 'What are you?', there were several other questions people always seemed to ask Lili sooner or later.

How do you remember which language you're speaking?

Are you from the same country as Milan Kundera?

What language do you dream in?

She did not, she believed, dream in language at all; or perhaps her dreams contained all her languages simultaneously. Just as she appeared in her own nights as a mother of two with dark hair, or in sparkling underground forests which represented the city of Paris, just as an Asian man she spoke to might be at the same time her father and François Mitterand, she would dream in a universal rush of concepts, a perfect and panlinguistic clarity that would translate itself, later, into the language of any person to whom she might tell a particular dream. But she did not often tell anyone her dreams.

She was walking through a city which most resembled Brussels, grey and square and solid, though at times she would find herself at the shore of the Adriatic, the pedestrian city opening up onto the shimmering turquoise, the waves trembling under summer sunlight. She was looking for the courtroom, opening heavy wooden doors with big dark nails, iron hinges, metal rings attached. She was looking for the courtroom. Doors persisted in opening towards the wrong rooms, living rooms for instance with red and orange rugs, large families watching television and eating crisps. There was some concern in this, but it seemed not to be a large problem, an irritant at worst. The city contained a court, she was sure of that, it was just that time seemed to be moving very slowly.

Sitting in a room, possibly a schoolroom, an individual addressed her, saying, in no language or in many, What are you looking for?

That isn't right, thought Lili, that isn't the question as it went in the Grail Quest, and she began to leaf through a large book looking for Simone Weil's exegesis, or maybe it was the Iliad she was thinking of, this book was not well indexed.

A nation as such cannot be the object of supernatural love. It has no soul. It is a Great Beast. A nation cannot be an object of charity.

Which was good, but not what she was looking for at the moment.

A future which is completely impossible, like the ideal of the Spanish anarchists, degrades us far less and differs far less from the eternal than a possible future, so long as it is conceived of as impossible.

Yes, though much of Weil's political thought was questionable. And that was also not the passage she was looking for, though perhaps it came closer.

What is your wound? That was the question, that was how it went.

She closed the book and tried to decide which question she should be answering.

Justice, she said at last. Justice.

Wide awake at one in the morning, Daniel packed up his little blue Volkswagen Golf, checked out of the hotel, and drove across the bridge and north along the Vrbas. He liked driving at night, the quiet, the headlights sweeping over pine trees, the occasional light of a distant farmhouse. Insulated in his small warm car, littered with road maps and sandwich wrappings, a leather bag with his camera and notebooks and micro-recorder on the seat beside him, a thermos of coffee leaning against it, the faint smells of plastic and gas. He put a tape into the car's sound system, and sang along with it, alone in the world.

Daniel was a cheerful person at heart, optimistic in his deepest instincts. It was the only way you could keep on doing this and survive, really; that little well of hope, embarrassing sometimes, even inappropriate, that would always eventually fight its way through bitterness and exhaustion, through what had become a deep and thorough cynicism, suggesting the possibility that people, a certain kind of people, would never be wholly destroyed. That the Women in Black would stand in Trg Republike protesting the wars for ever if they had to, that people in Sarajevo and Tuzla would rebuild, that they would not become narrow and fervent and violent, that even Republika Srpska would open up again someday, let the world back in. He did not believe these things because the evidence was particularly persuasive, but simply because that was how he was, Daniel Bryant, an improbable cowboy stringer with an uncertain address and a collection of tapes on the dashboard of his car.

At the Croatian border, he drank coffee from his thermos while a variety of heavily armed men sorted through his belongings and studied the stamps on his passport, the white customs booths casting circles of light on the dark road. Finally they waved him through, and soon he was at the turn-off for the *autocesta*, the Motorway of Brotherhood and Unity. The signs at the ramp insisted that the eastbound road led no further than Osijek. He remembered the odd shock of the road signs during the war, how he had got onto the roadway and found that, overnight it seemed, violent slashes of black paint had eliminated every indication of the distance to Belgrade, while a few kilometres away graffiti artists were equally engaged in wiping out any trace of the existence of Zagreb.

He pulled onto the motorway, readying himself for the long haul through the plains of Slavonia, and slid a Joy Division tape into the deck. He liked Joy Division for night driving, the heavy bass and the blurred voices, the undertow of beauty. '*Love*,' he sang, tapping his fingers on the wheel, '*love will tear us apart again*.'

1980 that song was recorded, practically the last thing Ian Curtis did before he killed himself, but Daniel was eighteen years old and solemn then, a philosophy student at the University of Toronto, and he didn't listen to a lot of popular music, wouldn't have approved of the band's gothic romanticism. Anyway it didn't come out on an album until 1988, which is when he bought it, being by then a much less serious person. He was working in that terrible job at the *South London Press*, a time redeemed solely by the fact that it was slightly less stultifying than working at the *Croydon Advertiser*. In his mid-twenties, too old and too late to be a genuine punk, he cut his hair so that it would look as if he had once worn a Mohican, and tried to create the impression of having an interesting past.

'Oh then love, love will tear us apart again.'

Was that the year he met Julia? No – that was the next year, at someone or other's birthday party. She was a painter from Edinburgh, her hair dyed jet black, bright, laughing, tall in a red blouse and velvet skirt. They moved into the flat in East Dulwich together in June, and in January he was in Romania, trying to call her from a bizarrely malfunctioning hotel phone that kept ringing him through to a confused woman in Luxembourg.

Julia over bad phone lines. In the end, Julia breaking up with him via the satellite phone in the Reuters room at the Holiday Inn, somewhere into the third year of the siege of Sarajevo.

'I'm not trying to be dramatic,' she said. 'I'm not even feeling very emotional about it. But you haven't been back to London for almost a year, and I just think it's time to confirm that we don't have a relationship as such any more.' The windows were rattling under the shelling, Daniel crouched down near the desk with a hand over his ear, trying to hear her voice. 'I'm moving to Islington,' she said.

'Okay,' said Daniel. 'Okay. All right.' Probably she was moving in with someone else. Tony possibly. He wondered why she didn't just send a letter through the Red Cross, and realized that it was costing him forty US dollars a minute to be dumped. Though of course she didn't know that. Another shell burst near by, and hairline cracks webbed out across one windowpane. He tried to think of something to say. 'Ah, could you sublet the flat? Would that be something you could do? Keep the lease in my name?'

He didn't know, then or later, why he held on to the flat. It wasn't like it was home any more, if it ever really had been. The young couple Julia rented it to had lived there, by now, much longer than Daniel ever had. He tried to go back only when he knew they would be out of town, visiting their parents or something, and still he felt like an intruder into someone else's life.

They seemed like nice young people, teachers. They had quite redecorated the place. Painted everything sunflower yellow and sky blue, not a colour scheme he would have chosen, but he supposed it wasn't really his business. Photos of themselves on holiday in Spain. Eventually, he guessed, they would have a baby and move somewhere bigger, and then he'd have to figure out what to do again.

The thing was, it was good to have a base, somewhere that was available to come back to. He was thirty-eight years old, middle-aged by any reasonable definition of the word (though there were people who wouldn't call themselves middle-aged until they were sixty, apparently anticipating that they would live to be a hundred and twenty years old), and he'd been covering these wars for close to a decade; something which stunned him when he thought about it, such a large part of his life sweeping by in what seemed like a year or two at most. One of these days he would want to stop. He would want to settle somewhere, presumably, and London would make as much sense as anywhere else. His career was secure enough now. He could write columns and commentary, be the detached voice of experience. One of these days he would surely want to do that.

It was odd to think that he wouldn't be in the Balkans, probably never would have got out of South London, if it hadn't been for Julia; if she hadn't told him to stop sitting in front of the television, watching the crowds streaming over the Berlin Wall and telling her that was where he wanted to be, and just get on a plane and go. It wouldn't have occurred to him that it was possible; if it had been left up to him, he'd probably still be working at a local paper and spending his weekends listening to the UFO man in Brockwell Park, a hobby of his which Julia had particularly hated. He should phone her sometime. She'd sent him a card last Christmas, it would be all right to phone her, maybe it would be a good thing if they could be friends again.

He changed the tape and kept driving along the *autocesta*, heading to the north-west.

And what did he think about, Nikola Marković?

He was a literary man at one time, but he had nothing to read that night except the pamphlet about the prison rules and complaints procedures.

It could not be said that he felt much guilt, but he did believe that things had gone somehow terribly wrong.

He worried about how his wife would manage without him.

He believed that he had no specific desires to hurt other people. It was just that sometimes things had become very difficult. Sometimes the range of things that he could choose to do had seemed very small.

And he thought that he had enjoyed power, of course, it was a natural human thing, and even in the love of a parent for a child, there was surely some pleasure in power.

He thought that he had some insights into his own behaviour, and that under those circumstances it was not very right to put him in prison. He was sure that the same things would not happen again.

Daniel took the motorway around Zagreb and crossed the next border easily into Slovenia. Such a pretty country, he thought, trying to decide what music was appropriate for this inky blue of pre-dawn. He never spent as much time here as he would have liked – he'd missed the Ten Day War in 1991, and after that there was nothing much you could sell a story about, just the straightforward life of a smallish country industriously pretending that it had never been part of Yugoslavia at all. He settled on the first Velvet Underground album, music he felt the Slovenes would appreciate.

The sun rose as he wound between the rising green hills, skirting the Krka river, the verge of the road thick with ferns and wild flowers, purple and gold. Bright white houses roofed with red terracotta were emerging from the mist, the early morning damp beading on his car's bonnet and windscreen.

He thought briefly of stopping in Ljubljana for breakfast, but he knew it would delay him, more than he could afford. Awake as he felt now, he would start to wear out later in the morning, and if he didn't reach The Hague by sunset he wouldn't be safe on the roads. This was age, the one thing aside from his hair he'd noticed so far, the inability to dispense with sleep for days at a time. Soon he'd be going on about his joints aching when it rained. He would stop past Ljubljana, in a small town or a service area nearer to the Austrian border, fill the car up again, get some food and more coffee.

He had one truly vivid memory from Slovenia, something that still turned up sometimes in his dreams – the day he saw the human fish. It was winter, the beginning of 1992, and very cold, and he was in Ljubljana, working on a story about EC recognition, and getting away from the war in Croatia. He already had his ticket back to London. He needed a break; this wasn't something, he thought, that he could do for more than a month or two at a time.

'Well, you must come and see the caves,' said Andrej. 'Okay, is like Slovenian Disneyland, I know, but what the hell, give it a try.' So he bundled Daniel into his car and set off for Postojna.

What did he remember of the caves? The images were brilliant and fragmentary, daggers and ribbons and veils of dripstones, icy white or smeared with orange and pink, iron salts. Electric light shimmering in deep caverns, passageways, shining off gleaming curtains of rock.

'*Zimska dvorana*. The Winter Hall,' said Andrej, reading from a guidebook as they shuffled along at the back of a Slovenian-speaking tour group. '*Lepe jame*. The Beautiful Caves.'

The bridge, built inside the caves by Russian prisoners of war. The burned room, the cavern without dripstones, walls charred where partisans had exploded a Nazi fuel dump.

'The man who lit the fire was burned all over his body,' said Andrej. 'And he wandered the cave for two days, alone. But he lived. Or so guidebook tells us, anyway.' Daniel didn't want to hear that story, necessarily. He had seen burned bodies in the last few weeks.

Beyond these caverns were others, the Black Cave, the Planina Cave, with pools and underground lakes. And that was where it lived, but there were two in the shimmering gallery, kept in a tank for a little while, soon to be sent back to the hidden waters.

'*Človeška ribica*,' said Andrej. 'The human fish.'

They were pink, tender, their colour almost exactly the same as the palm of his hand. They were half the length of his arm, they had tiny, fragile arms and legs of their own, little fingers on their infantile hands, creeping over the rock. They were pathetic and terrifying.

'They live in the darkness for a hundred years,' said Andrej.

He stooped down by the tank, watching the vulnerable creatures groping forward. They had both lungs and gills, Andrej explained. They were blind. They could sense electrical fields.

No one understood how they reproduced, though somehow or other they did so.

They lived in the darkness for a hundred years. Sightless, wandering, belonging to no one element. If they were taken out of the caverns, they would die.

He woke up that night in a cold sweat and wrote in his notebook, 'The human fish is mortal terror and isolation. The human fish is mortal hope.'

In the morning he looked at the scrawl and thought, right, that's a story AFP won't be wanting.

The Slovenian hills were becoming mountains now, as he drew up towards the Alps. He stopped at a service station for fuel and breakfast, and stood in the car park breathing thin, clear air; looking up at the fissured and jagged cliffs beyond him, snow patterning the higher surfaces in feathery lines, the peaks shining white in the early morning sun, circled by drifts of cloud. He ate buttered rolls and drank espresso with whipped cream, in the borderland between the Balkans and the Schengen Zone. Back in his car, he made his way along the mountain road, through the Julian Alps, climbing higher, until he reached the checkpoint at the Austrian border, the door to another country, to official Europe, post-war Europe. He opened his Canadian passport, collected his stamp and entered the Karavanke tunnel, far up in the alpine light.

Lili woke from the shreds of an early morning dream, in which she had been trying to get her microphone to work while UN employees in long orange gowns and flowery hats kept popping in and out of her booth. She showered, washed her hair, put on a blouse and skirt, ate a slice of bread and jam, poured a cup of coffee.

It was true that, strictly speaking, any apparent conflict of interest had to be reported to her supervisor. It was also true that if everyone took this literally, the head of the languages section would be doing nothing but arbitrating a string of conflict of interest situations, and that someone like Lili, licensed for seventeen years now, was expected to know her code of ethics and exercise some independent judgement.

She lit a cigarette and breathed in deeply, coffee and nicotine, breakfast for the nervous system. There was something about her situation with Daniel, she thought, that was fragile and private, something that didn't translate easily into words. *Social relationship with a journalist* didn't mean very much at all on its own, but she wasn't sure she could be more precise, whether precision itself would not be misleading in this case, drawing outlines more definite than the reality.

Or whether she was just being Jesuitical because she didn't want to talk to her supervisor about this anyway. She poured a second cup of coffee, drank it while combing her hair and pulling on her jacket. She did know the rules, she knew the boundaries, and she was fairly sure she could manage this, that it might not be what either of them wanted but there would be something workable, areas of safety were available.

As she walked along the edge of the park, isolated fragments of her earlier dream came back to her, a door, a rug, a series of questions. She thought of Simone Weil, and of her father. She thought of the building she was walking towards, the dry ritual of the law, its formal impersonal speech. Justice.

Things in the past you couldn't change, and what you could do about them now. A magpie, black and white like a court official, hopped along a vivid green strip of grass, under a willow tree.

At the security checkpoint, she picked up her copies of *Le Monde* and *Libération*. There was a photograph of Marković, kneeling on the ground with NATO soldiers above him, on an inner page of *Libé*. She checked the tiny credit – *AFP photo* – it must be in a number of papers by now, that was a bit of luck for Daniel. She paused at the top of the marble stairway to fold the papers and put them away in her briefcase, went into the office, and resumed her role.

Winding through the mountains to Salzburg, then across the German border, a Schengen border, essentially unguarded. He was tired, his eyes starting to burn, the coffee giving him only a deceptive surface alertness. To keep himself awake he put The Clash into his tape deck. No one could drift off to The Clash.

He was on the *Autobahn* towards Nuremberg. There could be something in that. He tried out an opening sentence – *The road from Banja Luka to The Hague leads through Nuremberg*. Might work. He was not quite sure what it meant, but it sounded like it meant something. Must write that down at his next stop for fuel.

A service station just past Nuremberg, hot sausage sandwich, more coffee. He sat at the table with his head in his hands for a few minutes. This was starting to seem like a foolish idea. It would hardly do to survive a series of wars and then wipe himself out in a conflagration on the *Autobahn*. But he'd come this far, and it was straight along the A3 now, just on through Frankfurt, Köln, Düsseldorf, over the Dutch border and a short pull along the A12 to the coast.

Lili, well, yes, Lili. He realized he'd been making a partly deliberate effort to keep her out of his mind, not sure how this would work out, but as he thought towards the end of this long drive she was there, perfectly vivid, her small chin and high forehead, the white blouse she was wearing the last time he saw her, hair like winter light. So yes, he supposed that was one reason he wanted to reach The Hague by evening, though Suzannah from the *Sunday Times* wouldn't expect him till sometime tomorrow. It would be good to see Lili again; he needed to sit down and talk with her in person, properly.

He could . . . and then there was the sound of shattering glass and a screen of adrenalin flew up over his eyes, instinct taking charge as he ducked for cover behind the table; catching himself partway down, remembering where he was, and peering upwards to see a young waitress, her face all bunched up in frustration, standing over a tray of smashed cups. Damn. He sat up and took two deep breaths, a nervous twitch in his limbs, the undischarged reflexes with nowhere to go. How do you live like this, someone asked him once, back in London. It's all right as long as I stay in a war zone, he said. In the middle of a war, it's perfectly appropriate. It's only in peacetime that it's a problem.

Better to do something, move around, work off the chemical hit; so he stood up and walked over to the little waitress, who seemed on the verge of tears. '*Kann ich hilfen?*' he offered, the best he could do in German. '*Danke,*' she said, and he bent down and started to collect the ceramic chunks and shards.

The lawyers arrived with a suitcase of clothes, and Marković put on a respectable, unfamiliar suit, dark grey, slightly ill-fitting at the shoulders but presentable if he didn't move his arms very much. It would take time for his own clothes to be sent.

Nothing here belonged to him; even the books, though they were the ones he had requested, were not his own copies, they had unfamiliar bindings and cover illustrations and didn't open in the same way. It was a strange detached feeling, locked in this little room, a patch of sky and clean air in the window behind him.

He took a ballpoint pen and wrote his name on his hand, NIKOLA MARKOVIĆ, in Cyrillic characters, and about half an hour later a guard noticed it and made him wash it off.

He had two lawyers, a Frenchman in an expensive suit and tie, and a younger man from Montréal whose parents, as he explained, were from Serbia; his name was Milan Lukitch, and he spoke the language fairly well. When he met them in the interview room, the older man did most of the talking, while the other one translated. It all seemed very distant. The room was pale and sterile like a disinfectant, and when he heard the word cleansing, *čišćenje*, he thought only about this, about the sharp smell of cleaning products, and none of this connected in his mind with the chaos and stench and confusion of the days in wartime. With the wild excitement, yes, he had to admit to that, the thrill of it, but that was before, he had been a man in a different state of mind, and after all there were reasons.

He tried to explain this to the lawyers, that it was not possible then to think clearly, but they didn't seem interested, didn't seem to find it relevant. 'He says that as for counts one and two,' the young one was saying, translating for the Frenchman, 'he cannot see that they have any *prima facie* case for genocide at all. Absent intent, their case collapses, and he does not believe they have any evidence of intent, so we are going to move to dismiss those charges immediately. For the rest, we will have more information after the arraignment, but he says that it all seems to rest on command responsibility, really a Yamashita situation he says, and he says that he has serious questions about the definitions they are using.' They sat at a table together in the interview room, but he felt a wall of glass descending between them, a transparent barrier of language.

His mind drifted, and he thought of the men who had come to arrest him. Wondered again if it had really been Daniel

Bryant at the end of the street, a small figure, distant behind a truck. Not that it meant much, the man seemed to turn up in the strangest places sometimes, but he was curious. It was something to think about, at least, something to take his mind off this little room, the echoing words of lawyers.

'. . . response to aggression, and what country would not do the same?' the young man was saying fiercely, and Marković realized he was speaking for himself now. He raised his eyes, and something shifted inside him – yes, these were words he could recognize, soothing like a cold drink. He sat up a bit and listened. 'The prosecution is never going to admit that there was Muslim provocation, but all that they have is some dead bodies, they have no proof about who killed them, and we need to bring in our own forensics. We can find experts who can say, right, these Muslims were killing their own people to provoke the international intervention—' The young man broke off abruptly and began to speak in French, apparently summarizing what he'd been saying for the other lawyer, who was frowning and looking at his notepad. Marković felt a sudden rush of happiness, as if he had already been pardoned, and his chest filled with gratitude.

The other lawyer said something brief, his voice dry and precise. 'He agrees this is a line of argument we could follow,' said the young man, and began outlining more strategies. Marković drifted away from his words again, content with the understanding between them.

'Do you know the journalist Daniel Bryant?' he asked suddenly, interrupting in mid-sentence. The two lawyers exchanged glances. 'I've seen some of his articles,' said the young man. 'The interview with you, of course, we've both read. Is there something about this we need to address?'

'Oh, not really, no. I was just wondering, I think I saw him when I was being arrested, and I just wondered if it was him.'

The man's brow furrowed. 'I'm not sure that I understand. You think he had some involvement with your arrest?'

'No, it's nothing. I'm sorry I brought it up. Never mind,' and he understood that even Milan Lukitch, though he was the closest thing to comfort that Marković had now, was here for a defined and limited purpose, not really to talk to him, not to be his friend. A wave of grief swept over him. He seemed unable to control his emotions in any way lately. Maybe they were putting drugs in his food.

'I can look into it,' the young man offered helpfully. 'I can see if there's anything questionable . . . I mean, he is a controversial writer, isn't he?'

'Is he? I suppose.' He looked down at the table and started singing under his breath. '*A song of love is a sad song, for I have loved and I know* . . .'

'. . . not that you ever expect to get an acquittal here,' the young man was going on; they seemed to be discussing an entirely different subject now. 'The defence is at a huge disadvantage, that's quite apparent, and . . .' The other lawyer made a small gesture to him, and he paused. They exchanged sentences in French.

'He says he wouldn't want to overstate this,' the young lawyer added, looking back towards Marković, and if there was a hint of anger in his voice it was not overt. 'He says there are issues around the principle of equality of arms, but he knows there have been acquittals in some instances, so he wants to tell you not to give up hope.'

But what they meant by hope, he couldn't imagine.

Lili walked back from the cafeteria, passing one of the straggly haired computer people who had been roaming the halls in recent weeks working on the Y2K Preparedness Project. She entered her booth in Courtroom One, adjusted her microphone and, as she did at least once every day, swore to perform her duties impartially, independently, faithfully, and with full respect for the duty of confidentiality.

A new witness entered and sat in the chair, a very thin man in his late fifties with heavy glasses and a wisp of beard. Rasim Efendić.

'Where were you born?'

Efendić named a town in the Drina valley. The lawyer spoke in English, Efendić in Bosnian. Lili spoke, in French, for both of them, alternating thirty-minute shifts with Alain beside her.

'And how long did you live there?'

'All my life until 1993.'

'What was your profession?'

'I was a chartered accountant.'

Efendić answered briefly, nervously, looking directly ahead at the judges.

'And your ethnic background?'

'I am a Bosniac.'

'Mr Efendić, do you know the accused, Cvjetan Obradović?'

'Yes, I do.'

'How long have you known him, and in what capacity?'

'I guess about fifteen years. He was the town librarian.'

'How would you describe your relationship?'

'I would have said we were on good terms. So that we would say hello in the street, you know. A friendly relationship.'

'Can you see him in this courtroom right now?'

'Yes. He's sitting over there. The one with the black moustache.'

'Mr Efendić, let's turn to the night of 28 April 1992. Did you hear any disturbances that night?'

'Yes, I did. I could hear shooting.'

'Did you know what was going on?'

'No.'

'Did you try to find out what was going on?'

'No. I was afraid.'

This was partially theatre, of course. Both the prosecution and the defence knew in advance what the answers would be. The prosecutor spoke in a hushed, sympathetic tone, providing a pathos that the witness himself would not evoke with his quick tense answers, the flat and elementary words of trauma.

'And what happened the next morning?'

'The next morning, a group of men came to my house and asked us to turn over our weapons. We only had one small pistol, and I don't think it even worked.'

'Did you see them prior to their arrival at your house?'

'Yes, I saw them going to other houses in the street.'

'Did they go to all the houses in the street?'

'No. They went to the houses where Muslims and Croats were living. I didn't see them go into any houses of Serbs.'

'And did they have a vehicle with them?'

'Yes. They had a tank.'

'Were they armed?'

'Yes.'

'Heavily armed?'

'Yes.'

'Did you see the accused outside your house?'

'Yes, I did.'

'Can you describe how the accused appeared?'

'He was standing on top of the tank. He was wearing a camouflage jacket, and a kind of a hat with a, with a kind of a crest on it, and he was holding an automatic rifle. He got down from the tank and pointed the rifle at me.'

'Did he say something to you?'

'Yes, he did.'

'What did he say?'

'He said, "You have to call me the boss now." He said, "From now on, we're in charge."'

Germany is a hell of a big country, thought Daniel as he drove along the tangle of roads north from Düsseldorf, exhaustion settling down into a numb determination, only a few hours left to drive; then realized that this was an absurd thing for a Canadian to think, Germany was just a bit bigger than New Brunswick, could fit tidily into a corner of Ontario or Quebec. He was getting too used to European scale, expecting to cross six countries in a day.

The *Autobahn* rolled out in front of him, congested with traffic, the summer heat dangerous, potentially hypnotic. He took one hand off the wheel and pinched his leg hard, letting the pain clear his eyes. Bored and irritable, tired of his tapes, he flipped around between radio stations, static resolving into bursts of jazz and reggae, news in several languages, and the inevitable Oasis and U2 tracks playing every hour. He wondered what Lili's restrictions would end up being, and how he would ever deal with this, confidentiality, conflicts of interest, it was worse than having an extramarital affair, and then he thought he shouldn't let himself think in those terms, he was presuming too much, he really needed to get some sleep.

The Dutch border at last. He filled the tank for the last time outside Arnhem, and set out in the gathering shadows as fast as he dared, on the excellent Dutch roads, into the lowlands.

At the end of the day, Rasim Efendić was sitting patiently in his chair while the judge argued with the registry officials over the number of days the court would sit next week.

'No, look, because I keep a diary at home, I write in it everything, even birthdays and when I go to a movie and whatever, and in my book I clearly wrote that we were not taking any breaks next week.'

'Yes, but it's a tentative schedule until we—'

'Well, listen, a tentative schedule is no good to me when we're trying to confirm witnesses! Don't tell me about tentative schedule any more!' Lili, her fingers steepled against her lips, smiled quietly to herself while Alain interpreted.

Finally Efendić was dismissed, cautioned not to discuss his testimony with anyone until the court resumed, and Lili and Alain left the booth.

'Some of us are going for a drink,' said Alain, as he packed an armful of books into a canvas bag. 'Would you like to come with us?'

She looked at the newspapers on her desk and wondered when Daniel would arrive, whether he would be phoning her that evening. But it hadn't been entirely clear what his plans were – a newcomer at the tribunal, still partly isolated, she didn't want to turn this offer down to wait for a phone call that might not come; anyway, he could always call her mobile number. 'Okay,' she said. 'Okay, sure.'

They met Vanja and Danica coming down the stairway from Courtroom Three. Alain frowned when Danica ducked into an office to find Ivo.

Ivo was a recently hired clerk in the prosecutor's office. He preferred Serbo-Croat to English, his wife had to live in Amsterdam where her job was, and everyone knew that he was often lonely and wanted to be with people who spoke his own language; but there had been a fairly heated argument between Alain and Danica over whether it was acceptable for interpreters to be seen in public with prosecution staff. It had got as far as the supervisor of the languages section, who had eventually decided that it didn't pose a serious conflict of interest as long as they met infrequently and in groups, but Alain was still not entirely happy.

'Are we taking the tram?'

'No, I think we can fit everyone into Danica's car.'

Alain took Vanja's arm as they walked through the lobby, and Lili thought that this was a good thing, possibly a very short-lived one but that could be all right. Ivo arched his eyebrows at her dramatically, pointing at them behind their backs, and she waved her hand dismissively at him.

'Leave them alone, Ivo. You're just like an old lady, you are.'

Daniel turned off the motorway, and drove into the crowded centre of The Hague. He felt slightly stunned and disoriented, back on city streets, fumbling with his map and taking a series of wrong turns until he staggered out of his car finally in a grey neighbourhood of housing projects at the south of the city, breathing in the cool evening air as if he were drinking water. He swung the leather bag over his shoulder and rummaged indecisively in the boot, taking things out and putting them back in again, unable to fix his mind on what it was he might need in the next few hours. Settling on his laptop and a holdall, he made his way into the cheap little hotel, where the desk clerk glared at him as he leaned against a wall. But he had cash and a credit card, which was all that a desk clerk generally cared about in the end, as long as you weren't shouting, or vomiting on the floor.

In the room, stationary at last though feeling as if the floor were still vibrating and turning under his feet, he pulled off his shoes and socks and located his mobile phone somewhere in his bag, falling back on the bed as he punched in the numbers. Lili's mobile wasn't picking up. He tried her home number – it took him a minute to remember it, his mind was moving slowly right now – but after three rings he heard the click of the machine. A short trilingual message, she wasn't able to come to the phone, please speak after the beep.

'Lili. Hi. It's me, it's Daniel . . . well, I made it into town, and I'm staying at the Aristo. I'm in room . . . hang on.' He fumbled around the bedside table for the key. 'Room forty-seven. Call me when you get home. I'll be here. So . . . I'll talk to you soon. Okay then. Bye.'

He put down the phone and thought that he would not go to sleep quite yet. He'd stay awake for a little while. In case she phoned. Because she'd probably be home from work – in the next hour maybe – and he should really stay awake for a while and . . . but before he could finish shaping the thought, it seemed to stall in his mind, and the words stayed there, half-formed, putting out odd strange dreamy branchings, like floating mental seaweed, and he was drowned in sleep.

Sometime during the night his phone began to ring, but by the time it penetrated his awareness, by the time he managed to recall where he was and to scramble down to the floor searching for the phone which had somehow fallen under the bed, by the time he actually found it and answered, the person on the other end had hung up.

V

The Blackbird Field

Date: 8 May 1997 14:09
To: danielbryant5@hotmail.com
Subject: Re: stuff
Reply-to: stambolovic_l@uparis.edu.fr

Hello Daniel
I can get Radio B-92 on my laptop now. Last night I couldn't sleep so I turned it on around two a.m. This is an exact transcription of what I heard, and yes it was in English.

Male voice: . . . cause, you know what, fuck. Like, you know, man? Cause I'm walking around the streets, man, and I see all these people and they're like, fuck, they're so . . . they're like ghosts, man, you see what I mean, it's heavy, it's really heavy.

Other male voice: Well, see, that's your trip, right? And maybe that's not my trip, but you know what, that's cool, man, because that's your trip. But if this headspace is, like, too hard for you, then man, you gotta change your trip, you see what I'm saying?

This continued for at least twenty minutes before I turned it off. Late-night Belgrade is obviously a very happening place.

all the best
Lili

Date: 6 November 1997 00:14
To: stambolovic_l@uparis.edu.fr
Subject: law and order
Reply-to: danielbryant5@hotmail.com

Hey there Lili
What do you think, is the tribunal finally getting serious?

Some young woman came around this week to take some kind of statement from me, and she was ever so serious, and very determined to reassure me that they really were going to start trying some major people soon. Anyway, I spent several hours being deposed or whatever it is they do, but it's probably just going to go into some kind of storage room. I know, I shouldn't be so cynical. They're actually making real-life arrests at last, and all that. But, well, as for getting up the chain of command in the courtroom, I'll believe it when I see it.

In other news, I met a man in a cafe & he said, 'Everyone else wants to get out, but not me. I'm an entrepreneur. I have a well-advanced plan to open the first sushi restaurant with karaoke in post-war Sarajevo.' Somebody's got to do it, I guess.

Written on a wall downtown: 'Don't be bad, this is only a tradition.'

talk to you soon

D

Date: 12 January 1998 23:45
To: danielbryant5@hotmail.com
Subject: Re: this & that
Reply-to: stambolovic_l@uparis.edu.fr

Hello Daniel
I'm sitting here in my hotel in Geneva, looking at a picture in the newspaper of Slobo and Lady Macbeth in their teens.

It's such a strange picture, very disturbing, and it's disturbing because honestly, if one looks at it, they are beautiful young people. They look shy and sad and pretty, and terribly in love. And one thinks that they are so endangered, that the world could be so hard on them, that time and power will inevitably take them away from each other and that this is the worst that could happen to them.

I wonder what is the worst thing that time and power can really do.

Do you know, I think that the two of them are still in love. Whatever one hears about them, everyone says that they are devoted to each other. I remember back when there was a pop-Freudian idea that a happily married person would never be a dictator. Much interest in Hitler's troubled sex life. But obviously this was pretty much nonsense. I guess that there is no human emotion which is guaranteed to save us from ourselves.

Did you hear that Mladic's daughter killed herself last year? It's said that she read a magazine article about some of the things her father had done. But that may be apocryphal, all one really knows is that she is yet another suicide, and it doesn't seem right to dwell on her a great deal, when you take everything into account.

All of this has been troubling me so much, I can't even tell you.

I'm sorry to be in such a dark mood, Daniel. I'm not sure why, perhaps I'm simply tired. I want to get back to my own flat in Paris, and cook myself a meal in my own kitchen. I know this is a long strange letter. But I just found myself writing these ideas down, and I couldn't think of anyone else who might want to read them.

Tell me sometime about growing up in Owen Sound. I'm sure you're right in not thinking much of it, but it does have an interesting name.

Anyway, Daniel, I've finished my contract, and I'll be back in Paris tomorrow. I'll call you when I'm settled in again.

best wishes

Lili

Date: 3 March 1998 18:35
To: danielbryant5@hotmail.com
Subject: where are you?
Reply-to: stambolovic_l@uparis.edu.fr

Daniel, where are you right now? I saw your by-line on a piece about the Drenica Valley, but your phone hasn't been picking up for days. Are you still in Kosovo? Are you all right? It sounds like a terrible business down there.

Lili

Date: 3 March 1998 21:13
To: stambolovic_l@uparis.edu.fr
Subject: Re: where are you?
Reply-to: danielbryant5@hotmail.com

This is Illyria, lady.

And yes, I'm quite aware that this line could drag me into all kinds of political controversies going back several thousand years, but let's just take it that it's a line from a play I always liked, though I confess to thinking that Viola would have been much happier if she'd run away with Feste. I never trusted Orsino at all.

Sorry if I'm being facetious. I'm honestly touched that you were worried about me, but I'm an old hand at this, I don't get hurt. At this exact moment I am in Pristina, I just got back from the funerals in Drenica. About 100 reporters are roaming around the valley trying to find the KLA, we will undoubtedly all find them at the same time, such is the way of things.

It is a bad situation. The family that was killed in Likosane was not KLA, not even close, I'm convinced of that & whatever KLA the police were after they didn't get them. They got babies and old women mostly. But as for me, I am threatened by nothing worse than an unheated room in the Grand Hotel & the questionable humour of Jim the Photographer. I'm keeping my phone turned off most of the time just because I don't get many chances to recharge it.

The story that went out on the wire under my name was chopped up beyond recognition. Don't believe half of it. You can sort it out, right?

If you want to send me some useful words and phrases in Albanian I'd be grateful. I don't speak a word & I don't have quite the feel of the ground that I've got by now in Bosnia.

Have you been in Pristina ever?

D

Date: 3 March 1998 23:49
To: danielbryant5@hotmail.com
Subject: Re: where are you?
Reply-to: stambolovic_l@uparis.edu.fr

Hello Daniel, and thank you for writing back so quickly. Here are some phrases for you. Obviously you must hire a local interpreter, but these may help if you are on your own.

I am a journalist = Jam gazetar
I am Canadian = Jam prej kanade
I am not armed = S'kam arme
I don't understand = S'kuptoj
I cannot speak Albanian = S'di shquip
Can you speak English? = A dini anglisht?
I can speak a little French = Di pak frengjisht

Perhaps you want to avoid speaking Serbo-Croat? But you could always try calling it Bosnian (Di boshnjakshe).

You are aware there are two distinct dialects of Albanian? These (very basic) phrases are in Gheg, which is what you will need. Most dictionaries will be in Tosk, I'm afraid.

The verb in Albanian has two moods which do not exist in English, the optative and the admirative. The optative is used to say e.g. 'I wish I lived in some other time', and the admirative to say 'how strange that I am living in this time.' I don't suppose you will need either of these constructions, but their existence has always made me happy.

No, I have never been to Pristina or anywhere else in Kosovo. My mother feels about it roughly as you feel about Owen Sound.

I'm going to Brussels tomorrow, but you can reach me there if necessary.

Take care of yourself

Lili

Date: 5 September 1998 03:29
To: stambolovic_l@uparis.edu.fr
Subject:
Reply-to: danielbryant5@hotmail.com

hello hello lili my dear
the secret police are sulking in the lobby of the Grand Hotel & the blackbirds are spinning around the square shrieking & Ive had too much to drink & I'm thinking of leonard cohen & wondering what i/m doing here at all

EVerything;s burning here. i saw a family killed today, I looked at the bodies & it didn't even bother me, i think theyre's some5thing wrong with me sometimes. serbian police smashing through everything, burning vllages, thousands of displaced people wandinerg around the hills. KLA fervent but strategicaly hopeless & spend much of their time killing other albanians who have irritated them in some way. filed two stories today, three others over the last few days, but theyre not getting used. Next week I'm going back to bosnia so they can stick my stories on the other spike for a change, thouhg probably it's all one big Balkan spike in fact.

oh i must stop throwing all my frustrations on you
write back soon, lili dear
and the rain it raineth every day
daniel

Date: 8 September 1998 21:13
To: stambolovic_l@uparis.edu.fr
Subject: surrey with the fringe on top
Reply-to: danielbryant5@hotmail.com

Dear Lili
I'm back in Sarajevo. My friend Emir's flat still doesn't have any windows, & the bars are full of internationals looking for women, but it feels almost like home. Compared to some places, at least.

Anyway, Lili, I wanted to thank you for phoning me the other day, and apologize again for troubling you. I really can't be sending you bizarre emails in the middle of the night whenever I get upset about something. But I did appreciate your call.

Well, on to other news. I'm hearing a lot of talk about the Hague, up and down the republics, which is a good thing in a general way. On the other hand, most of what I hear is pretty weird. A guy in Republika Srpska swears up and down that Serbs are being offered thousands of 'American dollars' to confess to things they never did; a guy in the Federation says that two of the judges are close personal friends of

Milosevic. No one has brought up the UFOs yet but I expect them any day.

And while we're on the subject of war criminals, Nikola Markovic now seems to think I'm his drinking buddy-cum-confessor. Every time I'm in Banja Luka he's waving me into his favourite bar. On the one hand as a reporter I can hardly turn down the chance to talk with a character like that, but on the other hand he's getting awfully repetitive. And once he's had enough to drink he starts singing songs from American musicals, eg the entire score of Oklahoma, which he professes to despise but nonetheless knows by heart, thus the header of this message. Much good advice regarding friendship between the farmer and the cowman, which should stand as a lesson to us all.

thanks again, and talk to you soon

Daniel

Date: 31 December 1998 23:43
To: stambolovic_l@uparis.edu.fr
Subject: the mad prophet of lambeth
Reply-to: danielbryant5@hotmail.com

Dear Lili

Here's a long story from the depths of South London, whither I have gone on vacation whilst my tenants are away.

I was walking along in Brockwell Park, and I saw this fellow up on a box giving a speech. Well, he's actually a kind of neighbourhood fixture; I used to go to the park and listen to him sometimes, so it's nice in a way that he's still there, though I should point out that one is really supposed to go to Hyde Park to do that type of thing. Tall man, very thin, rather dignified ascetic face, big hollow blue eyes. Vivid ideas about outer space.

So I stopped to listen for a bit, alongside an elderly Jamaican woman with her shopping in a straw bag, who kept shaking her head and whispering to me, 'That is one sad man.' He was into this long ramble about the Book of Revelation, some kind of numerological section about how there are seven kings, and five have been, and one is now, and one is yet to come, and actually there aren't seven, there are eight, and then actually in addition to those eight there are another ten, so in fact there are eighteen kings, and then he started tying this in with the UFOs in some way I couldn't quite follow, so it never became clear to me who the eighteen kings are, except that one of them was Hitler. Fair enough.

Then he got on to the subject of the Whore of Babylon and all the filthiness of her abominations, and this seemed to be a bit much for the woman with her shopping, who picked up her bag and left. Seeing that his audience had been reduced by half, our man began to lose his momentum, & eventually got down off his box and came over and shook my hand.

'Good day,' he said, very calm and polite. 'I'm Father Jamie Bennington. May I ask your name?'

So I told him my name, and he asked after my accent and whether I might be Irish, and I said no, Canadian, and he said, 'Ah!' Then he sighed a bit and looked around the park & said miserably, 'You know, there are all these great prophecies in the Bible, but I have a very hard time convincing people of them.'

'That's too bad,' I said, and he asked me whether I could think of anything he could do to improve his public speaking style.

'I'm not really a public speaker,' says I. So then he undertook to explain to me that on midnight 31 December 1999 the world was going to rotate on its axis, & this was going to cause some very serious events. Possibly planetary extinction, though he wasn't sure on that point. And then he said that it's not a well-known fact, but hypnotists are now finding that their patients are going not into their past lives but into the future and there's a lot of ice and the ground falling away and a general sort of things falling apart and the centre not holding. 'Okay,' I said, 'but it sounds like the present to me,' and this made him quite impressed with me.

'The present but MORE SO,' he said, and then he said there was some dispute about what was going to happen after that, but most probably the entire planet was going to die and then be reincarnated, I think as another planet was the idea. But 'certain people' will instead go to 'Planet X', where they will have 'the experience they have stored up for themselves' (I gather these are the bad people with the abominations of filthiness & so on).

I said, 'You do know the new millennium doesn't actually start until the first day of 2001.' And this is where he became much more like everyone else I talk to, because he told me I was just being pedantic and that technicalities were not the point. 'The planetary axis isn't moved by such things,' he said.

'Well, Father,' I said, 'I guess I'd better be going.' And then I asked him what kind of Father he was anyway, and he said, 'Church of England.'

'Really?' I said. 'You're a priest in the Church of England?'

'Thirty years last month,' he said. Then he sighed again and looked off into the distance. 'But I'm afraid my bishop thinks I'm a bit of a lost soul if I don't get some psychiatric help.'

And so ended my adventure in this exotic foreign land.

I tried to call you but then I remembered you were going to be at Dominique's party, so I'm sending this instead.

Happy New Year, Ljiljana

love

Daniel

VI

De retour sur la route 61

1968–1970

When she was nine years old, she smelled tear gas for the first time.

She was woken up in the night by her baby brother's yelling, and found that tears were running down her face. She thought maybe she had been dreaming of something sad. Her eyes were sore and there was a nasty taste at the back of her mouth.

Her mother came into the room and told her to put a wet cloth over her face, and that was really all the memory she retained from that particular night, sitting on the edge of her bed with the cloth across her eyes, hearing the layered textures of sound, Sasha crying, the students screaming in the streets, the roar of the police charge, boots hammering on the pavement, the faint crackle of fire in the distance.

She did not have a clear narrative recollection of that May, only incidents and moments. The schools shut down quite early on, her mother was engaged with the baby, and her father was talking endlessly to his comrades in order to work out the correct line on *les événements*. So Lili – Lilja, she was to her family – walked around some by herself, despite predictions that she would 'come home dead'.

Even now, it was mostly those images that she called up when she thought of a war zone. It was embarrassing, that her mental Sarajevo was furnished with details from the Boul'Mich in 1968, but there wasn't much she could do about that. The torched cars lying across the street, black and twisted. Smashed shops, paving stones torn up. Smears of blood on a grey limestone wall.

She hated the police automatically and without effort, because one simply did, and also because she had seen them, from her window, beating students who were lying on stretchers, one last whack before they would let them be loaded into the ambulances. About the students themselves her feelings were more confused. In the early days, she and her family had marched with them, but not comfortably. Her father did not approve of the barricades. It was important, he explained, to harness this revolutionary feeling and turn it in the proper direction, or everything would collapse into Cuban-style confusion. Lili was not certain what Cuban-style confusion involved, but there was no doubt it was an impressive phrase.

As they marched he spoke to her in Serbo-Croat, so that he could dissect the politics of the students for her benefit, without having to engage them in argument. 'They don't know anything about the workers or the Algerians,' he explained. He impressed on her that the only newspaper she should trust was *L'Huma*. She was pleased that her father spoke to her as if her thinking mattered; he was unusual that way, even after Sasha was older he continued to treat his Lilja as the intelligent child. The difficult one, by then, the one who troubled him with her arguments, but still the one with brains.

One of the things she did not admit, then or later, was that she was sometimes confused between *La Marseillaise* and *L'Internationale*, both songs set to music that made her want to stand up and salute, both soaked in the imagery of history transformed, *le jour de gloire, la lutte finale, debout les damnés de la terre, marchons, marchons*. The kings hideous in their apotheosis, a line irresistible to a young girl beginning to reckon with language as her calling.

But she could distinguish them, ultimately, because she knew she was not truly an *enfant de la patrie* – though they were hardly oppressed like the Algerians, her parents highly educated, professional, respected. She wondered if Sasha, born in Paris, was an *enfant de la patrie*, and also why *patrie* was feminine.

Her father had to meet some people at the Renault plant one day during the events, so he took her along; she remembered it as large and dark, grimy, and she remembered that the strikers spoke differently from the people in her neighbourhood or the members of her parents' Party cell. She had one mental picture of a vast room, black with dirt, filled with evil-looking machinery, but this had to be derived partly from literature, it was not probable that the Renault plant really looked quite that way. The police patrolled outside, grim, holding their nightsticks. Afterwards her father bought her a hot chocolate in a café, it was a cold spring, her hands were cold, she felt important and adult.

Streets filled with wreckage, soggy leaflets, bags of rubbish. The parks clogged with food wrappers, old socks, torn placards. Rain and wind gusting along the corners. She had a red raincoat that year. It had not been purchased as a political symbol, that was merely coincidental.

One memory, one night – a wall of fire on the boulevard; it wasn't even clear to her why she had been out that night. Maybe her father had gone to the barricades to argue with the students, and taken her along because her mother was tired. She was not afraid. Children at a particular age are not really afraid of these things, they are afraid of strange men perhaps, or afraid when their parents weep, but not afraid of fires and police charges and paving stones flying, rumours of revolution.

After a few weeks the Party broke decisively with the

students, and Lili was faintly disappointed, because it had been much more dramatic to be partially aligned with them. But she had to acknowledge that they did not show much discipline or long-term thought. She herself understood the importance of these things.

In August, Soviet tanks invaded Prague, though that was not exactly how they put it in *L'Huma*. She trusted her father that it was something unfortunate but necessary. She did know that people died. It didn't mean much to her when she was nine, people dying.

Two years later she went to the library, secretive and frightened, and found certain magazines, and opened them up to photographs of the end of the Prague Spring, and saw pictures of the bodies. And she knew what it meant when people died. She sat at a wooden table and looked at the photographs for hours, tendrils of sickness spreading from her stomach to her arms and legs as if her whole body was curdling. At eleven, she could begin to comprehend betrayal.

She lay awake that night, miserable, unable to sleep, crying silently so she wouldn't wake Sasha, thinking, if it's true, what hope is left for the world? If the Party was wrong – and it wasn't only those pictures, it was so many other small things that came together now in her mind, adding up to corruption, ruin, flaws too deep to be fixed – but if the Party was wrong, what was left except a world of oppression and misery? No chance that it would ever be better, no hope, no hope.

So at the age of eleven Lili left the Party – although that was a misleading way of putting it, because she was not actually a member of the Party; like certain Protestants, they did not accept infant baptisms. She did not, as some older people did, hope for change from within, looking to the reform-minded Italian CP. She simply walked away, alone, solemn, a girl with a striking talent for languages and a sense of despair for the world.

She lay on the floor of the living room, eating *pain au chocolat* and trying to work out Dylan lyrics with her English dictionary.

C'est comme la nuit, pas vrai,
Qui joue des tours quand tu essaies d'être bien tranquille. . .
Et Louise tient une poignée de pluie
Pour t'ammener à la défier

Too young to quite get the point about Louise and her lover and the visions of Johanna, but not too young to understand that there was something happening in this language as well.

So of course she did not despair entirely and for ever, though as a child you always believe that you will. She did well at school, she had friends. There were many contingent reasons for hope, Bob Dylan, for example. Poetry – Apollinaire and Rimbaud, she read in her early teens, and also Robert Frost, who seemed weirdly exotic. She read Camus, *La Peste*, and decided that it had changed her life, that she understood everything now, she would be honest and brave and deal humanly with the truth of things.

But she didn't want to look at her father and see a small man. Sometimes if it weren't for her father, for the way she could talk to him, she wouldn't have known where she fit in, slipping accidentally into French at home and Serbo-Croat at school, a fine-boned blonde in a dark family. An Illyrian girl, her grandmother said, her pale hair carried down from the earliest mythical Balkan people, but there were too many histories, and she couldn't belong to them all.

She didn't want to think that he was a narrow ideologue, that so gentle and loving and concerned a person could be so tightly tied down. His moods, his fascinations, his words and arguments, had made up the fabric of her life, and she had to excuse him, she had to find reasons to trust him.

She could see his sadness now, and his anger, and over time she could have learned to deal with both, as everyone does when their parents slowly become mortal. But she could not, she would not, see that deadly point of belief that sometimes crossed his eyes.

VII

Saints in Ivory

January–February 1999

'That is such complete bullshit, Nikola.' Daniel sat in the brightly lit bar in Banja Luka, holding his notebook in front of him like a shield. 'Have you ever been in Kosovo at all? Would you even want to go if you had the chance?'

'Once again you succeed to misunderstand me.' As the waiter set two glasses on the table, Marković started to pay him, but Daniel moved more quickly. There were certain rules he had established for himself to regulate these conversations – he would never let Marković buy him a drink; he would never shake his hand. 'When I use the metaphor of Jerusalem, I am not speaking of a pilgrimage or some such. I mean to say it is the, the matrix of the Serbian nation, our origin as a people, the womb if you will. Think of it, Daniel, could you bear to see your mother sleeping with a Turk?'

'My mother's playing bingo in Nevada right now. Sleeping with a Turk might be an improvement.'

Marković rolled his eyes dramatically. 'Are you entirely unable to understand the concept of metaphor?'

'I'm a journalist. I deal in particulars.'

'Well, if you want the particulars of our history . . .'

'Nikola, look, see how I'm not taking notes here?' Daniel turned his notebook towards Marković, *30 Jan 1999* scrawled at the top of an otherwise empty page. 'Because we've already been over the migration of the South Slavs in 600 AD. We've been over the glorious defeat at Kosovo Polje about a hundred times. What I asked you was, what does anyone expect to gain from driving the Albanians out of Kosovo, when the only Serbs I've ever met who actually want to live there are a dozen Orthodox monks who have no complaints against the Albanians at all?'

'And I am attempting to illustrate that this very question shows failure to understand. Serbian people are constantly threatened, harassed, all throughout history, but never destroyed, and finally we come together to protect ourselves.'

'Bullshit.'

'You have heard of the raping of nuns that has been going on there?'

'Yeah, I hear quite a lot about raping of nuns. It's an interesting look into the minds of some of your friends, but the thing is, it never happened. Do you know how long I spent trying to source this story? It didn't happen, Nikola.'

'Perhaps your problem is with journalistic concept of truth. Let us regard the raping of nuns as another metaphor, then. Say that Kosovo is a chaste and beautiful woman—'

'Oh, forget it,' said Daniel, draining his glass. 'I'm tired of your sexual fantasies about the Turks. I'm going back to my hotel.'

As they walked out, into a thin, stinging snow that shimmered against the darkness, Marković extended his hand, and Daniel stood blinking as if he saw nothing, a pantomime familiar to both of them.

'Well, Daniel, I hope we can speak again soon.'

'Yeah, sure,' said Daniel, hands in his pockets, moving away. 'See you in The Hague.'

He walked through the snow flurries, feeling drunk, half-sick, half-complicit, as he always came out of these meetings. The all-night burek stand across from his hotel was a shimmering patch of light on the dark street. At the front desk he asked for his messages, and the clerk told him there weren't any, in the truculent tone which almost always meant that there were, but they were being temporarily withheld to punish him for his objectively anti-Serbian articles. Back in his room, he searched through the pockets of his bags for his little immersion heater and an envelope of instant hot chocolate he'd been saving since his last trip to Croatia, and started heating a cup of water. Nestlé's, he thought, looking at the envelope, he was supposed to be boycotting Nestlé's over, what was it again, over something, but he could never keep track.

Men can't talk about war without talking about sex. He emptied the contents of the envelope into the hot water. Sex, rape, purity.

He knew that he himself had lived an almost monk-like existence since the guns went up around Sarajevo, protected at first by his increasingly theoretical relationship with Julia, and later by habit as much as anything else. He wanted to think it was because he couldn't stand this rhetoric, the verbal confusion of things; he hoped that it wasn't just because you didn't need sex when you had a war. Shortly after Julia broke up with him he had a two-week affair with an alarming Norwegian journalist named Inge who liked to leave her flak jacket on when they made love. If you could call it that. She had apparently had the greatest sexual experience of her life during the siege of Dubrovnik and was constantly trying to recreate it. He thought she'd gone to Chechnya later. It wasn't an interlude he enjoyed thinking back on.

Purity. He sat by the window and sipped his hot chocolate. The snow was gathering into a blizzard, and behind the glittering white veil that streamed across the glass, behind the sharp howl of the wind, it looked almost beautiful, Banja Luka. Any city in the winter, the burned-out neon and crumbling plaster wrapped in the muffled darkness and swirl, the streetlights dazzling.

Lili's voice came back to him, an exhalation of smoke at the other end of the phone line. '*Čišćenje*, cleansing, you know about this word? It used to be the colloquial term for abortion. You see, that's the point of this, impure births. Someone like me, you know. Half-*shqip* bastard. To make me not to have been born. *Čišćenje terena*. That's my mother, that's me, we're the terrain.' The tiny sound of her lighter. 'But I shouldn't really say me, should I? It's not like I'm in much danger here. That's exactly what they want, I should start to think of myself as ethnic categories, mixed-race for God's sake.'

He drank the last of his hot chocolate. Maybe he would phone Lili. Or maybe he shouldn't do that.

It was possible that he was in love with a woman he had seen only once three years ago, and that was really absurd. More ridiculous than all that time pretending there was still something between him and Julia; at least with Julia there had been the memory of reality, the flat in East Dulwich, the ends of her dark hair brushing his chest as she bent over him in their bed. Was he turning into someone who could only have imaginary relationships, defended by miles of space and several national borders?

He should go to Paris. He should go to Paris for the Kosovo peace talks, it was a perfectly reasonable excuse, something that wouldn't have to be awkward for either one of them; he could see her. Hold her. Maybe.

Of course it was as likely as not that she would be somewhere else; Brussels, Strasbourg, Geneva. He could never be sure where she would be at any given time. But it was at least a possibility. He picked up his phone. It rang six times before she answered.

'*Hmmm? Allô? Stambolović.*'

'Hey there you,' he said softly. 'I woke you up again, didn't I?'

'*C'est toi, Daniel? Un moment.*' He could hear the small sounds of her sitting up, collecting herself, a noise that was probably her clock being picked up and set down again. 'Oh, it isn't so bad. I think I just fell asleep a minute ago.' Even coming out of sleep her voice was crisp, neatly articulated. 'Did you get my message then?'

'Yeah, ah, yeah,' he said, quickly and he hoped not too awkwardly, wondering what message this was. 'Sorry it took me a while to ring you. I just got back from one of my interviews with the vampire.'

'Oh, indeed? And how is he today?'

'The usual. Destiny of the heavenly Serbian people and so on. I don't know why I even talk to him.'

'You could look on it as collecting evidence, I suppose. Anyway, Daniel. We need to speak about an issue.' There was a sharp edge to her voice, and he felt a small knot of apprehension in his chest, something not quite right. 'The peace talks in Paris, I don't know if you were planning to attend, and perhaps I'm making an incorrect assumption, but—'

'No, I was going to come, I mean I was thinking that—'

'Okay.' She cut him off and spoke briskly, officially. 'What I need to clarify is that I have been asked to work for the French delegation. I have to be very precise about this, Daniel. If you see me during the talks, you don't know me. Do you understand this? I'm sorry, but this has to be very definite.'

'Ah.' He sat holding his phone and trying to work out what was happening, wishing his head was clearer. If this was meant to be a conclusion or what. He thought about never being able to call her again. 'Ah, what if I see you outside of the formal talks?'

'Well, that won't happen, because I'll be quartered with the delegation throughout.' There was a pause, he thought she was reaching for a cigarette; yes, the lighter, that intake of breath. When she spoke again, some of the hard edge was gone from her voice. 'I am sorry. It's just, these talks, you know how delicate they are. If I were perceived to be a leak – anything could happen, Daniel. In the worst case I could lose my licence.'

'You know I wouldn't ask you to do that,' he said. But at the same time he was startled by the realization that of course she would have information, she would have almost unlimited access. He wondered if he was telling her the truth.

'Oh, anybody is a source. You can't really help it.'

'Lili, no, I . . . no.' He searched for something to say that wasn't stupid or dangerous, but she cut him off again.

'Anyway, that isn't the point. It only matters how it would be seen. Honestly, I didn't choose for it to be this way. Maybe another time?' Her voice was gentle now and he wanted to be there, tried to collect the scraps of memory from that one moment of touch, the smell of her perfume, the shape of her back, hopelessly confused with his own imagination and fragments of other women.

'Okay. Sure, okay. I, ah, I should let you go back to sleep.'

'Good night, Daniel.'

'*Laku noć*, Ljiljana.'

In the morning the desk clerk handed him his messages, thoughtfully dated so that he could see they had been held back for a full forty-eight hours. *Lili called*, said one. And, *Editor called, can you go to Paris talks?*

In Visoki Dečani, the monks lit beeswax candles and chanted. They watched the Serbian offensive, the looting and burning of the town. They took in people who came to their door, Serbs afraid of the KLA, Albanians afraid of the Serbs. They heard the gun battles as the Serbian forces advanced. Every Thursday, they opened the coffin of their founder and released into the air the scent of roses. They remembered the days when tourists came to look at their ancient frescoes, which were once reported on television to be paintings of UFOs bringing life to earth, our DNA seeded from outer space, and they thought that they had enjoyed those tourists despite it all. They chopped wood, cleaned the stables, and did HTML coding for their web page, where they implored other Serbs to talk to the Albanians, just sit down and try to talk. They prayed that, when the day came, and it might be soon, they would make a good death.

A little knot of journalists stood on the wide gravel path, men and women in winter jackets with cameras, boom mikes, notebooks. The delegates walked past them, coming from long cars, from French military jets, from taxis, the government ministers, the guerrillas out of the woods, the writers and lawyers, the advisors and secretaries, translators and interpreters, the security guards, the people who would cook and clean, the people who would monitor the video footage from every room, walking in the February chill. *Albanian delegation hours late*, wrote Daniel in his notebook, *problem?* and, *French aide talking to man from Le Monde. (?)* Someone leaking something then, but not one of his channels, it would reach him later, outdated. *Snow on dark windows*, he wrote, and then drew a line through it, turning aside to approach a man in a grey suit who was walking up the path.

'Almighty and everliving God, who hatest nothing that thou hast made . . .'

Father Jamie Bennington stood in London's Brockwell Park at dawn, his loose jacket whipped in the cold wind. His congregation, two giggling teenagers on their way home from a rave, sat on the ground in front of him.

'. . . create and make in us new and contrite hearts . . .'

He reached down to the ground and picked up a handful of cigarette ash and dirt, grinding it in his palm, spitting on it to form a thick paste. He stepped forward and knelt in front of his congregants.

'Remember that you are dust, and to dust you shall return.' Father Jamie pressed his thumb into the ash, and drew a cross over the forehead of the girl with glittery hearts on her cheeks, who dissolved in helpless laughter.

'Remember that you are dust, and to dust you shall return.' He pressed his thumb in the ash again, and marked the forehead of the smirking boy beside her.

'O Lord, hear our prayer, and let our cry come unto thee.'

Then Jamie stood, and saw a dark-haired young man beside him, his arms folded against the cold, hands tucked into the sleeves of his denim jacket. 'Good morning,' said the man seriously, with a small nod. Startled, Jamie hardly noticed the teenagers running away, hanging on to each other and whooping gleefully.

'I listen to you before,' the young man went on. 'Excuse me. My name is Paja. I must speak to you.'

'Of course,' said Jamie. 'That's why I'm here.'

'You know,' said Paja. 'You know about it. Terrible things coming.'

'About the judgement? Yes. But it's not so terrible as—'

'We must talk. I know about this things.'

Jamie frowned. 'A lot of people think they know. Most of them don't really understand—'

'No. I know about it really,' said Paja, shaking his head.

'About the end of the world. I am from Bosnia. I have already see it once.'

'So, then.' Daniel placed himself at the centre of the steps, blocking a lawyer from Whitehall who was trying to walk down. 'The talks were planned to last a week, and we're getting into the third week now. Can I take it things aren't going very well?'

'No comment,' said the lawyer, trying to dodge around him.

'Would you say you're optimistic about the meeting in March?'

'No comment. You can wait for the press conference.'

'Do you expect a climbdown by . . . ?'

'I told you, no bloody comment,' snapped the lawyer, pushing past.

'I'll take that as a negative, shall I?' Daniel called down the pathway as the man stalked away.

The French delegation left the building last, as the black cars of the foreign diplomats were driving towards the airport; the negotiators climbed into their own black cars, the assistants and interpreters into taxis. Lili asked the driver to let her out at the corner of St-Michel, thinking that she hadn't been home for more than two weeks, that she would need to buy some food, cigarettes, newspapers. That it would be a relief to walk for a few blocks through her own neighbourhood, then go back to her quiet flat where no one would talk to her, or expect her to speak in any language at all.

She knew with some precision just how badly things were going, worse than it seemed on the surface even, that something was coming which was dark and very large, not yet risen into a verbal shape. *Guerre*, she whispered. *Rat*. War.

The lights of the café at the corner were bright against the cold evening, and her eyes were passing across the windows with indifferent familiarity when she saw Daniel. She stopped, took a step back into the darkness. It had been a long time. Perhaps she was imagining this, she was tired, suggestible. But she didn't really believe that. It was Daniel, for certain.

He had lost some hair since the last time she saw him, and he had probably put on a few pounds. But on the whole he looked – in fact he looked younger, she thought, as she stood in the dark, off to one side a bit. Not so drawn and haunted. Just that same slightly worried air as he pushed his glasses up his nose, reading something from the screen of his laptop, a cup of coffee beside him.

She had no idea what to do. She should cross the street. She should go back to her flat. She stood and watched him as he tapped at the keyboard, and then he looked up and saw her. Well, there was nothing for it now, so she walked into the café as he was standing up from the table, closing the laptop, and then he put his arms around her and hugged her hard. And it was too late to prevent it, so she leaned against him, wrapping her own arms around his battered leather jacket, noticing that they were almost the same height, and she was so tired, it did feel good to be held, here in a little café on Gay-Lussac. She thought at the same time, there are advantages to a public place, we could be easily overheard, it demonstrates good faith, no intention of secrecy. Anyway there was surely no one here who knew him.

'I went by your place but you weren't there, so I thought I'd wait,' he said against her hair, and she pushed him away a bit with a sharp small noise.

'Did anyone see you?'

'Just the concierge.' She sat down across from him, made a point of smiling at the waiter, showing that she was here in the open in her local café, that she had no wish to be inconspicuous.

'Okay, I will have a word with her. But you shouldn't have done that.'

Daniel made a helpless motion with his hands. 'I'm at sea here, Lili. The talks are over. I thought it was all right.'

'It's not so bad. I only . . . Oh, it's done, no use to worry.'

'I'm sorry if I've made things difficult.' He leaned towards her, and she kept her head partly lowered. 'How are you? Can I buy you a drink?'

'Oh no, thank you, no. I'm exhausted.'

'How did . . . well, how were the talks then?'

He might not even be conscious of it, she thought, that edge of hunger in his voice, his knowledge of her knowledge. She sighed and pressed her fingers against her eyelids.

'They happened. I did the interpretation. That's all,' she said flatly. She didn't raise her eyes, but she could hear him inhaling slightly, catching himself.

'Okay,' he said, and there was something like an apology in the modulation of his voice. 'Okay. How are you feeling?'

She waited, and he said nothing else, and slowly her shoulders relaxed. 'Tired,' she said finally. 'Really just tired. It was, it was very, I don't know, intense. It was all consecutive, and nobody likes consecutive. For days and days. And the French were trading me over to the Americans, and the Americans were treating me like, oh, the Universal Translating Machine of *Star Trek*, you know?' She looked up at him and felt herself smiling, and he smiled tentatively back, an area of danger avoided.

'They'd just talk talk talk about two hundred words a minute and forget even to let me take a break,' she went on, talking too much now perhaps, but this was surely harmless, 'and then when they found out I have some Albanian they were trying to make me to monitor the Albanian interpreters, which I am in no way qualified to do. And when I could go to my room finally, the Serbian delegation would be under my window getting drunk and singing nationalist songs about, oh those liars, they say Serbia is small, Serbia is not small, Serbia is very big. Personally I just don't appreciate to be kept awake at night by someone who can't distinguish between Serbia and his penis.'

Daniel smothered a laugh. He might have been about to ask her something else, when his face suddenly fell. 'Hey.' He reached his hand towards her. 'What happened?' he asked, putting his fingers gently against her cheek.

'Damn,' said Lili. 'I thought I covered that up.'

'It's a nasty bruise, it's hard to miss.'

'Damn.'

'Tell me.'

'It's really not important.' He was still touching her face, people were going to notice this. 'Just one time during the talks when I was on lunch, I thought to go and buy some cigarettes, have a bit of a walk, and there was this demonstration out on the street. And somebody there apparently knew that I was, as he charmingly put it, the daughter of a *šiptar* whore. So he hit me.'

'Oh, Lili,' he whispered. He cupped his hand around her cheek and she thought that this was too much, she had to stop this, and she took his hand and put it back on the table.

'Listen, I must go. You can hear, I'm so tired I'm losing my English. I really need just to be alone and quiet.'

'Can I see you tomorrow?'

'I don't know. It's not entirely wise . . .'

'Lili, it's a big city. The delegates have all gone home. I'm not suggesting we drop by the Quai d'Orsay or the Reuters office, I'm just saying I'd like to see you.'

She looked across the table at him, his odd intelligent face, his lopsided glasses. 'Okay. But it has to be somewhere neutral and very public. It has to be clear we have nothing to hide.' Daniel shrugged, frowning only slightly. 'I'd say the Beaubourg,' she went on, 'but they have this eccentric idea to keep it closed until midnight December 31.'

'Which is not the millennium, by the way.'

'Yes, I know that.' She rubbed her temples, trying to concentrate through the echoing voices in her head, the compulsive tic that kept transferring his words into other languages – *Lili, veliki je grad*; *Je veux juste te dire que je veux te voir*. 'The Cluny, I think. There are always a lot of tourists at the Cluny. I'll meet you there tomorrow afternoon.'

'The word on the street in Zagreb is that Tudjman has a brain tumour, I mean that he's literally deranged now. Might serve him well if he could backdate that, there's not many alibis better than brain damage.'

'So, what, do they think he's going to step down?'

'Are you kidding? No, that's one thing he fully absorbed from communism. They'll be propping him up on the balcony with sticks until his flesh actually starts to decay.'

They walked through the high stone rooms of the Cluny, skirting clusters of German and Japanese tourists in the dim light. Past the battered heads of the kings, the stone faces resigned, tired, their noses and ears worn away.

Lili stopped in front of a glass case and looked at a tiny ivory carving of a saint, appealing and almost comical with his smiling cartoon features, his big round eyes and huge uplifted hands. 'Isn't that nice? I really like that.' She felt better now, she had slept well, the harsh words of last-ditch diplomacy no longer repeating themselves so insistently in her head, though the knowledge did not go away.

She noticed Daniel studying one of the gracefully elongated Gothic statues and thought, he's going to say it looks like me; men were always saying this to her, she could rarely go past Notre-Dame with a man and not get some variation on that line. She did not believe it was actually true, but supposed that all thin women with high foreheads heard it eventually. Daniel looked between Lili and the statue, but in the end he said nothing, and she was oddly pleased, as if some more original compliment was implied by this.

And he was being careful, at least trying to be careful, skirting the subject of the talks, redirecting the conversation before she had to do it herself. Maybe he had some residual hope that she would tell him what she knew, but it couldn't have been very much, it couldn't have been why he was there. It probably couldn't.

They came out to the entrance hall again, and Daniel went to retrieve their things from the cloakroom. He reached over the counter and picked up her shoulder bag, and his arm dipped downwards, unprepared for the weight. 'Gah. What's in this? Building materials?'

'Books,' smiled Lili. 'Law books, if you must know.'

'I thought you read poetry. Nice thin little books, you get with poetry.' He handed her the bag and she swung it over her shoulder.

'I need to work on my legal vocabulary.' She hesitated, feeling oddly shy. 'I put my name in at the tribunal, you see,' she said lightly. 'They're expanding their pool of interpreters . . . I don't know what will come of it, they have their own set of exams I would need to pass, and legal terminology is probably not my strongest field.'

'Well. That's great. I think that's great.'

'You don't have to say that. I know you have questions about its usefulness.'

'It's my job to be the sceptic, isn't it? I'd still rather it was there than not.'

'It's interesting, I think. Some of the legal precedents.' They were walking south up rue de la Sorbonne, a bit aimlessly. 'Did you know that simultaneous interpretation was invented at Nuremberg?'

'I never heard that.'

'Yes, you could say that I owe my entire career to Hitler in a way. It's actually quite a fascinating story . . .' Then she stepped off the kerb, lost her footing, and the heavy bag twisted on her shoulder and pulled her down onto her hands and one knee.

'*Merde!*' She stood and dusted herself off, inspecting her ruined stockings and chapped palms, and turned towards Daniel. 'Sorry about that, I . . . Daniel? Daniel, what's wrong?'

He was flattened against the wall, his face drained of colour, his eyes huge. She took a step towards him as he lifted his glasses and passed a hand over his eyes, blinking rapidly, his breath ragged. 'Daniel, I just tripped, it's nothing. *Mon Dieu!*'

'Oh Lord,' he whispered. He reached into his pocket for a worn handful of tissues and wiped his forehead. 'I'm sorry, Lili.'

'I don't understand.' She put a hand on his arm. 'What happened? What's wrong?'

He wouldn't meet her eyes. 'I thought it was a sniper,' he said softly, looking at a point in the middle distance.

'A sniper?' she said, and then, 'Oh.' She looked at him as he breathed in deeply, colour coming back into his face. 'Maybe you should sit down somewhere.'

'I'm all right. Honestly. I'm sorry, I just . . .'

'Okay, but let's sit down.' She led him around the corner to a small café, ordered two glasses of wine.

'You do understand that this is post-traumatic stress?' she said, watching him carefully.

Daniel, who seemed quite recovered now, gestured dismissively. 'Oh, for God's sake. I'm just so tired of hearing about post-traumatic stress. People tell me they've got post-traumatic stress because their car got bumped at a red light. Forget it.'

'You were in Sarajevo. I think that's a reasonable—'

'I was a *journalist*. I could get on a bloody UN plane and fly out any time I wanted. I could go to Croatia and sit on a beach. I could go back to London. It's not like . . . I wasn't there like *people* were there.'

'You're not people?'

'I was people with an escape route. It makes all the difference.'

'Nevertheless, it's not unreasonable to consider—'

'I'm familiar with the checklist, all right? Do you want me to run through it with you?' He ticked points off on his fingers as he spoke. 'Post-traumatic flashbacks: rarely, despite the dramatic show I put on back there. Nightmares and difficulty sleeping: yes, sometimes, but I can deal with that. Emotional numbing: definitely not. Depression and anxiety: no more than the average. Suicidal ideation: never. Impairment of daily functioning: no, although I admit the daily functioning demanded of me is somewhat abnormal. Overall I'm a pretty mild case.' But he drained his wine glass in two fast gulps, and his hands were nervous on the tabletop.

'Is it hard for you to talk about?'

'It's just not very interesting, that's all.'

'Okay, if you say so.'

'Besides, I'm a lot better than I was. The first time you met me, right after Dayton? I couldn't even cross a bridge at that point.'

Lili nodded, sipping her wine. 'You were a wreck, actually. I was rather concerned about you.'

Daniel frowned. 'Oh, what is this, then?' he snapped irritably. 'You just adopted me out of pity or what?'

'I didn't say anything remotely like that.' She touched the back of his hand. 'You're still upset.' He took her hand and wound his fingers gently around hers, and she thought, oh no, not this, not now. 'There are people here who know me,' she said quietly, slowly folding both hands in her lap. 'There might be people who know you.'

They sat for a minute without speaking. She looked past him into the square, the creamy marble of the fountain, a white froth of water.

'You're angry,' she said.

'Not angry exactly.'

'This is a difficult time. In a lot of ways.' She reached for her lighter. 'We both know there's going to be another war.'

'There's already another war.'

'Yes. It will get worse.' She kept her eyes on the burning tip of her cigarette. 'And we're both going to be involved in it somehow.'

'I guess so.'

She shrugged. 'It's just difficult, right?'

Daniel lifted his hands and dropped them.

'Probably I should go,' she said.

'I'd like to buy you dinner, if I could.' He played with his empty glass. 'I'm leaving tomorrow for Priština, I'd just . . .'

'We can have dinner. Somewhere bright, lots of people. But I have to pay for myself.'

'Yeah. Whatever.'

They ate at a crowded and mediocre crêperie, part of a chain, on the broad grey rue Soufflot. Behind them, a girl was talking about how much she had enjoyed her visit to the Parthenon just up the street.

'The worst thing about this,' said Lili quietly, 'is that she is not even talking about the Panthéon. The building she was actually in was St-Etienne-du-mont. But I suppose she's happy anyway.'

He walked up the hill with her to Gay-Lussac, as the dark blue evening settled on the small shops and bars.

'Goodbye, Daniel. I will call you.'

'I don't want to wait three years to see you again, okay?'

'No. I mean – of course we should see each other sometime. I don't know when exactly.'

'Sure. We'll talk.'

'Yes.'

She kissed his cheeks quickly and he looked almost as if it hurt.

An armed conflict is considered to exist, according to the precedent of the Tadić case, when armed force is employed between States; or, more pertinently to our example, when there is armed violence between state authorities and armed groups, or between armed groups within a state, for a protracted period of time (see 'Prosecutor vs Duško Tadić', Appeals Chamber, p 451, para 70). In the case of any armed conflict so defined, all requirements of international humanitarian law continue in effect beyond the period of hostilities until some form of peaceful settlement is reached.

She sat on the couch, the heavy book propped up on her knees, trying to absorb not so much the legal arguments as the formal, neatly pointed language, the rhythm of the sentences, how a thought was formed.

. . . principles of criminal responsibility incorrectly applied in the Mauthau sen Case (1946–7, Vol XI Law Reports, 15) . . . The Tadić trial approved the approach of the Zyklon-B Case ('Trial of Bruno Tesch and Others'), British Military Court, Hamburg 1946 (see vol. 1, 'War Crimes Reports', pp 93, 103)

Her hands were still slightly sore and red, her knee scraped, a bruise was fading only slowly over her left cheekbone. The transient physical index of distress. Small pieces of history.

In her dream she was in a kitchen, painted entirely in pink, a colour she disliked. She was undergoing some kind of interview, maybe an exam, maybe police questioning.

What do you speak?

Do you mean professionally or conversationally?

No, I mean, what do you speak?

As much of truth as I can.

Do you really believe that?

Mostly. Yes. I try.

Someone was making tea on the stove behind her, a woman in an apron, not anyone that she knew.

Why do you speak?

I don't understand that question.

And what did you say? When it was important?

I don't know what you mean.

Yes, you do. It was a long time ago, but you do.

I'm sorry, I can't answer that. I can't answer that.

The dream shifted to somewhere else, a shadowy stone room hung with blue strips of cloth, shot through with gold. She was sitting on a bench, waiting. The walls of the room shifted about forty-five degrees. Daniel was holding her, touching her hair, and it was very simple and warm and safe, and though she knew it was impossible for this to continue she didn't need to say so right away, not right away.

VIII

Attention

15 July 1999

Daniel was startled out of sleep by the blare of the clock radio, apparently set by a previous guest. Fighting his way through a tangle of sheets and blankets, he slammed the button on the top to turn it off, felt around until he located his glasses on the floor, and eventually managed to sort out that he was in a hotel in The Hague, that it was nine-thirty in the morning, and that he had been wearing the same clothes for more than seventy-two hours and both looked and smelled like a pile of garbage.

After a long, fiercely hot shower – Western Europe, he thought, the land of unlimited hot water – he shaved and changed into clean clothes, and for a moment seriously considered just throwing the old ones into the bin. But he really wasn't so well equipped for clothes that he could afford that, so he put them in the bath, tossed in a handful of soap powder from the little box he carried with him, and left them to soak. He felt, against all reasonable expectations, thoroughly rested and full of energy and ambition. He found his notebooks and his mobile, and flipped through his address book for Suzannah's number.

'Hello? Suzannah? It's Daniel Bryant from AFP here. Yes, how are you? Great. Yeah, I've got the tapes from the long interview, though I used almost all the material in that feature I wrote, and notes from a couple of other talks, for what they're worth . . . yeah, the background on the town as well, though you must have a lot already . . . Which version of the indictment do you mean? Have they . . . yes, okay, I've read that one . . . Two hours? Sure. Right at the tribunal building? Okay, see you then.'

Pointless to call Lili now – she would be at work, in the exacting confines of her booth, cut off from the outside world. It was possible that she would turn her phone on during lunch. He went down to the hotel restaurant and ate rolls and cheese and salami and hard-boiled eggs, drank two cups of coffee, syrupy with evaporated milk. A light warm rain was drizzling across the window.

In the courtroom, Lili was speaking for a witness, a British academic with a nasal voice and nervous hands.

'Well, the document we'd be looking at now – can you put it on the overhead? – this document would be the minutes of a public meeting in the spring of 1991, and the speakers here seem to be expressing concern that all Serbs should identify themselves as such, because there was evidently a feeling that they were, well, they were not so much doing so. And Mr Vuković is noted as saying, ah, that the problem, the problem is making Serbs realize that they are of Serbian nationality and not Yugoslav, and he was seeing this as a problem at that time. So you see we have a series of recommendations at the end here, such as, you see, every local board should hold a panel and convince people to declare themselves as Serbs, and there's some suggestion also of a radio programme to that effect, and finally you see a comment from Mr Vuković that there hasn't been, that there's been no actual, no real seizure of power. So he's seeing that as a problem at this time.'

Jean-Louis Ducasse came down the central stairway towards the coffee machine in the lobby, fidgeting with the white bib of his robe. The defence teams had no proper offices in the staff area, one of several things that irritated him, but he was aware that defending alleged war criminals was not a good way to make friends. Some of the lawyers compensated for this by developing warm personal relationships with their clients; Ducasse, however, was not inclined to develop warm personal relationships with anyone.

He was more of an academic than a courtroom lawyer, in any case. Picky, precise and self-contained, the type who had laid in bottled water and tins of paté in case of a Y2K computer crash, he was nevertheless a passionate believer in the right of every accused to the best defence, determined to ensure that judgement would have to stand up to the most ferocious probing of every possible ground of doubt. He had volunteered for this job precisely because he knew that hardly anyone wanted to do it, and so it had seemed to him, in his abstract way, like something that he should do. The politics, he thought, were none of his concern.

The Canadian who was assigned with him on the Marković case was someone Ducasse hadn't met before, someone who made him slightly nervous. He seemed impulsive, and certainly he had his own political opinions; it didn't do to give the judges the impression that one had an axe to grind. If Ducasse had been a different kind of man the two of them might have sat down and talked about this; but he was not a different man, and he didn't want to get into the discussion. It would never occur to him, even much later, that things might have happened in any other way than they finally did.

The director of the political section of the Scheveningen Detention Centre was a big hearty man, a former police officer, and a great believer in the rehabilitative value of team sports and forced ethnic mixing. The lawyers had delicately suggested to Marković that some participation, particularly in the latter, might be looked on well at sentencing, should the case go that far; so he had gone out of his way, that morning, to play cards with two Croats in his cell block, a disagreeable pair of soldiers charged with several counts of rape and persecution each, who cheated him out of half his tobacco ration. Some of these people, he thought as he waited for the van, were simply chaotic sociopaths who had taken advantage of a period of disorganization.

Of course there were others more like himself, surrounded by enemies, trapped in a certain set of circumstances; and not all of them were Serbs. He could acknowledge that, he wasn't a blind nationalist. That he loved his country, there was no crime in that; surely there was something wrong with a man who didn't.

Dejan Vasić, for instance. You could hardly call him a good example. He'd been thinking of Vasić lately; the effect of being around so many lawyers, he supposed. Not that Vasić – a fat, florid man whom Marković suspected of being a homosexual – had ever practised law at this level. He'd barely managed to keep his office open, rummaging through piles of dog-eared papers trying to negotiate an occasional contract, notarize a document, deal with a few civil suits involving disputes between neighbours about overhanging tree branches.

Possessed of many eccentric beliefs, he had at one time been the general secretary, and possibly the only member, of a campaign to save a particular small fish native to the Vrbas river, and at another time the Yugoslav delegate to a conference about the relationship between speleology and democratization. Exploring the Caverns of Community, or something like that. In much the same spirit, early in 1992, he'd tried to organize an anti-war protest, him and his friend Salihović; the entire turn-out, including themselves, was seven people, all of whom ran away immediately when the police arrived.

What could you do with a man like that, really? He remembered dropping by Vasić's office once, in January or February that year, and finding him engaged in a frantic attempt to telephone Boutros Boutros-Ghali at the United Nations in New York. Perhaps not surprisingly, it seemed that the Secretary-General of the United Nations was reluctant to accept a direct call from an unknown small-town lawyer.

That was the same day that Vasić had ordered him out onto the street and informed him that their friendship was over – Marković couldn't even remember now what he had said to set him off, something or other about Muslims; he hadn't thought that Vasić, as a Serb, would get into such a temper over it. But you never could tell with people, some of them turned out to have these strange attachments to the Muslims and the Croats. He even supposed that there was something admirable about it, futile but at least determined. Like Vasić standing outside his office later that spring, his pink face covered with sweat, yelling at a young paramilitary officer who was probably just too surprised and amused to shoot him. A comic, pathetic man, a failure, but a failure on his own terms, you had to give him that.

The van arrived, windowless, heavily guarded, and Marković was escorted inside for the drive to the courthouse.

Daniel, wiping rain off his glasses, went through the security booth, and up the low stairs into a lobby which bore signs of hasty renovation; ersatz columns and potted plants under a low ceiling, a row of small press offices thrown up along the back wall, white plaster partitions and unfinished plywood doors. Another set of metal detectors, attended by armed guards, stood in front of a dim marble stairway, with a piece of paper reading 'Courtrooms This Way' taped on the wall.

There were tables along the right-hand side of the lobby, where one or two people were working on laptops.

He peered into a couple of the little offices, computers and phones crammed onto narrow desks, and located Suzannah, a tall woman with a greying ponytail. She shook his hand energetically and launched into a summary of the interviews she'd finished over the last day, while eating instant chicken soup from a plastic container.

'I've been talking to some of his old colleagues in Ohio, and getting what I suppose is the academic equivalent of "such a quiet boy, kept to himself, so devoted to his mother". Didn't seem to take an interest in politics, rarely seen reading newspapers even. Nothing special academically, not much of a publication record, but he was popular with the students.'

'Very fond of Jane Austen.'

'Yes, a few people mentioned that.'

'It is a truth universally acknowledged, that a married man with a moderate fortune, must be in want of absolute power.'

'Hmm. Did you work on that one for very long?'

'Not really. It's pretty obvious.'

'Now, this story about his father dying in Jasenovac, did you verify that?'

'Oh yes. It's quite true. And his mother certainly did have cancer, breast cancer; nasty business according to the relatives, not properly treated, abscessed. There's a little uncertainty over whether she died of the cancer directly, one of the aunts claims that she killed herself when it metastasized to her brain. But I'm inclined to treat that as just family gossip.'

'Relatives brought him up afterwards?'

'Father's mother. No one has a bad word to say about her, nice old woman by all accounts, but certainly she was a Serbian nationalist of the sentimental weepy sort. I've always suspected he got this breaking into song business from his grandmother, but, you know, that's not something I can document.'

'Marković adapted to Tito just fine, though, didn't he?'

'Marković adapts to anything. He's what you might call a flexible thinker.' He checked his watch. 'Could I use your phone to make a personal call? They took my mobile at the door.'

'Is it long-distance?'

'No, no. Just a friend I have in town.'

'Sure, go ahead then.' But Lili hadn't turned on her phone. He dialled her home number and left a short message.

'Hey there. Don't know when you're going to pick this up, but I'm around and about. Call me after work, okay?'

He turned back to Suzannah. 'He used to go on about his connections with organized crime, but I'm pretty sure it was just bravado. I didn't really feel like testing it out when he offered me a cut in some kind of armed robbery profits, but he wasn't one of the serious mafia guys, not like some of them. All I could tie him to was a bit of petty sanction-busting.'

'Which is presumably why he ended up in court instead of dying in a mysterious shooting. He must have liked you if he was trying to cut you in.'

'He was short of literary company is what he always said.' Daniel picked up a pen from her desk and spun it around in his fingers, leaning against the wall. 'This is something that kind of fascinates me, actually, that you get from some of these guys. The literary-critical approach to politics. The production of the spectacle and all that. Marković was always quoting Baudrillard at me to prove that I was the one producing the spectacle, and meanwhile his lot were out there creating these things that were – you know, on the one hand they'd hide some things, the camps at least, but on the other hand it was almost like we had to find our way there eventually. The camps, the siege, they were practically constructed for us to, to align with literary parallels. Nothing happened in this war that hadn't been written out in advance.'

'I'm not really a literary person,' said Suzannah.

'Karadžić's poems are full of burning cities, destroyed cities, did you know that? Going back decades.'

'Haven't read his work. I'm not an academic, Daniel.'

Daniel spun the pen again, realizing he was drifting into free association. 'Yeah, well, neither am I. It's just I always thought there was some kind of article in that if I could sit down and write it, but I don't imagine I ever will. Anyway, is there any chance of getting an interview with Marković at this point?'

'Not a hope, absolutely not. Once he's in custody, he's off-limits to media. They're extremely strict about that.'

'Hmm. Okay.' He felt oddly put out by this, as if he had some kind of special right to speak with Marković, and this disturbed him; it wasn't concern about the man, not that exactly, but something nearer to concern than he really liked.

'His initial appearance is this afternoon, though,' Suzannah continued. 'It's a by-the-book kind of event, very routine, but worth sitting in.'

Attention taken to its highest degree, wrote Simone Weil, *is the same thing as prayer. It presupposes faith and love.*

Lili in her booth, tending to language with the professional's extreme care, the nuance of each colloquial phrase, how to move ideas from the context of one culture to another, to capture the assumptions, buried in the words, that the speakers themselves took for granted. She was a subject of interest to neurologists and cognitive psychologists. Her blood pressure and heart rate were significantly elevated. A CAT scan would show unusual brain activity, the organism stretched in one very particular direction, an effort of understanding created for the age of genocide.

Attention is bound up with desire. Not with the will but with desire – or more exactly, consent.

The translators and teachers and journalists who were drafted into the job at Nuremberg often believed, before they started, that the work would not be humanly possible. Of those tested for the position, only one in twenty could do simultaneous at all. But those who could found that, as a language act alone, it was not so bad, easier than consecutive in many ways; they had, it seemed, the necessary neural quirks, brain plasticity in the right areas.

What they could not always do, these original interpreters, was to bear the emotional weight of the speech. Some of them would break down crying, choke on sentences, refuse to interpret anti-Semitic diatribes, would have to be taken out of the booths and replaced.

They did not do these things, Lili and her colleagues, though the temptation was sometimes extreme. Their job was to speak with attention and accuracy, to believe that truth would ultimately emerge from the words, if only all the words were given their proper and equal due. It was the interpreters who were required, along with the judges, to hold the presumption of innocence untouchable. To place all their faith and all their hope in the fairness of the process, to create that fairness themselves, to hope that goodness would come from this.

To believe that language, any language, all language, deserved their meticulous love.

The courtroom was small, cluttered with tables and computer monitors, lawyers in black robes leaning over to talk to each other, while their assistants took notes or sifted through large binders. They sat at desks and chairs that were cheap, prefabricated; Daniel almost expected to see a 'Courtroom by IKEA' sticker on the sheet of bullet-proof glass in front of him.

Two guards led Marković into the room. He scanned the tables in a dispirited way, and then his gaze travelled over the public gallery and met Daniel's. He lifted his head, and moved one hand in an ambiguous wave. Daniel raised his eyebrows and twisted his mouth, a greeting unreadable even to himself – *Told you so? Ah well, bad luck, Nikola? Fuck off?* – then dropped his eyes, uncomfortable, aware of Suzannah's quiet laugh beside him.

The clerk called for everyone to rise as the three judges entered, robed in black and red. The British judge, incongruously and comically, had insisted on retaining his curled white wig, and it sat perched on his head like a bonnet, giving him an almost matronly air.

'The Prosecutor versus Nikola Marković, Judge Terezinha dos Santos Abreu presiding,' recited the clerk in a monotone as the lawyers sat. Each of them wore a set of earphones. Daniel hooked his own pair over his head and plugged it into a small handset, turned to the English channel.

'Appearances?'

'Good afternoon, Your Honour,' said a tall Irish woman at the right-hand table, rising again and speaking into a microphone. 'For the prosecution, I'm Claire McKinley, and I'm joined by my colleagues Peter Solomon and Richard Bonneville.'

'*Bonjour, Madame la Juge Abreu,*' and a neatly dressed man rose at the other side of the room. '*Pour la défense, je suis Maître Jean-Louis Ducasse, et Maître Milan Lukitch m'assistera.*' The words reached Daniel in English through the earphones, a woman speaking with a British accent, just a few seconds behind the lawyer himself. Perhaps only because he was reminded of Lili, the voice in his ears seemed strangely personal, closer than conversation, approaching the distance of thought.

'Can the defendant hear me in a language that he understands?'

Marković nodded.

'Could you speak for the record please, Mr Marković?'

'*Da, razumijem.*'

'Yes,' said the voice of the interpreter, 'I understand.'

'Mr Ducasse, have you reviewed the indictment with your client?'

'*Oui, nous en avons pris connaissance.*'

'Yes, we have reviewed it.'

'Does he wish to hear the indictment read out in full?'

Marković leaned slightly forward, exchanged some words with the younger lawyer, and informed the court that he did indeed wish to hear the indictment read in full.

The prosecutor began to read in English. The first several paragraphs were an abbreviated and somewhat academic history of the war in Bosnia, embedded in legal terminology, and Daniel started playing with his interpretation equipment. On the French channel, which he couldn't easily understand, a man's voice was running crisply through the long sentences. He switched to the Bosnian-Croatian-Serbian channel, and sat up in surprise when he heard Lili, unmistakable, absurdly familiar.

'What's up?' asked Suzannah. 'Problem with the earphones?'

'No, no, I just had the volume a bit too high.'

Her voice, normally quite soft in conversation, seemed louder and more definite when she was working. She continued through the items of the indictment, echoing the prosecutor's inflections, in a language which he realized he had rarely heard her speak, though it was her first language, the one she had learned before anything else. He looked up at the courtroom and noticed the sheets of dark glass in the wall on either side. So she was there, invisible to him and unaware that he was listening. It seemed so close, disturbingly close, the stark accusatory sentences and the nearly intimate voice, and Nikola Marković looking towards him from the dock.

... April 1992, Serbian forces seized physical control of the town of S. On or about 2 May 1992, Nikola Marković became 'President' of the 'Crisis Group', and later of the 'Municipal Council' ... had extraordinary executive and legislative power within the municipality of S during the time period covered by this indictment ... initiated a series of events which would result in the death or forced departure of most of the non-Serbian population of the municipality of S ...

He flipped through the printed indictment in his lap and listened to Lili speak.

... laws restricting the movements of the non-Serbian population, banning them from most forms of employment, from gathering in groups of more than three persons ... attacks on villages and areas inhabited primarily by Bosnian Muslims and Bosnian Croats sometimes began with heavy artillery bombardment ... populations rounded up and marched to assembly points for transfer to camps ... Some instances of killings at the detention camps involve the following: the killing of about 75 men in 'room one' of camp A in late July 1992; the killing of about 100 men and women taken off buses at camp B on or about 10 August 1992; the killing of about 60 men in a field at camp B on or about 11 August 1992 ... deliberately operated in a manner designed to inflict upon the detainees conditions intended to bring about their physical destruction with the intent to destroy, in part, the Bosnian Muslims and Bosnian Croats as national, ethnic or religious groups, as such ... By this conduct Nikola Marković did commit Count 1: genocide, punishable under Articles 4(3)(a), and 7(1) and 7(3) of the Statute of the Tribunal; or, Count 2: complicity in genocide, punishable under Articles 4(3)(e), and 7(1) and 7(3) of the Statute of the Tribunal.

Counts 3-5, murder/extermination ...

The indictment continued, through counts of persecution,

torture, deportation, inhumane acts, destruction of institutions dedicated to religion.

Marković sat looking straight ahead, expressionless. A few times he turned his head slightly in the direction of the public gallery, and Daniel found himself, without quite thinking about it, averting his eyes and staring down at the English words on the printed pages.

. . . participated in a joint criminal enterprise aimed at the permanent forcible removal of the majority of the non-Serb population from the municipality of S . . . Despite his awareness of the possible consequences, Nikola Marković knowingly and wilfully participated in the joint criminal enterprise . . .

Lili's voice disappeared, replaced by another woman, with lower and darker tones and a trace of a Bosnian accent. Marković was shaking his head, not so much in disagreement as, it seemed, in an attempt to negate the room as a whole, to make the construction of the court as such an error in the semiosphere, something that could go away.

The accused Nikola Marković, while holding the positions of superior authority set out in the foregoing paragraphs, is also criminally responsible for the conduct of his subordinates . . .

The prosecutor concluded, and Marković was asked to plead. He half-rose, leaning towards the mike.

'To count one, genocide, how do you plead?' asked the judge.

'*Nisam kriv*,' said his voice briefly in Daniel's earphones. Not guilty.

'To count two, genocide, how do you plead?'

'*Nisam kriv.*'

'To count three, murder/extermination . . .' And the judge read, expressionless, through the counts, Marković rocking slightly back and forth as he pleaded over and over, not guilty. Not guilty.

* * *

Daniel reclaimed his mobile at the door. 'Can I buy you dinner?' asked Suzannah.

'Oh, I don't know, I think I'm all right.'

'Come on, Daniel. I know it's early, but I also know you can't afford to eat in this town. I'm on salary, let me buy you a meal.'

'Ah, hang on, I'll just make a call first and let you know,' he answered, and walked a few feet away along the pavement to try Lili's mobile, then her house. No answer at either number.

'Good friend, is it?' asked Suzannah when he returned.

Daniel shrugged. 'Someone I haven't seen for a bit. Anyway, I guess I'm free for dinner.'

They went to an Italian restaurant in a hotel near the tribunal, and Suzannah inspected him over the tops of her glasses as they waited for their food.

'Could I ask you something, Daniel?'

'Well . . . sure, you can ask. I don't promise I'll answer.'

'I hope this isn't a delicate question, but why are you still working as a stringer?'

It wasn't what he had expected at all, and he smiled a bit with relief.

'I mean,' continued Suzannah, 'you surely must have had job offers.'

'Oh yeah, some.' He shrugged lightly. 'What, is *The Times* making one now?'

'I'm not saying we wouldn't.'

'Well, you know, what can I say? I like the way I've got things set up at the moment.'

'So what you're telling me is that you actively want to stay on the lowest rung of the journalistic ladder? When you're surely in a position . . . well, it's a perverse way to run your career.'

'Oh, I know, I know. I should have a staff position somewhere,

I could be somebody's bureau chief in a year, et cetera and so on. I hear this from various quarters. I'm just . . . I'm happy like this. I enjoy being an itinerant news gypsy.'

'You enjoy a complete lack of financial security?'

'It doesn't bother me especially. I mean, if I were somebody's proper staff, do you think they would have let me knock around in Bosnia for the last three years?'

'Well, I guess it's easier if you don't have a family.' Daniel remembered that she had two children, one of them with, what, some kind of difficulty – Downs, was it? – and he felt suddenly adolescent and foolish. 'Still, there is something weirdly self-destructive about it,' Suzannah went on.

'You could look at it that way.' Daniel toyed apologetically with his fork, trying to think of how he could make himself sound less irresponsible. 'Or you could think of it as a long-term plan to make me seem more eccentric and desirable.'

'Are we talking about editors here, or women?' smiled Suzannah. 'Or men, if you prefer, I don't want to make assumptions.'

'I was thinking of editors. It didn't impress my last girlfriend much.' It hadn't occurred to him that people found his personal life as opaque as his career decisions. This bothered him more than it probably should have, and he wondered again when Lili would call.

'Well, I've done my bit. I've put it on record that *The Times* thinks you could do better, and having said that, I can write this off as a business expense. Your choices are quite up to you.'

The waiter set plates of pasta in front of them. 'How's your family?' asked Daniel.

'Reasonably well,' said Suzannah briskly, looking at her plate. 'The girls are much as ever. Stephen's doing final revisions on his book.'

'Ah. Good for him,' said Daniel, and couldn't think of

anything else to add. They ate in silence for several minutes.

'So what's your impression of our man's mental state?' asked Suzannah finally.

'Confused, I think. I don't know, he looked pretty blank. Is that usual?'

'Well, it varies. Some of them take a lot of notes, or else they do the grim stoic gaze. Others yawn and giggle through most of the trial.'

'Nikola was always strange about it, about what he'd done. He'd get into this confessional mood like he was baring his soul to you, but he never actually told you anything concrete. I never quite understood what he told himself. What do you say to yourself about going from teaching university to, you know, mass murder?'

'You have to wonder how a man like that got into such a position.'

'Oh, I don't know. I mean, you look at Koljević, little old Shakespeare professor who said he didn't really know what was going on because he was too scared to travel out of his command centre. You look at the gang of grandfatherly doctors who took over Prijedor. It's . . . well, an opportunity came along to do these things to their neighbours, and the TV kept telling them it was all right, and . . . you know, sometimes I lie awake at night wondering what I'd do.'

Suzannah looked seriously at her plate again. 'I would,' she said slowly, at last, 'do whatever it took to protect my family. Whatever it took. I think I would do some very evil things, if I had to for their sake. Or if I thought I had to. That's my truth. I can't say otherwise.'

'There are days,' said Daniel, 'when I think I could do those things for no reason at all. If the circumstance happened to arise. Just for, you know, just for the sake of doing it.' He speared a piece of pasta with his fork. 'Because it would be forbidden things that aren't forbidden any more. Exciting things. Because it would be possible,' he said flatly, and watched Suzannah's mouth tighten faintly, another person deciding he'd come back from Bosnia crazy. 'I don't suppose everyone would, but I think maybe I would. I just try to stay aware of that. It's the safest thing.'

Suzannah raised her eyebrows and wiped her lips with her napkin. 'You know, Daniel, maybe you've been in the Balkans too long.'

He shrugged and smiled, trying to signal that he was going to talk normally again, like a sensible person. 'What?' he said lightly. 'You figure a tour of duty in Colombia would improve my view of human nature?'

'Italy. Lovely country. Peaceful and pretty, lots of corruption to ferret out.'

'Yeah, I'll become a Vatican-watcher. That'll work.'

'So are you heading back right away?'

'Soon, but not tomorrow. I drove for a full day to get here, I might as well poke around a bit and see if I find anything to write about.'

Daniel checked his watch again as they came out of the restaurant. 'I hope she rings you soon,' said Suzannah, smiling, as she left him at the corner.

'Worked out that much, did you?'

'You do understand that I'm curious, right?'

'Sure. And you understand that you get nothing from me?'

'Of course.'

'Then we have a perfect understanding.'

'Let me know if you turn up any new angles on our man.'

He walked along the tram tracks, under a canopy of deep green trees. He should have got Lili's address at some point, really. Not that she was probably home. But it would be nice to know where she lived.

The street, he realized, ran through a small wood, a real wood, not landscaped or manicured, and he turned off onto a path, deeper into the tangled bushes and birch trees.

Suzannah was right, of course, that he didn't need to stay in the Balkans. God knows no one else did. Even the wire services were mostly staffed by local journalists now; sometimes he ran into other internationals in Sarajevo, sometimes in Belgrade, but not often. In Goražde or Banja Luka there were city reporters, and there was Daniel, and that was about the end of it, while his colleagues flowed in a tidal movement after the latest explosions of violence around the world.

He wasn't immune. He knew the adrenalin rush, knew that after the war in Bosnia it was hard for him, too, to live without it. He knew that some dark oily part of his mind had welcomed the fighting in the Drenica Valley. Journalistic heroin, terror and hypnosis, the constant possibility of instant death. You can never quite be a normal person again when you've tasted it.

And there was always a good reason – certainly people should hear about East Timor, about Chechnya and Sierra Leone, although he saw no reason they should hear it from him, someone who understood no more about these places than anyone else on a Sarajevo street. But how did he explain that he had made a promise somewhere, somehow, to no one; that at some indefinable time in the wars he had vowed that he would see this through, and that no matter what anyone thought, it wasn't over yet.

He had seen a girl dancing in a Belgrade nightclub, a little girl with a tired, old face and ripped jeans, dancing like a fury in a cloud of smoke and pounding techno, and he knew that this girl, or somebody like this girl, still had a part to play, that there was an unfinished story in that dance.

At the top of a low hill he paused, took his phone out of

his pocket and decided to try the number just once more – and yes, this time she picked up, her voice slightly breathless at the other end of the line, Lili.

'Daniel, sorry, I just came in the door, I had some errands to run.'

'It's okay, I'm glad I got hold of you.' He thought of telling her he had heard her in the afternoon, but decided that might sound pathetic. 'So, I'm in some kind of park somewhere, and if I can find my way out I could maybe meet you or . . .'

'Listen.' His free hand clenched when he heard her say the word. 'I've really thought about this. Under the circumstances—'

'You're not going to see me.'

'No, I didn't say that. Just . . . I think that we can only meet in, well, groups of people. Group situations where, where everyone can hear what we say. Not . . . just talking to each other.'

'You're kidding.' He strode down the path randomly. 'You mean . . . I don't even understand what you mean.'

'Well, I'm arranging to see a couple of friends after work tomorrow,' she said weakly. 'Interpreters at the International Court of Justice, and maybe one guy from the tribunal. You could come and join us. That would be okay.'

'Jesus Christ. Every time there's new rules. Where is this heading?'

'Don't be angry at me.'

'I'm not, I'm not angry.' He turned a corner, heading towards the noise of the roads that he could hear in the distance. 'Well, okay, I am angry, but I'm not specifically angry at you. It's just this whole thing.'

'I told you long ago that things were difficult with us. Half the people in this town are either employed by the tribunal or reporting on it.' He could hear her lighter flick, she breathed in and exhaled. 'Please, Daniel. I would rather see you this way than not at all.'

'Okay. Yeah. Okay.'

'You're just walking around in a park?'

'Yeah, I'm figuring on mugging some joggers.' The streetlights came on behind a row of trees, and he saw a fence emerging from the dusk. 'I'm coming up to a thing here. Let's see. It's, ah,' he peered through the fence at dim shapes, some distance away, 'I don't know. It looks like a bunch of little buildings and things. Do you have some kind of theme park here?'

'Oh, yes, that's Madurodam. The tourist office loves that place.'

'It's ever so picturesque.'

'This man, Mr Maduro, his son was a resistance fighter who died in Dachau, so he built a miniature town in his memory.'

'His son died in Dachau so he built a miniature town? Is there some connection I'm missing there?'

'The Dutch have their reasons whereof reason knows nothing. Wait until you see the painter of sand dunes.'

Daniel leaned against a tree. 'I miss you, Ljiljana,' he said softly.

'Don't do this,' she said. 'It doesn't help anyone.'

'I just said I miss you. I do.'

'I'll call you tomorrow at lunchtime. *Bonne nuit*, Daniel.'

'Sleep well.'

Putting his phone back in his jacket pocket, he made his way down the slope of a hill to the road and walked slowly towards the tram stop, beside the green water of a broad canal.

IX

Çka ndodhi këtu?

24 March–10 June 1999

Dear Mme Stambolović;
Re your current assignment, please find attached the following background documents.

A) Security Council Resolution 1199 [Eng, Fr, Ger]; B) Allied Forces Activation Order of 12 October 1998 [Eng, Fr, Ger]; C) OPLAN 10601 – Allied Force [Eng, Fr; Ger to follow]; D) legal briefing prepared for British foreign office [Eng only] . . .
Lili sat on the train, leafing through pages of documents which she had printed out from her computer as she quickly packed her suitcase, made hurried arrangements with the concierge. There was language she needed in this material, there were phrases and concepts she had to assimilate, sentences that were urgent to have in her control.

. . . E) legal briefing prepared for French foreign office [Fr only]; F) text of interim peace agreement as signed by Albanian delegation [Eng, Fr, Serb, Shqip]; G) text of variant agreement proposed by Serbian delegation [Eng, Serb] . . .

Far away, too far away to hear, NATO planes were rising from the runways. The bombs were falling on Serbia, falling on Kosovo.

'For there were certain men crept in unawares, who were before of old ordained to this condemnation; ungodly men, turning the grace of our God into lasciviousness . . .'

A few people walking their dogs in Brockwell Park glanced at Father Jamie curiously as he read his text for the day, and a policeman nodded in his direction. Paja sat on a bench near by, frowning, his square hands spread across his knees.

'The Lord, having saved the people out of the land of Egypt, afterward destroyed them that believed not. And the angels which kept not their first estate, but left their own habitation, he hath reserved in everlasting chains under darkness unto the judgement of the great day . . . '

Father Jamie was not afraid of destruction. It was not that he had confidence that he himself would survive the Great Day; he understood that this would be a sin of pride, and it did not trouble him to imagine himself in darkness or in fire. He was not preoccupied with his own fate. He looked with longing to the cleansing of the world. This attitude was, he felt, the fruit of many years of discipline and mental prayer.

'. . . and the cities about them in like manner, giving themselves over to fornication, and going after strange flesh; likewise also these filthy dreamers defile the flesh, despise dominion, and speak evil of the dignities.'

He finished the reading, closed his book and sat down beside Paja, who turned towards him, his eyebrows lowered.

'You have see on television? The war?'

Jamie nodded. 'We knew this was coming, of course.' He took another book from the pile beside him, a paperback with a picture of a comet hitting a glacier on the cover; must remember to tie that comet in with the reading next time, he thought. 'The end time events . . . one tries to tell people how we're falling short, but they just don't care. And ultimately there has to be judgement, doesn't there?'

Paja sighed, running one hand over his face, and stared

at the ground. 'It is being everywhere soon, you know. I remember how it happens. This is something you think you understand?'

'It's all tied in with the laws of cosmic physics, really. You talk to people about sin, they think, well, you're simply making it up. But it's all quite scientific. The fire, the plagues . . . I mean, you have to die. That is, one has to die.'

'Yes,' said Paja grimly. 'Many people die.'

'But what they don't understand is the evolutionary leap in the solar system.'

Paja looked up again, starting to speak, and began to gasp suddenly, his breathing troubled. 'Excuse me,' he said, waving one hand impatiently. 'It is asthma, nothing else. Please excuse.' He coughed, then spoke again. 'It is coming here very soon, I think, the dying. For myself it is not a matter. But for my baby son I mind.'

'Of course,' Jamie pursed his lips thoughtfully, looking at the other man. He found it hard to judge the ages of young people these days, but Paja was certainly well under thirty. Hardly more than a child himself, Jamie thought. 'Of course you would, yes. But, you know, I don't expect he's done anything terribly wrong. I mean, if he's only a baby. I'd guess that it wouldn't be so bad for him.'

Paja shook his head. 'You are not one time being there,' he said. 'It is worse, you know. It is worse than you can think.'

Daniel stood on a small hill at the Albanian border, weighing the possibility that he was hallucinating.

All around him people, in suits and pyjamas, in flowered skirts and headscarves and jeans and slippers, doctors with white coats and no shoes, people wearing whatever they had been able to find, holding bits of paper with numbers, begging the little crowd of journalists for the use of their mobiles, and he handed his phone over, no idea how much this would cost him, it seemed inhuman to have the thought, as they passed it from hand to hand, calling Tetovo, calling Vienna, calling Dallas and Toronto, calling Belgrade even. And through the hills were more, a thick line of people stretching far beyond the limits of his vision, on foot, packed into trucks, clinging to the sides of tractors, too tired to weep, their identity papers torn from their hands as they crossed. He had seen the populations of towns trekking through the forests of Bosnia with their remaining possessions clutched in their arms, but this swift and wholesale transportation of an entire people was something new. It was the city of Prizren emptied out onto these fields, the city of Djakovica, dozens of villages whose names he tried to record in his tattered notebook, Jim the photographer perched on a higher hill above him, taking pictures of the endless human train.

Tents were going up in the muddy fields, NATO soldiers instructed to build refugee cities, spirals of steam rising where someone was boiling water. He scribbled down pieces of stories as they sat on the ground, his interpreter pale, wiping sweat from his forehead, transmitting fragmentary scenes that didn't always connect with each other, images Daniel had to struggle to assemble. It was like being disastrously stoned, though in a strictly chemical sense he had never been more straight and sober in his life.

'The Serbs were telling us to go to the border and shooting their guns in the air and we were going, and I saw these men in a field by a mountain pass. I think their hands were tied. A hundred? I don't know.'

'We got to the border and some of the police said, no, go back home, so they started us marching again and we got back to the village and all the houses were on fire and one of the other Serb men with the guns said, what are you doing here, send them back, so they marched us again.'

'I got up in the morning to feed the animals, and I went outside, and there were tanks all around the village. And I didn't even know anything was wrong up to that day, I don't read the newspapers, I don't know how to read, I just saw these tanks. And then they all started firing, and all the livelong day they were in and out of the village and we just ran away into the woods, and the ones who got away, they escaped, and the others were killed. I don't know why they did this, I don't know why.'

'We were told to go to the train station, and we were in the train station, and we heard the bombers and we thought, NATO, NATO has come to save us, but they didn't save us, did they? The Chetniks told us to get on the trains and we drove, I don't know where we drove, it was a long time.'

'I was hiding in the cellar and then I realized they were burning houses and I thought, I will be burned alive, so I came out and I gave them all my money so they wouldn't, so they wouldn't, so they would choose a different option, and they told me to go to the border. And there were a lot of people lying dead on the ground.'

'And then I went by this pass in the mountains on the tractor and I saw a pile of bodies. I don't know. Just a pile of bodies. Then they took three of the pretty girls out of our group and took them into the bushes, and honestly I don't want to think about it any more.'

'There was blood all over the grass. I don't know. I don't remember anything. I just saw the blood. That's all I can tell you.'

'Take this to The Hague,' insisted a man in a dusty tracksuit, thrusting a stained piece of cloth into Daniel's hands. 'I held this against my brother's chest while he was dying. They can do the tests, they can prove I'm telling the truth. Take it to The Hague and let them see.'

In Niš, in southern Serbia, three weeks into the war, he sat by a candle in a fourth-floor flat with Nina, a peace activist, and her boyfriend, an ageing punk who went by the name of Sicko. The bombers were overhead, the whistle and shudder of missiles shaking the building, orange flames scarring the darkened room into momentary visibility. Nina was crying in the corner while Sicko played his badly tuned guitar.

'They are bombing the chemical plants,' wept Nina. 'I will have deformed babies, I know it. Why do we have to live here? What did I do so wrong in my past life that I got born in Serbia?'

Sicko was singing Clash songs under his breath, 'London Calling', 'Spanish Bombs'.

'And I am so bad, I am so selfish, because I think about my Albanian friend in Kosovo and I know it must be so worse for her that I cannot imagine. We just are in a doomed history.'

The candle went out as the floor trembled under the bombing, and Daniel reached out with a match to light it again. He knew that these were brave people, exceptional people, that they could be punished terribly for having him in their house, for having those Albanian friends, that they were more profoundly courageous than he could ever be.

'I cannot stand to go to the shelters,' Nina went on. 'All night they are singing nationalistic songs and cursing Bill Clinton. Daniel, Daniel, what is happening in Kosovo? Do you think my friend is all right?'

'I don't know,' he said, wondering how much of the truth to tell her, thinking that everyone in Serbia needed to hear it all but Nina was not, perhaps, the best place to start. 'Probably she's in a refugee camp by now.'

Another missile struck, and the dull blaze of a fire ignited somewhere to the east. '*Yo te querda, o mi corazon*,' sang Sicko quietly.

'What if they kill me? What is the good in that? I hate Milošević so much more than they do. Oh, I want to get out of this stupid, stupid place.'

Maybe, he thought, she could get out on her own, she was a woman, just possibly they would let her cross the border and never return, but Sicko was draft age, he couldn't even leave the house, much less the country, had to hide in the wardrobe when there was a knock at the door.

'I worry,' Daniel said. 'I worry that I'm putting you in danger by being here.'

'Oh, forget about it,' said Nina with a wave of her hand. 'Look, we have cruise missiles in our back yard, we should be worried about danger from you? Anyway it is good. You are a good influence, to be so calm about the bombing. Accustomed to war, I guess.'

He didn't know how to think about it, that he could sometimes barely function in a city at peace, and move so easily through the centre of a war. He didn't want to think about what the last ten years had done.

There was the sound of a crowd of men coming out onto the balcony of the adjoining flat.

'Oh God,' said Nina. 'Now they are going to shoot at the planes again.'

He could see their shadows, half a dozen shapes of men swaying, pressed against the night, whistling and shouting obscenities at the bombers.

'They do this every time.' Nina shrugged. 'About this hour they get drunk enough.' Daniel saw the shadows of guns being raised, ducked his head as the volleys of rifle fire exploded.

'Did you see that?' shouted one of the men. 'I got him!

Fuck his mother's cunt, I got him, I'm sure of it! The fucker's going down!'

'Jesus Christ,' muttered Nina.

'Let's go get him!' screamed another man. 'We'll show him not to fuck with us!' And they ran crashing down the stairway, whooping and firing their guns, heading into the streets to search for the B-52 bomber they were convinced they had just shot down with hunting rifles.

'Okay, now it's official,' said Sicko, looking up from his guitar. 'This whole country is now completely insane.'

In Hungary one night he reached Lili on her mobile.

'I don't want to talk about the war,' he said, 'but I don't think there's anything else left that I know about.'

'So tell me where you are.'

'In a hotel in Budapest.'

'What can you see out your window?'

'You really want to know? There's a bunch of hookers hanging around in the street. One of them's wearing a bathing suit.'

'Okay. Well, let's see, they have an elephant in the Budapest zoo that does paintings. She has quite a successful career, I think. There's a gallery on the Île St-Louis that sells her work.'

'Does she come over for the hangings then?'

'I think that would be difficult. Anyway, there's kind of a story about how she got involved in this project of self-expression. What I was told is, she had started, well, they have some birds that wander around the zoo grounds, and the elephant, she'd take her food and put down a trail of bread crumbs, and then she'd stand at the end of the trail with her foot lifted up. And the birds would find the crumbs and come along, and, well, you probably can visualize the outcome.'

'Jesus. I never knew elephants were so intelligent. Or so bloody-minded.'

'But since they got her engaged in painting she doesn't do that any more. She's very fulfilled by her artistic endeavours. She's so happy she even got a boyfriend, which she wouldn't do before. So it was just an issue of finding the right line of work, in fact.'

'Well, I'm really happy for her.' For no reason he could imagine his voice choked, a sudden catch in his throat. He breathed in sharply and pressed one hand on his forehead.

'Budapest's very pretty in parts,' said Lili softly.

'Yeah, um, yeah it is.'

'This is all really hard.'

'Is it okay? That I don't even know what's right?'

'You think I do? Christ. I *am* the war, Daniel. You think I know what's right?'

Neither of them spoke for a minute.

'Where are you now?' he asked.

'In a hotel. That's all I should probably say.'

'All right.'

'I'm starting at the tribunal in June.'

'I'm glad. I knew they'd want you.'

'Daniel,' she said hesitantly. 'I just . . . I'm . . .'

'Lili? Are you okay?'

'Yes, never mind, I . . . it's not something I can talk about. I shouldn't have . . . Forget I said anything.'

'Sure, but are you okay?'

'I'm all right. I . . . sometimes I wish that I could see you. It would be nice if you were here, probably.'

'Hey, tell me where you are, I'll come. Honest to God, Lili.'

'Yes, well, you know how things are. I should, I should go, I have to work in the morning.'

He studied his Albanian phrasebook, the words for bomb, grenade, shell, minefield. The crucial phrase 'What happened here?' – *Çka ndodhi këtu?* Maybe you only ever needed that phrase, he thought. Maybe his whole career only took up that one line in a phrasebook. War crimes, *krime lufte. Ratni zločini.*

Brussels. It was early May now. Daniel sat through the briefings. He phoned for appointments and was refused. He stopped grim-looking men going into work and got nothing. Even his established sources were drying up, being coy with opinions and information, and he was reduced to haunting expensive bars looking for Eurocrats who'd had too much to drink, or second undersecretaries who wanted to talk. He found no one except other journalists working on the same strategy.

Giving up finally, he decided to take himself to a bar he would actually enjoy, La Fleur en Papier Doré, a long narrow crowded room, dull golden-brown, the walls and tables impastoed with scraps of papers, poems and doodles. Cats prowling along the benches. He opened the door into the thick smoky warmth. Lili was sitting at a corner table near the back, her face lined with exhaustion and unhappiness.

It hardly even seemed strange. She was just there, obviously Lili, there could be no one else in the world who looked like her. He slid onto the bench beside her almost without thinking about it, and she lifted her head slowly to look at him, those startling hazel eyes. She was pale, her forehead knotted with tension, a glass of brandy untouched in front of her.

'What the hell are you doing here?' she said, without much animation, her voice heavy.

'Interviews. I didn't know you'd be here.'

'Do you have any idea how damaging it would be if anyone saw us together?'

'No one's looking at us.'

She picked up her cigarettes, and swore under her breath as she opened the pack and found it empty. Her hands were shaking terribly. Daniel reached into his jacket, took out a pack and passed it to her.

'You don't smoke.'

'Do you think I would've gotten a single interview in Bosnia if I didn't carry cigarettes?' She shrugged and slid one from the pack, her hands so unsteady she had trouble holding on to it. He took a lighter from his pocket and stretched the small flame towards her, and she leaned forward.

'Thank you.'

She took one long starved drag, then set the cigarette down in the ashtray, where she seemed to forget about it entirely.

'You really have to go away.'

'Not right now.' He watched her as she stared down at the table. 'You can't tell me what's wrong, can you?'

She shook her head. 'You know that.'

'Yes.'

She pushed a strand of hair away from her face, and he didn't know what else to do, so he leaned over and kissed her. 'You can't do that,' she said, pushing him away.

'You can't do that,' she said again, and he saw that she was crying. Her cigarette burned itself down in the ashtray as she sat with her head in her hands, sobbing quietly to herself as if he wasn't even there.

He wanted to do something and there was nothing he could do. He thought about the taste of her lipstick, and the odd fact that he hardly ever kissed women who wore lipstick. On the table in front of him someone had glued a fragment of a poem. *Comment m'entendez vous? Je parle de si loin.*

The cigarette had burned out entirely, and Lili was not crying any more but taking small ragged breaths. He put his hand on her knee underneath the table, where no one could see.

'Come with me,' he said.

'Don't you understand? I was at NATO,' whispered Lili.

'I didn't ask where you were, and I'm not going to ask.'

'We can't. You know how it looks. We can't.'

'I'm staying at the Eperonniers. It's just a couple of blocks from here. No one's going to notice.'

'Daniel, people know who you are.' She wiped at her eyes with the tips of her fingers. 'You must go. You have to.'

He stood up, and with the sensation of someone throwing everything he owned over a cliff, he leaned towards her. 'I'm in room twelve. I'll be there. Please.' She pressed her hands to her face and said nothing.

He walked out of the bar quickly, into the spring night.

Doctors, priests, lawyers – people have some sense, however poorly understood, that these professions are bound, that they are answerable to a code that exceeds them, an impersonal necessity. No one thinks of interpreters, of the stringency and beauty of their work, their requirements of accuracy, neutrality, confidentiality. Faithfulness.

And Lili did believe. Not in the ineluctable force of history any more, not in the proletariat or the nation or the power of blood, but in her own sworn duty to be precise, to be a pure and trustworthy mediator of thought, subject to the laws of language.

What Lili was doing, as she walked into the hotel in Brussels, was not a material violation of her code. But even so, it was not the perfect faithfulness she wanted to maintain.

She closed the door behind her quickly and looked around the small bare room, a holdall open at the foot of the bed, a laptop and a little tape recorder on the table.

'I'm glad you came,' he said.

On the tape Lou Reed was singing a sweetly pretty song about his friend Candy the New York transvestite, about how she hated her body, how she was lonely and afraid of death, how she wanted to walk away from herself.

'Don't you want to know,' she said, 'the things I know?'

'Of course I do. How could I not?'

'Do you understand that I will never tell you?'

'Yes, I do.'

She put her hand on the back of his neck and kissed him.

Small sounds of the night city drifted up through the window, a distant high laugh, the heavy wheels of a delivery truck. She lay with her head against Daniel's shoulder, one arm across his chest, her body filled with a soft, slow pleasure. His breathing was soft and even; he must be asleep, she thought, or nearly asleep.

It would be so nice to stay here, to sleep with Daniel under the nubbly pink hotel blanket, to wake up in the night knowing she could smell herself on his lips and fingers, to drink coffee with him in the morning. But she knew that if she wasn't in her own room in the morning it would be noticed, it might be looked into.

She touched his face and kissed him quickly, moving away from his arms. 'I must go,' she said. 'I'm sorry.'

'Don't,' he said, his voice blurry, running his hand along her shoulder. 'Stay here.'

'No, I really can't. I wish I could. It was lovely, Daniel, but I can't stay.'

He sat up, fumbling for his glasses while she picked her clothes up from the floor. It took him a while to locate them, blinking vaguely, patting surfaces at random; finally his hand fell on them, and he set them on his nose, his face taking on a whole new shape and expression.

'I'm legally blind without these, you know,' he muttered.

'What would you do if you lost them in a war zone?'

'I carry spares.'

Everything was resolving into single suspended images, the small white buttons of her blouse, the structure of muscles in his shoulders and arms, a mole underneath his right ear.

She wondered if she needed to say something, to clarify that this was not the beginning of anything new, that it couldn't be a permanent change. She thought not. After all, it was Daniel, vagrant, obsessive, distracted Daniel. Even if he had wanted this to be more than it was, he could never keep it in mind long enough, driving from one conflict to another, filing words into cyberspace.

'I have to go to Tetovo in the morning,' he said hesitantly, as if in confirmation.

'Yes, I assumed so.'

He took her wrist, and she let herself be pulled back down. His skin felt soft and smooth, like silk, like cream.

'I can't convince you to stay?' he breathed against her ear.

'Almost, but no.' She kissed him again, and he nearly managed to shift around and pin her underneath him, but she laughed and pulled away. 'Don't try it, buddy.'

'That was very colloquial, Ljiljana. You see I'm a good influence.'

'Okay, but I really do have to go.' She stood up decisively and put on her shoes.

'Hey,' he said, just before she opened the door. 'Who wrote that line? *Je parle de si loin?*'

She stopped with her hand on the doorknob and smiled. 'You saw that, then. It's René Char. My favourite poet, maybe. That's why I like to sit at that table.'

'I'll talk to you soon.'

'Yes.'

Out in the street, the city was still and silent, with the chill in the air that comes just before dawn, and she realized with a shock that there was a narrow band of light on the horizon.

She would have to tell them that she was sick, a sore throat, a low-grade fever. It was impossible to interpret without sleep. The fine point of concentration wouldn't be there, wouldn't be available, her brain incapable of the effort that would be demanded. She didn't like to report in sick, she hardly ever did.

But she was still wrapped in contentment, walking quickly through the quiet streets around the Bourse, with its bizarre carvings of fruits and *putti*, she was still smiling, happy to have this, a private and treasured thing to store in her memory.

Back at her own hotel, she took off her shoes to walk the corridor, slid into her room, showered and changed into a dressing-gown, called her supervisor with a rasp in her voice. All of these were things that other people had done in similar circumstances. Her supervisor told her she should stop smoking, and she agreed that she should.

As she sat on the bed and lit a cigarette she started to feel tired, a headache creeping in around the edges of awareness, and she thought, nevertheless, it is dangerous. To be this close to him, a journalist after all. She could not entirely trust herself, she had nearly cracked several times this month, nearly started to tell him what it was like, interpreting discussions about permitted and non-permitted targets in the city where she was born, whether the likelihood of civilian death was tier one or tier three, if they should send ground troops in through Albania, where they would enter, whether that was too much of a risk on behalf of people they didn't like that much anyway. Accidental strikes on refugee convoys. And she could not say any of it was exactly wrong or exactly right, the alternative maybe only the gradual torture of her mother's people, a slow-motion massacre. She was charged only with accurately conveying the words, as the pieces of her heritage ripped each other apart.

Stubbing out her cigarette, suddenly anxious that an imaginary sore throat could turn into a real one, she went into the bathroom and gargled with salt water. Her muscles were aching a bit. She knew she should sleep for a few hours, get back on schedule, but she was distracted by fragments of her body's memory, his lips on her neck, his hands on her breasts.

She would be in The Hague soon, and in that hermetic world Daniel had to be treated with great caution; there would have to be more distance between them. Probably that was for the best in any case. She lay down, her forearm over her eyes, slipping into a realm of undefined sensation and trying to think, trying to focus enough to think about how she could explain this to him, whether he could understand how much it meant to her. That there were things she was making up for; and if he sometimes dismissed the tribunal as psychotherapy for European guilt about Bosnia, he wasn't likely to see the point of her more personal guilt – all the things she had never told him – that it was better not to tell him, and once again she was getting too close. She fell asleep thinking that she had to be more clear about the boundaries, and then she dreamed about him, of course, the warmth of his body. It meant nothing, it couldn't. She woke up, and looked at her mobile phone, and wondered how long she could keep it turned off.

On 10 June, Serbian forces pulled out of Kosovo and the NATO bombing ended. President Milošević announced to the Serbs, curiously enough, that they had won, and also that the entire nation had been a noble part of the war effort, 'from babies in maternity wards to patients in intensive care to soldiers in trenches'. No one asked the babies what they had thought about the war, if they were volunteers or conscripts, if they really believed in the glorious Serbian people, if anyone had offered them the chance to refuse.

X

Spanish Bombs

16 July 1999

In his cell in Scheveningen, Nikola Marković was singing, under his breath, not creating a disturbance. He was a well-behaved prisoner. He sang about the opening of the American frontier and the appeal of belonging to a Puerto Rican street gang, songs with a halo of distance around them, the slight golden haze of a foreign culture. He sang because he needed that tug of sentiment at his heart, the music surging tenderly up and down. Better that than the words of the indictment. Too simple, those words, stripped of nuance and ambiguity, even less real than childish American love songs. As if the world could be like that.

He wanted to think about the reassuring language of the young lawyer, the familiar stories, the realization that no one could be blamed for history, and him least of all. What he didn't want to remember was the hot rush of blood that had swept through him at times. There were times when he had told his men to stop. Not to do this or that. Some of them were sadists, he had no part in that. He didn't want to remember the exhilaration.

We all give in to temptation now and then, he thought. We would be less than human if we didn't. But he had imagination, he had feelings, he had often wept for individual Muslims, understanding that they were victims just like himself. Shouldn't that count for something?

The older lawyer had come back to the prison a few hours after the hearing, with an armload of binders which he tried to explain in surprisingly poor English. 'I am sorry,' he shrugged. 'I lack the, what is it, facility of languages. But I appreciate you to read the documents.'

'What are these?' asked Marković, not wanting to touch them somehow.

'Selections of statements of witnesses, or possibly witnesses. It is, um, partial now, but it is helpful that you can read. With particular attention, please, to the material of Mr Vasić.'

'Vasić? Dejan Vasić?'

'Certainly. He is, um, central in the case, it may be. So your consideration of the matter here is very much helpful.'

Dejan Vasić, God help us, that absurd man. He had a sudden mental image of him, that pink babyish face and watery eyes, on one of his pointless excursions into the courtroom in the summer of 1992. He couldn't quite remember why he himself had been there, but he did remember Vasić, furiously waving bits of paper at an impassive judge.

'This man is sixty-five years old! He can't see! Why do you keep sending him call-up notices? Are you all completely insane?'

'Mr Vasić, please. We are in exceptional circumstances, as you surely appreciate. When a people is at war—'

'At war? At war? Who are we at war with? Is some country invading us? Please tell me, who should we be at war with? Am I at war with my newspaper boy?'

As far as he could remember, that exchange ended with Vasić being cited for contempt. He was living in Belgrade now, wasn't he? Marković seemed to remember that. Working for some sort of pathetic human rights group. Certainly he had left, after his office was shot up for the third or fourth time. If Vasić was central to their case, they couldn't have much of a case to begin with.

But he didn't want to look at the binders. He felt uncomfortable putting his hands on them. They were heavy, and the covers felt rough and dirty, and after he had pushed them under the bed he had to go into the cell's little bathroom and wash his hands.

The prison guards urged him to keep himself busy, join the basketball team, take English classes, as if his English wasn't already better than theirs. He would rather watch television. The Orthodox chaplain was useless, practically illiterate, and he certainly wasn't going to deal with the Catholic, or the Wiccan whom he understood was on call for some of the regular Dutch prisoners.

The best thing to do would be to keep up his work. He could publish books from prison, a great tradition, that one. He had a paper in mind about the symbolism of the written word in the Serbian epic. The almost magical power of print, how it carried blessing and death. If something was written down, it would have to come true. There was no other way.

And when the written words come to Lazar
he sees the words, he drops terrible tears.

Lili entered the muffled space of the booth in Courtroom Three, checked the mike, and fitted her earphones onto her head, pushing them slightly sideways, off her right ear. She'd worn them like that for years, just because it felt better, but recently she'd come across a research paper explaining it in terms of cerebral lateralization among early bilinguals, so now she was self-conscious every time she pushed an earphone back.

The session, when it resumed, would claim her full attention. They were interpreting both for the lawyers and for the witness, a Swedish peacekeeper whose English was tortured and heavily accented, and which they had to transfer into

BCS with a reasonable degree of coherence, but without improving his words so much that they would create any false impressions.

She was glad of this, glad it would be a demanding morning. She needed work that would keep her mind off Daniel. She would see him, they would speak, they would spend a few hours in a crowd of people; that was enough. Perhaps it would be strange, but in the end it would be helpful, a step back towards the safety of their mediated friendship, the long-distance intensity that had threatened nothing.

Vanja came into the booth, rushed and apologetic, and Lili held up her hands lightly, *nema problema*, there was lots of time. She pushed a file towards her colleague, joked about the witness and his weird usage of English words, and in a moment the court clerk banged his staff three times, that strange archaic remnant of ritual. The judges entered in their robes like distracted ministers, and Lili leaned forward and began to speak.

Daniel had spent the morning more constructively than he had expected; succeeding, to his own surprise, in reaching Irina Marković on the phone. She spoke as if she were reading from a sheet of set phrases, and perhaps she was, perhaps the lawyers had already briefed her on what to say to journalists. That her husband was a good man, that he had never harmed anyone, that he was not a nationalist, had no political ambitions, and that the trial was – there seemed to be two conflicting lines of argument here – alternatively a terrible mistake or a deliberate conspiracy against the Serbian people.

'Have you talked to him since he was arrested?' asked Daniel, speaking in Bosnian.

'Yes, but just twice. He only has a pay telephone in the hallway, it's not adequate at all.'

'How is he?'

'Well, what do you mean, how is he? He's in jail, how do you think he is?' she snapped.

'I'm sorry if I put that badly. Language problem. How is he coping with the stress?'

The woman at the other end of the line – he had no mental image for her at all – paused for a moment. 'He's depressed,' she said, and she sounded for the first time as if she might actually be speaking to another person. 'He gets really very depressed, you know.'

He never talked about her, thought Daniel. I don't know anything about this marriage except its bare existence, and even that I didn't know for years.

'You knew him, didn't you?' she went on. 'He's a man with very strong feelings. A great determination. It's hard on him to be confined.' This was starting to sound like a script again. Were there any Serbian epics about prisoners? None that he could think of, but the basic outline wouldn't take much devising. Determination and endurance and noble sacrifice.

'But he is confident that he will be able to prove his innocence,' she was saying, and Daniel was thinking about their marriage, the entirely mysterious space they shared, a man he knew slightly and didn't want to know better, and a woman he couldn't even picture in his mind. Well, he should take his notes to Suzannah. Something could be done with them.

It was a warm day, and brighter, not so wet and overcast. At the door of the tribunal building he presented his passport again, walked through the metal detector, handed over his phone. He walked up the low steps and through the revolving door, and Lili was standing a few feet away in the lobby.

He saw her briefly before she saw him. She was standing

by one of the fake plaster pillars with her briefcase at her feet, reading a piece of paper, her face thoughtful, serious. She wore a short-sleeved dress in that blue-green colour she liked, some kind of silky material, and, quite incongruously, a pair of cheap running shoes. Certain French women could carry off anything, even old trainers with a silk dress, and she looked exactly as if this had been a deliberate fashion choice; but he knew without quite knowing that she had put them on because she was nervous and defying her own nervousness, because she felt better in them, and there was something so nearly childish and awkward about it all that he thought it might break his heart.

'Ljiljana.'

'Daniel.' She turned towards him, and there was no strain in her casual greeting, an old friend, nice to see you again, but she hesitated for a moment before she touched him. A light, tightly controlled hug; he held her nervously, trying to gauge how this was supposed to be, and she was moving away from him immediately, pulling back and reaching for cigarettes, something to occupy her hands. 'I didn't know you were in town,' she said brightly.

'Just for a day or two.'

It was a non-smoking area, so she could do nothing with her pack of cigarettes except play with it, turning it over and over in her delicate fingers. 'It's nice to see you. How have you been?'

'Okay, I guess.' He could actually hear his heart beating in his ears. This was insane, the whole thing.

'Well, I must go, I'm needed in court.' She started to walk away, and then came back. 'Are you free this evening? I'm meeting some friends at the Café Banka.'

He very nearly said that he wasn't free, that he was leaving in the afternoon, and then she reached for his hand, her fingers tracing a feathery motion across his palm and retreating. His breath caught in his throat. She stepped backwards.

'Yes,' he said. 'I could be there.' She turned and went quickly up to the steps, disappearing behind a wall of glass.

Daniel left the building, his nerves in chaos, and found himself, as he walked south, fiercely and irrationally irritated by the architecture, the sobre faceless brick buildings which stood stolidly along the wide streets, as if they had never in all their time wanted something they couldn't have. He didn't know how he had ended up here, in this respectable governmental city, so content with itself. He didn't know how this place could even hope to answer the tangled intimate conflicts of the Bosnian war, neighbourhoods dissolving into battlefields, genocide in pizza parlours.

So he was strangely relieved to turn a corner and find himself in an almost seedy area, a dusty-looking street with an occasional sign announcing an Erotic Shop, or a Spaced-Out Coffee House with dope fumes drifting through the window. The suggestion that The Hague was capable of at least minor vices made him feel slightly less alienated, and he wandered around a few corners, into a residential district that was a bit more affluent but somehow even more barren than South London, identical three-storey houses without gardens or trees or even windowboxes. A little boy with toffee-coloured skin and blond dreadlocks was sitting on top of a car singing a song in Dutch. All right then, this was tolerable, this was a place where people actually lived, not necessarily carrying on legal argument at all times.

He was prepared to accept that desire made fools of everyone, but he was completely unwilling to be thrown so off balance by her fingers on the palm of his hand, as if he had never touched her before, as if he didn't know how her body felt arching against him, what she tasted like for godsake. Which was something he had been trying not to think about too much, but it was getting increasingly difficult.

Prins Hendrikstraat opened up into a small plaza, tram tracks bending around a ring of tall trees, and inside them a little concrete park, another child standing on a bench, throwing bread at the pigeons. And in the centre of the circle, astonishingly, were five turtles made of stone, each of them nearly as large as a person. They were a soft shade of pink, and sweetly crude, their upturned heads blunt and eyeless, their feet a set of embryonic flippers. His face lit up in momentary delight, and he sat down on a grey marble bench and studied them; arranged as if they were creeping slowly in a rough circle, they made him feel curiously hopeful, as if he were after all in a place where things could happen for the best.

Perfection was always the interpreter's ideal, but it was an ideal that could never be met. Interpreters were human and limited and under considerable stress, and minor slips – missing articles, errors in tense and agreement, graceless word ordering, extra adverbs – had to go uncorrected. Difficulties with numbers were constant. Sometimes it was necessary to repair a serious mistake, a badly misunderstood word or expression, and thus fall further behind the speaker.

But the problem of interpretation went deeper than accuracy alone. It was not, in a strict sense, possible to say the same thing in different languages. You could not – and all of them knew it, at least half-consciously – you could not have the same thought in French and in English. The span of a whole speaking life, even the whole history of a people, would intervene. And so interpretation would always be approximation, even in its most accomplished and flawless form, for the speaker could not be remade, the world could not be recast, you could not ever go back and completely rethink a German thought into French, an English thought into Bosnian, Croatian, Serbian.

Lili sat in her booth, the court in recess, studying a document that was about to be submitted into evidence, but at the same time thinking again about Daniel's voice, specifically about the way he said her name, how odd it was that he had mastered the 'lj' sound, so tricky for foreigners, but still had that Canadian drawl on the 'a'. Her name sounded quite different coming from him, not the way her family pronounced it, not even the way a French person would. Or the short form, no difference between herself and the flower the way he spoke it, and she knew that this was correct in English, but it seemed strange.

And what did this mean, what did this mean in his world? She thought of lilies, their white waxy petals, deep folds and dramatic curves, and the sharpness of their scent, and their life in the wild, in wet green shadows.

She shouldn't have touched him like that. Absolutely she should not have. She had implicated herself, she had deliberately complicated things, instead of telling him clearly that their night in Brussels was just that, one night, and that it was no use asking what she wanted, that wanting didn't enter into it. She knew better, that was the point. The nature of law lay between them, the need of justice to be seen to be done. You could not change the lives that had put them here, you could not remake the world.

The palm of his hand, soft against her fingers.

The judges entered, the lawyers and spectators rose and sat, and the session resumed.

'Now, you told the court before recess that you saw the defendant, Mr Kovačić, at this meeting,' said the defence attorney.

'Ja, I did.'

'Had you seen him many times before?'

'Not so many, but once or two.'

'Only once or twice?'

'Ja, I said so.'

'Don't you think, then, that you might perhaps have mistaken someone else for Mr Kovačić?'

'No. I don't think. He is a very, um, distinguished man.' He must mean distinctive, *osoben*, not distinguished, *otmen*. Kovačić was recognizable mostly by his severe acne. But would that translation tip the balance ever so slightly against the defendant? She opted for *osoben*, but it worried her. Someone at the defence table, listening on the earphones, seemed to turn his head slightly towards the booth and make a note. Probably he would not challenge it – the judges didn't listen to the BCS channel anyway – but he would monitor her now for a pattern, saving it up against an appeal. She had made a bad call, it would have been the right thing to do at a conference or a meeting, but it was the wrong thing to do in court. She would have to be aware of this.

All these thoughts took her barely a second, she was on to the next question now, the answer, the gradual emergence of the story.

He couldn't sit with the turtles for ever, of course, especially not when he didn't even have a newspaper to read, so after a while, feeling somehow refreshed, he went back to wandering in the direction of the city centre, trying to distract himself with the image of Marković in the courtroom. It had been strange to look at him there, out of his context, drained, lacking in meaning, as if the bar in Banja Luka had been a fundamental part of his identity.

And it had been only a few days ago, really, or not much longer. Odd to remember that. It seemed so distant, but he'd been in the bar just a week before the arrest, the air thick as hot soup even at night, windless, hard to breathe. Daniel's shirt had been sticking to his back, trails of sweat trickling down the side of his neck. Cigarette smoke hovered in a cirrus layer around them.

'So. You care to comment on brutal NATO slaughter of innocent children and babies?' Marković said, waving to the bartender for a round of drinks.

'That's a hell of an opener for a conversation.' Daniel was exhausted by the heat, slightly sick to his stomach, sluggish. He could sit here and try to get a useful quote, or he could go back to his hotel and read a Belgrade tabloid explaining that Bill Clinton's brain was controlled by alien thought beams, or he could have another frustrating and inconclusive telephone conversation with Lili. The advantage of sitting here was that he didn't have to move.

'I just want to see if your legendary concern for civilian casualties is genuinely impartial. Or if it matters less perhaps when the victims are Serbs.'

'You read my articles, didn't you? You know I wasn't letting NATO off the hook.'

'Although as I recall, you were critical of strategic choices, rather than questioning brutal neo-colonial—'

'Whatever.'

'You know, my friend, you should one day face up to your role in the global panopticon.'

'I've pencilled it in for Wednesday. Do you suppose I could get a quote on the local reaction that doesn't come from Foucault?'

'A vast Western strategy in which over-information becomes equivalent of no information at all.'

'Reliable estimates of about ten thousand ethnic Albanians killed. Reaction?'

'You see? You send those vague numbers floating out there until no one is able to keep track of reality any longer. You are a tool of the globalist putsch, Daniel. And what about Albanians who are back in Kosovo and Metohija now killing Serbs?'

'I've written about that too. I and the public know, Nikola.'

'Those to whom evil is done do evil in return, yes, yes. People seem to find that saying very clever.'

'Okay, how about this. Milošević. Such a great protector of the Serbian people that you've lost just about everything now. Such a great military success in Kosovo that you'll never get it back, and even Belgrade's half destroyed. Feel like giving me a quote on him?'

Marković hesitated, ordered another drink. 'I will tell you a rumour,' he said at last, his voice lowered. 'What I hear said is that orders went out from Belgrade to the general of our army here. What I hear is that his orders were to engage the peacekeepers in Bosnia, in an attempt to tie NATO down. What I hear is that he refused these orders.'

Daniel was immediately wide awake, the heat fatigue vanished, reaching for his notebook. 'Source, Nikola. I need a source.'

Marković shrugged. 'The story is going around the streets. You did not hear it from me, of course. But it is possible that some military people have heard about this.'

'Names?'

'Oh, I think not. No, that is the extent of the favour I can do for you right now.'

'If I ask Branković . . .'

'I told you, Daniel. That is all.'

He scribbled a few sentences in his notebook and wondered if he should leave immediately to chase this one up by phone; but it was probably too late, better to start in the morning.

'Okay, fine. Let's get back to these casualty figures.'

'Why ask me? I was not there any more than I was in Belgrade. Perhaps they were all killed by NATO in a massive accident. What about your friend, that half-Albanian woman, what does she say?'

'Don't talk about her,' snapped Daniel, putting his glass down a bit too hard. 'Just don't you talk about her, okay?'

'Well. This appears to be a sensitive subject. Could it be you are finding that even your supposed friends must challenge your Western hegemonic views?'

'You don't know shit, Nikola.' Daniel laughed, realizing that Marković's understanding of him was as narrowly political as, well, as his own understanding of Marković. But he knew he had committed a cardinal error, he had let himself be drawn, and by a man who regarded his involvement in the murder of thousands of people as a kind of social faux pas. Things could only get worse from here, and the interview, such as it was, should be terminated as quickly as possible. He put down money for the drinks and stood up. 'Have a great night with the global panopticon, eh?'

He walked south as far as the Mauritshuis, checked his watch, and turned to take a different route back to the north end. He had never been terribly interested in art history, so visiting the Mauritshuis didn't occur to him as a way of spending time. If it had, he might have gone into one of the small rooms where he could have seen an odd and disturbing painting, a collaboration by two artists whose styles jarred against each other. A moment in time in which something had occurred, in which a peaceable kingdom of animals had suddenly woken up and begun to fall apart. On the crowded canvas, a wolf looked with sudden hunger at a white deer, one fish lay dead at the feet of a heron, and the bull and the lion turned heavy and mournful eyes towards two tigers, who began to tear at each other with their claws and teeth. Small dogs barked fiercely, birds rushed across the darkening sky, and the other creatures turned in surprise to the shadow of a tree, where the hands of two human beings touched around a bitten apple.

He saw them as he turned the corner. They were walking to the bar in a small group, Lili in her raincoat and running shoes. When he caught up with them, he saw a quick wild flash of emotion in her eyes – panic, longing, he couldn't separate himself from the moment enough to know. Her impeccable calm fell back into place almost instantly.

'Daniel, hello.' She introduced him to the others as her friend, a writer, and as they walked into the tiny smoke-filled room she gave him a list of names: Marie, Ivo, some others he didn't really catch.

'What do you write, Daniel?' asked a woman with red hair and a round face, pushing her way towards a small table by the back wall. He shrugged, not sure how he was supposed to answer. Lili pursed her lips and raised her eyebrows.

'Stories,' he said vaguely. 'Short, you know, little stories. About people.'

'I had to interpret for Schreiber today,' Marie was complaining. Someone was pulling over chairs, the group of them crammed into one corner, beside an unused fireplace. The room was noisy, crowded, with dull-coloured landscapes and still lifes framed on the walls, and plastic pennants from a beer company strung along the ceiling.

'Oh God, what a nightmare,' said someone else. 'Is he still clearing his throat into the mike every five minutes?'

'I thought my eardrums would burst. Then he started actually to blow his nose in front of the mike and I had to halt the session, it was mortifying.'

'Could I get you something to drink?' asked Lili, looking towards him.

'I guess so, um . . . whatever. Scotch, is that okay?' She stood up and walked behind him, towards the counter, and for a second as she passed he felt her fingers brush the back of his neck, hardly touching, something close to an accident of proximity. He wanted to tell her to stop doing that, he couldn't bear it, but then she might actually stop.

'Schreiber needs to see a nasal specialist.'

'Well, Schreiber needs a lot of things.'

Lili was walking back to the table. He reached into the pocket of his jacket for change, and his hand closed on a worn fragment of paper. He took it out and spread it on the table in front of him. The people nearest to him were talking in French, and no one was really paying attention to him. That was all right. Lili sat down, pushing his drink towards him, and he offered her a handful of guilders but she waved them away. He looked at the scrap of paper again, and thought, yes, this is a good idea.

'Does anyone speak Spanish?' he asked, and an immediate cheerful buzz of conversation broke out. After an animated discussion which allowed him to put together a few more names and faces, they achieved consensus on the opinion that Mandy, the redhead, had the best Spanish.

She scanned it quickly. 'It doesn't mean anything.'

'Aw, don't tell me that.'

He'd been given the scrap of paper back in Niš, not long before, standing in Nina and Sicko's tiny flat as Nina rushed around, her face a patchy flush, her eyes puffy, trying to sell everything they owned in a desperate attempt to bribe their way over the border to Hungary. Daniel had given them all the Deutschmarks he had, which wasn't much help.

'Who knows, I hear all these rumours how much you need,'

said Nina, packing pots and pans into a box for a woman down the street. 'For the TV we did okay, and the computer also, I just think, every bit we can sell, the more probability to make it through.' She wiped her nose with the back of her hand. 'We just got to get out right away.'

Sicko was moving stiffly, painfully, as he walked to the door with his guitar, taking it downstairs to a neighbour who'd offered the equivalent of five dollars for it. A week ago he had been snatched by the police when he went out to buy a newspaper. He wouldn't say much about what had happened. Obviously he had been beaten; once he had told Nina something about death threats, about his body turning up in the Danube. After three days, he had signed a statement implicating several people, including Nina, in a US-funded conspiracy against the government.

The door closed behind him and Nina sat down in the last remaining kitchen chair. She sniffled, wiped at her nose again. 'You know, I forgive him, of course,' she said abruptly, her voice wavering. 'I understand he had just no choice at all. For sure they would have killed him, just poof, disappeared. So I have to forgive him, it would be inhuman not. Right?'

Daniel didn't know what to say, so he sat on the floor beside her and patted her hand. She was young, Nina; maybe twenty-four or so. Thick black hair, all in tangles now.

'I still love him, you see. Of course I still love him. Just some days I think, ten years from now, twenty years, will I wake up in the night and remember this? I don't know. Will I tell our children? Should they know about this?'

'What can I tell you?' said Daniel. 'No one can endure everything, Nina. Sometimes people do things they really don't want to do.'

'Yes. Yes, I know,' she said, pushing a dark mass of hair

from her face. 'And sometimes people feel things they really don't want to feel.'

Sicko came back into the room before he could ask her if she was talking about hate or love.

Nina jumped up and started packing again, and Sicko lowered himself slowly to the ground. He held out a little handful of bills towards her, and she took them silently and stuffed them in her pocket, turned away, then turned again and kissed him quickly, without comment.

Sicko sat looking at the floor. 'Could you do one favour for me?' he asked Daniel quietly.

'Of course.' He expected Sicko to need something, maybe something only a foreigner could easily get. Dinars changed into hard currency? A message passed on to someone in Croatia or Kosovo? Maybe just tobacco.

'Could you find out for me the meaning of the refrain in "Spanish Bombs"? I always wanted to know.' And he had taken out the record sleeve with the lyrics printed on it, and copied the refrain onto a scrap of paper, and Daniel had put it in his pocket, and recalled it as he sat in a bar in The Hague.

'Okay, I'm exaggerating,' said Mandy. 'It's not that it has no meaning at all, parts of it mean something. But it's not real Spanish.' She took out a pen and began to mark the piece of paper. 'If we take out this *r* then the first phrase is fine, *yo te quiero*, "I love you", very straightforward. As for *finito* – we're verging towards Italian here, but I think it's like "I love you, and finished", you know, "it's finished, it's over". And this second line is just strange, because there's no such verb. *Querda*, I don't know.'

Jean-Michel looked over her shoulder. 'Are you sure about the *r* there?'

'That's how it was on the lyric sheet,' said Daniel.

'*Cuerda* means rope, okay?' said Mandy. 'Which gives us "I

you rope",' and I think we can rule that out as an intended meaning. Now, it would make a kind of sense without the *r*, but not much sense. At least it would be a real verb, *quedar*, to remain, to stay behind, but it shouldn't be transitive. I stay you behind? I remain you? Maybe he's trying to say "I'm leaving you" and he got it backwards, but it's kind of weird. Plus it would have to be *quedo* to agree with *yo*.'

'Could it be *recordo*? I remember you?'

'He's moved on to remembering kind of instantly, if so. "Spanish bombs, I love you and finished, I stays you behind, oh my sweetheart."'

'You're going to have to consult Joe Strummer about this one,' said Lili.

'What if he actually sang *infinito*?' suggested Marie. 'That could change the whole sense of *querda*, then.'

'Joe Strummer is infinite? I think not.'

'I'm assuming he meant it adverbially. I mean, it's still wrong, but it's at least slightly less wrong.'

'Where was he from again?' asked Louisa. 'Because the regional accent could be a factor here.'

'London, isn't he? Estuary?'

'The basic message seems to be, it's all over, honey.'

'Love ya, but.'

'Is he leaving her to go off and fight a war? I hate that.'

'It is not so explicitly narrative,' said Ivo from his corner of the table. 'More imagistic. About Spanish civil war and modern political violence and loss of love.'

'Fredrico Lorca is dead and gone,' said Daniel.

'Precisely.'

'Ivo's our music guy,' said Lili.

'My wife more than myself, really. She made rock videos in Sarajevo. Now she has mostly to film television commercials.'

'*Yo te querda*,' said Lili thoughtfully. 'I rather like it. It's a private language of some kind, I'd like to think, an idiolect. Leaving and staying behind at the same time. Want, leave, stay, remember, all at once.'

'First and third person at the same time?'

'Sure. That's the entire nature of relationships.'

He looked in her direction but she avoided his eyes. He wanted to tell her about Nina and Sicko, he wanted to tell her about Irina Marković, about the turtles in Prins Hendrikplein. And probably the only way he would be able to tell her about any of these things would be to go back to his hotel room and call her on the phone.

In a council flat in Lambeth, as the sun went down, Paja stood over his baby's crib, singing in a soft whisper. He wasn't sure the boy was breathing properly. Could you inherit asthma? And what did asthma look like in a little baby, could he just stop breathing, would anyone even notice? He leaned over the bars and poked Marko gently with his finger until the boy woke up and cried, and that was better, he was clearly alive now, Paja could pick him up and hold him, warm, heavy. Something terrible was coming, they would have to run, they would have to be prepared to hide, to climb over rocks, he would hold his baby tight against his body but if the baby wasn't healthy it would all be worse. He knew that Annie took the baby to the clinic, and they told her he was fine, but you couldn't trust too many people. They'd tell you all kinds of things, and then turn around and cut your head off.

She tried hard, Annie, she really did, and he knew how much he owed her, more than he could ever repay. It was unbelievable almost, that the red-haired girl who had hitch-hiked through his town the summer before the war, who had sent him cards and letters until the post stopped, would still have been there when he had scratched his way finally out of the war to London; something he had imagined without ever daring to hope it would really happen. He owed her everything, he knew that, but she didn't understand what it was like to crawl across the mountains covered with blood, with other people's blood. She didn't know how easily children were lost. How important it was for their father to protect them.

And in Montenegro, as darkness fell, people were seeing flying saucers. Hundreds of people reported loud noises, huge illuminated objects, twenty or more, hovering over their heads. The objects dipped and turned, changed their shape, and flew far up into the sky and out of sight. Witnesses insisted there were no discos or hi-tech facilities in the area which could create these phenomena. The aliens were among us again, scattering genetic material, scattering hope and confusion between the wars.

Daniel drank Scotch because that was what war correspondents drank in books; he'd known that for years. He also knew that he was drinking too fast, and that the only thing he'd eaten since breakfast had been some chips with mayonnaise.

A series of conversations was clattering around him, in languages he had given up on following a while ago. He tried to take some comfort in the fact that Lili was speaking English, presumably for his benefit, but they were on opposite sides of the table, and though she looked towards him sometimes, she wasn't really talking to him, mostly exchanging professional anecdotes with Mandy and Louisa.

'No, because I am not conscientious objector as such, but selective objector,' Ivo was saying, yes, he'd asked Ivo a question, hadn't he, 'so our chances of asylum were materially reduced. That is the great thing really about this job, legal residency. And lucky for me, war crimes in my country are growth industry.'

Lili stood up and walked to the bar. He watched her, he saw no reason to pretend he wasn't watching her, her slender hips, the way that her dress moved softly across her back. He wanted her so much. He should never have come here. Ivo was talking, but in a way that suggested he knew Daniel wasn't listening, that he was really musing to himself about how he would usually be in Amsterdam with Milenka at the weekend, but she was travelling on a shoot. A butter commercial. She was out somewhere in the green fields of Germany, putting Dutch-girl plaited wigs onto cows.

Lili came back to the table with a small glass of beer and a fried egg on toast, pulled a chair over next to him and sat down, putting the plate in front of him. 'You should eat something,' she said.

'I'm not hungry.'

'Still you should eat. Come on.'

He took a bite of the egg. She was sitting close to him; when she leaned towards him their heads were nearly touching. 'Are you okay?' she asked softly, the coloured lights of the bar in her solemn lovely eyes.

'Oh sure, I'm great.' He swirled the Scotch in his glass and drank, then ate another bite of egg. He thought about Nina and Sicko, underground in Budapest, destitute, illegal, chained to each other for ever by forces greater than love or hate or law. 'I need to tell you about my friend,' he said, pushing the plate away. 'The one who wanted to know about the Clash lyrics.'

'So tell me.' She was so close to him that her hair was almost brushing against his face, the familiar smell of perfume and nicotine, and if she was trying to avoid anyone noticing them she wasn't doing a very good job.

'No. No, not here.' He reached out and touched her hand. 'Come outside. Walk with me, please.'

She hesitated, and he put his fingers against her hair, and he knew that most of the people at the table were indifferent, caught up in their own conversations, but Ivo, objective, married Ivo, was seeing everything.

'Okay,' she whispered.

The air was gentle and cool, out in the street, and they walked beside the narrow houses of Soematrastraat, not touching. He didn't ask where they were going.

'I know a million things have happened that are worse, much worse. I just . . . something about them, I can't stop thinking about it. I wrote a piece, I thought it might help with their application for asylum, but AFP spiked it.'

'You could try somewhere else.'

'Yeah, I don't know, I've been calling around, but no one really thinks it's much of a story. I mean it's not, in news terms it isn't, it's this one little guy in a little town who got roughed up a bit, who the fuck cares?'

'Roses in Murano glass vases are sinking,' said Lili. He raised his eyebrows.

'It's from a poem,' she said. 'About Bosnia. I guess it's like your Clash song in a way. Small beautiful things that are lost.'

He thought that if he were just slightly more drunk he would tell her that he loved her, that he needed her, that he would give up his job for her, but the last part wasn't true, and without that the rest of it was useless.

They stood for a minute at the corner, looking at each other, then Lili looked away, reaching into the pocket of her raincoat for a cigarette, the orange flame of her lighter attenuated by a soft gust of wind. 'Let's go this way,' she said, and led him onto a path by the canal.

He didn't know how long they walked, lights reflecting in

the dark green water. He watched the small cloud of smoke that spiralled out from her mouth.

Slowly, a red and grey brick wall rose up along the left-hand side of the path, shielding them from the street, muffling the noises of the traffic. The bank of the canal was overgrown, tangled with weeds and grass. He looked up, seeing something lit by floodlights. The elaborate metal waves of the Madurodam entrance rose above the wall, not far in front of them.

'Would you look at that. No matter where I go, the miniature town comes after me.'

Lili tossed her cigarette butt into the canal and scuffed one foot against the bank.

'My father killed himself, you know,' she said.

He moved close to her, as she reached for another cigarette and cupped her hand around the flame of her lighter.

'I don't know why I'm telling you that. I don't often tell people. Somehow that dumb miniature town always reminds me. Hard to say why.' She inhaled, blew out smoke, looking across the water. 'He jumped in front of a train at Drancy. Where the concentration camp was. I guess that's the connection.'

'When did it happen?'

'1975. I was sixteen years old. Of course Drancy wasn't a concentration camp as such. Technically it was a transit camp. People didn't so much die there as they got sent on to Auschwitz to die. So the Vichy government could say it wasn't their fault.' She shrugged, her face faintly outlined in the darkness by the lights on the opposite bank. 'For years I tried to figure out why he chose Drancy. He was a Partisan in the war, he was practically just a boy then, so I thought, maybe it was some kind of post-traumatic thing, or maybe it was a statement about the revival of fascism in Europe. I guess what

I wanted to think at the time was that he'd finally seen the connection between the camps and the gulags and actually felt bad about it. But now I don't think it was any of that. Probably Drancy was just coincidental.'

'I'm so sorry,' he said, his voice sounding weak and stupid to himself.

'It was a while ago, wasn't it? Things happen. I guess he didn't die instantly. But pretty fast. That's what the doctor told me. He was dead quite a while before I got to the hospital.' She turned around, looking straight at him. 'You can't fix these things, Daniel,' she said, suddenly fierce. 'You can't fix any of this. Look.' She bent down, picked up a handful of dirt. 'You know what this is? Bones, Daniel. Bones. You don't understand that in North America. You think you can start all over, you think history doesn't have any power over you. You don't know what it means to walk on bones.'

'That isn't true,' said Daniel. He jammed his hands into his jacket pockets, and he was angry now too. 'Don't pretend you're so much wiser than me. I'd tell you to ask the Beothuk about bones, but you can't, because we killed them all.' He kicked at the dirt of the canal bank. 'I'm not trying to fix anything. And I don't believe that I'm outside of history just because I was born in Owen Sound. You want to talk about bones? Jesus Christ, Lili, you know where I've been. I'm part of all this. Ask me about bones.'

She stood absolutely still on the path for a long time. 'Oh, fucking hell,' she said at last, threw her cigarette to the ground and crushed it with her foot. And then she kissed him, so that he staggered back against the wall, the world tilting around him, and her skin was warm, he folded his arms around her and they were a tangle of heat, her skin, the inside of her mouth, warm like sunlight or blood, her hands in his hair, and later in a dark room he moved his mouth across her body, kissing her ankle, the back of her knee, the inside of her wrist, and at some point he grabbed her hips and pulled her hard against him, deep inside her, her skin hot and slick, and she bit his shoulder, a wild sound in her throat, and the pain was exquisite and essential.

He didn't think that he had fallen asleep, but suddenly the room was filled with light and Lili was no longer there. He listened for few minutes to the small sounds of birds outside, and then he heard her, moving quietly, in an adjoining room. Blue quilt, white walls; he couldn't see much more than that, and he sat up and began to search for his glasses.

Lili appeared, a pale shape in the doorway, and she walked towards the bed and picked them up from the floor, fitting them gently onto his face, so that she sprang into focus, in a white dressing-gown, her blonde hair tangled.

'I don't know,' she said, kneeling beside the bed. 'I don't know what the hell we're going to do now.'

Part Two

LAW

XI

Aurora Borealis

6–8 November 1999

'Have you ever seen the human fish?' he asked her.

She was in the kitchenette of her flat, making hot chocolate. He'd just come inside and he was sitting on the sofa, shivering in his leather jacket – he didn't seem to own a proper coat, and she wondered how he managed in the hard Bosnian winters.

'Not really. Not exactly,' she said.

She'd stopped counting the number of times he had turned up, calling her from a service station on the A12, or just waiting in the bar downstairs until she got home from work. As if there was a tacit agreement between them that he would not tell her in advance, that he would not give her the opportunity to refuse.

'Tell me about it,' he said, his blue eyes intense, slightly magnified by his glasses. Certain things in the world were inexplicably important to him. She gave him the mug of hot chocolate, and he held it high up against his chest, closing his eyes and letting the slight curl of steam run over his face. 'I know I shouldn't have come.'

This was part of the ritual; there was no need for her to respond. She sat down beside him and looked at the cup in her own hands, its shiny orange glaze.

'It was the summer after my father died,' she began. Her uncle in Rovinj had invited them for the summer; he was her father's brother, he felt responsible for the family, Lili and Sasha and their mother Vjosa, without an adult man now.

Sasha was still just small, very interested in American comics, particularly *Batman*, and the trip to the caves had probably been for his benefit mostly.

They drove up to Slovenia, three adults, three children, and two teenagers, all crammed into a station wagon, Lili sitting by the window with her book, trying to pretend she was alone.

Anyone else would have asked her about grief. Would have been stricken by the image of that moody skinny girl reading poetry in the car, tapping her cigarette ash out of the window, surrounded by cousins, her little brother saying, 'My papa died, you know,' at half-hour intervals. Daniel wanted only, and quite genuinely it seemed, to hear about the human fish, as if he trusted all necessary truth to emerge from that.

'We didn't go to the Postojna caves, too many tourists. We drove up to the Planina Lake area. It's part of the same cave system, but not so well known. They're water caves at Planina, you have to go in with torches, I mean flashlights, and big black boots. It's very dark. Further on you have to get in rubber rafts. The torchlights reflecting on the water, all broken up, so you see the people lit up only in fragments, half of somebody's face, an arm.' He shifted his mug into one hand and began to run the fingers of his other hand through her hair, bending towards her to kiss her just behind one ear.

'The sounds – it's all water sounds, water dripping down the cave walls, the lakes breaking on the rocks, quite softly,' she went on. 'Though the truth is, we were with these noisy kids, so I only heard the proper sounds of the cave here and there. An echo, a bit of an echo. The human fish really lives in the wet caves. That's their real place, moving around in the pools. Breathing air and water. But they hide from people, of course. They don't like something about us. I don't know if they can hear, so maybe it's vibrations more than noise.' She leaned against him, wrapping her legs around his, the smell of the night air still on his skin. 'They die if they have to be near us,' she said. 'But there's a lot of caves that no one can get into. They just go back into those caves, then they're all right.' He was holding her, sliding his hands under her blouse. 'You said you kind of saw it, though,' he whispered.

'Perhaps in a way. I would hear, when we were going along the water, these sounds that I didn't have a source for. Not the sound of the rafts, or the dripping water, or the water on the rocks. Small sounds a bit like a pebble falling. I had this idea what it was, so I was looking around for the source. And sometimes I would see small circles in the water, silver because the torchlight would pick them out, a distance away. It could have been anything, of course. And chances are that I invented it all. But I always believed. I just decided to believe that it was the human fish, swimming towards safety.'

'I can't even tell you how much I love you,' he said.

She pushed his jacket off his shoulders and started to unbutton his shirt, kissing the hollow at the base of his throat. There was no way he should be here. She wasn't even supposed to talk to journalists, for God's sake. But that wasn't the most serious problem, the most serious problem was that he understood everything she said, that there was no one else who understood things the way he did, and the temptation was almost more than she could bear.

He had court accreditation from AFP now, another laminated card to wear around his neck and a limited set of privileges; he could take a mobile phone and laptop as far as the lobby, and attend the press briefings if he happened to be in town.

He tried not to report on the courtrooms where she was working, tried to go to the building when she was off shift as far as possible.

Daniel didn't rate his success as a truth-teller very highly.

Being a stringer for a wire service was like that; you could send them as much of the truth as it was possible to tell, but by the time it got through the editors and went out on the wire it could be something quite different, something *objective* and *balanced* and fundamentally dishonest. There were some features he'd written for the papers that he thought better of, but how far did that go, after all – about as far as the next recycling collection, most of the time.

Still, what he did, what he had always done, was to try to tell the truth. He was surprised, then, to find out how easy it was to lie when he wanted to.

It was many years since he'd studied philosophy, but he retained fragments here and there, including a long argument over Plato's proposition that no one willingly does wrong, that all evil is a misdirected attempt at good. He'd liked this idea when he was a teenager. It sounded reassuring in theory, but Plato, he had to assume, lived in a world populated entirely by pure ideologues and the clinically insane, a world that would be even more terrifying than the confused and human evil of the gunners above Sarajevo – no one but Karadžić and Tudjman pursuing their visions of good to the end of the earth.

He didn't mistake his actions for goodness, going to Lili when he knew that she was pressing at the edges of her code, that she believed herself to be doing wrong, conscious and deliberate wrong. He loved her and he was hurting her, and he knew all this. It would be better not to come back, but of course he would come back, he would come back for as long as she would let him. Aristotle at least allowed for moral weakness, even if he had bizarre theories about women's teeth.

The taste of her skin, the sound of her voice against his ear.

Sometimes she woke in the night and heard him crying, in the choked way that men cry, as if they had a bad cough, and when she touched him he jerked upright, pushing her arm fiercely away. He never remembered this in the morning.

One morning when her alarm went off, she found him sitting in the living room, huddled over on the sofa, his face in his hands. 'It's nothing,' he said. 'Not anything important. Forget about it.'

She had lived under confidentiality for her whole working life. It was fundamental, almost a reflex. When she really needed to talk about something and could not, she wrote in a journal, which she then burned, regularly, on 1 January every year.

There were exceptional restrictions at the tribunal. That was understood, it was part of the job – there were precautions layered on top of the conference interpreter's normal precautions; a requirement not to talk about pending cases at all, not to mention the names of her colleagues in the languages section.

But even so, it shouldn't be so difficult. It hadn't been like this with her other lovers – and some of them, yes, she had genuinely loved. There had never been this need to say things, like a pressure against her chest, a constant withholding that she was always on the verge of breaking. There was something wrong with this, it wasn't appropriate or healthy.

It wasn't just that she wanted to tell him when her day had been shattering, when she had spoken for a protected witness who had been tortured in the camps; everyone felt like that sometimes, and it was a comfort you learned to live without. It was something more than that, it was how badly she wanted to tell him about little things, insignificant things. He understood the importance of the way a bird flew up from the ground. She wanted to tell him about small issues with words, or the quality of a defendant's voice. This was all wrong, it was intolerable. Of course if she did he would be careful, he would never deliberately use the information. But he was a journalist, and in his world information existed only to be shared. He wouldn't realize he was doing it, but facts would find their ways out, tiny ways, and there would be no controlling them, no limiting the damage that they might, without anyone's intention, finally do.

He was sometimes alone in her flat, when she went shopping, or some days when she was at work. This was probably another violation; he might have looked through her papers, read her journal.

There were measures she could have taken. She could have locked the drawers of her desk, she could have started to write her journal in German instead of its current mixture of Serbo-Croat and French. She made a conscious decision not to do these things.

In which way will you choose to betray people? You will always betray them one way or another. Which way will you choose?

He brought pastries from Bosnia wrapped in soggy wax paper, baklava and kadaif. They ate omelettes and crunchy syrupy sweets, and every time he touched her she felt like she was going to break apart. The taste of his mouth, pistachio and honey, his fingers sliding inside her.

And words didn't go away, for certain people words never went away, though they might fragment, falling from sentences into an open depth, pounding in the ears like the rush of her own pulse, skin trembling, and not only the obvious words, *oui*, *ne*, *c'est ça*, but words that had no contextual meaning, the ones that shaped the tongue in a certain way, sounds that vibrated with the nerves at the top of her skull, and all tangled up with Maureen Tucker's little childlike voice on the tape deck saying close the door, I wish, I wish, ah, *impossible*, ah, *clair*, ah, *clair*.

She knew things that he would never know, that he longed to know. When he touched her he was close to her knowledge and impossibly far from it, a shimmer of contradiction over her skin.

When she came home, he didn't ask her how things had gone at work. When he saw her at her desk with a stack of papers, he didn't ask her what she was doing. He tried not to think about how she spent her days, tried to forget that when the courts went into closed session and the audio feed cut off, the interpreters were still hearing every word.

She stood in the park in the November wind, smoking and watching the waves on the tiny lake, as red and pink streaks of light stretched out behind a mass of clouds, sunlight spreading like oil over the choppy water.

She thought about it now and then, a future of some kind with Daniel. It wasn't a realistic prospect, but she couldn't help thinking about it. She didn't imagine it in any concrete or specific ways; it was just that it would be nice for both of them to have a fixed point to come back to. She wanted to picture Daniel working on his laptop in her flat on Gay-Lussac, while she read a book or made notes on a document. Something that simple. Distant and tiny, like a scene watched through the wrong end of a telescope.

She had anticipated for some years now that she would always live alone, and she was not greatly troubled by the prospect. But she wished that she could think of Daniel as if this would last a while.

As Daniel drove towards a red sunrise, he had a fleeting memory of the day he saw the Northern Lights. It was an anomaly, of course, something strange enough to get into the newspapers, an electromagnetic storm driving the aurora down the south shore of Georgian Bay. He was lucky, he happened to look out of the window at the right time; and for some reason he ran outside and got on his bicycle, riding up and down the dark winter streets and seeing that amazing thing above the houses and stores, sheets of deep red and green pouring down over the sky. They even saw it in the United States, and in some places alarms went off and people ran for their fallout shelters, thinking that nuclear war had come at last. It was the seventies, after all, so any strangeness in the sky had to be nuclear war.

Daniel knew enough about the Northern Lights to recognize what they were, though his teachers had carefully explained, in history and geography classes, that Canada lay on all the important flight paths, and that if the US and the Soviet Union started firing at each other it would be Canada stuck in the middle, exactly where the anti-missile missiles would shoot the nuclear devices down. But an attack wouldn't look like this, like candy syrup running across the night.

He rode around the city, out to the highway and back, the lights fading slowly, and for a few days his determination to move far away from Owen Sound took the shape of a plan to go and live in the north, where he could see the aurora borealis and live among polar bears and oil pipelines and the tiny flowers of the brief arctic summer. He should tell Lili about this, his short-lived ambition to do vague and frontier-like things up on the tundra; she would enjoy that image.

He drove on into the afternoon, through the diminishing autumn day, and stopped at a service station in Germany to plug his laptop in beside the coffee urns and type up a few pages of notes. Somewhere in Austria he rang the office, and promised to file two stories later that night.

It was dark again by the time he arrived in Ljubljana. He parked his car near an army barracks that had been converted into an artists' squat – he'd written a piece about them last year – and under the circle of brightness from a streetlight he saw a wall where someone had painted, *Give them just what they need, water and poetry*. Reaching into his bag for a notebook, he scribbled the line down, imagining a cupped hand filled with clean water, a treasure.

He checked into a cheap hotel, bought a kebab and a bottle of Slovenian beer and carried them up to his room, setting up his laptop and flipping the pages of his notebook. He tried to ring Lili, but she wasn't home, so he made a few directory enquiry calls, and then tried a number in Belgrade.

'*Molim*,' said a young woman's voice.

'Good evening,' he said, in his most polite Bosnian. 'Is this Stana Marković?'

'Who is calling, please?' asked the woman in English, an edge in her voice.

'My name is Daniel Bryant. I'm a journalist, and I'd like to talk to you about your father. I understand this might be difficult for you,' he was speaking as quickly as possible, knowing that the longer he kept her on the phone the less likely she would be to hang up, 'but I really want to hear the more personal side of his story, not only the politics, but the human aspects, the things that only his family can tell me.'

'You spoke to my mother?'

'Yes, that was me.'

'We did not like that article at all. It was full of lies.'

'Okay, then maybe you can clear things up for me.'

'There's no point talking to you if you are only going to print lies.'

'Then tell me what you think I should be saying.'

'Look, I know how you guys operate. You sound all sympathetic now, but anything I say you will twist around and make us to look like criminals. It's not just the Serbs who were doing bad things, you know.'

'But you do admit that some Serbs did bad things?'

'Some in every group. It was a war.'

'Do you think your father did bad things?'

He heard a hiss of breath through the phone and thought, now she's going to hang up, but she didn't. 'No,' she snapped. 'My father is a good man. You don't know, you don't even know him. These things they say about him, he is not capable of things like that. I know this, Mr Bryant. He is my father. I *know*.' She spoke angrily, but without hesitation, without a tremor.

'Were you with him during the war?'

'Part of the time. I went to Belgrade more at the end. I would have stayed with him and Mum but they insisted that I go, for my safety. I would have stayed with them to the end of the world. You don't know, Mr Bryant. You don't know about families. We love each other. We know each other.'

'So you saw nothing? Nothing that would make you wonder? Question what he was doing?'

There was a pause, and a small sound that twisted Daniel's heart automatically, even before he consciously recognized it, the click of a lighter. 'Let me tell you a story,' said Stana Marković. 'When we came back to Yugoslavia from Ohio I was fourteen years old. I spoke with an American accent, and of course I did not know anyone in my class. So I was bullied. Called names and so on. Cliques of girls would make circles around me in the schoolyard and laugh at me. One day my father came to pick me from school and he saw this. And he walked right over and said, "If you want to give trouble to my daughter, you go through me first. Because she is my child, and I can tell you she is worth a hundred of you. If you would laugh at someone for the way they talk, you make yourself worthless."' He heard a catch in her throat. 'Of course the other children were even worse to me after that. But I mean to say . . . a man like this . . . and the things they accuse him of . . .'

'You don't believe he could do these things.' This was sentimental, ridiculous; he could hear Marković clearly in his daughter's voice, that same complete abandonment to half-fictional emotions, to edifying stories that always saved the teller. But there was something touching in it, even so.

'Of course not. Of course not.'

'What if he is convicted?'

'At that court? It means nothing to me.'

'Okay. But what if there was something? What if there was evidence, evidence you really believed, that he had done even part of what he's accused of? Could anything convince you, ever?'

She inhaled softly, and spoke, calm now. 'To love your father is like breathing, Mr Bryant. Even you must know that. No, there is no evidence that could convince me. I know him, as a person, as a father. No evidence is stronger than that.'

Three walnuts therefore, and a bowl and the guest
who is gone, whose basic absence
fills the hollow in the chair as if it were a soul.

Daniel reached Lili late in the evening, and she sat up for a while after that, longer than she probably should have, reading a poet from Sarajevo.

In his cell in Scheveningen, Nikola Marković sang himself to sleep, trying to keep certain images out of his mind with songs about love and loss and rain on American windows. He thought of the times he had sat up late at night in Iowa, watching the musicals on television, the innocence of it all. That girl and her hand puppet – who was the actress again? – he couldn't recall her name. He remembered her as a blonde dressed in a sky-blue skirt, with big wide eyes, but he had no confidence that this was precisely true.

He'd already handed in his notice to the university and bought their tickets back to Yugoslavia, the night he saw that movie. He might have been packing to go home. And he had thought, this is the last I will see of America, this weird little story. The girl and the puppet lamented the sadness of love, and he knew that it was true in a way that the Americans themselves would never understand; that he wasn't going home because he would be happy there, but because he had to, and that was a kind of love too, wasn't it? A certain kind of love.

Before the sun rose in London, Father Jamie stood on the concrete walkway outside the door of his flat, watching his congregation. Families were coming outside, women shoving children into jackets, giving them bags of books and lunches; some shiftworkers were just arriving home, turning to doorways soft with light. On one of the tall bare walls, someone had sprayed the message, *WE HURT YOUR MUM BEHIND YOUR BACK.*

They were here, the multitude, and he could hear their many languages around him, and he was among them too, the Lambeth crowd. He had to hope, he had to trust, even on the days when it wasn't easy. For Jamie wanted all his people – and they were his people, whether they knew it or not, the mothers and babies, the men walking their dogs – he wanted them to be chosen, to survive the coming judgement, to be among the hundred and forty-four thousand, the ones who would be saved for the best new lives.

He lifted his hand against the branches of the distant trees and spoke, the words of morning prayer, and for a moment he was calm, in that impersonal contentment of ritual, the power of certain things he could still do.

It was all up to him, to believe, to explain it, to help them see. To see that a special planet was prepared for them, these little ones, if only he could make them understand.

And he cried with a loud voice to the four angels, to whom it was given to hurt the earth, and the sea, saying, Hurt not the earth, neither the sea, nor the trees, till we have sealed the servants of our God in their foreheads.

Things are getting worse, said Annie, as Paja pulled on his jacket and went out in the grey maze of the city. I'm worried about you, you're drinking too much, and why do you keep talking to that lunatic in the park, she said. I don't want to hear any more about apocalypse, why don't you go to a doctor? Okay, said Paja, this is good thought, go to a doctor to cure the war, this makes very good sense. And he didn't want to be angry with her but he couldn't help it, thinking that this was all of him she really knew, this scarecrow man, that she must barely remember who he was when she met him back home, when he had a motorbike and two other girlfriends and steady work rewiring houses.

Why don't you go to church, she said, or a mosque or whatever you go to. Oh yes, he said, another excellent thinking. Because is very good here. Very helpful, for certain.

He wasn't even sure what religion the man in park belonged to. Something British, sort of Christian he supposed, nothing he recognized. But that really didn't matter. What mattered was that he knew about the end of the world. He knew what it looked like, the death, the burning. He knew it might start in one small country, but it would come to everyone soon.

When the war came to his town he couldn't fight, they couldn't make him a soldier because of the asthma, so his job was to find the bodies, to go out when the shooting stopped and bring them back to be buried. Fishing the bodies out of the river, women, children, the flesh falling off them. The sweet thick smell. Scrabbling up into the hills after dark and dragging them back, bloody, draped over his body.

He wheeled Marko's pushchair down Brixton Road and the dead people followed him, their feet making soft sucking noises against the pavement, it was awful, he wanted to warn everyone around him, so they could run away before it was too late. It was unfair, their not staying buried, a dirty trick. But he knew what these sneaky corpses had to tell him. He did understand.

Bad things had come with him to London; he had brought them here. And the one truth Paja knew for certain was that they would find his son. That his son would die.

There was no place in this landscape for God or the friendly spacemen. He himself, he alone, was charged with the attempt to save his child, an attempt which could only fail, over and over until the final failure, but this one charge, in a world of death, he would not lay down.

Dawn came slowly, the light diffusing through a pile of thick clouds, as Daniel crossed the Croatian border, driving through the morning and eating a greasy day-old burek with one hand while the car moved swiftly, straight along the *autocesta*. By afternoon he was in Republika Srpska.

There was no clear point at which he crossed the war's front line, because the front lines in this war had been everywhere, had run between the homes of every town, between brothers in a single family. But it was just before the Bosnian border that he began to see the gutted buildings, the smashed walls and the houses pocked with bullet holes, the remains of the cleansing. Abandoned gardens, overgrown among the wild flowers, where whole communities had gone up in flames.

The poet René Char, married to a Jewish woman, fought with the *maquis* during World War Two. In his journal, he wrote of watching, in a village where he was hidden, the arrival of the SS in search of him, seizing one terrified young man and beating him with rifle butts, demanding to know where Char was hiding. Char wrote that he had calculated that the young man could hold out for about five minutes before he talked. He sat in his hiding place and hoped that the SS would kill the boy more quickly than that.

Then, he wrote, a crowd of women, children and old men appeared, moving slowly and deliberately from every street, streaming over the SS and paralysing them, all the while looking calm, compliant, as if they were simply obeying the soldiers' summons to gather in the square. The SS men, furious and disgusted, stormed away.

I loved my fellow human beings that day, he wrote, loved them beyond sacrifice.

He wrote as well about how he sat crouched in the woods one day, permitting a friend to be executed so that another town could be saved. Knowing that he could save him, that the men around him were silently begging for a signal to open fire, he held back. He chose the community of strangers, to be saved at any cost.

Qu'est-ce qu'un village? Un village pareil a un autre?

In 1962, Char published a poem titled 'The Library is on Fire'. Thirty years later the Sarajevo library was hit by incendiary shells, fired by the soldiers of the poet Karadžić, and thousands of books, Char's possibly among them, burned into ash. The fire engines came right away, but the water supply to the city had been cut off three hours earlier, and while they tried to pump water from the Miljacka river, the hoses were shot full of bullet holes. Under sniper fire, the people of Sarajevo formed a human chain to pass the most precious books from the burning building, as the elegant columns of the reading room blazed and exploded.

Water and poetry. A town like any other.

After another hour of driving, through winter fields and low mountains, Daniel turned onto a side road leading into the city, in a little flurry of snow that seemed very like soap powder, tiny white pellets rattling against his car, and drove slowly around corners, looking for a parking space. He had certain instincts which rarely misled him, and his impulse this time was to leave the car some distance away from the ceremony.

Locking the doors and getting out, he walked through the streets of the old town, a normal post-war city by the standards of Republika Srpska, depressed and impoverished, with an exceptionally high suicide rate, and stubbornly refusing the erasure of the inter-entity border, though it was the one thing that might put the country on the road to being functional. He arrived after a few minutes at a patch of open waste ground which had once been a mosque. He could see buses, some civilian UN personnel in white jackets. A double line of blue-helmeted peacekeepers, small arms in holsters at their waists, holding back a crowd. He spotted Jim standing off to one side, two cameras around his neck, and he waved to him, walking in that direction.

It was not one crowd, he could see as he drew closer, but two, quite distinct from each other – one a small huddle of people, mostly Muslim, mostly old, former residents who had been brought in on the buses. They stood to the side of the square, keeping close together. On the other side were several hundred of the people who lived here now. It was on this side of the square that the peacekeepers stood with their legs braced, their arms joined.

One of the UN civilians had a megaphone, another a large stone. They were not beginning the reconstruction of the mosque in any serious way today; it was winter in any case, there was snow on the ground, no one would really start putting up a building in this weather. This was only the ceremonial stone-laying, and perhaps it was wise to keep it separated in time from the actual rebuilding.

'We're going to get some action today,' said Jim, tipping his head towards the angry side of the crowd.

'Oh, great,' said Daniel sourly, but he started moving towards them; the magnetic pull of 'action', any action, working on him as strongly as on anyone else. A UN police officer unobstrusively fell in beside him, quietly ensuring his passage up to a certain point. 'I'd stop here if I were you, sir,' he muttered finally.

'I'd like to ask them some questions,' said Daniel, pointing to the people who were pushing, now, at the line of peacekeepers, creating an irregular surge back and forth.

'I don't think they're in a mood for talking.'

The clamour of the crowd was drowning out whatever was being said by the man with the megaphone. On the other side of the square, among the frightened group of Muslims, he saw one of the cameramen he remembered from Sarajevo, and a woman reporter he hadn't seen before, interviewing someone. The noise level was rising, the arms of the peacekeepers straining as the crowd pushed again, again, men with red faces, suffused with anger and confusion, forcing themselves forward, people he knew from restaurants and hotels, people he had talked to, and the man with the megaphone tried to raise his own voice and say something else, and at that moment the crowd broke through.

'Jesus Fuck!' he heard the UN police officer shouting, and Daniel was knocked to the ground, rolling quickly into a protective position, his hands on the back of his neck as feet in heavy boots came racing past him, running over him. He couldn't make out distinct words in the screaming. He heard a single gunshot.

Pushing sideways, he broke out of the worst of the

confusion and struggled up onto his hands and knees. Miraculously, he had not yet lost his glasses, and he could see one of the peacekeepers on a concrete block, his pistol raised, firing a second warning shot, uselessly, the crowd oblivious. There were iron bars in the hands of some of the men, and bricks they had seized from the construction site, and guns, yes, he could see guns. Jim was lying on his back near by, propelling himself backwards with his feet and still firing off his cameras. The crowd was heading towards the group of Muslims.

'Get them out of here!' screamed another peacekeeper. 'Get them inside!' He heard the shatter and soft whoosh of an explosion, and twisting his head he saw a car going up in flames. A small knot of local police officers were standing on the corner, chatting casually, as if they were quite unaware of anything out of the ordinary.

'This is Serbia!' a woman was shouting, he turned his head, an elderly woman, furious, waving her fists as she stood on the construction site. 'This is Serbia! We don't need a mosque here! Go away!' Daniel stood up, and saw that the buses were burning now, saw people running, their heads down, into a community centre across the corner, peacekeepers forming a corridor against the crowd. Someone grabbed his arm. 'Come on now, sir,' the man said with a soft Indian accent. 'Let's get you in where it's safe.' And they ran together, chunks of brick sailing past them, across the rough ground. One rock hit the side of Daniel's face, knocking his glasses off, and he felt his feet crunch over them as he ran, through the line of blue helmets, dashing into the building, the door slamming behind them.

They were inside now, an echoing space, maybe a gymnasium. His legs turned suddenly to water, and he sat down on the floor, reaching into an inner pocket of his jacket for a second pair of glasses. Beside him, a civilian UN worker was holding a blood-soaked handkerchief against a gash on his head. Women in flowered headscarves sat weeping in a small huddle. He felt the abrasion on his own temple – it was bleeding a bit, but nothing serious. He had to be bruised over most of his body, though.

Looking up at the window, he saw a man's face pressed against it, hot and distorted, yelling at them about Muhamed's mother being fucked by a horse and the Hague prosecutor being fucked by wild dogs and various other acts of unnatural congress.

'What do you think?' he said, turning to the UN worker. 'Reconciliation not completely achieved yet?'

'Don't be such a smartass,' snapped the other man.

'Sorry.' Black clouds of greasy-looking smoke were billowing past the windows now, an orange light behind them. He could hear rounds of gunfire, but he knew that it was only the triumphant crowd shooting into the air, in the grip of a fury carefully cultivated among them, nurtured for years, a toxic soup of propaganda and frustration and the games of powerful men. 'Definitely Plato's kind of evil,' he muttered.

'Didn't I tell you to shut up?' The UN man stood and walked away, calling for a medic. Some of the journalists were already filing by mobile phone. Daniel located an electrical outlet, plugged in his laptop and started to type.

By the time they were allowed to leave it was almost dark. He walked past the burned wreckage of the buses, the litter of the riot, hats and gloves trampled into the mud, spent bullets. His car, when he located it, was essentially safe, although someone, seeing the British plates, had painted *KLINTON = HITLER* on the passenger door. He decided that, all things considered, it might be a good idea to drive into the next town and sleep there.

XII

Double Helix

12 November 1999

The indictment did not allege that Nikola Marković had spent much time inside the camps. It was enough that he had planned them, set them up, appointed the guards, been informed of what went on. He didn't have any official functions there, unlike the Crisis Group's vice-president, who had been more than pleased to take on the job of supervising operations. Marković mostly only received reports from the guards, former policemen who liked to use nicknames such as Hitler and Psycho, and from his vice-president Miloš, an enormous man who had previously been a real estate agent, carried two ammunition belts strapped around his chest at all times, and favoured a Michael Jackson T-shirt.

He himself was very busy with developing an overall strategy, because there were a lot of villages in the municipality and each of them presented its own challenges. He was busy sorting out the work of the Bureau for Population Removal, because it was better to do these things in good order, not just chase them out any old way – get them to hand over their property first, get their documents, have them pledge that they weren't coming back. If you did it right one time, you wouldn't have to do it again.

He didn't carry a weapon every day, not like some people. Of course he owned guns, and he knew how to use them. And often it was safer to have a pistol inside his jacket. But not every day, and not just for fun. Only when it was necessary for protection.

He had used his guns the night they took over the municipal offices. But there had not been much fighting, and not many people killed. None on their side; they were better prepared and better armed, obviously the ones who should take control.

I am a man who never knew my father, he thought, as he led the meetings of the Crisis Group. I never knew my father, I have achieved manhood on my own, I have no memories to care for. I will create memories from the open space of possibility and care for these. He felt the soft and not unpleasant pain of history in his heart, a poignant throb.

In a society which was largely pre-literate, written words naturally seemed to carry an almost magical power of compulsion.

He tried not to think, as he wrote that sentence, of the blackboards in his office in the municipal building.

It seems that this compulsive quality now adheres to the televised image, though the written word may still have an additional air of sobriety and authority. The status of the spoken word is variable.

He waited at dawn for the windowless court van to arrive. The pile of binders under his bed was growing, and the French lawyer had spoken to him impatiently about reading them. But he was feeling tired lately; even a short walk down the corridor seemed to require an effort. Depression, he could recognize depression.

He edged one binder out with his foot, and pushed the cover gingerly open. The first thing he saw was a photograph from one of the camps. He closed the cover again. Words written on the outside of the binders: Camp A, Crisis Group, Vasić.

Nothing seemed to matter very greatly. He had overheard his lawyers arguing in the corridor outside his cell, and it seemed to him that this was probably not a good sign, but it was less important than sleep.

It was a difficult time. He said this to himself again. A very difficult time. We all have regrets. Yes. Everyone does.

What was it, exactly, that the lawyers had in those binders? More photographs, newspaper stories, testimonies from this person or the other? Things which laid claim to a fixed version of reality. Things which didn't address the tangled knot of his feelings. I never knew my father, he thought again, lying on his bed in the cell. Surely, allowances should be made for that.

It seemed best to Daniel if he didn't get to know anyone here too well. He avoided conversations with the other journalists – not that there were very many of them, most of the time. Like Suzannah, they tended to be in and out, arriving for initial hearings and the beginnings of trials and then leaving for other assignments. They were aware, he supposed, that he came and went on his own unpredictable schedule, sometimes sitting in on the most tedious sessions of legal manoeuvring, keeping to himself, working alone at a table in the lobby instead of using one of the press cubicles.

He was there one morning, typing up a story about a case from the Krajina which would inevitably be spiked by the office, when Ivo came out of the staff area, walking casually, with his long stride, towards the coffee machine. Daniel noticed this because you didn't often see people from the prosecutor's office in the public lobby. It wasn't unprecedented, but it was rare. As Ivo passed the tables, his eyes flicked over Daniel, who was studiously quiet, remembering the other man in the bar, and his own vague explanation about writing short stories.

Ivo fed a handful of coins into the machine, took his little plastic cup of coffee, and came over to the table where Daniel was sitting.

'So. Mr Daniel Bryant, AFP,' he said, glancing at Daniel's press card. 'We meet again. Do people call you Danny?'

'No,' said Daniel.

'All right.' He sat down across the table, and Daniel glanced at him warily, not moving his hands from his keyboard. Ivo smiled and raised his eyebrows, sipping from the plastic cup.

'Well, Mr Daniel Bryant, you like The Hague?'

'Not especially, but it does happen to be where the court is.'

'True.' He took another sip of coffee. 'Do you know Lilja lives in the dope-smoking neighbourhood?'

His initial confusion was genuine; it took him a moment to realize that Lilja was Lili. 'Excuse me? Why should I know this?'

'No reason, of course. Now, she would tell you she lives on north-east perimeter of dope-smoking neighbourhood, not directly in, but I have my suspicions.'

'Do you really.' He stared at his screen as if he had pressing work to do. 'I don't know what this has to do with me.'

'Nothing at all. I just have theory that Lilja is actually co-ordinating drug ring in her spare time.'

'Well, maybe you should tell her about that.'

Ivo shrugged. 'Lilja is anxious kind of person. I do not want to trouble her. I only mean to say that some things, in my own opinion, are not my problem.'

Daniel raised his head slowly and looked up at the other man, his unkempt dark-blond hair and loose tie. 'Okay,' he said.

'Well, that was all that I had to say.' He finished his coffee and stood up. 'I just think it is interesting theory about the drugs.'

'I guess it is.' Daniel tapped his fingers against the keyboard. 'Ivo?'

'Yes, Mr Daniel Bryant?'

'Thank you.'

'No trouble to me,' nodded Ivo. 'Perhaps I will see you later.'

Lili bent towards her microphone, taking over from Alain, who leaned back and opened a binder of notes. She scanned the room, anticipating who would speak next as Milan Lukitch sat down, adjusting his black robes around him.

Lili knew many people who didn't know her, who had at best an approximate awareness of her as a voice, and Milan Lukitch, who appeared for several defendants, was someone she knew surprisingly well. Of course, interpreters always paid particular notice to anyone who spoke an unusual dialect like Quebecois; but Lukitch presented other complications, insisting at least half the time on using Serbo-Croat, in which he was not completely fluent. There was more than a little irony in the fact that Lili and Alain were, in today's session, interpreting his words into French.

They heard other things too, the interpreters. With Lukitch, they could hear the undercurrent of tension, of rigid determination, as he spoke his parents' language with a foreign accent; and Lili was not the only one among them who recognized this. They knew how hard this smart, ambitious young man, who wore wool socks and Birkenstock sandals under his legal robes and whose friends actually called him Mike, was clinging to family stories, to a willed identification with a ghostly history.

The judge cleared her throat, while McKinley and Ducasse glared across the room at each other, leaning over their desks. It was only the second pre-trial hearing in the Marković case, but the normal elaborate civility of the courtroom seemed on the verge of breaking down. The judge, in response, had adopted an air of almost febrile joviality.

'. . . and my goodness, when I saw an English transcript today, I had turned suddenly into Judge Ablu, so we won't be making any assumptions about the perfect accuracy of the transcript, if I may say.'

'Your Honour,' said Ducasse, rising to his feet, softly exasperated, 'leaving aside the issue of the transcript, I have to say that the prosecution is continuing to imply that we are trying to obstruct this trial, and the defence absolutely does not accept these implications. If I were that way inclined, I might have said that it was rather the other way around.'

McKinley rose, and the voice that Ducasse received through his earphones was Lili's, following the lawyer's controlled anger. 'Your Honour, I must make it clear that I absolutely respect the right of the defence to do whatever they can to defend their client as effectively as possible. That said, however,' and Ducasse began to rise again, 'that said, there are questions that simply must be asked and answered.'

'Okay, okay, now.' The judge gestured towards both sides of the room. 'Everybody will be calm while I read you my decision – reminding you again that we must have respect and courtesy between you in this courtroom, and I would urge you to try to work out your differences before you come back in front of me again the next time. Because when we are all day talking like this it is, you know, the money of the global taxpayer we are spending.' Both Ducasse and McKinley began to rise again, but she waved them back down. 'Now. The prosecution has put before me a motion for an order directed to the defence counsel, that they should respond in clear terms to the question of whether they have been interviewing certain refugee individuals in Amsterdam, specifically in order to uncover the identity of a protected witness.'

Ducasse picked up a pen and began to scribble fiercely on a piece of scrap paper, which he slid across the table towards Milan Lukitch. Lukitch glanced down at it, shrugged lightly, and pushed it away with one hand, then leaned over and whispered something to Ducasse. The older lawyer shook his head almost imperceptibly.

'Now, Ms McKinley, I will have to deny this motion. I can give you my written decision in due course, but in summary we have to accept the principle that, even in the event that a member of the defence team might be alleged to do this thing, and therefore perhaps incur a charge of contempt, he or she would be entitled to the same presumption of innocence as anyone charged before the court; and the question you have asked would seem to demand self-incrimination, against which of course any defendant would be protected. So I don't allow this.'

'Thank you, Your Honour,' said McKinley stiffly, bowing slightly.

'At the same time, I would take this opportunity to note that, if the defence were to pursue such a course of action, well, this would be a very risky strategy indeed. And I hope we're all aware that if there were to be more evidence of this, it would be, you know, potentially something with extremely serious consequences.'

Ducasse slid the paper in front of Lukitch again. He folded his hands over it without looking down. Ducasse frowned, and then rose to speak.

'Thank you, Your Honour. I welcome your decision on this motion, of course, and I welcome also your additional comments. I do have to say, in this connection, that while this course of action would, of course, not be one that I would ever contemplate pursuing, Your Honour should know that the defence team is feeling some intense frustration around the question of the witness protection measures, and the wholesale manner in which they are being employed by the prosecution. And this is not even to broach the question of the documents in the hands of Mr Vasić.'

Marković sat in the dock, looking as if he was nearly asleep, massaging his forehead now and then.

'We've made clear our position on Mr Vasić's documents.' McKinley rose, her black robe swirling around her legs. 'Mr Vasić maintains, and we agree with him in this, that his files are covered by lawyer–client privilege, and we submit that they cannot be given to the defence on these grounds.'

The judge turned off her microphone and conferred quickly with her colleagues sitting on either side of her. Ducasse jumped to his feet again, but the judge waved him down.

'Okay, Mr Ducasse, you can sit, because I'm upholding your position again. If Mr Vasić plans to discuss these documents in court in any way, they must be filed with the court. This is elementary, Ms McKinley, I don't see how there can be any question about this. If there are individuals who may be at risk, the prosecution can apply to me on a case-by-case basis. All right? Are we all happy? Because if we are not, well, you must find your own ways to deal with it.'

'Your Honour—'

'No, Ms McKinley, I have made my decisions. Now, we have been sitting for two hours, with the great indulgence of the interpreters, and there is another trial scheduled to move into this room for the afternoon, so I say that we all go to lunch, do some deep breaths, eat a good sandwich, and close this conference. If you want to file some more motions, you can easily find me, as I know all too well by now.'

Lili paused at her desk to exchange a file, then turned the

corner into the hallway. McKinley was throwing papers in her office. On the marble stairway, Lukitch was leaning against the wall, arms folded, refusing to make eye contact with Ducasse. 'Fine, fine, I have nothing more to say,' Lili heard Ducasse snap as she walked past. 'I want you to bear it in mind, that's all.'

At the back entrance, Nikola Marković was led into the windowless van, shivering in the damp November chill. Mr Vasić's documents, he thought. It looked like Dejan had become quite a star with the prosecutors. Probably he should read that material. Sometime when he wasn't so tired.

A hot day in late August, in 1992; he remembered the vertical white burn of the sun against the pavement outside Vasić's little office. He had been alone inside, flipping through a stack of books, writing notes in the margins.

'Well, well. Here you are, Nikola,' he said bitterly, glancing up. 'What have I done to deserve the honour of personal surveillance by our so-called civic leader?'

'Don't be dramatic. I'm paying you a visit, it's not surveillance.'

'I'm not an idiot. You turn up in court when I'm there, you turn up in my office. I'm not afraid of you, if that's what you're hoping to accomplish.'

'You're imagining things, Dejan. I just happened to be walking by.'

'Of course, of course you were just walking by. Well, by all means make yourself at home. You want brandy, cigars, a few more people you can ship off to forced labour?' There were patches of sweat under his arms and along his back, and the collar of his shirt was frayed. 'Want to expropriate some of my property? God knows I can't stop you.'

'Oh, fuck you, then.' Marković leaned against the wall,

where the plaster was flaking away around a bullet hole. 'I thought we were friends, once.'

'Get out of my office, Nikola. Just send your men to watch me from across the road like usual.'

An APC ground down the centre of the street outside, the gunner aiming the muzzle randomly and singing in a thick, slurred voice. When it had passed, a man came out of his shop and poured a bucket of water onto the pavement; it fell in a wide shimmering arc. He had been washing down dust, or washing away blood, it was no longer possible to remember the details exactly.

'Listen, Dejan,' he said, 'you don't need to be so fucking stubborn. Just back off a bit and I can look out for you, right? You need some kind of favour? I can arrange things.'

Vasić looked up at him in a kind of amazement. 'You're genuinely crazy, aren't you?

'Well, Christ, it's nice to see you're so grateful.'

'Okay.' Vasić stood up and started shuffling through the papers on his desk. 'Okay, you want to do me a favour? Tell me this, then. Where is Ibrahim Salihović?'

He could hear the roar of the fighter jets overhead. There was a pulse beating in his head.

'Did you hear me, Nikola? Ibro Salihović, remember him? Tall fellow, member of parliament? I'm asking because usually, you know, people will know where an MP is. People involved in local government, it's the kind of thing they usually know.'

It was a hot day, it was too hot, and he blotted the sweat from his forehead with a handkerchief.

'Here's what I have so far, if you think that might help,' said Vasić fiercely, his mouth curled with anger. 'He was rounded up in a mass arrest in June, you may recall that incident. And this is where the paperwork stops, Nikola. He's not on any Red Cross list of prisoners. His family isn't getting any postcards, if you see my point.' He tossed the papers back onto his desk, into the middle of a chaotic stack of files. 'Of course I just happen to start with Ibro. We could try a few others. Adil Velkić? Muharem Hotić? Ring any bells, Nikola?'

'Oh, just fucking forget it!' shouted Marković. He remembered the sound of the door slamming, then swinging open again behind him. The puddle of water in the street, his feet walking swiftly through it, so that wet footprints followed him, dark at first, but fading soon to pale outlines under the scorch of the swelling sun.

'Was there an occasion in 1992,' asked the prosecutor in Courtroom One, 'when men came to your house demanding money?'

'Yes, there was.' The witness was a man in his late thirties, a farmer, dark-haired and sturdy, in an ill-fitting suit and worn shoes.

'Could you describe it for us?'

'In June, some men arrived at the door, paramilitaries from Serbia. Arkan's men.'

'How could you tell that they were from Serbia?'

'The accent. It's easy to tell. And they had an emblem of the Tigers on their arms.'

'Did you learn the names of any of these men?'

'Not their actual names. The commander told me that his name was Mister Chetnik.'

'Were there any local people with them?'

'Yes. I saw Mr Todorović with them.'

'On what terms did he seem to be with them?'

'He was laughing with them.'

'And other local people?'

'Mr Samir Imamović.'

'And what condition was he in?'

'Very bad condition. He had blood all over him, and bruises. And the one called Mister Chetnik said if we gave him ten thousand Deutschmarks he would let Mr Imamović go.'

'And what did you do?'

'Well, we tried to find the money, but it was impossible, it was a huge amount of money, we put together everything we had and went to the neighbours, but we couldn't come even close. We offered them some jewellery as well, but it just wasn't . . . well, they went away with Mr Imamović, and I don't know what happened to him after that.'

'You didn't see him after that?'

'No. I never saw him again.'

'Was your house damaged?'

'Yes, they broke the television set with a knife, and, I don't know, I guess they broke all the furniture and took the radio and some things. And, you know, I really wanted to know what happened to Mr Imamović. I really wanted to know what happened to him, because I feel very bad that we couldn't find enough money. I really, really feel badly about that.'

'If I could ask you, what was your relationship with Mr Todorović prior to 1992?'

The witness frowned, his hands moving nervously. 'I would have said . . .' He paused, gesturing weakly.

'Go on.'

'I would have said it was a friendly relationship. I mean, I would have said he was my friend. You see, this is something I can't understand. I saw him in the café all the time, we used to talk. We used to bet on sports sometimes. I would have said he was a friend of mine. I wish he could explain to me how these things could happen, because I don't understand it at all.'

* * *

Lili sat at her desk during the break, drinking coffee and thinking about Paris. This was a mental exercise she had developed, trying to picture the precise details of the little grocery on her corner, where they shelved the biscuits, what kind of yogurt they usually had in the cooler, the bottles of juice and wine, the shelves of cat food and baby formula. Her beloved *fromagerie* on rue St-Jacques, the wheels and pyramids of cheeses piled on the wooden shelves, the deep, salty, melting smells.

She imagined walking by the Seine at night, and the sudden blazing illumination of a *bateau-mouche* going by with its kleig lights, the street shocked into white light as if it were noon, and she thought how oddly lovely these moments were, that she was really fond of the tasteless *bateau-mouches* in a way. And the elderly women with their little dogs, trotting up and down the pavements.

After twenty minutes she returned to her booth, to more stories about Mister Chetnik and Mad Dog, about men who beat their neighbours until they died, or sent them into camps and forced-labour brigades, or held them down on couches and made them drink entire bottles of whisky for no comprehensible reason.

'You talk about this work obligation,' said the defence lawyer. 'Isn't it true that Serbs also had a work obligation?'

'No,' said the witness. 'No, they didn't.'

'Could you explain to the court what you think is wrong with having a work obligation?'

'Because I didn't go of my own free will.'

'But wouldn't you agree,' the defence lawyer spread out his hands, 'that in war there is no free will, and the state decides what needs to be done?'

'Well, sir, that may be so,' snapped the witness, pulling himself up and breaking from the formal impersonality of courtroom testimony, 'but, my God, I never heard that in front of a bunker between two front lines who are shooting at each other, it is necessary to the state for me to mow the grass!'

She wanted to go to the lobby, to walk through the glass doors of the staff area and go to where Daniel was probably sitting, to take hold of his hand and say, tell me, tell me how we can survive these things. But she was able not to do that.

Nikola Marković sat at the desk in his cell, smoking, tapping the fingers of one hand against the surface, wanting to look out of a window and see something other than a small corner of sky. Or else wanting something brutal, definite, something to fight against. Just not this, not these walls again, not the bland accusatory guards urging him to attend a pottery class.

He had felt the cold clear satisfaction of a job done well, the decisive pleasure of colours shifting on a map, the weight of a gun at his waist. But only because it had to happen, there was a force of history behind him, if it had not been him it would have been someone else, anyone else, history would have its way.

Safety. A sense of safety. That certain people, certain things were being pushed further and further away from him, that he was in a place of clarity and light.

'No one in that courtroom has been through a war,' the young lawyer had said that morning, brushing a strand of dark hair from his oddly delicate face, 'and they presume to judge you? They think they understand what you had to sacrifice?' And he thought, yes, that was the way of it, it damaged me as well but I was willing to do this, it was something I had to do for my people.

There were photographs that had crossed his desk, yes, it was true, as part of the status reports, so he had seen many photographs, dead bodies, women with their faces blown off. They were terrible, tragic things, but he could not be said to have chosen this. That could not be said. He was being pushed forward by centuries, by the death of his father, by his mother's tumour, but not by his own desires, he denied that, he would have lived a quiet life if it had been up to him.

He should get back to his essay, he should do some more work on that. He had been both exhausted and agitated recently. There was a pressure at the back of his skull. Maybe he needed some Prozac, but he wasn't about to deal with the Dutch doctors over it. Dutch doctors, he knew perfectly well, were keen on euthanasia, and it wouldn't do to let them get too close. Everyone was so convinced he was a villain now, they would probably find the temptation irresistible.

He lay on his bed and read *Persuasion*, but he felt irritated suddenly with Jane Austen and her world of individuals, people who seemed to move briskly through their lives with no awareness of history or war – all love and money and manners, and there was Napoleon in the background, clever little Jane apparently considering him below her notice, as if he had existed for no other purpose than to complicate the love affairs of Wentworth and Anne Elliot. *There was a very general ignorance of all naval matters throughout the party*, indeed. He put the book down and started to pace the length of his cell, but had to sit down quickly, out of breath.

They don't know what it's like, he thought. They just don't understand what it's like.

And in Tuzla, they were thinking about DNA.

In a small house converted into offices, doctors were cataloguing samples of bone and tissue from the mass graves. The bodies themselves lay in tunnels under the hills, a second city beneath the streets, the people of Tuzla walking on these memories, thousands of missing gathered together in their last community.

The doctors had filed report after report on their computers, interviewing survivors about what their husbands and sons had worn, where they had dental work, any bones they might have broken in a football game years before. They attempted to match descriptions of buttons with small dirty fragments exhumed from the mud. But it was slow, too slow, the survivors would grow old and die before they found out where their lost ones were. So the doctors had placed their hope now in DNA.

They took small amounts of blood, red and living blood, from those who were searching, and they sent these carefully packed tubes, along with the bone samples, to laboratories in the United States for the extraction of mitochondrial DNA.

To extract mitochondrial DNA from a sample of bone or tooth, the exterior surface is sanded to remove dirt and other contaminants, then a small amount of the sample is ground into a fine powder. In the case of a tooth which is not fresh, the dentin layer is used. The powder is placed in a solution, exposed to a variety of organic chemicals which will release the DNA, then spun in a centrifuge. After it has been spun, the top watery layer of the mixture is filtered and concentrated, then heated to separate the two strands of the double helix. The scientists have now untied the fundamental knot that creates a living thing. They take the two template strands and produce many million copies of each one, ready for sequencing, this last microscopic trace of an individual person, rewritten over and over on their blank field of inquiry.

Mitochondrial DNA, however, can only demonstrate a link between a mother and a child. Many of the searchers were mothers, of course, so that was not a great problem. And two children of the same mother may be identified that way, so if a sister or a brother was searching, they could expect success from this method.

To link a father and a child is more difficult. This can only be done with nuclear DNA, and nuclear DNA is not easy to extract or analyse. If you were searching for your father, your hopes had to be much smaller. If you couldn't match an identity card, or an unusual personal item, or something notable about the teeth, you would probably not find your father again.

Lili walked out of the revolving doors into a drizzling afternoon, wet leaves falling heavily to the pavement. At the foot of Carnegielaan she walked down a stone stairway to a round pond, so thickly overgrown with algae that drinks cans and sweet wrappers were suspended above the water, on the layer of bright green scum. She sat on a bench and waited in the gathering darkness until she thought that she could look at Daniel and not fall to pieces, not tell him about Marković rubbing his eyes vaguely in the dock, not ask him if he knew what had happened to a man named Samir Imamović.

'You're cold,' he said, pushing back the hood of her raincoat when she met him in the little bar downstairs.

'It was a hard day somehow.'

'Okay.' He knew by now that he could not ask why.

'Really,' she said, touching the scab on his temple, 'what were you doing, standing in front of the riot with a KICK ME sign?'

'I was just in the right place at the right time. It's a talent I have.'

They walked upstairs together, and inside her flat she kissed him so hard their teeth collided, and they fell back onto the bed and were lost in this, the taste and smell and feel of each other, and though neither one of them could move or speak without invoking the ghost of a war, there were moments against the backdrop of history that seemed almost clean and pure.

In Lili's dream she was a girl of indeterminate age, standing in an ornamental garden by a crystalline glacial lake, as if she were in Geneva with the city itself removed. The garden was extensive; she crossed hills and found it emerging again from the hollows, an arrangement of laurel hedges and roses, chrysanthemum and iris, pebbled walkways, small fountains.

You are alone with this in the end.

She was aware that there were measures she needed to take, but she was unclear what they were or why. Swimming in the lake, fish in brilliant jade and turquoise colours, and she reached in and removed one, holding its heavy, fleshy bulk in both hands, then returned it to the cold water.

She was an adult woman, herself although not quite herself – her hair was reddish-brown – and at the corner of Laan van Meerdervoort she was trying to explain to someone about Daniel. *But the problem is, I have to take this to court*, she said. *And I'm not sure it's actionable.*

Did you ask your father? said the other person.

Of course not. He's dead.

Oh well.

She thought, *there is a legal book about this, but I'm not sure what library it would be in.*

The dream circled round again to herself as the girl at the lake, and it seemed as though it was going to repeat itself several times with minor changes, as her dreams often did, but the girl said, *leave me alone*, *all right*, *leave me alone*, and she woke and it was day.

XIII

North Sea

14 November 1999

There were times, Paja knew, when things had been getting better. At first it had been terrible here, he was lost in this loud hollow city, struggling with the language, insulted by clerks in the Home Office; and he still had no official papers, no legal existence, no proper job. But then there was Annie, remarkably wanting to be with him. Their days together, almost safe. Almost like a home. He got some work now and then, in London's own grey economy; mostly fixing people's disastrous attempts to rewire their flats, muttering under his breath, 'So, I see you have ambition to die in giant fire,' and taking payment in cash. He wasn't shooting up in a Soho doorway like some of his old friends, he drank sometimes, that was all – drinking was not so bad, not like the drugs, and it was only to calm his nerves. There had been times – weeks, even months – when he had believed, stupidly, dishonestly, in the possibility of peace.

He should never have let himself think that way. It only meant that more people would suffer, in the end. It was dark in the street outside, a single siren winding northwards, the throbbing light of an ambulance reflecting against the walls of the room. He couldn't sleep, he never slept any more; he lifted Marko from the cot and held him, feeling the baby's thin hot breath against his neck.

And outside the window a mouth, pressed to the glass, its

outline blurred and thick with bright red blood, waiting for him to turn and see. A wet hand sliding down the pane.

One night during the fighting, Paja had gone into the hills to look for the dead. It was in summer, early summer. There were flowers, there was pollen in the air. It wasn't good for his asthma. He had been breathing badly, too loud, his chest aching with the effort. He cut his knee on a rock. The men who were trying to kill him were out there somewhere, but they didn't like to waste their ammunition in the dark, shooting at a distant rasping breath in the rough grass.

He found some bodies. And he found something else. There was a man there and he wasn't dead. Or he was dead, in reality he was dead but some part of his brain had not yet understood that fact. With his little torch Paja could see this. He could see the man's internal organs lying in the grass, he could smell them, faecal and nauseating, but the man was still moving, gasping, he didn't realize that he had to be dead.

It would have taken a long time. It might have taken a long time, a lot of pain, the man's eyes were staring at him and he moved his mouth, and Paja put the torch down so he couldn't see the man's face. It could have taken for ever, they could have been out there in that field, it was dangerous, someone could hear the man making wet noises, fish noises, someone could hear Paja's ragged breathing, see the small light.

He had a knife in his pocket. In his hand. He knew where to find the artery, and once he made the cut it took only seconds, there was no pain, it was quick, the man was still.

Paja was never even sure what side the man had been fighting on.

It had been the right thing, the kind thing even, for him to do. But he knew, he never stopped knowing, that he would pay for it. There had to be justice.

Because of this, because of this. Because his town went up

in flames, and they ran into the mountains, Paja drowning in his own bad lungs, fainting, crawling. Because there were times that he thought he had escaped, but he always knew it wasn't true, that it would follow him here to London, the war, the terror. That it would follow him and anyone he loved, for ever. Would follow him to the end of the world.

Father Jamie was taking a break between readings when Paja arrived at the park, with Marko asleep in a pushchair. 'Excuse me,' he said. 'My wife is at work, so I look after the baby.'

'Not a problem at all,' said Jamie, looking at an ancient painting of aliens in one of his books. 'I'm glad you could come.'

Paja sat on the bench and began to move the pushchair back and forth with one foot. 'You see, he is such good baby. This is why I am afraid he should suffer. Is not fair to him.' Marko's sleeping face was puckered in infant concentration, a knitted cap pulled down over his small head, his fists clenched.

'Well,' said Jamie, 'it's all for a greater good in the end.' He turned to look at Paja, who was pale and nervous, his eyes red with small exploded veins. 'I don't like to see people so worried, you know. It's only a transient stage we're discussing, just something that we have to go through.'

'I understand necessity,' said Paja. 'Is not Marko's fault, is all.'

'No. No, I'm sure that it isn't. But it's not really a question of fault, is it? It's simply a period of testing. Tribulation.' He flipped a page in the book and looked at a carving of a UFO on a pyramid, and thought about people he had known before, people who didn't talk to him now.

'There's always some sacrifice,' he added. 'If you have a goal, if you have a duty, you have to be prepared to sacrifice. In the end, it will all be worth while.'

'Sacrifice,' said Paja, pronouncing the word thoughtfully. 'Yes. That is true. There must be.' He stood up from the bench.

'Really, are you all right? You don't look terribly well – your health problem . . .'

'Is okay. Thank you. That is good insight. I speak to you again later.' And he walked away, under the bare trees, wheeling the brightly coloured pushchair in front of him.

Ducasse paced up and down in his small rented office off Statenlaan. 'You are obsessing on this witness, Milan, and it is extremely unproductive.' He turned to look at the younger man, rocking a bit on the balls of his feet. 'You did listen to what Abreu was saying, didn't you?'

'Yes, I did listen, and she said among other things that I was entitled to the presumption of innocence. I think I am also entitled to have you refrain from implications about my professional conduct.'

'Somebody talked to those people in Amsterdam, Milan.'

Lukitch shrugged. 'So then, somebody did. I would of course have no need, since thanks to the documents from Mr Vasić I believe that I now have the name.'

Ducasse threw up his hands. 'But why do you need this name so much? This is not a key witness, this is not a witness, in my opinion, who has high credibility, even without looking into identification. So one traumatized, damaged person says that he saw Marković do this or that in the camp. So he gives so many details it looks like an obvious confabulation, he wants to make some investigator happy, and it's not even relevant to the core issues. Even if I found him completely believable, this is a minor, a very minor incident compared to the overall picture.'

'Surely not so minor.'

'Compromising, for sure, yes. But it's an uncorroborated story from a single fragile individual, and I don't believe it will hold up.'

'No, I don't believe you can make so little of this.'

'You're getting all caught up in an emotional response. Just because something makes an exciting story doesn't mean it carries weight in the courtroom.'

Lukitch snorted in frustration. 'Fine. Condescend to me if you want. I'm the one with courtroom experience, and I know which lines of inquiry I'm going to follow. What about Bryant? Are you looking into him?'

'He's not even on the list yet.'

'He will be. And he's making me very suspicious. It's not only his partisan politics, you know. How is he there when our client is arrested, why is he phoning the family almost every day? How is he coming up with all these stories he writes? This man has personal interests we need to uncover.'

Ducasse shrugged. 'Well, Bryant's material is an interesting dilemma. I'd like to talk to you about—'

'You don't take me seriously, do you?'

'I was just about to ask your opinion, as a matter of fact. If you want to go off on lunatic tangents of your own, there's little I can do about it.'

'No. I think that you're refusing to consider my lines of inquiry, because you have a problem about working with me.'

Ducasse took his glasses off and stared at the other man, perplexed. 'Excuse me?'

'I don't know if it's because I'm younger than you, or because I'm a Serb, but you're being frustrating and uncommunicative, and frankly, yes, it is unprofessional that you won't treat me as an equal partner in this case.'

'Well. This is just silly.' Ducasse replaced his glasses. 'If you want a lot of sharing and hugging, Milan, you should look into a career in social work, not the law.'

'All right. That's it.' Lukitch stood up and began packing files into his briefcase. 'I'm going to be out of town for a week or so. I'm going to be working on building up a support team so that I can actually defend my client. Call me when you think you're interested in doing the same.'

Nikola Marković watched the shiver of rain against his window, massaging a random pain in his shoulder. Tentatively, slowly, he lifted the binder marked *Vasić*, flipped the heavy cover back and skimmed through the pages, stopping to glance at a copy of a letter Dejan had sent to his office through a courier, in the autumn of 1992.

. . . attached a print-out of the Nuremberg judgement, which you may wish to study at your leisure . . . Getting to my main point, and submitting that habeas corpus may be regarded as emerging into the status of a non-derogable right of universal application . . . given the termination of court proceedings on this matter in a remarkably abrupt fashion, I am addressing to you personally another request for information as to the whereabouts of Ibrahim Salihović, member of parliament . . . opportunity to speak to you as a human being, Nikola, but I don't expect that to come about again. I just want you to know that I have decided to live as if we were still under the rule of law. How you choose to live is up to you.

He turned the page, and continued to scan the documents. He did not feel well, but he could manage this. It was simply a dispute about certain issues. No more than terminology, in some cases. And in the end, the courts had upheld his side of it, hadn't they? Job-termination notices, draft notices, none of these seemed so very important.

A song of love is a song of woe, don't ask me how I know.

More blurry photocopies. He looked at the top of one of

them, badly typed on ledger paper. *Affidavit filed by Hotić, Muharem. Dated 9 December 1994, Tuzla. Bosnia-Herzegovina.*

He shut the cover of the file, pushed it back under the bed, and reached hastily for another book, grabbing randomly and opening, as it happened, a copy of *The Third Man*, inexplicably given to him by a well-meaning prison librarian who didn't read English.

'Was he in great pain?'

'He was dead. I looked right down from my window here and I saw his face. I know when a man is dead.'

He threw the book across the room.

Sunday morning, filled with clear early light. Lili and Daniel walked down to the pretty little green space of Anna Paulownaplein and ate pancakes in a café called The Flying Saucer, as the wind blew brown handfuls of willow catkins against the window.

'This is so cool,' said Daniel, studying a copy of *The UFO Book* which he had taken from a rack behind the table. 'Look, it's Dr R. Leo Sprinkle, UFO expert. Have you ever seen anyone who looked more like an R. Leo Sprinkle in your life?'

It had taken him weeks to convince Lili that it was all right to walk around in her neighbourhood, and even now she wasn't completely at ease, glancing nervously at the doorway whenever someone came in. He touched his fingers to the back of her hand, the only kind of contact she would allow him in public. 'Take a look, okay?'

She smiled softly at him, flipping through pages of blurry photographs of frisbees and hubcaps. 'Do you see a lot of these things?' She was drinking cappuccino from a white ceramic cup, a thin line of foam on her upper lip.

'UFOs, or R. Leo Sprinkles?' He ate his last forkful of

pancake and pushed the plate to the side. 'Actually, the answer in both cases would be no, but I live in hope.'

Somewhat to Daniel's disappointment, Lili wiped the foam off her lip with a napkin. 'Making the universe safe for gamma rays.'

'How's that then?'

'Oh, I just heard someone saying that last week. You see, I have nearly everything I need in this neighbourhood. A café, a tree, crazy old men who try to talk to me in the street. Well, he said it in Dutch, of course.'

'Oh God, do you speak Dutch now?'

'I already spoke German. They're closely related. Anyway I'm far from fluent.'

'Did the universe used to be dangerous for gamma rays?'

'You'd have to ask the crazy old man.'

She was reaching for a cigarette when her mobile phone rang, and she pulled it out of her coat pocket. *'Allô? Oui, c'est moi . . .'* Balancing the phone against her shoulder, she shook a cigarette from the pack with one hand. *'D'accord . . . Ah, oui?'*

Daniel picked up her lighter from the table and flicked it, stretching the flame towards her. She arched her eyebrows at this, as if it was too intimate for a public place, but leaned forward anyway.

'Oui, c'est possible . . .' She took out her diary and flipped ahead one or two weeks. *'À quelle heure? Je serai au tribunal jusqu'à quinze heures.'*

He wondered who it was on the other end of the line. Obviously it wasn't personal, he knew her professional voice by now. She blew out a thin cloud of smoke. He looked at the small rose in a vase on the table, a pale off-white outside, deep orange at its heart.

She was more right about the neighbourhood than she

knew. It seemed so dangerously easy to live here, shop in the little stores, walk on the plain cobbled streets, watch the parents playing with their children at the corners. So easy to think of her flat as home, though this was no good, this was inexcusable, and besides it wasn't even properly hers, all those decorative bits of lace and wicker that she would never have allowed into her Paris flat.

And he thought of the slender elegance of the old neighbourhoods in Sarajevo, coming slowly back to life, the steep cobbled streets and low archways, the pastry shops and bookstores and the sharp taste of Bosnian coffee. He thought about standing in the Baščaršija marketplace, hundreds of pigeons flying up around him like a storm.

'*D'accord, seize heures. Je te retrouverai au tribunal? Bon, au revoir.*' She disconnected, and slid the phone back into her pocket. 'You were saying about UFOs?'

'Never mind.' Of course she couldn't tell him who it was, what the call was about, she couldn't tell him anything. He picked up his coffee cup and sipped; it was starting to get cold. 'Did you read my article about Stana Marković?' he asked, sounding abrupt even to himself.

Lili raised her eyebrows again, and reached out to tap the ash from the end of her cigarette. 'Let me think about that.'

'Yeah, yeah, okay, I'm sorry.'

'It's cutting a bit close to work, you know?'

'Forget it. I shouldn't have said.'

She inhaled, breathed out smoke. 'As a matter of fact I did read it, though. I think she is an exceptionally stupid girl.'

Daniel shrugged. 'It's a whole nation in denial. You can't really expect her to—'

'Don't make excuses for her, Daniel,' said Lili, her voice cold. 'She is a stupid, stupid girl. Now please can we drop this subject.'

Both of them sat for a moment looking at the table, the window of the café rattling softly in the wind.

'You're making quite a career out of Marković.'

'More a leitmotif than a career, really,' said Daniel uneasily.

Lili rubbed her temples and nodded.

'His lawyer was asking about me, apparently,' Daniel added, knowing this too was probably a forbidden topic.

'What, Ducasse?'

'No, the other one, the one who looks like he's fifteen years old. According to Suzannah he was up and down the lobby looking for me. Says I'm causing his client stress and strain by phoning his family, something like that.'

'Well, goodness, we can't have that,' said Lili, taking another drag on her cigarette. 'I'm sure he's a man of very delicate feelings.'

Daniel pushed the ashtray closer to her, paused, and then ran his finger along the edge of her cup. She looked at his hand and smiled.

'Are you leaving tomorrow?' she asked quietly.

'Tuesday, if it's all right.' He drank more of the cooling coffee. 'I have some interviews set up in Zagreb, but not till mid-week. I can, well, never mind what I might do on Monday. Just some stuff.'

'Yes, it would be nice if you could stay.'

He touched the back of her hand again, briefly, almost invisibly. 'Could we go for a walk somewhere?'

'I can't think where.'

'The beach? It surely couldn't be very crowded this time of year. Anyway, I don't think lawyers go to the beach.'

'You'd be amazed at what lawyers do. But I guess it might be okay.'

She sat in the window seat of the tram, looking out as they climbed the small hill towards Scheveningen, and thought that for most people here that name meant primarily a beach, not a prison.

'They were just making it up, weren't they?' she said, out of nowhere. 'Those guys in the Balkans. Like, they just sat down and thought, what can I do that would be really bad? And those were the kinds of things they came up with.'

'Depends what you mean,' said Daniel. 'You know there was an overall plan at the top, an overall ideology. But way down on the ground, yeah, it seemed pretty much improvised a lot of the time. Kind of like Beavis and Butthead with heavy artillery. He said Muslim, huh huh huh, BANG!'

'I was just wondering, is it good or bad that their imaginations were usually so impoverished? I mean, that most of them could only come up with stupid brutal things.'

Daniel tapped his fingers on the top of the seat in front of him. 'Did you know,' he said, 'that there was a Russian novelist who came to visit the gunners around Sarajevo, and they asked him if he wanted to fire off a few shots, and he did? Just down into the city. They got that on film. Damn, could have been when I was crossing the street. Sometimes I'd be in a doorway, you know, taking cover, and I'd have time to wonder who was shooting at me. Novelists, literary critics, professors. Creating this terrible movie in their minds.'

By the time they stepped off the tram the sky was dark, heavy with clouds. They hurried through the towering masses of the shopping arcades and casinos, towards the water, Lili in her dark coat, Daniel in his leather jacket.

'You should buy a real coat, you know.'

'I'd just have to carry it around with me all the time.'

Down the stairs from the concrete promenade, they walked past rows of abandoned deckchairs, trudging heavily through the sand in winter boots. The North Sea stretched out beyond them, into a featureless mist.

'It's beautiful,' said Daniel, looking across the empty bank of sand, the dark waste of the sea along the curve of the world.

Lili bent and touched one of the thousands of tiny shells embedded in the wet sand, white with black stripes, brown stripes, grey shells, small and shattered.

The stone pier was coated with seaweed, a vivid deep green covering it like grass, a muddy brown layer drying beneath it. It was not as slick as he had expected, his feet found an easy grip as he walked to the end of it. The rocks were thick with little black shells.

'There's nothing alive in the tide pools,' he said.

'Should there be?' asked Lili, crouching beside him.

'I don't know. I guess it's just the way the North Sea ecosystem works. It's not what I'm used to is all.' He folded his arms around his knees, squatting on the rocks. 'I expect anemones and things, little pink and white creatures. But I guess this is just how it is here.' He took a ballpoint pen out of his pocket and tapped one of the black shells. 'Do you think these are alive?'

'If they are, you aren't doing them any good hitting them with your pen.'

'Yeah. I wish I knew, though.'

'I expect they are. If they were dead they wouldn't be so tightly closed. I'd guess they're alive.'

Daniel stood up and slid the pen back into his pocket. 'Okay, then.'

They walked back to the sand, leaning into the wind, a light sharp rain whipping against their faces. There was no real shelter from the wind, except for the high steel pier with the games arcade, and there would be people there, it wasn't a place they could go. Daniel sat down, thinking it would be less windy near to the ground, and pulled the collar of his jacket up. 'I mean, we don't have to stay here if you don't want.'

‘No, it’s nice here in a weird way,’ said Lili, sitting gingerly beside him, folding her coat underneath her. He could feel the warmth of her body, though they were not quite touching. For a few minutes neither of them spoke.

‘What do you dream about?’ she asked in a light careful voice.

He shrugged. ‘Very predictable stuff, really. War dreams. I don’t expect you need the details.’ He pushed his glasses up on his nose and looked at the long bleak green of the sea, thinking how banal, how obvious, his dreams were still; mortar fire and shattered bloody skulls, women running for cover as the bombs exploded, rotting bodies in the mountain passes. But he wanted to tell her something.

‘There is one dream,’ he said, and she turned her head towards him. ‘There is one dream I remember – and it’s pretty much a cliché still – but it’s a dream about having five minutes to pack and leave. You know, the paramilitaries in the doorway, I can pack one bag and run before they burn the house down . . . I, well, a lot of the time I’m sorting through these piles of computer disks, pictures of my family, some books, but I can’t carry everything and there’s only a few minutes left, everything’s burning, and whatever I leave, whatever I can’t hold in my hands, it’ll be destroyed. I’m trying to hang on to all these things to save them . . . And kids’ toys sometimes, I don’t know why, but I’ll be holding on to this stuffed rabbit or something, holding it against my chest, and these photographs that keep slipping and falling on the floor, and the time’s nearly up . . .’ his voice trailed off. ‘It’s a trivial dream really, isn’t it? It’s just . . . it’s not even about fear. It’s about this, this sadness, such a huge sadness. Everything . . . . I don’t know. Everything falling away.’

She reached out and touched the side of his face. ‘I’m all right,’ he said. ‘I am all right. It’s just a dream, that’s all it is.’

His lips were dry and cracked from the cold, and when she kissed him she was aware of the faint metallic taste of blood.

She rested her head in the crook of his shoulder while he stroked her hair, and time was briefly suspended, gentle. She thought of him in other cities, in that former country where she was born, and simply the knowledge of his existence apart from her was poignant and beautiful.

'Thank you,' she said, 'thank you for telling me,' and she was not sure what she was speaking of.

His hand on the back of her neck, he could feel the long exhalation of her breath, the tension rising and subsiding in her shoulders. He kissed along the fine line of her jaw, the cold wind around them, and he knew that she could not go on like this for ever and that he could change it, there were decisions he could make, he had choices. He could choose her. But he didn't say it, he waited on the verge of speech and said nothing, in the fragile equilibrium of this temporary home.

XIV
The Prisoner

1992–1996

There were certain things that Daniel remembered about Sarajevo.

No one stayed in the south-facing rooms of the Holiday Inn; they were in the direct line of fire, it was impossible. The north-facing rooms were the safest, but if your room faced east you could see more, you could look right into the tortured centre of the city and record the greatest number of casualties without having to leave the hotel.

Daniel's window faced west, towards the university buildings. Across the street he could see, at an angle, the National Museum. Sometimes he would sit on the bed with his ancient, useless Baedeker and think longingly of the old Roman statues, the prehistoric stele, the dusty peace of stones worn down by age instead of bullets. He would dream of walking among the glass cases, looking at amphorae, ancient bits of cloth, fish in bottles.

The city was like a mosaic of terror. Privileged, halfway protected, the journalists would race from the hotel in cars, wearing flak jackets and helmets, and wherever they stopped they would find something vivid and terrible, fire, death. He was ashamed to realize that it was more than a year before he knew the layout of the streets, before they were anything more to him than a series of flashing images, interlocking when he closed his eyes to sleep.

He knew that Sarajevo was a kind of modern icon, a word that people threw out to symbolize this concept or that, mostly ideas that they didn't really understand themselves. Some of the buildings had become familiar, almost tired photographs – the wrecked Parliament, the Oslobodjenje tower – and of course they were part of his time there as well.

But later what he remembered most was another building, a small house squeezed between ugly Tito-era apartment blocks in a Serb-controlled zone. One of the things about being a journalist was that you could go there, you could go into Grbavica or up to Mount Trebević, and watch the snipers shooting down at the people in the streets; you could, like the Russian novelist, be offered your own chance to take a few shots.

The house, though. He noticed it when he was in Ilidža being refused interviews, at the end of 1993, because a Red Cross van was parked out front, and that was unusual. He asked around the disconsolate market, where women sold cigarettes, spread out on blankets, one at a time, but no one was interested in telling him about it.

A week or so later, he was heading back into Sarajevo from somewhere, with his driver/interpreter Alija and a photographer named Lucy, when they were flagged down about a mile from a roadblock by a Danish woman in a white flak jacket and bare feet. Two men, also barefoot, were sitting at the edge of the road, smoking and scowling.

'Red Cross,' said the woman, pointing at her armband. 'Our truck was hijacked. Can you give us a lift?' She was a small woman, pretty, fine-featured with a little turned-up nose; probably that was why she'd been put in charge of hailing the first passing journalists. They crammed into the little Volkswagen Golf – Anna, Dennis, Slavko. Alija narrowed his eyes a bit when he heard Slavko's name.

'ICRC,' whispered Daniel. 'I'm sure he's okay.'

'I know, I know, but just . . .'

'We're cool, yeah?'

'Yeah.'

The Red Cross was not a very reliable emblem in this war; the Red Cross of Republika Srpska was said to be occupied, among other activities, with running its own rape camp and driving its trucks over the legs of prisoners in Keraterm. But the workers with the International Committee were usually sincere and innocent; and anyway there wasn't really much choice. They could hardly be left on the road, unarmed and barefoot in the snow, trying to walk across the front lines into the city. The sky was already darkening; by the time the car reached the outskirts of Sarajevo it would be night, and Alija would have to turn off the headlights and gun the car blind through the firing zone.

The Red Cross workers were trying their best to look simply bored and irritated, not like people who had had guns put to their heads and been left on the road for target practice. Journalists and aid workers did die here, but not at the same rate, or in the same exquisitely torturous ways, as the locals, so it wouldn't do to make too much of it.

'What kills me,' said Dennis, 'is the idea of those frigging Chetniks running around in our van.'

'Don't say Chetnik,' said Anna. 'It's a term of ethnic abuse.'

'They frigging call themselves Chetniks, Anna. I don't mean Serbs in general, I mean specifically those goddamn Chetniks.'

'Just stop it. You are representing the International Committee of the Red Cross.'

'The hell. Whatever.'

Daniel filed this exchange away, noting to himself that while Anna might be more pleasant company, it would be Dennis who would tell him more. But in fact, later that evening in the relative luxury of the Holiday Inn restaurant, it was quiet Slavko who explained what the truck had been doing at the house in Ilidža.

'There is a prisoner,' he said, hungrily eating a plate of greasy meat and cabbage. 'Part of our prison visitation programme. A very tiny prison. Very personal, you could say.' He looked around the restaurant. 'Kind of like Sarajevo, I guess.'

He was always and impenetrably an outsider. He knew that. He was not under siege, not truly, and he never would be.

Sometimes he took scraps from the hotel dustbins and left them outside for the little grey feral cats. He would crouch in the back doorway and watch them eat. But really, the cats were clever, they could eat mice and cockroaches and crawling bugs. Dogs had a harder time finding food; what often happened, in the end, was that the dogs ate the cats.

But people did try to feed their pets when they could, there was even a vet who still kept office hours. Water was a bigger problem than food.

So much of life in the siege was about water. The swift, shallow Miljacka river ran under the treacherous bridges, lovely and undrinkable. People risked their lives carrying plastic jugs to the intermittently working public taps, collected rainwater in buckets at night, even wandered the streets with dowsing rods, reaching out towards the buried life of water.

Once, just one time when he was in Sarajevo, he had thought about dying on purpose. Not about killing himself exactly, but about walking slowly down the centre of Sniper Alley, without his protective gear, hands at his sides. It was the middle of winter and people were dying regularly outside his window from shells and bullets, and other people were freezing slowly in the old folks' home. The UN troops were sitting in the airport, watching the city perish. It didn't seem entirely appropriate to be alive.

The snow was beautiful, dazzling handfuls of light thrown off the white landscape, and he thought that he could walk there and watch the light around his feet, lift a hand to the brilliant sun, and then stop. He wasn't so naïve that he expected a quick or clean death, but still it seemed that it would be somehow restful.

He didn't get out to Ilidža again until the summer. But when he rounded a particular corner and realized where he was, he simply, in a moment of wild speculation, knocked at the door of the house. He must have been feeling invulnerable that day, magically protected from harm. It was like that in the summer of 1994. There was a shaky ceasefire around Sarajevo and for a few months it seemed like life was beginning again. People took chances.

A small round woman answered the door – white-haired, her plump body collapsing on itself like a loaf of bread left to rise too long. '*Ko si ti?*' she asked suspiciously.

'*Izvinite. Ja sam novinar*,' said Daniel, trying to smile in an unthreatening way. He stumbled through a few more sentences, making up a story as he went along, about how he was interviewing people in Ilidža to get their opinions about the war, wanting to know what ordinary folks were thinking. Could he come in and talk to her for a few minutes?

She watched him with keen, dark eyes, but to his surprise she opened the door more widely and ushered him in. Another woman was sitting at the kitchen table, around the same age but taller and thinner, her face angular and severe. She stood up and began taking biscuits out of the cupboard and arranging them on a plate.

The smaller woman's name was Sonja, the taller one was Mirela. Sonja seemed to be the one who did all the talking. He thought that he should have brought an interpreter, that he kept overestimating how well he was learning the language, but he could make out enough to take some notes as Sonja launched into an extensive complaint about the world, about how everyone had betrayed and mistreated her, how she hated the Muslims, hated the Bosnian government, hated most of her fellow Serbs as well, would stab Karadžić in the heart if he came into her kitchen, hated the UN above everything. He noticed an axe behind the kitchen door, and interrupted to heap praise on her flour-and-oil biscuits.

It was Mirela who made them, she explained. From the humanitarian supplies. He offered his pack of cigarettes, and the women reached for them eagerly, looking at him with a new level of respect.

He watched the two of them, Sonja with her softly subsiding face, a few hairs growing from her chin, and Mirela, pouring cups of plain boiled water, long grooves by the sides of her mouth, pale blue eyes. He wondered where the prisoner could be – an attic, a basement? – and indeed who. Anything seemed possible.

Sonja excused herself to the tiny back garden, explaining that she would pick some radishes for them and return in a moment. When she went out of the back door Mirela was silent.

'Is there anything you'd like to tell me?' ventured Daniel; one of the sentences he had memorized early on.

Mirela stretched her arms towards him and rolled up her sleeves. He could see a pattern of fading bruises leading up from her wrists.

'She beat me sometime,' she said in English.

Sonja opened the door, and he expected Mirela to push her sleeves down, but she left her arms lying loosely on the table.

He looked at the bruises, at the loose flesh, the brown marks of age. Mirela stared at the smaller woman as she came back into the kitchen, her hands full of radishes and dirt.

'Is she complaining again?' snapped Sonja. He guessed that only Mirela knew English, but her arms, spread out on the table, made it clear what she must have said. 'Don't believe everything that one tells you. She gets good treatment here. Like a sister, I treat her.'

'You are a prisoner?' he asked Mirela softly, in English.

'Yes,' she said, and then turned towards Sonja, washing radishes in a bucket. 'I told him I am a prisoner,' she explained.

'You better tell him the whole story.' Sonja kept her back to them, scrubbing the radishes furiously with a small brush.

'The government taked her daughter,' said Mirela in English, her stern face turned towards Daniel. 'They taked her into prison. So the Chetniks taked me and bringed me here. She ask for a prisoner exchange. Red Cross tell us it is difficult. Problems on talks.'

'How long have you been here?'

Mirela sat calculating to herself. 'One and a half . . .' she said finally, groping for the next word.

'One and a half months?'

'No, not month. Year. One and a half year.'

That time, that one time, he went slowly down the stairway of the Holiday Inn and stood at the back door. All I need to do is walk around the corner, he thought. He stood there for some time, listening to the crackle of the guns. He knew, he had seen from his window, that there was at least one person lying dead in the street already, outside the Faculty of Philosophy, half-covered by the blowing snow. All I need to do is turn the corner, he said to himself, looking at his worn boots, their artificial fur lining thin and grey.

He knew how he would look to a sniper, because he had been there too, among the sandbags, as a man with a heavy beard and hugely dilated pupils waved his rifle back and forth above the streets. He would look small, toy-like. A simple thing to snap apart. He would fall, and bleed, and stop.

He had not stayed in the sniper's nest to see the man pull the trigger, but as he made his way back to the centre of the city, he had heard the crack and the whistle of a bullet. That man, or some other. And the people who died that day began to die.

When he got back to the Holiday Inn he found a message waiting for him at the front desk, the Red Cross workers – who seemed to be very well informed – more or less begging him not to write about Mirela and Sonja, explaining that it could endanger months of negotiations, that they might be on the point of freeing Mirela and he surely wouldn't want to ruin that. He wrote a story but didn't send it to his editors, thinking that he could sit on it until Mirela was freed.

A month later he went back to the house, and only Sonja was in the kitchen. 'Is Mirela well?' he asked. He expected to hear that she was back with her family.

'She was bad,' said Sonja. 'I had to put her in the cellar.'

'Oh.' He had to swallow hard to get his mouthful of biscuit down. 'What did she do?'

'She said a nasty word,' said Sonja. 'I don't want any of that here. I run a decent house.' She poured him a cup of weak tea, made from some unidentifiable kind of leaves. 'She's a very bad one sometimes.'

For the next half-hour he drank ersatz tea and tried to follow the anarchic processes of Sonja's mind, which seemed to circle mostly around her resentment of everyone. The Muslims were going to force Christian women to wear chadors if they won the war, she explained. Also they would feed Christian Orthodox babies to dogs. Izetbegović had six wives – 'not many people know about this' – and she hated him and every one of those notional spouses. Also she hated the Croats, somewhat by way of an afterthought, but she hated Milošević nearly as much.

'If he came into my house I would cut his throat, like *that*, right here in my kitchen,' she announced, and Daniel found this entirely believable. General Mladić, she allowed, was a real man, and she would not actually murder him if he should happen to stop by.

'Could I see Mirela?' he asked hesitantly.

'No. She needs to learn her lesson.'

He nodded and sipped his tea, then reached into his pocket and laid a fresh pack of cigarettes on the table. Sonja smoked her way through several of them, thanking him absently, before he could turn the conversation back to Mirela again.

'If you let me see her, I promise I won't stay long,' he said, feeling like a ten-year-old negotiating a visit with a sick friend. Sonja considered this thoughtfully, the light falling from the window on the pale skin of her soft face.

'All right,' she said at last. 'But only for a minute.' She stood, reached for a key on one of the shelves, and unfastened a padlock on the basement door. 'You go down yourself. I won't talk to her until tomorrow.'

At first he could see nothing in the basement, only a narrow and unstable wooden stairway stretching downwards. He stepped onto it nervously and plunged into the musty darkness; but it was not quite dark, there was a small window set high in the basement's stone wall, and as he reached the foot of the little stairs he could make out shapes. A furnace, boxes. Mirela.

She was sitting on the dirt floor, quite still, quite calm. As he walked closer, he could see that there was a thick fraying rope tied around one of her legs, the other end of it knotted over a water pipe. He knelt down beside her, and saw a fresh purple bruise on her face.

'My God. Are you all right?' he whispered.

Mirela sighed and rocked her head back and forth. 'Is nothing unusual,' she said in a low voice. 'She will let me out next day.'

'We have to tell the Red Cross.'

'They know it. Is nothing to be done.'

'This is awful, Mirela!'

She shrugged, her grey hair stringing over her face. 'She has a trouble from her nerves. She know I am not guilty, but she get very upset. I only . . . I only am afraid one thing.'

'What is it?'

'Just that I go crazy before I get out of here. I hope not to go crazy before I see again my family.'

'That's long enough!' shouted Sonja from the top of the stairs. 'You have to come up now!'

'Mirela, I'm so sorry,' whispered Daniel, trying to think through his appalled confusion towards something he could do for her. 'I'll come back. I'll . . . I'll try to keep an eye on her. If I can do anything . . .'

Mirela shrugged again. 'Is nothing to be done. I just try to hope. Someday, maybe, war will end.'

'I said, get upstairs!' called Sonja.

'I'm coming!' shouted Daniel. He turned to Mirela again. 'Can I take a message to your family? Bring you something? Anything?'

'I don't know where is my family now. If you cannot make an end of the war, there is nothing for you to help. Just go.'

His memory of that day at the back door of the Holiday Inn was a true and accurate memory, but it was also a screen, something he remembered in place of things that were too much to bear, days he allowed into his mind only when he had to write about them, and then as briefly, as narrowly as possible. As if he could reduce the feeling of a dying man's blood all over his hands into a neatly formed sentence. Or the leg of a small child, lying by itself in the street.

The person he had been before the wars moved in his mind, stiff and distant, like a character in an animated film. He had no understanding of how that person thought.

He did return sometimes to the little house, in between everything else, between the multi-front war in Bihać and the shelling of Goražde and Tuzla. And the day after his visit, every time, he would find a message from the Red Cross at his hotel, asking him not to write about it yet, assuring him they were still negotiating, that there could be a breakthrough at any time. He didn't argue; filing the story wouldn't have helped Mirela anyway, and it wasn't as if he was short of material to write about. He felt ancient and numb and ravaged, and he was not yet thirty-four, and it was wrong to think about how he felt, in the midst of these things.

There were poets in the hills, firing mortars. And there were poets in Sarajevo, still writing, obsessive and concentrated, survivors like the cats, pouncing on spiders.

He came to the house with a packet of coffee, and Sonja and Mirela were watching television, a show that could be referred to more or less as news, which consisted mostly of extended shots of mutilated bodies. Sonja went into the kitchen, and he sat on the torn cushions of the couch, scanning the room so that he wouldn't have to look at the screen. An old woman's house, cluttered, worn at the edges, a lace doily on top of the television, and little ceramic dogs sitting up and begging. A dead plant, a small icon perched high in one corner of the wall and another on a shelf. Photographs in ornate brass frames – a younger Sonja with a heavy-set man, a dark-haired woman who must be the daughter.

He looked down and saw a few fat drops of blood drying on the floor.

'Mirela?' he asked softly. 'Are you all right?'

She nodded, her stern face expressionless.

Sonja returned with coffee and glasses of water on a tray, and sat down beside him, her gaze returning hypnotically to the TV.

'Awful,' she whispered. 'It's so horrible.'

'Yes,' said Daniel. The droning announcer was saying something about Muslim atrocities, Croat atrocities.

The blue light of the television played across the photographs, across the sad jewelled face of Christ.

'Is that your husband?' he asked, pointing to the picture of the man.

Sonja's soft mouth twitched and tightened. 'Branko,' she murmured.

'Is he still alive?'

'He died long ago,' she said, and her voice turned almost dreamy. 'Before all of this. So long ago.' She lifted her coffee cup. 'I was all alone after they took Vesna. If they hadn't brought me Mirela, I suppose I would have died of loneliness.'

'It's hard to be alone,' agreed Mirela, her voice sounding strangely thick. 'When you get older. It's hard.'

Daniel drank his coffee, trying not to let his eyes return to the blood at the edge of the carpet.

'I knew Branko a bit,' Mirela added. 'He was a good man, wasn't he, Sonja?'

'A good man,' nodded Sonja, still vague and drifting. 'He gave me a good life.' She raised one hand to wipe her eyes.

'Oh, I'm a stupid old woman. Somehow I feel like, if he had only lived longer, none of this war would be going on. You think these things . . . it doesn't make sense, but you think so.'

'Why do you think the war started?' he asked carefully.

Sonja held up her hands in a defeated gesture. 'Who knows?' she said. 'It's just a terrible thing that's happening here. Like a fire that no one can stop.' She reached for her water glass.

He looked over at Mirela, and as she opened her mouth he realized that one of her front teeth was newly missing, and his eyes moved again towards the blood.

'Some people could have stopped it,' she said.

Sonja began to shake all over, the glass of water unstable in her hands. 'My nerves are bad,' she said. 'My nerves are very bad.'

Mirela nodded, and touched her lips with her long, age-marked fingers. 'No one in this house is guilty,' she sighed softly. 'Not one among us here.'

Daniel stood up, feeling suddenly ill, and walked towards the window. The sun was setting outside, across a deserted playground, an expanse of gravel with one broken swing still standing. He would have to drive through the line of fire in the dark to get to his hotel.

'We are people who have nothing,' said Mirela.

He turned around again, touching the notebook in his pocket as if it were a charm. Sonja raised her eyes to him in some kind of appeal.

'My daughter is a lovely girl,' she said.

He walked out into the dusk, and looked back into the lighted window. Sonja sat on the couch weeping, Mirela patting her back.

* * *

He had not walked into Sniper Alley that day, of course. He was still standing at the doorway when an Italian cameraman passed by on his way to the hospital to film casualties, and his greeting had broken Daniel's dream-like trance. He waved to the cameraman, turned around and went into the hotel restaurant and ordered a glass of brandy, and a few hours later he went out in a car, with someone from an American paper, to follow up on another story. But it was then, he thought, that he had pledged himself to this. If he didn't die with the people of Sarajevo, at least he wouldn't leave them until this was over, until there was some point he could call an end, a conclusion to the wars.

There was a sense, he knew, in which he had not left yet.

He got a ride back into the valley in a NATO truck, after the peace agreement was signed, and there were no roadblocks, no snipers, as they entered the wreckage of the winter city. Little groups of men and women, thin and exhausted, were trying to clear the rubble from in front of their houses, to fix what small things they could, dreaming of one day living again in a place with a post office, with trams that worked and a streetlight here and there, a huge distant dream of an ordinary life.

He saw children, blank-eyed and speechless, curled up in cots, their best imaginable future a slightly renovated hospital, or perhaps that they might be cared for by people whose own hearts were not irreparably hardened; and he was glad that he wasn't a cameraman, because it would be obscene to film these children but he would do it if it was his job, if it was his way of telling the world, *this is what went on here. This is what happened.*

Mirela was back with her family, in an apartment with plastic sheeting on the windows and occasional running water. Her husband was dead, shot down by a sniper in a queue for water, but her children were alive, and it was by the standards of war a happy ending.

'Do you think that you can ever live with Serbs again?' he asked her, as he had been asking everyone. And like the others, she paused for a long time before she answered.

'I am an old woman,' she said slowly. 'I will not live much longer. Sometimes I ask myself, why could not I died a few years earlier? It is not right, that this war should be the last thing I know on earth. I did not need to know such things before I die.' She held on to her son's hand, and Daniel saw that her son was old now as well. 'So you ask me this question, it is hard to answer. I cannot answer this question.'

Her son shook his head. 'They were our neighbours,' he said quietly. 'We went to parties at their house, they came to ours. We were happy that way. And if they were here now, I would kill them with a rusty knife.' He ran a hand through his short grey hair. 'I think I hate them most because they made me want to kill them.'

Mirela lifted her pale blue eyes. 'Tell me, have you see Sonja?' she asked anxiously. 'Is she doing good? If you see her, tell her please that I think about her. I wish from my heart her daughter is let go.'

The last time he saw Sonja she was sitting in the back of an open truck, clutching her axe, part of a convoy about to move deep into Republika Srpska, away from the city where they had been Bosnians.

'They tricked me,' she told him bitterly, as she waited for the trucks to begin moving. 'The Red Cross came and took Mirela away. It was an evil trick to play on me.'

'But your daughter did come back. She did get out of jail.'

Sonja bent her head. 'She's angry at me. I don't know why. She's angry at everyone. We're getting out of this Muslim city now. Fuck them all. Maybe if we're somewhere safe, with other Serbs, she'll start to feel better.'

'Mirela sends her best wishes,' said Daniel.

Sonja hugged her axe like a pillow. 'Is she all right?'

'I guess so. Yes.'

'You know a funny thing? I wish sometimes that she was coming with me.'

Daniel wrote his story about Mirela and Sonja; in fact, he sat up most of one night, writing it and then deleting it and then writing it again, astonished by how thin and meaningless it looked on his computer screen. It was published eventually, some version of it, in a couple of newspapers, and later on he thought of it sometimes, and hoped that Lili hadn't seen it. He wanted to tell her about it in some other way, in a way that would make sense and contain the Holiday Inn and the snow and the way that the boundaries of the war were as mobile and soft as weather, the way that he no longer knew what age he was. How the first time he had gone back to England after the war he had screamed at bus drivers for no reason, had smashed his tenants' crockery against the wall and told them it was an accident.

What he wanted to tell her was something true, and there was no form of words that wasn't in some way a lie; but maybe it would have been better to tell it anyway. Not that it would have changed the way things happened, in the end.

XV

Witnesses

25 November 1999

Ducasse walked across the lobby dragging a small wheeled suitcase full of documents.

'Thank you for agreeing to do this, Mme Stambolović,' he said, shaking her hand. 'I would normally have my co-counsel translate, but he's out of the country for a short period, and I do need to speak to my client.'

'No problem,' nodded Lili, as they walked down the steps and into the security booth. 'It's a normal part of the job.'

'Well, it's a great help to me.' They left the security booth and made their way down a spiral staircase to the underground car park, Ducasse hefting the suitcase with both arms. It seemed to weigh nearly as much as he did, and he exhaled with relief as he dumped it in the boot of his car.

'By the way,' he said, as he unlocked the passenger door, 'you look rather familiar. Do I know you from somewhere?'

'Quite possibly,' said Lili, who had recognized his accent immediately as Parisian. 'I live in the Fifth and I teach at the school of interpretation, does that help?'

'Oh yes. I've seen you around the university, I suppose.' He fastened his seat belt, and then, apparently moved by meeting a near-colleague, burst out, 'He's taken himself off to Bosnia in a fit of temper is what he's done.'

'Ah,' said Lili. You could say anything to an interpreter, and people sometimes did.

'Oh well, never mind. Let's be on our way.' They drove out of the car park, then north and east along the main streets towards the prison.

'Obviously I understand the frustrations of acting for the defence around here,' Ducasse went on, as if he were talking to himself. 'One doesn't get invited to a lot of parties, as it were. And I do think we're scandalously under-resourced compared to the prosecution. But that's no excuse for pulling stunts.'

'Of course.'

'I just want to get things under control, so I can get back to Paris before Christmas. I'm spending far more time here than I'd anticipated. The sort of complications coming up . . . I don't think much of the behaviour of the prosecution in this case. Usually there's a more cooperative attitude to evidence.'

He flexed his hands on the steering wheel. Lili was familiar enough with this situation. She didn't fully understand why she inspired these outpourings of confidences from men who had no one else to confide in, but she knew that her job was part of it, that she occupied an area somewhere between a priest and a mechanical device.

Ducasse seemed to have got everything off his chest now, in any case. His narrow shoulders relaxed very slightly, and he was silent for the rest of the drive.

Marković felt heavy and sleepy as the guards led him down the corridor to the interview room. The French lawyer was sitting at the table with someone he didn't recognize, a woman in early middle age with faded blonde hair. The other lawyer, the Serbian man, wasn't there. There was a sharp disappointment in this. He wanted to go back to his cell.

'Good morning, Mr Marković.' The lawyer began in his heavily accented English. 'I will introduce to you Mme

Stambolović of the languages section. She will be translating for us in this talk.' Then he slid back into French again, the blonde woman watching his face and scrawling notes on a small pad while he spoke.

'I've brought a new set of documents.' She spoke in Serbian when Ducasse paused. 'Have you had an opportunity yet to review the previous binders? You probably remember our earlier discussions about this. It is of some importance.'

'I looked at them a bit,' he shrugged.

'Je les ai consulté rapidement,' said the woman, and he was taken aback to recognize the vague sluggish disinterest that suddenly appeared in her voice.

'I see. How much is a bit, then?'

'I flipped through the Vasić folder.'

'All right. That's very good. Now, could you tell me your impression of the reliability or the accuracy of any of that material?'

'No. Not really.'

Ducasse narrowed his mouth. 'Mr Marković, please, I'm your lawyer. I am not trying to persecute you. We'll make much more progress if we have a relationship of trust. If you're hostile to your own lawyer, you're going to find this process extremely difficult.' He paused. 'I'd like us to work together,' he added.

Marković made a limp hand gesture. 'I'm doing my best. I just can't get very far with these papers. They don't, they don't seem to have much to do with what it was like.'

'All right.' The lawyer jotted a note in his book. 'There's a larger picture that's missing. Can you help me fill that picture in?'

'Probably not,' said Marković. 'You're weren't there.'

'That is why I need you to help me,' repeated Ducasse, articulating each word sharply.

'I'm tired. I don't feel well.'

Ducasse put down his pen. 'Okay, Mr Marković. Would you like to see a doctor? Is there a problem with the prison conditions? I'm certainly prepared to make a submission if something needs to be changed, and absolutely you should have medical attention.'

'I don't want a Dutch doctor. Can you get my doctor in from Banja Luka?'

Ducasse exhaled softly. 'I will make a submission; but I must tell you that's likely to be difficult. If you don't feel well, you probably should see one of the doctors here in the interim.'

'No, I don't think so.'

'Well, I will take up the issue of bringing your doctor here.'

'I don't want to talk any more today.'

'Mr Marković, I made arrangements, I hired Mme Stambolović to be here, because we need to talk. I have to go back to Paris soon, we won't have many more opportunities before February. I will do everything I can to get you looked at by your doctor, but it's really very important—'

'Can we do it in a couple of days? Or a week?'

Ducasse glanced towards the interpreter, who nodded briefly. 'All right. I will arrange a time with the prison.' He unzipped his suitcase, reached inside, and began piling binders onto the table. 'I'm not asking you to read all of these in the next week, clearly. If you can get back to Vasić, that will be fine. But just for your information, these are the most recent materials from the prosecution. They haven't confirmed their full witness line-up yet, but this should certainly give you an idea. If you can find time to look at them.' He stood up, taking the handle of the now-empty suitcase with one hand and extending the other. 'Good day, Mr Marković. I do hope that you're feeling better next week.'

* * *

Daniel had spent the last ten days mostly in his car, driving around between Zagreb, where Tudjman, though hospitalized and very possibly comatose, was still running for re-election, and Djakovica, where he interviewed three terrified elderly Serbian women who were living under round-the-clock UN guard while their Albanian neighbours shot at their windows. Back in the damp fresh air of The Hague, waiting for Lili to come home from work, he sat in the lobby of the tribunal after the courtrooms closed for the day, revising a story, and writing some odd fragmentary sentences about the fountain in the plaza out front, how it looked like a circle of men holding spears and machetes, what this might mean. He had been coming up with these essayistic bits and pieces lately, quite unusable, more like a diary than anything else.

Finally he realized that he was starting to become conspicuous, that nearly all the staff had left. She was off on one of those mysterious Special Services Agreements, might not be at her house for a while, but he supposed that he could wait in the bar.

When he went out of the revolving door, he saw Ivo standing by the stairway, sheltering from the cold rain under the overhang of the roof and smoking. He waved and smiled when he saw Daniel.

'Hello there, Mr Daniel Bryant. Back in town again.'

'Seems that way.' Daniel walked over to the lamp-post where he stood, a litter of cigarette butts on the ground at his feet.

'I hope that you are having good luck in finding things to write about.'

'Oh, I always do.'

Ivo nodded, brushed some wet hair off his forehead, and cleared his throat. 'There is a matter that you might find interesting.'

'Is there, then. What kind of matter?'

'Of course I am not supposed to talk to the press. My superiors would not be pleased that I am speaking to you. If I would say certain things, I could easily lose my job.'

'Yes.'

'That must be a bit hard for you, I imagine.'

'It can be.'

Ivo took a drag on his cigarette and looked thoughtfully across the plaza towards the tall white hotel that faced them.

'I guess you travel quite a bit, Mr Daniel Bryant.'

'Some, yeah.'

'Do your travels ever happen to take you to Tuzla?'

Daniel shrugged. 'I can go where I want. I go to Tuzla if I think there's a story there. Why do you ask?'

'Oh, no reason.' He dropped his cigarette to the pavement and ground it out with his foot. 'It just seems that sometimes you can run into certain people in Tuzla. If you happen to be there. Or so I have heard, in any case.'

'Have you.'

'You hear this and that, around the place.'

'Well.' Daniel pulled his jacket around himself. 'I couldn't really say. I haven't decided where I'll be going in the near future.'

'No trouble. I just thought I would mention this.'

'I'll keep it in mind, though.'

'It is entirely your decision.'

'Yes.' He nodded. 'I'd better go now, hadn't I?'

'I think so.'

'Perhaps we'll talk.'

'Perhaps. But I often read your stories in the papers anyway.'

It was no more disturbing than anything else around the tribunal, but it was odd to be interpreting for Nikola Marković, odd to see him sitting across the table, a large pale man with purple shadows under his eyes and a Bosnian accent, not a character in an anecdote or an article but a man with fleshy hands who sat in a wooden chair, accused of genocide, and did not seem to grasp the scale of this.

'He's a troubled person,' said Ducasse absently, turning onto the motorway. 'Not very well emotionally, I suspect.' They drove in silence for a while, and then Ducasse sighed, as if some of his client's exhaustion had been transferred to him.

'I'll be quite honest with you, I don't really expect an acquittal.' Suddenly, he remembered that he was actually speaking to someone, and turned his head towards her. 'This is in complete confidence, of course.'

Lili nodded. 'Everything I hear is in confidence. I take it for granted.'

'That's a refreshing attitude.' He sighed again. 'Well, as I said. But I do think that I can aim at lowering his sentence. I see a great deal of exculpatory material, I really do. It's not as clear-cut as the prosecution likes to make it.' He shook his head a bit. 'Well, I would say that, wouldn't I? But I think it's true. They believe the Bryant material supports them, for instance, and in some respects it does, but there's a good deal in it that's exculpatory.'

Lili didn't move for a moment, then turned her head to face the window. 'Do you mind if I smoke in the car?' she asked slowly.

'Of course not. In fact, I'll join you.' He reached into the glove compartment for a pack of cigarettes and handed one to Lili. She lit it and breathed in deeply.

'Would that be Daniel Bryant? The journalist?'

'Yes, the one who interviewed him. You probably saw that article? The prosecution hasn't formally called him yet, but clearly they're intending to do so. If they don't, I'll do it myself. It wouldn't be very orthodox, but I do see value to the defence in some of his statements.'

Lili took another drag on her cigarette, keeping her free hand clenched so that it couldn't shake. 'That would be an unusual strategy,' she said thoughtfully.

'Well, perhaps. But it's really only a wild conjecture. He's going to be a prosecution witness, there's not much question there.' Ducasse turned to look at her again. 'This *is* in confidence, right?'

'Of course. Always.'

They drove over the canal and onto the road that ran through the woods, a few dark pines among the thin bare branches.

'Actually, why don't you let me out here?' said Lili, when they had gone a bit further. 'I can walk home from here.'

'It's raining outside. I was going to offer you a lift to your house.'

'No, really, I think that I'd rather walk.'

'If that's what you prefer.'

She stepped out of the car in the dark afternoon and headed into the woods, her head down, brown leaves scattering in front of her feet and a magpie cutting through the sky above her.

When Daniel got to the building on Laan van Meerdervort, the street door was unlocked; so she must have come home not long ago. He went inside, locking it behind him, and climbed the narrow stairway to her flat.

She was sitting at her little work table, smoking and staring at the floor, her hair in damp strands around her face.

'Love? What's wrong?'

She didn't look up when he spoke to her, and he stood with

his back against the door, water soaking through from his wet clothes to his skin.

'I can't explain to you,' she said softly. 'It's just . . . something has come up. It isn't your fault.'

'Oh God.' He took off his glasses and put one hand over his eyes.

'You don't need to go right now. I don't want to create a big melodrama. You're here now, it doesn't make much difference, just . . . when you do leave, it's better if you don't come back again.'

He slid down the wall, sitting back on his heels. 'Goddamnit, can't you tell me anything?' he snapped, hating his tone of voice.

'I've gone this long without breaking confidentiality for you, I'm damn well not going to do it now,' she said, her voice high and tense. 'I mean, you're supposed to be an investigative reporter, work it out yourself. Do you think that when those people from the tribunal interviewed you back then, it was just for fun?'

'Good Lord.' He lowered his hand, looking at the blurred shapes of the room, the flicker of Lili's outline. He felt slightly protected by his myopia, the world's impact muffled. 'I'm being called as a witness?'

'I can't confirm or deny that.'

'Is it Marković?'

'I think it would be a fair guess that you're an object of interest in that case. But that's not necessarily the only one.'

'Okay, okay.' He shifted uncomfortably in his wet jacket. 'But what would that mean? Theoretically?'

She stood up from her chair, an uncertain white form. 'I could not possibly work on a case where you were a witness. A journalist is bad enough, but a witness in a case – that's not even . . . So if people don't know already, when I start recusing myself from cases they'll definitely work it out. And it wouldn't stop there. In that theoretical instance. Once it started to get around, every defence attorney, plus everyone out there with an axe to grind against the tribunal, which is a great many people, would be going through every one of your articles looking for information I might have given you.'

'You never gave me any information.'

'You know that, and I know that. Do you think anyone else would believe it?'

'I'm being called as a witness,' he repeated idiotically, aware of a looming mass of questions that he would have to look at later, not now, there were only so many things he could contain in his mind at one time. He leaned his head back against the wall, looking at the blobs of colour that surrounded him, wishing that everything could really be that soft and unthreatening. 'You know,' he said, reaching for some kind of distance, 'speaking as a professional, I just don't see a big story here. Honest to God, if I stumbled across this one I wouldn't bother to file it. So a minor reporter has a relationship with an interpreter, it's not exactly Iran-Contra.'

'I'm sorry to break it to you, but most of your profession is not exactly Iran-Contra. You might recall they're in the process of bringing down the American government because the president had it off with a girl in thong underpants.'

'Yeah, but that's *America*.'

For just a second she started to laugh, and he was hit by a temporary surge of warmth, bittersweet and dishonest. The laugh collapsed into something close to a sob. 'Do you think I want to do this, Daniel? And take your stupid jacket off, for God's sake.'

He didn't know what he was going to do in five minutes, in half an hour, where he would be, but he slid his jacket off, and left it lying beside him on the floor.

'I want to tell you a story,' she said, sitting down on the couch. He put his glasses back on and looked at her, folded over with her arms wrapped around herself, her eyes rimmed with red. 'This is something I've never told anyone. Not that it's professional confidentiality, but I always felt it wasn't really my story to tell. But I think it's important for you to hear it.' She breathed in deeply. 'It's a story about how my father murdered somebody.'

She started by indirection, talking in a disjointed way about her father and the Party. How she had wondered, for a while, at the way he had avoided any real trouble in Belgrade; how she had realized that he could not have been nearly as fervent as he liked to think in his pro-Soviet opinions, or he would have ended up doing a term in Goli Otok, or at least losing a job or two. How she had, years later, come to understand something about the nature of exile, and to realize that even as fortunate an immigrant as her father, with his fluent French and his several degrees and his editorial job at *L'Humanité*, would have felt the cold glance of exclusion. If she knew that she was, in a small way, not a child of the country, he would have known it much more sharply. But the Party had accepted him, had taken him in, his origins in even a questionably Communist country an advantage with them, and the fact that he had come to them because he found them more ideologically sound hugely flattering both to them and to him.

'So it mattered to him, the Party. I mean, he was an ideologue anyway, sure. I can say that, I know that he was, he had this little narrow ideological mind, but he was also just a man who was looking for a home.' She rubbed her forehead. 'God, Daniel, I was a child when I saw through them, and even so there's a little bit of me that misses the Party.'

He nodded, and thought it was better not to speak; moved toward the couch and sat down beside her.

'So. Anyway. There was this man at the Russian Embassy. His name doesn't matter, you wouldn't recognize it. The thing is, he had some contacts with the PCF, my father and the other people around *L'Huma* knew him. And as a matter of fact I knew him as well. I still went to a lot of the Party events at that point. It was, it had to do with not upsetting my parents, I suppose. This man had a son about my age, a boy I used to see at these things. I liked him. I wouldn't say we dated as such, but a few times I went to their house.'

'This was when?'

'I was fourteen, so it was 1973. Now, I had some idea that there was something, how should I put this, something a little dodgy in their house. I mean, I would see books there that such a man shouldn't have in his house. He was low-level at the Embassy, not a bigshot, not the kind of person who got away with things, so it was strange to see those books. And little comments he would make. Something strange. I think that was maybe part of what I liked about the boy, this sense of mystery around his family, this sense that there was some kind of challenge going on. Well, I had no idea. No idea what this man was really doing. If I'd been older, if I'd been old enough to put the pieces together . . .' She reached for a cigarette and lit it, sitting silently for a minute.

'What was he doing, then?' asked Daniel.

'Samizdat. He was passing information to a group that smuggled books into Czechoslovakia. Telling them where there were border guards that could be bribed, that kind of thing. It was a little operation, not on the scale of Jan Kavan or anything, probably one of the smallest pipelines they had, but any route was important, you know?'

Her hands moved nervously, the cigarette shedding ash on the carpet, on her shoes.

'Well, then. Here's what happened. My father shopped him.

That's the English expression, isn't it? He shopped him to the KGB. And the family was very suddenly called home to the Soviet Union and he disappeared. There you go. I don't know for sure if he was executed, or if they maybe just put him in one of those mental hospitals.' She exhaled sharply. 'Did you know a little while ago they published some poetry that was smuggled out of one of those places? I had this wild thought, maybe it was him. He was a literary man. But it doesn't really matter. It was him, it was anyone.'

'What happened to the boy?'

'He's still alive. I was able to find that out. I don't know anything more than that. Who knows, he's probably selling old vegetables in Moscow.'

Daniel turned the story over in his mind, unable to stop being a journalist entirely, looking for the gaps and questions. 'How do you know it was your father who turned him in?'

Lili laughed bitterly. 'One of his old friends told me, as a matter of fact. A few years later, just after he killed himself. Would you believe he was trying to make me feel better? Like, these are the noble things your father did for the cause? Some of those people were just, you know, there was something wrong with them. Of course it's not like it was illegal, what my father did. Just a little questionable thing in a big criminal landscape, there were millions like him. You can't get them into court over it. Not here, not anywhere.' She looked towards him, her face pinched and hollow. 'But here's the real problem, Daniel. How did my father know? How did he know? Did I say something? Did he find out from me?'

Daniel frowned. 'But . . . don't you know the answer to that?'

'That's the whole fucking point,' said Lili sharply. 'No, I *don't* know. I was fourteen fucking years old. I didn't know what was dangerous and what wasn't. I can't *remember* what

I might have said.' She buried her face in her hands. 'I have thought about it over and over so many times. Anything I think I remember now is probably invented. I will never, never know.'

He reached out and put his hand on her back, lightly, tentatively.

'Because I wouldn't have necessarily been careful,' she went on, her voice low and fast. 'I wouldn't have believed that my father could . . . that he would betray someone that way. I loved my father, Daniel. He was a good father and I loved him. But he did this thing. And maybe, maybe I could have given him the information he needed to do it. I just don't know.'

She stood and walked to the window, staring out at the night. 'I love you, Daniel, I really do. You probably don't know how much. But that doesn't help, it doesn't have anything to do with what's right. I can't even be sure how much I've told you, one way or another. What I say, what I don't say. Effectively I broke confidentiality for you ten minutes ago. And I'll do it again. You know I will. It can't go on.'

He got up from the couch and put his arms around her, breathing in the smell of her hair.

'I'd better go,' he said, hearing his voice crack.

'I would like it if you could stay till tomorrow,' she whispered.

'I don't know . . . I think I should . . . I could, ah, get a hotel or . . .' He swallowed hard, twice, pressing his eyes shut. 'Oh, fuck it,' he said fiercely, falling back on anger because it was available and safe, letting her go and stalking towards his jacket, picking it up from the floor. 'Fucking . . . just . . . I'm just going, okay?'

Lili was motionless in the centre of the room. 'We could

talk on the phone? Sometime later?' she said, her voice arcing in nervous interrogatives.

He stopped in the doorway and leaned his head against the frame. 'Oh, what do you think, Lili? Of course I'll call you. I'll just go on and on like this until . . . never mind. Forget it. I'm leaving now.'

He ran through the rain to the street where he had parked his car, knowing he would get in it and drive, too fast, to some city he hated – Rotterdam, Utrecht – and find a bar and drink until he couldn't stand up, and the next day he would get back in his car and drive to Tuzla, in the hope, the fervent hope, that something terrible would happen there.

XVI

Directions

28 November–3 December 1999

Lili went down the stairway of her building late at night, her footsteps echoing slightly in the silence, and walked, under the bare trees of the park, drifts of cloud pale against the dark sky, reflecting back the lights of the city.

She had always inhabited words, and she walked now reciting poems to herself, not for the meaning so much as the movement and lift of the language, the rhythm of her legs striding along the path, the rise and fall of her breathing.

She knew all along that this had to happen. There was little room for surprise or anger. Only the knowledge that certain things were required of her, that she had taken on responsibilities, and if she wanted to be a faithful custodian of language she had to respect them.

Je suis parti pour longtemps. Je revins pour partir.

Mostly what she felt was empty; strangely blank and drained. There was never much hope in it anyway. They were people who had never been very good at this kind of thing, too solitary, too stubborn, too much inclined to settle nowhere. Attached to disconnection.

She stood at the edge of the pond, looking at the dark trees on the opposite bank, her arms wrapped hard around herself.

La terre nous aimait un peu je me souviens.

* * *

So you are sitting in a café in Tuzla and thinking about being drawn right into the centre of that legal theatre, and you are thinking about what you should do.

This was almost certainly the stupidest lead he had ever followed in his life, waiting aimlessly in Tuzla to see if he ran into some completely undefined people whose importance he might or might not recognize when or if he saw them. So he sat at a small table in a corner, irritable and hung-over, writing notes to himself. He had been writing a number of useless things; in one of his jacket pockets was a long, rambling, maudlin letter to Lili, which he was not about to post and also not about to throw away.

You think about real consequences. The possibility that they'll ask you to reveal a source, that once you are up there in the box there's no protection for you, and everyone knows that you guard a source even if it means going to jail, but nobody wants to go to jail. The possibility that you could never go back to Republika Srpska with any degree of safety. The possibility that no one will trust you enough to speak to you again.

He had done as much as he could think of to do, in pursuit of this phantom story. He'd had a pleasant but pointless conversation with the mayor, an old communist who had been governing Tuzla apparently since the dawn of recorded time and had managed, for all his limitations, to keep his city somewhat multi-ethnic and somewhat safe throughout the war. He'd phoned the local NGOs. Nothing out of the ordinary was happening in Tuzla, that much seemed clear.

Since he had no reasonable expectation of income from this trip, he was staying in a hotel with unrepaired bullet holes in the window and pictures of topless women pasted to the wardrobe door. The café, pleasant and unremarkable as the city itself, was a clear improvement. It was mid-morning, a cold day, the windows slightly misted. Behind the bar, a waiter in a Che Guevara T-shirt was flipping through a paperback book, and a handful of other men sat at a table by the window, smoking and arguing passionately about football. It was very improbable that they were the people Ivo was interested in, but he didn't feel much like walking around the streets in the late November wind.

Of course he was free to leave. He could leave Tuzla, he could leave Bosnia, he could leave the Balkans for that matter. He had almost nothing but choices.

You think that Nikola Marković will hate you. That doesn't matter. But should it matter? The fact that it doesn't matter, does that mean you've lost something in yourself? Or does it mean you still have some grasp of right and wrong? You don't know about that part.

He didn't miss her in the form of specific images. There wasn't really a picture of her that he called up in his mind, no more than a fragmentary impression of pale hair and the delicate bones at the top of her spine when she bent her neck. Missing her was more of a sensation in his body, a soft tense pain, an intermittent wave of anxiety like a brief sickness.

He could rewrite the letter so it was less of an illegible drunken effusion. It wouldn't be hard. He could tell her that he would go and write commentaries on New Labour for the *Guardian*, or any number of other things that wouldn't be a conflict of interest with her work. There were a lot of good reasons to do that.

Mostly, you think about neutrality. That we're supposed to be under this blanket, with the Red Cross and the UN, that it is, or so we say, why people will give us interviews and why they don't kill us. You think, if journalists go into the court for one side, and we throw that blanket away, how long will it be until journalists start to carry guns? Until people make us carry guns and fight for one side or another, or until we decide to do it ourselves.

The waiter brought him another cup of espresso. '*Hvala*,' nodded Daniel.

'*Jesi li ti Amerikanac?*'

'*Kanadjanin.*'

'Ah, Canada. I have uncle in Canada. Vancouver.'

Daniel sometimes wondered if there was anywhere you could go in the world where you would find someone who didn't have an uncle in Canada. Burma, perhaps. But he smiled, chatted a bit longer with the man – Muharem, his name was – about the weather in Vancouver, and about Cronenberg's *Videodrome*, which had made a big impact on Muharem years ago, and given him slightly inaccurate ideas about Canadian culture in general.

You think about the UN troops shining spotlights on the Sarajevo airport runway, and helping the killers separate the men from the women at Srebrenica. You think about what Nina told you, that the Red Cross gave lists of Serbian refugees to Arkan's men so he could kidnap them and drag them back into the war. You know that mostly these things were accidental. They were failures of imagination, an inability to recognize evil, but they happened, and they weren't neutral events.

It did not escape him that this argument with himself about testifying was strangely ironic, given that he was effectively in Tuzla on an errand for the prosecution, though he was pretty certain that the Office of the Prosecutor as such knew nothing about it. He would not have to do anything overt beyond coming here – if he found the story, and if it was a real story, he would write it because that's what a journalist does, and if his editor thought it was a story it would go out on the wire, and it would do whatever it did in the world, as all his stories would.

You think that you are born not breathing, and you have to act in order to breathe, and if you do you've made a choice that isn't neutral, a choice for life against death, and every other choice will follow on that. You think that there's never been a neutral action in the world.

They had come into Tuzla when Srebrenica fell, the few men who survived; stumbling out of the woods, emaciated, bloody, their eyes hollow and empty, like death, like something beyond even death, the utter black absence of shrieking space. Like nothing he had ever seen. Years later he had watched the investigators digging up one of the graves, carefully lifting out a single Nike shoe, and then a skull.

You think that the tribunal is a flawed and sometimes ridiculous institution which was set up to make people feel better about letting genocide play itself out under their noses. And you think that anyway, you will testify, you will go there and testify when they ask.

And then Lili. He put down his coffee cup. He would deal with this story first, with whatever he had to do here; he would give himself that much time. But he had the letter in his pocket, and somewhere at the back of his mind he was aware of the faint but definite shape of a decision. It felt right, it felt clear and promising.

And you think that it's the best we can do, something so limited, so constrained. You think, this is an attempt. An attempt, in the face of murdered children, in the face of rape camps, in the face of the mutilation of corpses. An attempt, partial and imperfect and terribly human, to proclaim the continued existence of the world.

In fact, when he found the story, or the story found him, he was playing a silly game with a statue. Tuzla didn't have a lot in the way of tourist attractions, but at the bottom of the Korzo there were two statues of local worthies, a painter and a writer, both of them in heavy overcoats and looking full of ennui. He had put his hat on the writer's head and was trying to fit a cigarette into the painter's bronze hand when he saw the young man walking past him, and there was that momentary sense of slippage, transparent plates improperly aligned, that happened when you met someone you vaguely recognized, but in the wrong place. Marković's lawyer. Of course.

It took only another second to realize that this must be what Ivo had meant, and he moved away from the statues and composed his face into an open, sociable expression, walking towards the lawyer as if he were a bit curious, a bit embarrassed.

'Excuse me,' he said, 'you probably don't remember me.'

But clearly he did, because he turned around with a glare of complete and sudden hatred that actually drove Daniel back a step. There was no room for indirection here. They were enemies. The look of pure ideological hate was something you didn't forget.

'I know you,' Lukitch said briefly. 'The journalist who wants to exterminate Serbs.'

It was entirely, irrecoverably the wrong thing to do, but Daniel laughed.

'I could destroy you,' Lukitch hissed, his voice with its slight Quebec accent vibrating with fury. 'If you do anything against my client, I will end your career.'

'Oh, I don't think so,' said Daniel mildly. 'It's not really that easy. Is that why you're here, then? Keeping an eye on me?'

Of course he wasn't that easy to trap. 'Is that a joke? You know that you're following me. And I'm warning you again,' he said, fixing Daniel with ice-cold eyes, 'do not touch my client's case. You have no business here.' He turned away, and got into a car a few metres up the street. Daniel watched him go, thoughtfully, leaning on a streetlight in an unconscious echo of the statues. He couldn't very well leap in a taxi and tail the car, but Lukitch had been coming from the pedestrianized centre of the city for a reason, and in a city this small the reason had to be something he could find.

It didn't even occur to him to worry about Lukitch's vague threat. He had heard this often enough before, how his reputation would be ruined, how no one would ever again read a word he wrote. It never came to anything. The gunners over Sarajevo at least had understood that the only effective way to destroy journalists was to shoot them.

He walked back into the centre. Probably Lukitch had been at another lawyer's office, something like that; there were a few places he could check. He couldn't think yet what it might all mean, but at least there was a direction to follow now.

Then he walked by the café, paused outside without thinking about it, and through the plate glass of the window he saw Muharem meet his eye and pull back. He opened the door and walked inside, and the waiter was staring at him – at Daniel, Canadian Daniel – with a sudden wild mixture of confusion and fear, and at that point he knew, almost in detail, what the story would be.

This would not be quick, he could not do anything that would frighten this man further, could not push him too hard. But the story was there. It was only necessary to open it up, unfold it like a greetings card and read the message.

'Excuse me,' he said, sitting down at the bar. 'Could I speak with you for a minute, please?'

It wasn't a big story – it could have been spiked, and then he would have had to make a decision about telling Ivo. But it wasn't spiked, it did go out on the wire, and one or two papers picked it up. There was no other action needed on his part.

'I can't believe you could be so stupid,' said Ducasse, pulling his car violently onto the motorway. 'I simply can't believe this. I don't know what I'm doing on this case sometimes.'

'You're not even going to listen to my side of it, are you?' said Milan Lukitch, looking out of the passenger window. 'This man, who is universally known to be biased, says I was intimidating the witness, and you don't even ask me if it's true.'

'I don't care if you were recruiting the witness for a football team, Milan. You do not wander off to Bosnia and chat with the prosecution's people. You *know* that.' Lukitch continued to stare out of the window. 'At any rate, I did my best for you in the hearing, but you're under formal investigation, and your courtroom privileges have been suspended, so you're now serving as my legal assistant, and you take no actions outside of that role, are we clear?'

'Perfectly clear. Thank you so very much,' said Lukitch bitterly. 'I'm sure you're not shedding any tears about that arrangement.'

'Milan,' said Ducasse, almost pounding his fist on the steering wheel, 'listen to me, please. Can't you understand that you aren't here to fight your father's wars?'

The young man turned to him with a level gaze. 'What else is anyone doing here?' he asked.

Ducasse was appalled at himself for speaking so personally, and almost couldn't summon a reply. 'Upholding the law,' he said finally, his throat constricted with effort. 'Upholding the sanctity of the law.'

Lukitch looked at him as if he were insane.

They drove silently into the car park, and walked at a slight distance from each other up the stairs and towards the security booth.

Inside the grey-glass walls, several people were putting their coats through the metal detector, someone else was sorting through a pile of newspapers. The guard behind the desk glanced at their staff passes, nodded them through and then paused, reached up towards a Post-it note on the wall of his booth, and signalled to the guard at the metal detector.

The second guard, a tall man, blond, stepped in front of them, his hands reaching casually for his baton. 'Sorry,' he said briskly, in accented English. 'This one cannot come in.'

'*Non, vous vous tromp* . . . you make a mistake,' said Ducasse, shaking his head. 'I have talk to registrar, is no problem.'

'No. He cannot come in.' The baton was up against his chest now, and when Lukitch took a step forward he moved it, just fractionally, just enough to push him back, then touched the radio on his shoulder. 'Bravo One,' he said softly into the static, then spoke several sentences in Dutch.

'This is stupid,' snapped Lukitch, and stepped sideways. Before Ducasse could register what was happening the guard moved as well, and suddenly he had Lukitch pressed up against the wall of the booth, holding the baton hard against his chest and shouting in Dutch while Lukitch shouted back in French. 'Please,' fumbled Ducasse. 'Is not, is not . . . we have need to . . .'

'*Puis-je vous aider?*' said someone quietly, and he saw the interpreter, Mme Stambolović, who was watching the collision with astonishment from behind the newspaper table. 'I had an arrangement with the registrar,' he explained hastily, relieved to be speaking French. 'I don't know what's gone wrong, but he isn't supposed to be barred from the building, I . . .'

'Okay,' said the interpreter, and moved towards the guard, speaking in rapid soft English with some Dutch phrases, suggesting that they should call the registrar's office, that things could be sorted out, but the guard and the lawyer were paying attention only to each other now, still spitting mutually unintelligible insults. She turned to the man in the booth, and he picked up the phone to call the registry, but at the same time the guard pulled Lukitch's staff card from his neck, leaving a scraped red line on his skin, and threw it on the ground. Lukitch stiffened in anger as the guard ostentatiously put one hand on his gun.

'You go out now,' said the guard in English, his teeth clenched, and Lukitch stepped backwards, pushed by the man's hand on his chest, launching a long stream of Quebecois profanities, *mon christ de chien, touche-moi pas, tabarnac, lâche-moi, mon hostie de chien sale* – and Lili, in professional mode now, couldn't help but ransack her mind for the English equivalents, *you motherfucking cocksucker, get your fucking hands off me*, and before Lukitch was quite out of the door he saw Lili, leaning against the wall with one hand on her mouth, and spat, still in French, *You think you're going to get away with this, bitch?* Lili stepped backwards and thought, he's just saying things at random, this doesn't mean anything, he doesn't even know who I am, and turned in the other direction, out of the door and up the stairs into the building, leaving Ducasse in the security booth in a wreckage of emotions, holding his head and wanting only to open up a law book and escape.

Around the world, computers were running through a series of drills designed to take them through their own small digital Year Zero. And in London, wheeling Marko's pushchair to the shop, Paja took a deep breath and understood finally what it was that he must do.

It would require a plan, of course, a plan of some intricacy. There was always a knife, there was always an artery; but it was no good that way, with his own hands again, you couldn't cancel out justice that easily. It had to be properly done.

There was no one he could turn to for help; not Annie, poor thing, who still thought the war was something far away, something that ended long ago. Not even the man in the park who knew some things, a few things, but didn't understand that it was Paja, that he had brought the apocalypse with him in his blood, limping out of his burning country, guilty and already dead.

There is always some sacrifice.

It was Paja's responsibility. The man in the park spoke of rescue by the spacemen, and it was a good dream; but there would be no rescue from outside this world. Paja would have to create his child's rescue himself, and it would cost him everything, but that was all right, he was glad, he was joyful. There would be no price too high to pay.

XVII

Ten Other Places in the World

December 1999

'I've never seen a trial fall apart quite like this,' whispered Alain. 'And it's not even a trial yet, properly speaking.'

Lili looked through the window of their booth towards the courtroom, where Ducasse was attacking a piece of paper with a ballpoint pen while he waited for the status conference to resume. She wondered if Daniel's name would actually be spoken in the courtroom. So far it had not been. The story hadn't appeared under his byline, it was simply an anonymous wire-service feed, though it seemed that everyone knew who had written it. Calls had been made to AFP, of course.

Her desk was covered with pieces of paper, motions under discussion about the status of Milan Lukitch, about whether Muharem Hotić's testimony was now contaminated and inadmissible, about the performance of the defence team as a whole, about the performance of the prosecution, and Daniel hadn't come up yet, but he was on the witness list too, this would have to enter into it.

Judge Abreu and her colleagues returned and sat. 'Well,' she said, and Lili followed the forced cheer of her voice, 'have we all been getting ready for the Christmas spirit on our break? The charity towards each other and so forth? Very well. So now I will ask again if the defence and the prosecution have been able to reach a certain sort of factual agreement about, well, actually I would be satisfied with an agreement about anything, not even touching to the facts of the case yet.'

McKinley and Ducasse glanced briefly at each other across the room. 'I'm not entirely sure to which matter Your Honour is referring,' said McKinley, rising, 'but I don't foresee very many grounds of agreement between myself and my colleague at this time.'

'Well, I can say only that it is getting late in the proceedings to be at this difficult point, and I don't say any more about it for now. But I take it that means you are both still wanting me to decide on every one of these very many motions here.'

'Your Honour,' and Ducasse rose in turn, 'I really have to address the court again about the difficulties the defence is having in preparing this case. I'm, I have to be simply looking around for staff at this point, after the shameful display which the security personnel put on with regard to my colleague Mr Lukitch, which was really, Your Honour, very ugly and intolerable, and in the face of this it's very difficult for me even to find legal assistants, and I just have to ask again for a mistrial here on the grounds that the principle of equality of arms is being persistently violated.'

Abreu rubbed her eyes with her fingertips. 'Can you suggest a remedy for this, Mr Ducasse?'

'Well, the remedy would be a mistrial, Your Honour.'

'I don't really see that as a remedy. Would you like us to delay the proceedings some more? Assign you some new staff?'

'I'm asking for a mistrial.' Ducasse was tense, visibly agitated, and even Lili could recognize that his legal arguments were getting very shaky.

'Well, I'm not going to grant that, so let's look towards remedy, because clearly this situation isn't beyond—'

'Then I'm asking for the disqualification of this trial chamber on the grounds of bias.'

Abreu folded her hands. 'Okay. Let us be calm here for a moment.'

'I will be filing this as a written motion.'

'Well, you have that right, Mr Ducasse. You can ask for me to be taken off this case if you want, but I think you need to put some evidence. Your motion will go to the appeals chamber for a decision as you ask. I just say to you, I suppose they will want some evidence.'

Lili checked her clock, and looked at Alain with a grimace. He rolled his eyes and shrugged. No knowing how long this would go on.

The interpreters couldn't help but be affected by the mood of the courtroom, so by the time the hearing had worn itself down in a flurry of motions and recriminations, Lili and Alain were both edgy and irritable, worn out in a way quite different from the end of a day of testimony. Lili was trying to breathe deeply as she walked down the wide white staircase; and then she saw Ivo at the bottom, with a copy of *Politika* in his hand and his face tight with suppressed emotion. He gestured her away from Alain, who went on towards the lift, and handed the paper to her without speaking, folding it to an inner page.

She read it, and then clutched her arms around her chest, closing her eyes. Ivo put a hand on her shoulder and said something, reaching out to take her into a hug. She stood stiffly with his arms around her.

It was dark when Daniel walked into Prins Hendrikplein. A tram, the windows a promise of light and warmth in the cold wind, curled around the circle behind him. Lili was sitting on one of the stone turtles, her feet drawn up, her arms around her knees. He stopped a short distance away.

She glanced up at him, then put her head down again. 'You

never explained that New Year's story to me,' she said, her voice drained and flat. 'About ten worse places in the world?'

'It's not all that great a story.' He tucked his hands into the sleeves of his jacket. 'It's just, I was in Sarajevo on New Year's Eve in 1992, and the UN Secretary-General was visiting. I don't know if he thought we wanted him to wish us a happy new year or what, but anyway people were following him around all day yelling, "Killer, killer, fucking killer," which I couldn't help but more or less agree with at that point. And then he had this bizarre press conference, where this young woman got up and started asking him what would it take, how many deaths would it actually take before the UN did *something*, anything, and he kind of turned on the room and said, "Listen, you're better off here than in ten places in the world, I can tell you ten places in the world that are worse than Sarajevo." And I just thought, which ten, you know? And why ten exactly? Do they rank them daily in New York or what?'

'Number eleven with a bullet.'

'More or less.'

She didn't say anything else. He walked closer towards her. 'I'm sorry,' he whispered, and she looked up, sighed and reached into her pocket for a cigarette. 'It never occurred to me . . . I should have thought . . .'

She shrugged. 'It's not your fault.' She took out her lighter and flicked it, circling the flame with her hand. 'You're a journalist, you did your job. It's just something that was bound to happen.'

He sat down by the turtle's eyeless head, watching her draw on the cigarette, not looking at him. 'Is it really so bad? I mean, that bad? It's *Politika*, after all, it's not like it's a paper anybody takes seriously. And they didn't actually say, I mean right out say—'

'It is that bad. Yes.'

He shifted on the cold pavement, running the text of the article through his mind. He could remember it by now almost word for word. 'Look, of course I have sources. I have lots of sources. So I knew what was going on inside the Kosovo talks, so did every journalist who deserves to be working. So I know some people at NATO; so somebody told me they were doing an arrest raid. I didn't even know it was Marković until I saw him. Lukitch has this grand unified field theory about my stories, like every bit of information I ever got came from one place. No one could possibly believe that.'

Lili tapped the ash from her cigarette onto the ground. 'Can you prove that it isn't true?'

'Well, I could.'

'Yeah? And how would you do that?'

He looked down at his feet. He knew there was only one way he could do it. He could reveal his sources. There was no other way to prove that Lili wasn't one of them, that she wasn't the central one. And you never reveal your sources.

He picked up a pebble from the ground and turned it in his hand.

'How would you do that, Daniel?' she repeated.

He thought that he could try to answer her honestly. He would go to jail to protect a source, but if she asked him he would do it, he would break that trust. That the particular sources he would have to sell in order to save her would not pay with their lives, but they would come down hard, jobs would be lost, people would be hurt, Ivo among them, and he would do that if she asked. And this was the wrong answer. If he told her the truth, she would never forgive him.

'Okay,' he said. 'Okay. I can't.' He pressed the pebble into his palm, a small sharp pain.

'Anyway, I've already handed in my resignation,' continued Lili, leaning her head on her knees again. 'As far as the tribunal goes, this is a tiny scandal. It'll blow over, no real harm done.'

'But?'

'Well, it's possibly the end of my career, isn't it?' she said without looking up. 'I have to take it to my professional association, and most likely I'll be suspended. Even if I'm not, my reputation is pretty well ruined. People are going to think very carefully before hiring me for, well, almost anything.' She was quiet for a few minutes, and he realized that her shoulders were shaking, that she was crying again, silently, hopelessly.

'This was my whole life, Daniel,' she said, so quietly he could hardly hear.

He thought about helpful suggestions – that academic conferences surely didn't care much about confidentiality, that she could always teach, or translate books, that she could write books for that matter – but he knew that saying any of these things would be stupid, worse than stupid. Like the men who sat around London parks yelling, 'Cheer up, love, it may never happen!' at total strangers.

The tram returned, a capsule of brightness isolated in space, gliding around the other side of the circle.

'I really am sorry,' he said. 'It's my fault, I know that.'

'No. I knew what I was doing. I broke my oath. I don't actually deserve to work again, to be quite honest. I had a trust, and I didn't keep it.'

'You never told me anything.'

'That's not the issue. Anyway, I would have. Someday I would have, for sure.' She wiped at her eyes with the back of her hand. 'Look at me. Jesus. Me and Stana Marković and the Mladić girl. Good daughters, all of us.' She lit another cigarette. 'Working here – I thought that was a useful thing to do with myself. Repairing a few things, here and there, perhaps. Trying to make some good, some justice, come out of at least one situation. But look at what happens. I can't do it, Daniel. I can't make up for what he did. Everything falls apart.'

Unable to touch her, he turned sideways and stroked the stone turtle's smooth head.

'What about mercy?' he said, not even sure as he spoke what he meant to say.

'That's an excuse,' said Lili. 'That's just like . . . this wasn't so bad, you can violate your trust here and there, nobody got hurt – you start there, and then you say, well, what my father did wasn't so bad, he didn't break any laws, he didn't even lie, he just told certain people things that happened to be true. You keep on like that, you end up saying, you know, that Radovan Karadžić, at least he was fighting for something he believed in. You can't just let everybody off the hook.'

He put his forehead against the cold stone, trying to reach for the right words. 'Listen. I've seen things, Lili, horrible things. I've seen bodies in the streets, little children, dying. People I thought of as my friends, they died too. I want justice for them. I have to believe that there might be some kind of justice, and you know that when I've criticized the tribunal it's because I don't think it goes far enough. But – but even so . . .' he held one hand up helplessly, 'I just think that somewhere there has to be some place for mercy.'

'What?' said Lili bitterly, tossing her cigarette to the pavement. 'You want to turn them all out of prison or what?'

'I don't mean that. I saw – after what I saw, I want Marković to stay in jail for the rest of his life. I don't know if they still want me to testify after all this, but if they do I'll come, I'll do my bit to put him away. I know there are people, good people, who can only go on by thinking about him spending the rest of forever in hell, and maybe he will, I'm not a religious person,

I don't understand these things. But there's a part of him, Lili, there's some tiny part of him that knows what he's done. He hates that part of himself, but it's there, I saw it. I guess . . . I would just like to think that there could be someone who would understand it all and – not let him off, not let him go, but just forgive him. Not me. I won't, I can't. I don't even have the right. But I can wish that someone would.'

She didn't say anything, sitting in the darkness.

'Ljiljana, darling, you don't need to judge yourself for ever. You aren't guilty for the world.'

She stood up abruptly, pulling her coat around herself. 'I have to go,' she said. 'Look, please don't call me, okay?'

'It's up to you,' muttered Daniel.

'All right. That's what I want. I have to go back to Paris and see what I can salvage of my career. It's better for both of us if you don't call me again. It would just keep on ending the same way anyway.' She walked away quickly, her hands in her pockets, her head down.

Daniel stayed sitting on the ground, his head on the turtle's pale pink neck, and he thought that he hadn't cried when he had seen dead children in Bosnia, and it would be very inappropriate if he started to cry right now.

No one told him anything; he was, after all, only the defendant. But he did hear stories in the corridors, he knew that something had happened on his case, even if he didn't quite know what.

The guards brought him down the hallway. Ducasse was in the interview room with a new interpreter, a man. When he passed on the lawyer's greeting, Marković could hear a strong Croatian accent. Very well. He could work around that.

'So,' he said in English. 'What is this kind of problem you've been having?'

The interpreter frowned, and spoke several sentences in French. The lawyer spoke again, and the interpreter turned to Marković. 'Stepping out of my role as interpreter, I have permission to tell you that, although I am able to interpret from English, I can be more accurate if you speak in Serbian.'

'Wouldn't you rather have me speak in Croatian?'

The interpreter sighed slightly as he exchanged words with the lawyer. 'I can understand both Croatian and Serbian,' he said patiently, turning back to Marković. 'I am a non-partisan professional employee of the languages section.'

Marković shrugged. 'I think that I will speak in English.'

'If you prefer.'

'Back to our subject then. I heard about some problem, and I would like to be informed. What has happened to the other lawyer, the Serb?'

'Mr Lukitch has been reassigned, I hope temporarily, to work as a legal assistant,' said Ducasse through the interpreter. 'I hope to have another co-counsel assigned within a few days.'

The intensity of his loss amazed Marković. He had met the man only two or three times and didn't know him in any real sense, but it was as if he had been told that he would never see his family again, that he would be alone in a tiny room for ever, and he could barely hold himself together.

'Oh, really?' he snapped. 'Is it possible he was too determined actually to defend me? Or is it only that I am to be denied any contact with Serbian people now?'

'It was an unfortunate incident that I hope we can clear up in the near future,' said Ducasse, looking through the papers on the desk.

'I heard that it was about Muharem Hotić,' said Marković, and Ducasse looked up sharply.

'Where did you hear that?'

'Nowhere special. Is it true?'

'I suppose that it is, yes.'

His stomach knotted, a sick feeling coursing up his throat. 'Hotić is a fucking liar. Whatever he is going to say is a pile of lies.'

Ducasse nodded thoughtfully. 'That's interesting, Mr Marković. Could you tell me more? Is there something I need to know?'

'Are they calling him as a witness then?'

'Certainly they are, as it says in the documents which you have,' said Ducasse, unable to keep an edge entirely out of his voice.

'Well, what is he going to say? What could he say except shitheap of lying?' He could feel the heat rising in his face, his chest.

The lawyer pursed his lips. 'He will speak, as it says in the files, about certain allegations regarding the camps. He will allege that you entered one of the camps and—'

'Never mind. Never mind.' Marković ground his fists against his eyes, against the picture of Hotić, the black stare burning in his gaunt face, the blood on the walls, the stench.

'Mr Marković, please. We need to discuss this case together. If you have any information that might cast doubt on Mr Hotić's testimony, I want to hear about it. If he's likely to say something I'm not prepared for, I'd like to hear your version first.'

'No. No, nothing,' muttered Marković. 'Well, he could say anything, but that hardly could make it true.'

'It didn't happen the way he said, then.'

'Who cares what the fuck he said!' Marković slapped his hand down on the desk, and it hurt, his palm stinging with little needles. He was seized with a huge pity for himself, rocking the hand in his lap. Everything was determined to hurt him.

'Mr Marković, are you all right?' asked the lawyer in English.

'Fine, fine.' He waved his other hand in a gesture of dismissal. 'I need to think. I want to go back to my cell.'

'Are you all right?' asked the lawyer again. 'It is better that you will tell me—'

'Marš vani!' shouted Marković, and was startled momentarily to hear the interpreter's echo, *'Vas-t-en!'*

Ducasse stood up, stiff and precise. 'Certainly, Mr Marković. If that is what you wish. We speak again after.' He summoned the guard, and Marković entered the corridor, and it stretched out in front of him into an indefinite distance, white, and at the end of it, as he walked, a dark room filled with blood.

XVIII

Ibro Salihović

December 1999/July 1992

He entered the room.
The smell of shit and vomit and sweat.
He turned his head and spoke.

Miloš was driving the jeep towards the camp, his belly swelling out under his T-shirt, his eyes red. Nikola had been drinking, at a certain point he had started drinking more or less constantly, but you couldn't say that he was drunk as such, only that it was a hot day, the air damp and thick, and the borders of things were blurred.

They stopped the jeep at the gate of the factory and he saw the figures in the yard.

It was not like seeing people. They looked horrible, their bones jabbing out at angles, their skin a strange yellow brown, and their movements were jerky, idiotic, irrational.

Miloš held his pistol to the man's head and turned to Nikola, raising his eyebrows in a question.

The floor of the building was sticky with certain substances.

In the corner, Goran Jović, formerly a policeman, was holding a rifle, casually, amiably. He spat, and pushed something aside with his boot. The thing was possibly still attached to the rest of the body.

In the clean white cell in Scheveningen, at the verge of the North Sea, he sat with the binders open in front of him and read over the text of the indictment, the words he hadn't really listened to when they were read in court, a little mosquito voice in the earphones, and he saw that somewhere in that long text was the name of Ibrahim Salihović. In a small subpoint, not a count by itself, but there it was, among the other names, dates, strange turns of phrase.

Mostly he didn't go into the camps. Mostly he stayed in his office.

Dejan Vasić, his fat pink face, his intolerable air of moral righteousness. But Vasić had never been tested, had he? No one had offered him power, no one had come to him with power in their hands like a flame and handed it towards him. He would not have turned it down. No man would have turned it down.

To be able to say, I will draw this line here, and these people will be on the other side of it. Apart from us. So that we can be alone, and pure, and safe, and these people will be the darkness on the other side. No one who had not had this chance could understand the sweep of it. The exaltation.

There was a large room, and then many small rooms.

A group of dull staring figures, skeletal, in a room. The stench was terrible. It was shameful that these men allowed themselves to be put in this room, that they weren't fighting, that they didn't lunge for the door when he opened it, it was shameful, they should not smell like that, it made you want to hit them.

There were no women in this room, they were held somewhere else. He heard a woman's voice in another room.

He did hear that. But he had his limits. There were things he didn't want to think about.

They were very changed, and he did not recognize anyone right away, and he did not care to recognize them, but yes, some of them he knew. Hotić, the boy who worked at the casino, pressed against the wall, black eyes hollow in his face. Šušak, the doctor, standing, arms hanging loose, his jaw sagging. Salihović, taller than most of the others, his skin a sallow grey under a layer of filth. He remembered Salihović, months ago, in another world, talking to the newspapers, saying there would never be a war. Wrong again, wasn't he?

Nikola took a step towards him. The tall man rocked backwards, into the bodies packed tight around him, his face blank.

The smell, he couldn't get over the smell, you wouldn't think that human beings would smell worse than animals, the smell of their shit and blood all thick and cloying and suffocating.

Nikola was still staring at Salihović. A small shiver of electricity ran through the room, the guards enlivened by it, awakened. They could see what was beginning now. Their jobs were hard and tedious. There was sacrifice involved, Nikola knew this, he was proud of them. This was what made it worth while.

'Hey,' called one of them, 'if you're an MP, where's your suit and tie? Shouldn't you be wearing a suit?' He smacked Salihović with the back of his hand. 'Where's your suit, motherfucker? Where's your fucking suit and tie?'

And they were turning like iron to the north, recognizing that Salihović stood at that intersection of privilege and weakness that was irresistible, tasting again the delight of bringing him down.

The birds gather, he thought, a phrase coming from somewhere and nowhere. The black birds gather. Saliva filled his mouth, his nerves twitching with excitement, and he spat into the mess on the floor.

The room was dark, there was no electric light, only a small window, far up. A dark room. There were a lot of things he couldn't see entirely.

There was not much room to move, but the other men drew away as far as they could, leaving a tiny margin of space around Salihović, understanding that he had been identified, named, that the focus of the drama had moved onto him now, and it was possible that the rest of them would temporarily escape.

He would have thought that Ibro Salihović was better than that, that he would have somehow avoided this degradation. You would think he could have avoided this in some way. You would think any man would find a way, not to be brought so low. Nikola stood in the doorway, in the dirty light from the hallway's larger windows; the sun was at his back, he knew himself to be a centre, a densely packed focus of strength. He was breathing fast and deep, and seemed to himself to grow in height.

It's not as though Salihović didn't have friends. People liked him. Nikola hadn't known him so well but he knew this. Good company in the bar, wicked sense of humour by all accounts. Not much sign of that now.

But he was like Vasić, he took things too seriously.

'You're a motherfucking jihad warrior, aren't you?' shouted Jović, hitting Salihović with the butt of his gun. 'And you thought you'd get away with it, didn't you? You thought we couldn't stop you.'

Salihović fell, caught his breath, tried to stand up. 'I haven't been in a mosque for thirty years, you fucking idiot,' he muttered. He should have known better than that.

That stupid demonstration he and Vasić had organized. People get themselves into this kind of trouble. There were ways to make things easier for yourself.

It really was quite dark. If you asked him today, he couldn't tell you a lot of what had happened in that room. There were so many things he couldn't really see. The noises were terrible, the smell was terrible, but he could feel a fierce pride in his men welling up in his chest. They would do what was necessary, what had to be done. They were hard, they were strong. No one would defeat them again.

At the desk in his cell he sat with his shoulders hunched over, flipping quickly through the pages of the binders. His arm was hurting and his stomach didn't feel well.

No one understands the kind of things you have to do. That you have to be tough. That the weight of events will push you into a corner and you will have no choice. That's when you really have to be tough.

A song of love is a sad song, hi-lili, hi-lili, hi-lo.

There were some odd things in here. Like a random collection of clippings in some places.

Article about Salihović from years and years ago. That stupid book he wrote. Fuck his stupid book. No one wanted to publish Nikola's books. And then those Muslims tried to claim that everyone was discriminating against them. Fucking whiners.

Article by Bryant about something or other. Population movements. Picture of a lot of people walking from somewhere to somewhere else. It was a shame about Bryant. He'd be someone you could talk to if it wasn't for his politics. He just bought that whole Muslim line, right off the plane. The thing about foreigners. He'd be someone you could talk to, otherwise.

He rubbed his eyes, feeling tired, weak as a child, and flipped through a few more pages, not really seeing them. No one understands what a war is like. I wouldn't have done these things if I didn't have to. I am not a bad man. I'm just a man who was in a particular place.

A song of love is a song of woe, don't ask me how I know.

Or came back to a particular place. Where I was born. Where I had to be.

In the room, as he remembered it, the men had turned their faces away. Most of the men.

Nikola never laid a hand on anyone. He was aware that his men were watching him. He could feel the current flowing from the small movements of his hands and eyes, that he and Miloš, who was laughing, leaning against the wall, his mouth wide open, that he and Miloš were at the centre of everything, but he never laid a hand on Salihović.

Some things he remembered only as shapes moving in the darkness. A man above another man. The sound of something breaking.

And that sound was like the final barrier that had confined him. His father had been held in a place like this, had been shamed and shattered, but Nikola had won now, he had beaten that story down. A great tide of sweetness filled his body, as if every bad thing in his life was settled. All of it paid for, all the badness washed away.

Another man moved towards the man on the floor.

Nikola inhaled slowly, and for that one moment he knew what it meant to be at peace.

The soft sound of a boot striking flesh. Miloš was moving now, taking one of his guns out of its holster. And the good feeling began to diminish.

'What do you think?' said Miloš. 'About time to wrap this one up?'

He couldn't recall if he had answered.

Miloš, huge and bulky, was kneeling down on the floor, in the liquid on the floor. It must have soaked into the knees and the turn-ups of his trousers.

Nikola wasn't feeling so well now.

Miloš held his pistol to the man's head and turned to Nikola, raising his eyebrows in a question.

Muharem Hotić, his small body held smaller, in the corner, dark eyes moving back and forth.

Miloš turned to him for instructions.

In his cell Nikola thought of the words *command responsibility*. He thought of the word *genocide*. He thought, how can you talk of genocide when each of us dies alone? You can kill eight thousand men, and every one of them will die alone.

Miloš looked towards him. He turned his head and spoke.

'Yes,' he said.

Miloš pulled the trigger.

The amount of blood was really surprising. Everyone in the room was covered with blood.

He clutched his stomach and moved unsteadily towards the bed in his cell. He was not well at all. He thought about calling a guard, a doctor. He would just lie down for a while first.

He never wanted to hurt anybody. It wasn't that this had been anything he wanted. He wanted to teach, write books.

But the problem was making your life worth while. Doing something special, something important. Not dying in shame. Not the way his father died. And not the way he would have died if the war hadn't happened, a mediocre man, someone who left no mark on the world. Who would go away without a trace.

He was in a lot of pain. It didn't seem possible to get up from the bed.

He thought of Salihović, and he thought how strange that this man's death should follow him so far. You wouldn't have thought that anyone would survive who knew or cared.

He would not lie about it. He knew that something bad

had happened in his country. He knew that something bad had happened in that room. But it had been necessary for him to take a stand. To do what he had to do.

There was a darkness coming in around the edges of his vision. This wasn't right. It was a shattering pain, consuming. His mind was coming apart under the blow of the pain. And of all things the image that kept clinging was Dejan Vasić's stupid face. A man who thought he was stronger than history. A failure. A man no one would remember.

For good or ill, they would remember Nikola Marković. They would remember him. He was falling apart. There was only a small point of vision remaining. A guard would arrive soon. Surely. Yes.

He folded into the pain, nowhere to go. In a small dark room.

What do you think you were proving, Dejan?

I never laid a hand on anyone.

There was one thing. There was this thing. His mind reached for the thought and pulled away, and the thought was out there in space, in front of him.

They asked me and I spoke. Anyone would have done the same.

How you choose to live, Dejan had written. How you choose to live. Dejan in his office, turning away. Turning away from that summer's awful light.

The thought hung in front of him and he did not know if he would accept this thought. It stood in front of him like a single word.

It stood in front of him and it wavered and dissolved, and dripped like a liquid into the darkness, and he flowed down beside it, the pain seemed to be lifting, that must be good, and the darkness was very great, and he ran like blood down the side of the darkness.

Part Three

MILLENNIUM

XIX

The Wind

26 December 1999

There was no good reason for Lili to be out at this hour, under the great dark wall of Notre-Dame. It was a cold night, windy, and even the men who were normally cruising around the park seemed to have stayed inside. Maybe it was not the done thing to go cruising on Christmas night. She had come back late from dinner with her mother – now living in the Nineteenth with an ancient Trotskyist named Bruno – where they had discussed, as usual, her brother Sasha's unsettling determination to pursue a career in surfing, and she hadn't felt like going to sleep, so after a while she put on her coat and went back outside.

The wind was rising, her hair flying into her eyes, her mouth; the branches of the trees creaked and swayed as she walked along the *quai* and over the bridge. She thought that if the millennium clock were still at the Beaubourg she could have gone and watched it count down the last few days, but they had irritatingly moved it to the Opéra; and anyway, the wind was getting too strong, she had to put her head down and force her way forward, bent almost double. Better to turn and go home.

She wedged herself against the wall of the Hôtel de Ville by the post office, looking for a bit of cover, and reached into her pocket for her cigarettes; but as she was lifting one out of the pack, the wind blew up in a violent gust, swift as a fist, and the cigarettes flew out of her hand, and when she made a grab for them she lost her balance, one ankle giving way and her shoe falling off, so she had to lean against the wall to stay upright.

The gust wasn't ending, the wind continued to swirl around her, thick as water, and she saw her shoe tumbling across the square. She took off the other shoe and ran after it, the cold pavement biting into her feet, and the wind was sweeping her forward, seizing her under her arms and driving her onward, her shoe now out of sight in the darkness, and she suddenly realized that she had no control over her own speed, that she was not so much running as being carried by the wind, in the night, in the direction of the river, and a surge of adrenalin sickness rushed up her throat. She stiffened her legs, stopped, fell forward as the wind slammed into her back. She had let go of her other shoe, and it too was vanishing, and she saw a current of wind grab hold of it and throw it far up into the air.

She had to stay down, close to the ground. Small and light, she offered little resistance to the wind, and it was clearly not going to stop, the darkness suddenly loud with the crash of shutters, thrown open and battered against the walls of buildings, the metallic clatter of dustbins rolling down the streets. A tree branch flew above her, landing two metres away. Rising, bent over, she walked towards the bridge as slowly as she could, the wind rushing her steps, pushing her too fast in the direction of the frothing Seine as she clung to lamp-posts, to the railing of the Pont D'Arcole. Step by step, tense and meticulous, she crept over the bridge, seeing the river full of debris, unidentifiable, tossed in the waves, and my God the wind was still rising.

She had made it onto the island. Another, larger branch flew just above her head, and then there was a gust, and she fell, deliberately, rather than let the wind throw her forward, crouching on the ground, her breath torn out of her mouth, watching a heavy metal postbox fall and cartwheel, end over end, slowly along the broad street. Her feet were aching with cold, and it was stupid in this situation to worry about her stockings but it bothered her that they were ruined. In the distance she could hear the grieving wail of the emergency vehicles, rising on the wind, and then there was a howl and a great breaking noise, and a tree shuddered and fell and the ground shook, the whole body of the tree spread out on the pavement. And then another. The streetlights went out.

Blind now, she staggered forward along the rue D'Arcole, sheltering against the wall of the Hôtel-Dieu, thinking only that she had to get home, that she had to get out of this. She reached the Parvis-Notre-Dame, and it seemed that there was still some light here from somewhere. She should have gone straight ahead, the church would have been some shelter, but she was frightened, it was dark, and she could only imagine her usual route, her usual bridge, diagonally across the square. There was nowhere she could take cover, the shops closed, doors locked, even the front of Notre-Dame blocked up with scaffolding; and then some of the scaffolding came free and crashed to the ground. There was a sound like an explosion. She took a breath, dropped to her hands and knees and began to crawl across the square.

She could not imagine how long she crept over the stones, blind, her coat flapping around her. Her hands struck concrete steps, struck bushes, she made her way forward by instinct, following the sound of the river smashing against the bank. Something hit the ground just in front of her, black fragments flying, and later she would realize it had been part of the roof of Notre-Dame. The sirens were wailing. She could not see another human being, only the detritus of the city racing south, chunks of wood and tile, chairs, wooden shutters, all cascading in the wind. A car horn was weeping somewhere, the skid of brakes, another crash.

She reached the Petit-Pont, and pulled herself onto it, and yes, the walls, the blessed stone walls, they did create a partial shield if she stayed low. She pressed herself against the stone, curled up at the centre of the bridge, her eyes closed, and surely it could not be swaying, a stone bridge, a hundred years old, it could not be swaying in the wind as if it were made of rope and planks, but she felt it.

Bridges aren't invulnerable, she thought, but she couldn't imagine leaving the partial shelter of the low wall. Carefully, she lifted her head, pushing her hair from her face, and on the opposite bank a tree rose in the air, turning slowly like a dancer, the roots tearing free, and then it fell, and the roof of a house shattered beneath it. Behind her she heard a woman screaming. Shaking, she let her arms go, and lay down.

Bridges could fall. She had no idea how hard a wind could blow, if it was possible to strike down a solid bridge, if the wind could turn into a mortar and crush the stones. But there was nowhere she could be safe, she could only rely on this bridge for now, hope that it would hold out, its small expanse supporting her above the froth of the Seine.

She lay in a dark world of sound, the crash of objects flying and falling, the shattering glass, the sirens somewhere on the other side of the wind, and she remembered Daniel telling her how he had been afraid to cross the bridges, how he had thought of the old bridge in Mostar reduced to rubble, the bridge in Višegrad slick with blood, bodies tossed into the river beneath. The Višegrad Bridge, the bridge at the centre of Andrić's beautiful misused novel, a nucleus of hope and hatred, and despite it all she was trusting this bridge, her bridge, in her *quartier*, in the city where she had lived since she was a tiny child. She remembered Daniel, wherever he was in the world. She didn't know what she could say to him now.

Was the wind dropping? She sat up; then carefully raised herself, braced against the wall. Yes. Yes. She could stand, the wind was still strong but it had weakened. She could walk, slowly, carefully, to the end of the bridge, and the river was still high and foaming, but no more trees were falling. She stepped delicately, her shoulders set, around fallen electrical wires and heaps of debris. Her stockings were dissolving into a network of runs, her knees scraped and bleeding. Barefoot, she made her way onto rue St-Jacques, south past the shattered windows of the shops, the pavement full of glass and branches. It was calmer now, a wind that seemed almost normal, and there were lights on in some buildings, a few streetlights working, though others were bent and broken, as if they had been made of clay, not metal. Her teeth were chattering; when she tried to hold her jaw still, her body began to shake so hard she couldn't keep walking.

Finally, finally she turned onto Gay-Lussac, stepping over a shop's awning that lay spread out on the corner, and the last few yards to her building; found her key, wonderfully safe in her pocket, opened the door and fell down on the steps in the dark little foyer. Breathe. Just breathe.

Supporting herself on the banister, she stepped towards the lift and pressed the button, and oh thank God she heard the gears begin to work, there was still electricity. She rode up in the tiny cage, opened the door of her flat and pressed the light switch. There was electricity, there was heat, the telephone was working; one window was broken, a shimmering fan of glass on the living-room floor, but her flat was otherwise intact, and it was all so miraculous that she sat down on her couch, dropped her head to her knees and wept, her face hot and slick with tears, her hands wet, fat tears falling onto her ruined stockings, home, safe, saved.

It was nearly light when she got up from the couch, changed her clothes and brushed the nest of tangles from her hair. She phoned her mother – she and Bruno were all right – and turned on the radio. People had died, the newsreader was saying. No one was sure how many, but there were reports of deaths. Buildings destroyed. The storm was still moving.

She thought that people would be waking up soon, people she knew in other cities, and they would hear the news on the radio, maybe right away, maybe later on. They would want to know how she was. She thought that she didn't want to pick up the phone. That he would phone her, and she couldn't deal with that.

She pressed the record button on her answering machine, and spoke calmly, in her professional voice, in four languages, explaining briefly that she was unhurt, that the storm had left Paris now, but she could not at the moment answer the phone. She completed the message and turned away from the machine, going into the kitchen to make herself a cup of coffee, and it was only then that she realized that she had, without even thinking about it, spoken in English first.

The phone rang. She looked at the clock, and thought about the morning news on the BBC World Service. She walked into the living room and sat watching the machine as it clicked on, the tape revolving.

XX

The Feast of the Innocents

28 December 1999–1 January 2000

When someone died in custody, there had to be a post-mortem. But this was relatively straightforward most of the time. When someone had only just died, and all the parts of the body were still together, not extracted bit by bit from the earth, chewed by animals, reshaped by wind and snow. After a post-mortem, the body could be returned to the family, travelling in a small plane over the mountains and hills of Europe, across the borders, across the inter-entity line.

It was a grey day in East Dulwich. Of course it was grey in East Dulwich for a great part of every year, so you couldn't make too much of that. Probably it was also a grey day in The Hague, where they had finished cutting open Nikola Marković and were preparing to dispatch him to Banja Luka.

. . . *Although suggestions from the government of Republika Srpska that poison had been added to his food have the virtue of being entertaining, the autopsy actually suggested that Marković had suffered a previous, probably unrecognized, heart attack some time earlier, and that a second and more serious one was close to inevitable. He was alone in his cell when he died, and had probably been in cardiac arrest for about twenty minutes when the guard first became aware of a problem.*

Daniel knew perfectly well that he was rambling; that it was old news anyway, and his editors would be irritated with him. It wasn't worth more than the few sentences that had already gone out on the wire, the night that Marković died. Still, it was something to keep himself busy with.

He flipped through a small pile of papers, balanced uneasily on the arm of the round wicker chair where he was sitting, near the window. He couldn't use the desk in his flat without shifting great piles of documents belonging to the holidaying teachers, some of them marked 'Confidential Student Records' and all of them covered with oversized Post-it notes reading 'Please Do Not Touch'.

He wondered why he had ever thought it would cheer him up to spend the holidays in a city where he knew almost no one, and in a flat where nearly any move he made seemed to infringe on Becky and Stuart's privacy.

One war crimes defendant committed suicide in his cell last year, and others have made serious attempts. However, no evidence was found that Marković's death was due to anything other than natural causes.

He saved and closed the file, and he remembered, maybe for the last time, Nikola Marković in the bar, trying to figure out what had gone wrong, why it had not been the way he expected.

His wife and daughter would meet the body in Banja Luka, and for now at least he would become a hero, a martyr. Another skeleton for the pile of heavenly Serbian bones.

Daniel shifted in the blue cushions of the wicker chair and opened another file. The pile of papers fell onto the carpet.

He couldn't call her again. Once he knew from her answering machine that she was all right, he couldn't come up with any acceptable excuse to call her again.

I can understand it, I guess, he wrote, *this unseemly haste to get the twentieth century over with. We're hoping, we can always hope, that we'll do it better the next time.*

Because it's out there right now, the twenty-first century, still untouched; we haven't yet managed to fill it with Auschwitz and the Khmer Rouge and Hiroshima. We think maybe we can keep it clean.

You have to hope. You have to hope that we have some things now, we have some tribunals, we have an evolving body of international human rights law, a key to break the locked code of the sovereign state and tell a new story. You have to hope it means something.

So we set off our fireworks a year in advance, racing towards the future, wondering if we can change.

When he went out to buy groceries, he was aware that he was walking through London as if it were an unknown country, inspecting with fascination the cramped little houses and their pocket-size gardens, brown now in the winter; studying shelves of Patak's Pickles and Cadbury's Flakes like an explorer examining strange animals. He had to look twice at the coins to remember which ones were which.

There was something refreshing about this. It added a certain edge to daily errands, and allowed him to experience a recurrent surprise that everyone in this odd place spoke English.

'You're wearing glasses, then,' said a woman in a newsagent's. 'When did you start to wear the glasses?'

He could not remember ever being in the shop before. 'I've worn glasses since I was six years old,' he said.

'Ah. I thought you didn't wear glasses.'

'That was probably someone else.'

'Probably so, love. Must be your brother.'

He didn't have a brother, but he could see that the conversation would get very complex if he admitted this, so he nodded and smiled.

Past the small shops of Half Moon Lane, he reached

Brockwell Park. He heard the voice first, and felt strangely reassured.

'The city shall be full of boys and girls,' said the voice, 'playing in the streets thereof.' Daniel turned around and saw the UFO priest on his box, still thin and grey, much the same as always.

It was a nice phrase. The city full of boys and girls. He tried not to let his mind throw up images of mortar fire. He walked up the path towards the priest, his hands in his jacket pockets, and stood a small distance away, listening.

'. . . that it might be fulfilled which was spoken of the Lord by the prophet, saying, Out of Egypt have I called my son. Then Herod, when he saw that he was mocked of the wise men, was exceeding wroth . . .'

Daniel didn't know the Bible terribly well, but at that point he knew what was coming next, and for some reason, though it was only an old plain story, he felt his hands clenching. You'll be okay with this, he told himself. Certain stories, certain sentences, could do this to him. There were pictures that just came back.

Children, that was the thing. A strangely jolly carol started up in his mind, a brief flash of himself, a pudgy nine-year-old, cheerfully singing, 'All the little boys he killed, at Beth'lem in his fury.'

'And sent forth, and slew all the children,' said the priest, and Daniel was clearing his throat and thinking that he had to get this under control when he heard a cry like the deepest grief of the world, and he froze.

There was a young man on the bench, someone Daniel hadn't noticed before, and he was bending forward now, weeping; and the sobbing sound was a relief, it was almost ordinary, not that awful bereft wail. Daniel took a step closer without thinking about what he was doing, as the priest dropped his book onto the ground and rushed towards the man, kneeling in front of him, talking quickly and softly.

'Please, don't be upset,' the priest was saying. 'It's going to be all right, really. It's nearly time, that means your problems are over. Finished, it's just a matter of . . .'

The young man lifted his head, his eyes swollen and terrible. 'No,' he said, with a strange calm in his voice. 'It doesn't end. Wars never end.'

'Oh,' said Daniel, involuntarily, and the priest looked up and saw him, and looked at him imploringly, as if there was something he could do to help.

'You know what is happening,' said the man. 'You just read it yourself.'

'No, no, that's not the idea, it's not what people think. I mean, if our proper incarnation is on another planet—'

'Never mind,' said the man. He began to cough raggedly, folding his arms around his chest, then recovered himself and shook his head. 'Excuse me. Thank you for everything.'

Wars never end, thought Daniel, standing rooted to the spot, thinking that only the thinnest of lines was separating him and that man on the bench. There was something in him that could break like that.

'The important thing about DNA,' said the priest nervously, 'is that certain elements of it can only be explained by alien intervention.'

'I must go,' said the man, and his voice started breaking up again into his difficult breathing. 'I have to . . . I have to be ready, I have to . . . Excuse me.' He stood up, and even as he rose his body seemed to shrink into itself and draw away, into the air, into the distance.

'Listen. Would you like to talk to someone else? A doctor perhaps?'

The man shook his head. 'There is no time.' He looked

up, and saw Daniel, and it seemed almost as if he were going to say something else. Daniel, not really thinking about what he was doing, started to hold out a hand.

'I'll call someone for you,' said the priest. 'Let me call someone.' Then he turned suddenly to Daniel. 'Excuse me,' he said, in a startlingly polite voice. 'Would you happen to have a mobile telephone that I could use?'

Confused, Daniel reached into his jacket and handed over his phone, imagining as he did a crowd of London's homeless materializing around him, calling for help, calling Dallas and Toronto, calling Priština perhaps.

The man was gone, vanished into the grey morning.

The priest sat down on the bench, and spoke into the phone, holding a hand over his other ear. 'Hello? Hello there? My name is Father Jamie Bennington, and one of my parishioners is ill . . . No, well, no, but he's in a bad way, and I thought if you could . . . Well, not so much as – upset is what I would say. He's quite upset . . . Yes, I understand . . . No, but I'm concerned because . . . I don't know. He said he has asthma . . . I'm sorry, I don't know . . . No, not now . . . No . . . No, I couldn't say . . . Nothing at all? . . . Very well, thank you anyway.' He disconnected, and sat with the phone in his hands, looking down at it. 'They weren't terribly helpful. It's a bit distressing,' he said vaguely.

'Yeah. I guess,' said Daniel.

The priest looked up. 'Oh. This is yours. Thank you very much.' He handed the phone back to Daniel, who tucked it into his pocket. He had the momentary thought that he should walk up to Cardboard City and start passing it around, and then he remembered that Cardboard City had been cleared out to make room for an Imax cinema, and he was such a stranger to London he didn't even know where the homeless men slept any more.

'Perhaps I shouldn't have read that passage, but one does try to keep to the lectionary for the day, especially on feast days,' the priest went on. 'Of course, it was never a real historical incident. Perhaps I should have explained that right away.'

'It wasn't?' Daniel felt curiously put out by this. 'I kind of thought it was.'

'Oh, I don't think so. No, most scholars would say not. I mean, it would have left some trace in the historical record, wouldn't it?'

'I don't know. Maybe not. It might not.' He had never anticipated that he would find himself defending biblical inerrancy to a priest, but he felt suddenly stubborn about the point. 'You'd be amazed what people forget.'

'A colonial ruler killing every boy baby in an entire province? Oh, I don't think they'd overlook that.'

'They would,' said Daniel. 'Yes, they would. I promise you, people would, people do.' And he knew that he wasn't really arguing about Herod's innocents. He thought of the children whose names he had never known, never written down. Maybe he would spend the rest of his life making a list of the children. He was full of useless plans.

'Well, it certainly is one of those things that we can never know for sure,' said the priest, pacific and conciliatory. 'It's an interesting discussion. Thank you very much for the use of your telephone. I'm afraid I must go now.' He picked up his box and tucked it away under a tree, then set off down the path.

Back at the flat, Daniel decided that he was a person without scruples, and started looking through drawers in Becky and Stuart's bedroom, but he found nothing of even passing interest, except what appeared to be Becky's ovulation chart, and he didn't particularly want to think about the menstrual cycle of a complete stranger. He didn't know what he'd expected to find. He was going to have to come to terms with the fact that not everyone was involved in international crimes.

There were people he could phone. It wasn't that he had to be isolated here. Julia and Tony had sent him an invitation to their Christmas party, even; he could certainly phone them. He had a clear mental picture of Tony saying, 'You know, I never know what to think about Yugoslavia, it seems so *complicated*,' and Julia trying to find out if he was seeing someone so that she wouldn't have to feel any residual guilt about him.

He called the *Guardian* instead, and managed to get himself attached to their Y2K team, charged with hanging about one of the South London hospitals at midnight. With any luck, the critical care equipment would malfunction and there would be enormous loss of life.

What did he think when he died? Did he know he was dying? Did he ever understand what had happened?

Tudjman, Marković, going out with the century.

And what can I say about me? That I just didn't think about what it might do to her, that I just never thought about it. My safety and my credibility have always been my own problems. I've always done this. It never even occurred to me that there was anyone else involved.

If you're that used to being alone, it's got to tell you something.

And she's the one who paid. I'm fine, no one can touch me, same as ever. She never did a thing to cause it, and she's the one who's going to keep paying.

It's not that I don't know this.

In London they've put up a giant wheel. Apparently you can watch people all over the place from the top of it. They call it The Eye. Am I the only one who finds this creepy?

'They're trying to get a Serb and an Albanian to shake hands on the bridge in Mitrovica at midnight,' said Adrian at the foreign desk. 'I can't tell you any more than that. If they throw each other over the edge instead, I guess that's NATO's problem. I'm doing my best to have a camera there, but we may be too short-staffed.'

'Any plans in Bosnia?'

'Not that I've got on my desk today. More handshaking, I expect. We've got some kind of prayer service scheduled between the Koreas, you want any details on that?'

'Thanks anyway.'

By the evening of the pretend millennium, he was starting to think that he wouldn't have much to do. Midnight had come and the lights had stayed on in Singapore, where the crowd was terrorized by a Ricky Martin impersonator and three barely dressed young women singing *La Vida Loca*; and in Hong Kong, where Jackie Chan fell upon them with giant wings. In Yogyakarta, a team of performance artists crawled around a cave shaking pieces of skeletons, in what the television informed him was intended to be a parable about greed and consumerism.

He wasn't due at the hospital until eleven; though the administration had decided this would be a good piece of public relations, the staff had made it clear that they were less than happy about a reporter haunting the hallways waiting for disaster, and that they were planning to limit his access as far as they possibly could.

At ten, just before he left, he turned on the TV again to see if they would have anything from Bosnia, and found himself sitting for longer than he had intended. There was some kind of contemporary music being played in Egypt, the pyramids all backlit and symbolic; in Greece, three choirs of monks were chanting on the Parthenon, and in Bethlehem they were releasing doves; there was nothing very surprising, but he thought, *we are really trying here. Trying something.*

Then the transmission moved to another country, and this was something quite different. On the screen, a handful of frail old men walked down a narrow corridor, and as they walked, a group of young dancers stopped, and moved to make room, and bent down before them as if they were bowing. They were plain men, wearing no special distinctions, but of course one of them he recognized right away. He had forgotten South Africa was in this time zone as well.

The famous old man stopped in the corridor, and walked through a door into a tiny jail cell, and he paused, and looked around. He reached towards a table, and picked up a candle, and he lit it, and passed it outside the bars of the jail cell into the darkness, and the candle outlined his face as he smiled, sadly, quietly. Where he stood, it was midnight.

We would like to believe that we can do something new.

When he arrived at the hospital, midnight was reaching most of Europe. He talked to Adrian, who said that NATO had assured him that a Serb and an Albanian had stood on the Mitrovica bridge at the same time, but they could not confirm whether a handshake had been successfully completed. In Sarajevo, Emir told him rather sternly, they were just having a party like normal people, not putting on some kind of show for the BBC. 'I think that we have entertained the BBC for quite long enough,' he added.

In Belgrade, on the Orthodox calendar, it was not yet New Year's Eve. This would happen later – a crowd would gather in Trg Republike, blowing on their frozen hands, but no bands would come onto the stage. Thin streamers of cloud would whip over the bright moon; young people would be standing near the back of the stage, doing something with their equipment, but still it would be quiet.

At midnight the stage lights would go out, and images begin to play across a screen. People who had died. People who had died in the wars, their faces lighting up the screen one by one. The screen would go black, the stage lights would come on. Then a girl with a ripped leather jacket and neon-pink hair would step up to the microphone, and speak to the crowd. 'This regime has ruined our country,' she would say. 'It is the year 2000 and nothing has changed. You have nothing to celebrate. Go home now.'

It was after midnight in Berlin, Madrid, Brussels, it was after midnight in Paris, and Paris seemed to be the big hit of this time zone, the TV in the doctors' lounge playing and replaying the footage of the Eiffel Tower sizzling with light, a brilliant pure white cascade of dazzle. She would be in Paris somewhere, but he couldn't say where, what she was doing, whether she was with someone.

A young woman doctor showed him out of the lounge after a brief interview, and sent him to sit in the waiting room of the casualty department, rather as if he were a patient himself.

Most of the people in the waiting room seemed to be extremely drunk; a haze of alcohol fumes floated around the plastic chairs, where men were holding paper towels against their bleeding heads and noses. In one corner, an exhausted young mother was pressing her fingers against her eyes while her tiny child, who had no doubt been quite sick an hour ago, jumped up and down on a little white table, screaming, 'It's time to go home! Home! Home!'

'Shu'th'fuck up,' moaned a man with blood on his mouth.

'Forty-t . . . forty-two min-minutes to go,' said another. 'Big bang. Computers are all going apeshit. You heard about that?' Then they fell back into silence, the stiff stillness of people who have been waiting so long they have stopped expecting anything, only the child still jumping and shouting.

'You need to look at this baby,' said someone.

Daniel turned, and saw him. He had just come in the doorway, and he was standing at the desk, the young man from the park, with a baby in his arms.

'If you'll take a seat, love, a doctor will—'

'You need to look at this baby now!' said the man, and though his voice was not very loud there was something in it that was dangerous.

The nurse at the desk put down her pen. 'Sorry, love, but you can see how busy we are. If you'll just—'

'No time is left,' said the man, and Daniel could see that there was sweat on his face, that his breath was coming hard. 'No time is left, you must look at him, you must look at him now.'

'Is he looking bad? All right, let me see him, then.' The nurse came out from behind the desk and held out her arms, and Daniel stood up, knowing that something was about to go terribly wrong, not knowing why.

The man looked down at the baby. 'I need to sing him a song,' he said softly, and the nurse frowned; but then the man seemed to change his mind. He fretted with the baby's blanket, leaned in and whispered a scrap of melody, but then he raised his face again, and moved towards the nurse, and placed the baby very carefully, very gently, into her arms.

Then he took a gun from his pocket.

Daniel was the first person to recognize it. Even the nurse, seeing it right in front of her, blinked for a moment, as if she could not make sense of this image. Then her mouth dropped open and she made a little animal sound, strangled.

'Take him away,' said the man, his voice torn up by his

ragged breath. 'Take him to a safe place. I need him to be safe.'

'Put the gun down,' whimpered the nurse. 'Please put the gun down.'

'Take him away!' said the man, and his voice cracked with a sudden sob, and then he said something else, the words barely discernible as he coughed and wept, but Daniel could tell that it wasn't English.

A doctor came into the waiting room, a small man, thin. He didn't initially understand what was happening, and he crossed to the desk, thinking maybe that he would help, and then the man moved, and had an arm around the doctor's chest and the gun against his neck.

Daniel was standing a yard away from them. He sat down on the floor. The man was talking, the sounds coming broken from his throat. Daniel recognized a word, and then another.

The nurse held the baby against her and moved backwards. And someone must have triggered an alarm, because security guards were arriving now, and one of them was talking to the man, and Daniel heard more words he recognized but they were fragmented, meaningless, because everyone was talking now, and someone was screaming, and his blood was rushing in his ears, and the security guards were pulling people away, moving them past the desk and beyond a door, but Daniel was sitting against a wall, too close to the man, they were trying to create a perimeter but they could not get everyone out of the room. They would seal the area, and he would be inside, with the man and the gun and the doctor, and another nurse and the police who were now arriving, and the man with blood on his mouth, who was unpredictable, who might do anything except that he was, thank God, asleep.

He sat on the floor, in a scramble of languages as the police tried to talk to the man, and then the man's eyes ranged frantically around the room and met Daniel's, and he knew again that they were not such strangers to each other.

Wars never end.

He saw this like a jagged landscape that every one of them would be moving across until they had all died; and he thought that there had to be something he could do, something he could say to the man, the words of that knowledge.

Moving in a crouch, he inched forward towards the nearest policeman. 'I understand the language,' he said.

The policeman didn't turn around. 'I understand the language,' said Daniel, louder this time. 'The language, the language that he's speaking, I know it.'

'Quiet!' snapped the policeman abruptly, moving his arm to push Daniel back. 'Stay down!'

'Listen to me,' said Daniel. 'The language, I know it, I can talk to him.'

'I told you, be quiet and let us do our job!' He pushed Daniel again, forcing him back against the glass wall of the entrance, never turning to face him.

Waves of red light poured across them, cars gathered outside now, and he saw a van arriving, and men were getting out who were carrying guns. They had sent for armed police. They had sent for snipers.

All that Daniel could do was watch, from a small distance, his hand against the glass, as helpless as he had always been.

He balanced his notebook on his knees and reached for a pen.

Across the street, Father Jamie Bennington knelt at the kerb in front of the barricades, praying that the final moment would come before Paja could hurt himself, praying and clenching his hands and choking every minute on the rising fear that it would not come at all, that the UFOs were not coming, there would be no new earth where they could start over in innocence, and at the kerb in the darkness he bent his head and wept for everything that he had ever wanted.

pol neg – no need for this, let's talk, etc etc, Daniel wrote.

man – no choice, have to (coughing, unclear)

nurse in next room – shd I bring in baby, parents will always focus on b; pol says no

m says, Marko has to be safe, have to end this – dr is calm but moving head, m jams gun

nurse crying in next room, cn I help dr vikram? pol no, nurse asks to come in w/o b, pol no

man breathing v. difficult, problem?

pol neg – we have yr wfe on phone

m, pls no, lve her alone

Marko again (baby?) – to stop the war, I am from the war, not Marko. Not guilty (Marko?) ???

can't see armed pol – where?

man – war is not going away, is following (coughing), in Eng says something about mnight?

pol neg – what about mnight? man – (unclr , wheezing) justice – I killed (?) – judgement ?? (can't get words)

pol, do you need medical attention

man, go fuck yrself

man in Eng, I am to make this stop. Stop.

pol neg – make stop? what?

man – you have to sacrifice always something. For child. Is for child.

nurse – I'll talk to him about b, pol no, sound of nurse struggle w/p??

cn see sniper in hallway

doors closing

11:56 by hosp clock

outside hosp, sounds of ??
dr says, yr gun not in a very good place
2 snipers in hall, 11:58
And his pen arced across the page as he dropped for cover.

The sounds he would remember in sequence, the crack and whine that drove him to the ground, the shattering glass, the dull echo of falling bodies, but only one visual image would stay frozen in his mind, stationary, as if they had been seized and held like that, the man bending his head back, the doctor sagging, and the spray of glass like a waterfall as the bullets came into the room.

He rolled under the chairs, pulled himself around.

'Hostage-taker opened fire and armed unit responded,' someone was shouting into his walkie-talkie. 'Hostage-taker opened fire . . .', but the crack and flash continued, blood curling across the floor in thick streams as the nurse pushed her way past the officer, a man lifting the small doctor and leading him away, and he realized that it was the sound of fireworks. Somewhere outside the window of this room, midnight had come.

The nurse was kneeling now over the man, pulling open his shirt, reaching her hands into the blood. A policeman took her arm and she turned, her face twisted with anger, shouting, 'Get the hell away from him!' And the doctor was back in the room, blood-smeared, pushing a stretcher, the police trailing him, and he and two nurses lifted the man and ran with him down the hallway, obligated, bound to his life.

The gun had fallen from the man's hand into the thick spreading pool.

A police officer lifted it.

He was young, with red hair and bad skin.

He lifted the gun, and his face went grey and he sat down on the floor.

Daniel crawled out from under the chairs and stood.

'It's a toy,' said the policeman, speaking to no one. He put his hand on his head, lost.

'It isn't real. It's a toy.'

Outside the window, the pop and flare of the fireworks.

Daniel walked past the policemen, his right foot landing in blood and leaving a smeared trail behind him. He was no one, hardly visible. He went down the hallway to a trauma room and looked in the door. They were stepping away from the man on the stretcher. The man lay still. There was nothing more to do.

Daniel remembered, at one point, sitting in the waiting room again with a cup of coffee, everyone seemed to have coffee, the drunks and the young mother and the doctors, this must be some kind of ritual.

He had never believed that he was in danger. This was part of a war correspondent's essential equipment, an irrational belief in personal invulnerability. He simply wasn't one of the people who died. He was the one who stood and watched them die. But someone kept bringing him coffee anyway.

They wouldn't let him ring the paper until he'd been interviewed by the police, and it took a while, and they seemed to ask the same questions far too many times. They insisted on praising him for his self-possession, his grasp of visual detail. They didn't want to hear about the language the man had spoken. Then after a while he was standing in a corridor, phoning the story in to the *Guardian*, and Isabelle said, 'You must carry something around with you, don't you think? Everywhere you go, someone starts shooting the place up.'

The nurse walked slowly out of the hospital with the baby in her arms, police officers on either side, her eyes red. She stopped in the reception area and looked around. 'The baby's perfectly fine,' she said, to no one in particular. 'There's nothing at all wrong with the baby.'

She walked out of the door, and Daniel saw her climbing into the back seat of a police car.

If he thought about it, he could probably work out what order these things happened in.

By the time he went through the sliding glass doors it was morning. He stood on the pavement, clutching his notebook against his chest, the sky white and cold over a wasteland of broken bottles and blown fireworks.

He took out his pen and wrote, *The first thing I saw in the new year was a man being killed.*

The grey-haired priest was sitting on the kerb, his head in his hands. Daniel sat down beside him.

'You don't need to tell me,' said the priest, his voice low and hollow. 'I already know.' He sighed. 'You were right about the millennium not happening this year, it seems.'

'Maybe not,' said Daniel.

'It's my fault,' the priest went on. 'I do realize that.' He wiped his eyes with the tip of his thumb. 'I killed him. I might as well have held the gun myself.'

'I'm sorry.'

'I thought I knew . . . it seemed so – so good . . . I thought I'd got it worked out finally. There has to be a meaning, doesn't there? Something we can make sense of?'

'Isn't that kind of what you guys do?'

The priest sighed again. 'I suppose that it is. I was just never very good at it.' His voice caught in his throat. 'There's nothing left now. I can't do anything.'

Daniel looked at his hands, thinking that there must be

something he could do to help this sad old man at least, to help somebody, somewhere. 'You could hear my confession,' he said. He was astonished at the words as soon as they left his mouth, coming from some quite foreign place, offering an idea he didn't even believe in to the most inappropriate person he could imagine. But it had been the right thing to say. The priest's worn face furrowed for a moment, but then he smiled, suddenly calm.

'Yes,' he said. 'I could do that. We don't do very many individual confessions in the Church of England, but I could do that.' He put his hand on Daniel's shoulder. 'I understand that I'm mad, you know. But I am still a priest.'

Daniel wasn't sure if he was meant to kneel – he didn't think he could manage that – so he only lowered his head, and reached into his memory for the proper sentence, familiar in a perfectly useless way from television shows and films. *Bless me, Father, for I have sinned.*

He couldn't remember later exactly what he had confessed to. He didn't know how it was supposed to work, whether detail was expected, and he didn't want to tell this peculiar man too much about his life in any case. It wasn't what you could call a good confession.

The priest put his hands on Daniel's head and recited a set of words. Then he lifted his hands, and stood for a long time, his eyes closed.

'Thank you,' he said at last, quietly. He gathered up a pile of books from the pavement. 'I think I should go and speak to my bishop now.' He started to walk away, and then turned back. 'I don't believe I ever got your name?'

'It doesn't matter. I won't be staying here.'

'I suppose the millennium could still happen next year, couldn't it?'

'Sure. You never know.'

The priest walked away, and Daniel reached for his notebook again.

The computers didn't fail, he wrote. *I think we forgot about that at some point, that we'd all been so worried about the computers. The computers are managing okay for themselves.*

And as for us, we have damaged our history from the first possible moment. We will go on doing damage. We will go on.

We want to make things that are fine and lovely, just and kind, somewhere between the wars.

Crass, foolish, beautiful, we hold out the best of our gifts for a false millennium, as years before we sent Glenn Gould into hopeful space, sent him travelling for ever towards our dream of loving alien hands.

He had obediently kept his mobile turned off in the hospital. Now he pressed the power button and watched it light up, a pale electronic blue.

Je parle de si loin.

It will keep ending the same way anyway, he thought. It was surely the worst thing for both of them; he could expect nothing better than phone calls and small violations of trust, hurt and confusion, trouble that neither of them could ever sort out completely nor quite let go.

The human fish does not live for ever; it dies like every mortal thing will die. It survives in the darkness for a very long time, blind and crawling forward. We don't know exactly how long.

Talk to me, Lili, he will say. Talk to me. Talk to me.

Acknowledgements

First and most importantly, I would like to thank those who shared their experiences with me: Bojan Aleksov, Zlatko Arslanagić, Ivana Balen, Howard Clark, Srdjan Dvornić, Marko Hren, Biljana Kasić, Boro Kontić, Violeta Krasnić, Lepa Mladjenović, Vanja Nikolić, Zoran Ostrić, Christine Schweitzer, Goran Simić, Vesna Terselić, Dorie Wilsnack, Staša Zajović, and many others, including some whose full names I do not know.

Thanks as well to those who have written about the Balkan wars and war crimes. While I visited the former Yugoslavia several times, I also drew on many printed sources in my research, but primarily the following whom I would especially like to acknowledge: Roger Cohen, *Hearts Grown Brutal*, Random House, New York; Michael Collin, *This is Serbia Calling*, Serpent's Tail; Francesca Gaiba, *The Origins of Simultaneous Interpretation: The Nuremberg Trial*, University of Ottawa Press; Michael Ignatieff, *Virtual War*, Chatto & Windus; Tim Judah, *The Serbs*, Yale University Press and *Kosovo: War and Revenge*, Yale University Press; Peter Maas, *Love Thy Neighbour*, Alfred A. Knopf, New York; Christopher Merrill, *Only the Nails Remain*, Rowman & Littlefield Publishers; Carol Off, *The Lion, The Fox and the Eagle*, Random House Canada; Erna Paris, *Long Shadows*, Bloomsbury; Geoffrey Robertson, *Crimes Against Humanity*, Penguin Books; Laura Silber and Allan Little, *The Death of Yugoslavia*, Penguin Books; Eric Stover and Gilles Peress, *The Graves*, Scalo; *The Sarajevo Survival Guide*, FAMA; and various articles by Ed Vulliamy and Julian Borger of the *Guardian*.

For information about the profession of interpretation, Casha Davis and Veronica Kelly, and for other linguistic help, Zlatko

Arslanagić, Professor Eric D. Gordy, Andrea Hila, Borivoj Radaković, Goran Simić, Vannina Sztainbok, and especially my long-suffering brother-in-law Claude Royer; for insight into the life of a war reporter, Ian Timberlake; for information on the Hague Tribunal itself, Carol Off, Ted Scudder, JustWatch, Tribunal Watch, the Institute for War and Peace Reporting, and Joanne Moore and the Public Information Service of the ICTY.

Some of these people may not agree with some of the opinions expressed in this book, but I'm grateful for their help nonetheless. All errors are of course my own.

Thanks as well, for reading and commenting on the manuscript, to David Helwig, Kate Helwig, Judy MacDonald, Erika Peterson, and particularly my husband Ken Simons, who talked ideas through with me at every stage; to Marcella Edwards and Noelle Zitzer; to my agent Lesley Shaw; and to my editors, Louise Dennys at Knopf Canada, and Alison Samuel at Chatto & Windus.

I'd also like to thank the Ontario Arts Council for financial support.

CREDITS

'A song of love is a sad song . . .': quoted from 'Hi-Lili, Hi-Lo', by Bronislau Kaper and Helen Deutsch, © 1952 (renewed) Metro-Goldwyn-Mayer, Inc. All rights controlled by EMI Robbins Catalog Inc. All Rights Reserved. Used by Permission. Warner Bros Publications U.S. Inc., Miami, FL, 33014.

'Love will tear us apart again': quoted from 'Love Will Tear Us Apart'. Written by Peter Hook, Stephen Morris, Bernard Sumner and Ian Curtis. Published by Zomba Music Publishers Ltd (PRS) and Fractured Music. All Rights Reserved. Used by permission.

'A nation as such . . .', 'A future which is completely impossible . . .', 'Attention taken to its highest degree . . .' and 'Attention is bound up with desire . . .': all quoted from Simone Weil, *Gravity and Grace*, translated by Emma Craufurd, © 1952, Routledge and Kegan Paul. Used by permission.

'C'est comme la nuit . . .': translated from Bob Dylan's 'Visions of Johanna', © 1966, Dwarf Music; French translation by Maggie Helwig and Claude Royer.

'*Yo te querda, o mi corazon*' and 'Fredrico Lorca is dead and gone': quoted from 'Spanish Bombs'. Words & Music by Joe Strummer, Mick Jones, Paul Simonon, Topper Headon. © Copyright 1979 Nineden Limited. Universal Music Publishing Limited (100%). Used by permission of Music Sales Ltd. All Rights Reserved. International Copyright Secured.

'*Comment m'entendez vous . . .*' and '*Qu'est-ce qu'un village . . .*': quoted from René Char, *Feuillets d'Hypnos*, © 1946, reprinted in *Fureur et mystère*, © 1948, Editions Gallimard. Used by permission.

'I and the public know . . .': quoted from 'September 1, 1939' by W.H. Auden, from *The English Auden*, © Faber & Faber Ltd. Used by permission.

'Roses in Murano glass vases . . .': quoted from 'Why Venice Is Sinking' by Abdullah Sidran, translated by John Hartley Williams, in *Scar on the Stone: contemporary poetry from Bosnia*, © 1998, Bloodaxe Books.

'And when the written words come to Lazar . . .': quoted from *Marko the Prince: Serbo-Croat Heroic Songs*, translated by Anne Pennington and Peter Levi, © 1984, Duckworth. Used by permission.

'Three walnuts, therefore . . .': quoted from 'Good Evening, the Guest is Gone', by Ferida Duraković, translated by Nuala Ni Dhomhnaill and Antonela Glavinić, in *Scar on the Stone: contemporary poetry from Bosnia*, © 1998, Bloodaxe Books.

'*Je suis parti . . .*': quoted from René Char, 'Éprouvante simplicité' in *La Nuit talismanique qui brillait dans son cercle*, © 1972, Editions Gallimard. Used by permission.

'*La terre nous aimait . . .*': quoted from René Char, 'Évadné' in *Fureur et mystère*, © 1948, Editions Gallimard. Used by permission.

'Was he in great pain? . . .': quoted from Graham Greene's *The Third Man*, © 1950, Heinemann.